into the

stories of magic and romance

CW00495007

edited by deadwoodpecker

Into the Mystic:
Stories of Magic and Romance

Published by Stillpoint/Eros (StillpointEros.com)

Book design by David Kudler and Stillpoint Digital Press

Title typeface: Luxembourg 1910 by Peter Weigel. Used through an Open Font License.

Dingbat typeface: Jugendstil Ornamente by Typographer Mediengestaltung. Used through a Free for Commercial Use License.

Cover design by Andrea Gonzales

Cover art: "Spring Scattering Stars" by Edwin Blashfield

Story art:

"Changelings" — Catherine Hiley

"Better than Fine" — Shannon Meyers

"Real," "Sasha Shutland," & "The Witch of the Margins" — JaneG

"A Tree of Life" — Melody Cunningham

Print ISBN 978-1-938808-56-2

version 1.0

*To all the members of
the Ginny Lovers Discord server,
without whom our lives would be
much more boring.*

Contents

Foreword

If you have wandered into this book without knowing some of the history of it, first: welcome! We are excited you're reading this. Second: we hope you enjoy this for what it is: a collection of novellas written by mostly first-time authors.

When I first had the idea to do this, honestly it was because I've felt a yearning most of my adult life to write and publish an original work of fiction, and I know the other authors in this collection (except one, who actually is published) felt the same. And how better to do it than have a group of people working toward the same goal? It worked better than I expected, as we ended up with the collection you are reading at this exact moment. *Into the Mystic* was a group effort at every turn, as we cajoled and challenged and encouraged each other across the finish line.

It's not that none of us have ever finished anything before — we are writers, we've just mostly been writing fanfiction. It is how we met; fanfiction is the backbone of the community we have created. You will find the DNA of that remaining in some of the pen names we've chosen: LegendDairy, TheWordsInMyHead, and deadwoodpecker. But what I found surprising was that despite how much we all have been inspired by one particular fandom, our original works vastly differ from one another.

The only real requirements I had for the stories was that it contain a bit of fantasy and a bit of romance. With such loose guidelines, I really shouldn't be surprised that these stories range so widely from one another. We have romance explored in a triad; soulmates discovering one another; a witch who falls for a mermaid; a Watcher who yearns for the woman he watches, and more. Each was a unique discovery and a joy for me to read, as I hope you will feel upon reading these stories.

But I know there may be some of you who do know us from around the fandom, and I am so grateful you've done the equivalent of buying one of us a cup of coffee. What you're reading is a dream come true for all of us.

Thank you for being here!

deadwoodpecker

into the mystic

stories of magic and romance

CHANGELINGS

K.D. West
(as Antosha Chekhonte)

Prologue

Remembrance

The saying went that one death was a tragedy, and three thousand a statistic.

But when you knew so many of the dead — knew their names, knew their faces, when they were your friends, your teachers... Your friends' parents. The first girl you ever kissed. The last one you've kissed.

When it was you that opened the gate that let the creatures who killed them in...

Then each and every one is a tragedy.

Ari knew where he would find her. Up the sere slopes of the Devil's Knob he stumbled, his dress shoes sliding through the muddy, dead grass, to the spot where he had come across her twice before, right at the top of the hill.

There she was, sitting wrapped in her scuffed black dress and overcoat, weaving a garland of dried flowers. "Rosemary," she said, "that's for remembrance..."

"Hey, Annie," said Ari.

"No," she said, shaking her tangled locks. "It's not hay. It's straw."

"It's... What?"

She held up a length of dried grass. "Straw," she said.

"Ah," said Ari, peering not at the brown grass, but at Annie's otherwhere eyes. He knelt next to her, moisture chilling his knee. "How are you?"

"There's rue for you," murmured Annie, pulling up a withered green-and-white flower from her skirts and threading it into the garland. "Doesn't look much like Rue, though...."

Rue.... Eyes wide... Cheeks flushed...

The day before, at Rue's memorial — his sweet, beautiful girl-friend's *funeral* — Ari had wept and told Mrs. Finneran he hadn't loved her half as much as she'd deserved.

Rue's mother had taken it as a compliment, which it was. It was also a bald statement of fact.

"No," Ari agreed, and put his hand on her arm to still it. "Annie, how are you?"

More a startled woodland creature than a girl, she jerked her head back and looked at him. Then tears came to her large eyes, and with them, a touch of humanity. "He's gone," she said. Her face, usually so serene, crumbled, sorrow distorting it and her voice until they were almost unrecognizable.

"I'm so sorry," Ari sighed, and wrapped his arms around her.

She sobbed into his shoulder, and he could feel the wet blast of her breath gusting against his neck. After several minutes of unrestrained weeping, she howled into Ari's shoulder, "He said he'd never leave me!"

Ari felt as if his lungs were being ripped out. He knew what it was like to lose parents. "I know he didn't want to."

Annie wept.

There are times when people cry and you feel uncomfortable because you know you're supposed to do something for them. This was not one of those times. Ari knew there was nothing he could do beyond what he was doing already, letting her tears and snot dampen his coat and holding her as tightly and as gently as he could.

He had wondered at one point if Annie might be part Fae — a changeling. She certainly had the otherwhere personality, the magical talent, and the odd, ethereal looks. But Ari had seen pictures of her pale, grey-eyed mother, had met her wonderfully odd father...

Her father, face black....

Ari shuddered, and stroked Annie's hair.

After some time — ten minutes? A half hour? — she began to subside, slowly losing steam. When she had calmed to merely gasping every few breaths, he kissed her on the top of the head — nothing romantic, just caring. Then he had tried to back up, but she had held him fiercely.

"What will I do?" she said into his collar. "Where will I go? I'm so *alone*."

"You've still got your home, Annie."

For the very first time since he had met her, hesitancy crept into the blonde girl's voice. "I... I don't think I could go back there."

He nodded. He had avoided going back to his parents' graves all these years. He could certainly understand. "Timi's moms... *mom* was really worried about you when you left the service," he said, wiping her wet chin with his sleeve. "I know Professor Schuler would love to have you stay at their house for as long as you want."

Her eyes drifted north, to the horizon. She shrugged. "I don't know that she would be terribly happy for me to be there. Not after her wife and Joe. And... Jim..."

Their funeral had been just the day before. Timi and her mom, Professor Schuler, weeping, and weeping, and... Their funerals. Joe. And Jim. And their mom — *mum* — Professor Schuler's wife Brigid.

And Rue. And Sam. And...

A tragedy.

My fault.

Ari hugged her close again, and he could feel tears rumbling up inside her once more. He was crying himself. "Trust me, she wouldn't mind at all. They'd want you there. Annie, listen to me. You saved their lives, and Timi loves you like a sister. I know. We've talked about it. You will never be alone so long as one of us is alive."

Ari was ready for her to weep again, and would have understood if she had. But Annie didn't. She looked at him for a long moment, her pale blue eyes washed almost silver by her tears and the overcast winter sky. Then she looped the bedraggled garland around the crown of her head and stood. "No," she said, "I suppose I won't."

Together they walked down the hill into Sundown Valley, back to the O'Danan's house.

Chapter One

Better Days

It wasn't until she returned to campus the next September that it really hit Timi. She was alone.

After the first day of classes, rather than wander up to the library, or back to the dorms, she found herself meandering down the lawn to the lone cedar that overlooked the river. It had been a favorite spot for the whole bunch of them to hang out, and as she sat down in the damp grass, she found herself searching for some lingering sign of their presence, of their laughter.

None there. Only in her memory, which was layered with images like a forest floor littered with leaves.

Jim, Joe, and Sam, all gone. Somehow, in this place, that was even more devastating than the loss of her own mother, a loss she knew she would be mourning for the rest of her life.

Ari, still so strange and distant, huddled there in his house down in the valley, looking up at her when they had both managed to stop crying and telling her, his dark eyes flat and lifeless, "I don't know who I am anymore."

Chancellor Levy and Professor Nolicherri, dead on the steps of the castle itself, right there.

Death and destruction, blood and terror, and somehow it didn't feel as if they had won, even with the Fae sent back to their home. Even with Oberon truly and finally defeated.

Fae. Fairies.

She had spent her whole life wrapped up in her brothers' lives, Joe's and Jim's — their ambitions, their battles, their struggles, their friendships, their loves, and their hates. She had rooted them on when they needed rooting and yelled at them when they needed yelling.

But none of it seemed to matter anymore.

Jim, Joe, both dead. And Mum. And Sam, the poor bastard. And Chancellor Levy, and Professor Nolicherri, and Kathy Kamayama's dad Tom, and Cindy Phelan, and Liz, and TJ, and Rue Finneran, and… and the Li sisters, and the Avaya brothers, and so, so many others. All dead.

And Ari as good as.

And all of the love and joy that had warmed her way through the difficulties of the past three years like some sort of magical furnace was melted away, less substantial than the mist that was dampening the grass, and swirling through the tree limbs.

She felt as if she were a changeling, an alien inhabiting this peaceful, beautiful landscape.

She sensed rather than heard someone settling down behind her, smelt a mixture of vanilla and sulfur. "Hey, Annie," she said. "Just come from Summoning?"

"Yes," said Annie, airily. "I tried to show your mother a different way of drawing a summoning circle. Daddy was researching an article. Before."

Before. Mirthlessly, Timi laughed, just because it seemed called for. "What did Mom think of that?" She and Mom, who were almost strangers to each other now...

"Oh, I never presume to know what people are thinking. But Professor Schuler didn't look particularly happy."

"I bet not," Timi sighed.

"For that matter," said Annie, "neither do you."

"What?" Timi said. Turning around, she saw Annie's eyes gazing at her in that steadying, infuriating, knowing way that she had. "Oh, all right, fine, I'm not exactly happy."

"Ghosts?" Annie asked, who knew something about ghosts.

"Yeah, I suppose. But it's more, you know, the *absence* that's eating at me just now. I thought coming back here would be coming back to all the laughter and the *purpose*... But it's all just empty, you know?"

"I think so," said Annie.

"It's like... realizing, last year, that the college was built here just because this was a place where the boundaries between the planes was thin... I mean, that's really wild, but somehow it made the Mountain... *less* magical. More just a place. And now, to come back, when there's so much missing... It feels so..."

"Empty," Annie finished, and handed Timi a tattered handkerchief.

"I mean, what's the point? Take classes, pass tests. Why? What does it matter? Go on dates to down in the valley? Learn silly spells to turn yourself into a bat or make the leaves of an aspen turn purple? Whoop-dee-fucking-doo. And so many people are just *gone* and it just all doesn't seem to matter at all, what happens, what I do. I mean, what the hell is the point of it all?"

Annie took back the handkerchief, limp and dry in Timi's hand, and dabbed gently at Timi's damp cheeks. "Oh, there is a point. I don't know that we ever get to see it, but there is a point."

Timi snorted. "What the hell is that supposed to mean?"

"When *my* mother died, I spent a lot of time thinking about the same sorts of things. Daddy, of course, wasn't much help, because he was just as devastated as I was. The two of us would barely remember to eat. And what I came to realize was that there is more than just what you can see and feel and hear at work. That there is some sort of gigantic game being played out, and we're only aware of part of it — that it goes on outside the realm of our senses and beyond our sense of time and place." When Timi scowled at her, Annie went on. "You've taken Metaphysics, Timi. You know that what they try to study there, all of it, is finally unknowable. Time, morality, the mind. Death. Love. These are dimensions that we can guess are there, but there's no way to say, 'Ah, this is how this works, this is what this means.'"

"You're full of shit, Annie."

"Perhaps. But I've been thinking about this for a long time." She looked out, down the long, winding valley carved by the Elysium River, her silver-blue eyes mirroring the overcast sky perfectly. "My mother used to say that the meaning of life was whatever you make of it. I never knew what she meant by that. But I think it had something to do with playing the game fully."

Timi rubbed her temples. She hated it when Annie got philosophical like this, because it left Timi feeling as if she were looking at the world through a wool scarf. "It's not a *game*, Annie."

"But it is, Timea. You love baseball, don't you?"

Timi shrugged bleakly. The fierce ecstasy on Joe's face as he caught the final out last year, her and Ari and Jim running over with the rest of the team to hug him. He would be dead less than two hours later.

Annie stared down at the river gorge for a moment and then went on. "I never really cared much for it. It always seemed rather pointless, you know, a bunch of people running around, throwing things and hitting things and catching things. But then, the year that you and Joe were first on the team, it all suddenly made sense to me. *You have to pick a side* for it to be any fun at all. You have to pick a side and pretend that it really matters: then it's actually exciting."

"Not most of the games we played *that* year," groaned Timi.

Her friend simply continued, "It occurred to me that most things are that way. If you play the game fully, then there's pleasure in the doing of it. Of course," Annie said, resting a hand lightly on Timi's leg, "then you also get the pain of losing. But it all matters." Annie's strange eyes filled with tears.

"You okay, Annie?" asked Timi, startled.

"Do you remember when my mother died?"

Timi nodded her head.

"You came over to play at my house every day for months. And I *couldn't* play. So you would play in my room, giving my dolls tea parties, brushing their hair, brushing *my* hair... And I would just sit there and watch you. And listen to you. For months. And the stories that you were spinning began to whirl around in my brain, and all of a sudden, I found myself *in* the games, playing along with you... Timea, it was the nicest thing anyone ever has ever done for me. Even nicer than the time Sam gave me that chocolate unicorn horn and kissed me under the mistletoe."

Timi didn't have any idea what to say, so she looked down at Annie's hand splayed across her leg.

"I'd like to try to return the favor," said her friend. "Come on, let me show you something." And she pulled Timi to her feet and onto the rope bridge across the Elysium towards the nearby forest.

"Uh, Annie, what... Where are we going?"

"You'll see," Annie said airily as they passed into the first trees in Grey Forest.

Timi looked around nervously — she'd been here before, but never without Jim, her brother, and Ari. "I don't know if this is a good idea, Annie, there's a reason we're not supposed—"

"Last June," Annie said, an uncharacteristic look of determination on her face as she pulled Timi along a narrow track, "you fought off two Greater Duh and the Fairy Queen. At this time of day, I don't think there's anything in these woods that *you* need to be afraid of, apart from the wolves. And the wolves still don't come to this part of the forest often."

Looking around, Timi was vaguely aware that they were, in fact, headed into the part of the forest where the Fae invaders had held their Great Hunt. Several of the trees seemed to have had their tops ripped off. "Can't blame the wolves," Timi muttered, "Oberon didn't like them very much..."

"No," Annie agreed, and then she held up her hand. They had come to a clearing. "Ah! Timea, I'd like you to close your eyes for a little bit."

Timi looked her friend dubiously; the determined expression was still lodged on Annie's face, however, so Timi merely shrugged. "I wish I'd never told you my full name. No one ever uses it."

"I do," said Annie — which made Timi want to laugh, thinking how annoyed Jim and Joe used to get at Annie. Which made Timi want to cry. Annie put her spindly fingers over Timi's eyes, and Timi dutifully closed the lids. "I think your name is lovely." Annie now lowered her hand and took Timi's. "I'm going to lead you now. Don't open your eyes."

"But..." Timi began.

Annie simply walked her forward. They were in the clearing, Timi knew, feeling the sunlight on her face and the thick grass pulling at her feet.

"Here," Annie said. "Kneel down."

Still dubious, eyes still shut, Timi did as she had been told.

After a minute of silence, Annie spoke. "Magic isn't just funny words, and squiggles on parchment and disgusting brews and such. Magic is part of what we *are*, part of everything — not just the creatures and us magical folk, though we have the sensitivity and the power to use it, but everybody, everything. The magic is spread across the face of the earth, but nobody sees it."

Timi felt a warm weight lay across her thighs — Annie's arm, she assumed.

"You should open your eyes now, Timea," Annie said, very softly.

Perplexed, Timi did so. A unicorn, impossibly white, was kneeling beside her, its golden horn laid across Timi's lap. A warmth flowed into Timi, filling an emptiness she had only begun to perceive. "Oh!"

Annie's hand rested lightly on Timi's shoulder, then began to run gently though Timi's hair.

Not so alone.

Chapter Two

Camera Obscura

It had seemed like a good idea at the time: step Outside down into Sundown for the afternoon with Annie, and cheer Ari up.

Ari's last letter had been so terse, so devoid of *Ari*, that it had taken Timi's breath away. When it had concluded, *It's nice that you're feeling happier,* she had thought, right, you bastard, we've got to do something about you, too.

Nice.

So she had decided to pop down to town at the beginning of the three-day weekend. Nobody would miss them, and they could be back in time to clear the new Dean Professor Crotchett's basilisk glare before bed check.

She had raided the last of the great O'Danan store of alcohol behind the clock in the student lounge — one bottle of moonshine and another of some rum that Jim's pen-pal in Brazil had sent him few years earlier that was supposed to turn your hair purple. *That should be entertaining,* she thought.

When Annie met up with her in the entry hall, it occurred to Timi for the first time to wonder what had possessed her to ask her friend along. True, Annie had never made Ari as furious as she had Jim or as nervous as she had made Joe....

Thinking of Jim and Joe suddenly left Timi feeling as if a bucket of ice water had been poured over her, and, unbidden, images of the two of them crumpled together on the floor led to images of her mother, dead on the front lawn of their house, of Tommy Kamayama, dead in the lobby of the Metaphysics building, of Professors Levy and Noli-cherri on the steps she was about to walk down, of TJ at Christmas, and Liz Garcia, and Rue Finneran, and the Li sisters and...

The touch of Annie's hand on her shoulder broke the spell. Timi realized that everyone in the line behind her was staring at her, as were Dean Crotchett and the chancellor. Chancellor Harrington placed a dry hand on Timi's other shoulder. "Are you all right, Miss O'Danan?"

Almost in spite of herself, Timi nodded. "Flashback," she murmured, and saw those behind her nod too. Everyone knew. Everyone thought they understood.

The chancellor gave her the thinnest of smiles, and waved Timi and Annie through the huge doors.

The two of them were the last members of the original group that had worked with Ari after he'd opened the rift to Tir na Nog left at the school. Thirty students had been in the group, including, of course, Timi's brothers. Most had died. Or graduated. Or just left. The Avayas, of course, the only other sophomores that year — they were among the dead. So that left just Timi. And Annie.

Everyone knew what Timi and Annie had done and what they had seen. And, of course, everyone at school had suffered their own losses.

As they walked down the road to the school gates, breaths barely ghosting the crisp October air, Timi considered her friend, who seemed to be reciting "The Walrus and the Carpenter" under her breath. Her wide, grey eyes scanned the world with an equanimity that Timi could only envy and wonder at.

In front of them, a group of freshmen were laughing, bursting with excitement at getting to leave the Mountain for the first time, some going home, some visiting the valley for the first time, chattering about where they could buy beer in town. It stunned Timi to see them acting so *normally*, when all she could think of as they walked through the gate was Professor Nolicherri riding on dragon-back against an armored squad of Fomorians. The top of the gate was still scorched black.

As the younger students sprinted down towards the train station, Timi lead Annie off in the other direction, down towards the railroad tracks. "Come on," she said, trying desperately to keep the sense of fun and adventure with which she had meant to infect Ari's gloomy home. "Let's step Outside from over here. We cleared the wards."

Without showing much concern one way or another, Annie nodded and the two of them disappeared without a sound.

Of course, they still had to enter the house by the battered front door. Annie reached out and rapped with the knocker. Cringing in anticipation of some explosion, though she couldn't say why, Timi was greeted instead by a quiet squeak as the door opened.

Eight enormous green eyes peered down from the lintel. "Miss Timi, Miss Annie! What a delightful surprise to see you two!" Anton, the fierce-looking, gentle-spirited cacodaemon who had attached him-self to Ari even before the rift was closed, was dressed in what looked like an attempt at a butler's black suit. As it was, he looked like a huge spider caught in a black circus tent.

He led them into the front hall.

Hanging opposite the door was the portrait of Ari's parents that TJ had been painting, just before he died. They waved down at Timi. She had watched her boyfriend painting this as a Christmas gift for their friend. Timi had filched the photo from Ari's photo album, so Gabe and Lyndsey Sundown's portraits knew her well. TJ hadn't even been able to sign it. But at least he had cast the charms that brought the figures to life.

"TJ died to save me," said a colorless voice from behind Timi's ear. "It was the least I could think to do to honor him. I think my parents would have approved." The Sundowns in the painting waved.

Timi spun to find Ari peering up at his parents from the bottom of the stairs. "Ari!" she said, but the excitement that had leapt to her throat died there as she saw his ashen complexion, the dark circles under his eyes. The redness that showed that — even now — he had been crying. "Oh, Ari."

Ari's eyes bathed her in their dark flood for a moment, then flicked to Annie. Annie, however, was looking abstractedly at Timi.

"So," Ari said, finally, "what brings the two of you down to this house of mirth?"

"We've come to cheer you up," Timi said, as brightly as she could manage. She felt as if she were playing the *role* of Timi O'Danan, Every-one's Little Sister: bright and plucky and always cheerful. *Cheerful* wasn't what she felt at all at that moment.

At least Annie gave a vague smile of support.

"Ah," Ari sighed, his face impassive, his black suit without a tatter, stain or ornament. "Kind of a tall order, don't you think?"

"What?" Timi said in what she hoped sounded like mock indig-nation. She pulled the bottles from her book bag. "A couple of college girls show up on your doorstep bearing booze, and that doesn't even merit a *little* smile, Mr. Sundown?"

"You're kidding. I've only been out of school a few months myself," Ari muttered, though the corners of his mouth did lift almost imper-ceptibly. The *idea* of a smile, but it would serve. "What did you have in mind? Two Truths and a Lie? Spin the Wand?"

"Now *you're* kidding," Timi teased, relieved that he was at least playing along. "I don't think we had any idea what we were going to do once we got here, but..." She looked to Annie again, but her friend was now staring off into the ether, that maddening Annie smile on her thin lips.

"But what?" Ari asked.

"But... It's been horrible being back at school, really. They've scrubbed away all of the blood, but I know where every spot was..." The two of them were staring at her now, both level-gazed, silver eyes and brown. "And I would have gone crazy these last two months if I hadn't had Annie there. She's kept me sane. And I thought... That is, we... I thought, and Annie agreed, that maybe we could do some of the same for you...." Her little speech petered out under Ari's empty look. Not so plucky, not so cheerful. Kind of bleak, really, but the truth.

Ari nodded, looking from Timi's face to Annie's. "Have the two of you had lunch?"

They both shook their heads.

"Hey, Anton!" Ari called out.

"Yes, Mr. Sundown, sir? What can I do, sir?"

"Would you mind bringing something to eat in to the dining room?" Ari asked.

"Would I mind, sir? Oh, it would be my greatest pleasure, sir!" The huge cacodaemon seemed to be vibrating with excitement.

Timi was feeling a bit alarmed. "Nothing too fancy, Anton, please, just some sandwiches or something...."

Anton scowled down at her as if she'd slapped him. *Funny,* she thought, *his eight eyes are almost the exact shade of Mum's.* Then the demon smiled broadly. "Miss O'Danan will have her little joke, miss. I will have luncheon out immediately, miss!" With that, he disappeared into the kitchen.

"Well," Ari said, the uncertain attempt at a smile still playing on his lips, "I can't have two lovely young ladies drinking..." He peered through his glasses at one of the bottles hanging limp in Timi's grip. "*Rum Cabelo Roxo* on an empty stomach. Not very hospitable, to begin with, and your mom would kill me, besides, Timi."

Before Timi's ire had a chance to peak, Ari meandered into the dining room. "When Anton says 'immediately,'" Ari said, "he means it. Look — he's already served out the first course...."

Timi and Annie trailed behind their friend and Timi was stunned. The last time she had been here, in mid-August, this room had still born the traces of having served as an operations center — shreds of parchment, torn maps on the wall. Anton had just started working for Ari then, and the transformation was astonishing. The chandelier glittered, a painting of Rhea Levy smiling down from the wall, and the rosewood-inlaid table was polished to a blinding sheen, sporting three places laid with silver and crystal and china. Three salads that looked so fresh and crisp that Timi almost couldn't bear the thought of disturbing the plates. Two goblets filled blood-red. One clear.

"Wow," Timi said. "Beats the Wyvern."

"Miss O'Danan is too kind to say so," Anton's muffled voice called out from the other side of the door that led to the kitchen.

Ari stood behind the tall chair at the head of the table and indicated that his guests should sit. Slightly awed, Timi did so, stowing her bag and the alcohol beneath the table. Annie seemed to notice the table only then; she too sat.

Again, Ari seemed to consider smiling before gravity sucked him back down. Timi's insides twisted as she watched that happen. *Damn you, Sundown...* He picked up his goblet, the clear one. "I hope you like the wine," Ari said. "The cellars here are still very well stocked, my mom... Now, if you don't mind, a toast: To friends, and to the joy they bring."

The twist worked its way up into Timi's throat as she and Annie lifted their glasses to answer the toast. The wine was dark-flavored, rich and almost chocolaty. "Mmmm. Ari, that's really... I mean, what do you say? It's really yummy," Timi said, feeling it spread through her. "Thought you didn't want us drunk on an empty stomach? And what are you drinking, Ari?"

The little warmth that had shown in Ari's face drained away. "Water. I... I really can't be drinking right now. Anton's worried that I sometimes get pretty bad."

"Oh." Timi wanted to take the two bottles at her feet and throw them out of the window. "I, uh... I guess that makes sense. That was stupid of me."

Ari shook his head, and began to eat, not looking up.

Timi looked down at her own plate, at the glistening china and the perfect arrangement of bright, crisp greens. "Jesus," she muttered. "I almost don't want to mess it up. Poor Mum would have loved to be served like this. She never felt as if her meals were..." Timi stopped before her throat seized up entirely.

Annie looked up, tilted her head to one side, and spoke her first intelligible words since leaving the school. "The meals at your mothers' home were the most wonderful I've ever had."

Ari peered at Annie for a moment, then nodded solemnly to Timi. "All those years of eating with you and your family, Timi, I never once failed to get up from the table feeling better than when I'd sat down."

Timi covered her face with her napkin, then took a breath and lowered it. "Even the time I dumped my curry in your lap, that first summer?"

That merited something approaching a true smile, even from Ari. "Even then."

Now she began to eat, looking for any distraction from the crushing sadness that every conversation with this man, every memory of this place seemed to visit on her.

"I remember having dinner at your house right after my mother died," Annie murmured. "Your mum made cheese soup, which I thought sounded rather odd. But it *tasted* happy. Or maybe it was all of you laughing and smiling...."

"That was the night that Jim and I..." Timi gave a weak, snorting giggle, "tried to convince Joe that 'fork' was pronounced *'fuck.'*"

And they all laughed, even as they all thought of the fact that Jim and Joe were not there.

They passed the rest of the meal in companionable, sad silence.

As Anton brought out the cheese course, even Annie groaned, standing up to examine the sleeves on the Levy portrait's formal academic robes.

"Anton, you've outdone yourself," Ari said. Turning to the girls, he sighed, "Poor Anton doesn't get much of a chance to dust off his skills. Haven't had many visitors..."

"Not true, Mr. Sundown, sir!" said the cacodaemon, pouring out tiny glasses of port that Timi thought tasted like sweet liquid smoke.

"Last week we had Miss Lambert and Miss Forest and Miss Partridge. The week before that it was Miss Fawcett and Miss Paris...."

"Sarah...? And Cricket Paris?" Timi said, even as dread settled heavy in her stomach. "You've been seeing *Cricket Paris?*"

"No!" barked Ari. "It's nothing like that! It's... nothing like *you* two. Not one of them came here as a friend. None of them stayed for a meal, which was, Anton, you meddling demon, the point that I was trying to make. They were all here to steal a march on the most eligible bachelor since Elysium Territory was first settled. Cricket came intending to seduce me, I guess — which made her stomach turn as much as it did mine, I'm sure — but she was much more passionate about the idea of our 'two great family lines merging' than she ever was about *me*." He glowered down into his water.

Damn you, Sundown, Timi found herself thinking again. How was it that he could humiliate her and inspire her sympathy, both at the same time?

"Come on," Ari said, "Let's go up to the living room. I've got another painting I want to show you." He turned to Anton. "Thanks, Anton. That was wonderful."

The girls murmured in agreement.

The cacodaemon wrung the hem of his tent-sized coat, large tears forming along his wide nose. "Mr. Sundown, sir, misses, you are too kind... Perhaps, Mr. Sundown, sir, I should not take my—"

"No, Anton, come on, we go through this every week. It's your evening off. Draw your pay and leave. If I see you before tomorrow morning — or if you spend any of your damned pay on *me* — I'll dock your salary."

"I am sure you intend that to be amusing, sir. Very well. I shall try to... divert myself this afternoon and evening. Once I have finished cleaning up from this meal, sir."

Timi moved forward. "Let us help you clear, at least, Anton."

Suddenly the demon looked deeply insulted, his tusks showing. "Oh, *no*, miss. Do not take from me the honor of my service, miss."

"I, uh, wouldn't dream of it," said Timi, nonplussed.

As they followed Ari's dark form up the stairs to the living room, Timi watched his parents in the front hall painting following her with their eyes, smiling.

Annie's hand tucked itself into Timi's elbow as they walked behind Ari into the old living room. He led them down to the far end, where once a huge map of Elysium Territory had taken up most of the wall. Now there was an enormous canvas, with nearly thirty very familiar figures milling around.

"It's the research group, that first day in Mom's lab!" Timi gasped.

Ari nodded. "It's not exactly the same, of course. Look."

Timi and Annie walked up to the painting. They were seated around the big table in the Summoning lab. In the background lurked Timi's mothers: her mom, Dolfy Schuler, in dingy black work duds; her mum, oh, Jesus, her mum, Brigid O'Danan, resplendent in an emerald green dress that matched her eyes — Timi's eyes, too, though she'd never have the figure to pull the dress off like her mum. In the foreground, around the pushed-together tables, were Dan Farmer, TJ Williams, Liz Garcia and Becky Smith, Rue Finneran, Ernie Curry and Jason Fleischer, Karina and Kailey Li in jewel-toned Chinese jackets. In the front row were Sam, Joe in his favorite dark blue Yankees shirt, Jim in a red Niners jersey, and then Ari, Annie and Timi themselves, all in black school robes. *Silly fucking European affectation...*

Timi's emotions were bubbling again, looking at all of these people she had fought with and cared for. She touched a finger to Liz's smiling face and Liz giggled as if tickled; she was dressed in sapphire silk, which Timi was fairly certain she hadn't been wearing that day.

"*We're* wearing black," Annie said, airily.

Timi looked again, and saw what Annie meant: the dead members of group, nearly half of the total number, were dressed in bright colors. They were looking happy, grinning and sipping at beer. Ari, Timi, Annie and the others who had survived were glummer, and they were all dressed somberly in their academic robes. Even Bill and Gus, the relentless clowns, looked as if they would really like to hear a joke.

Timi realized she was crying only when she felt two sets of hands on her shoulders.

"I'm sorry," Ari said. "I thought you would enjoy it. I didn't mean for you to—"

"No, it's all right." Timi shook her head and smiled, or tried to. "It's just... I think this is just right. The bunch of us that are left, everywhere we look is a reminder, isn't it? Even a celebration is an act of mourning..."

Ari backed away, his face in a grimace. "No, I'm so sorry. I feel... I feel like a fucking changeling. A monster. Everything I touch right now turns to ash. You came here to cheer me up, and all I can manage to do is make you cry."

Later, Timi would realize that her response had been building all day, all month, all year — ever since the week before Christmas the previous year, when the Fomorians had killed TJ and his family, and they had all been devastated, Timi especially, and Ari had been furious with himself, certain that TJ's family would never have been targeted if it hadn't been for for him, for the fact that *he'd* opened the rift, that TJ was trying to help *him* close it.

Nonetheless, standing there in the living room, the reaction caught her — and her friends — utterly by surprise.

"Don't you dare! Don't you *DARE* take away my right to call my grief my own, Sundown! You arrogant fucking self-obsessed beautiful fucking *asshole*. We came here today because we *love* you, you stupid prick! We think you're the bee's fucking knees, and without you we'd all be fucking *dead*. But that doesn't mean that my being sad is *your* fucking fault. You lost some people, did you? Two best friends, a girlfriend, a *former* girlfriend, a couple of parents a ways back, a bunch of pals? Fine, you arrogant fucking jerk-off, I'll see that and raise you. I lost *my* best friend — aside from the two of you — not to mention two brothers, a mother, two boyfriends and more friends than I think I can stand on any given day, including, as near as I can tell, *you*, Ari, and what did *I* do this morning, instead of going with Annie down to the Wyvern and flirting with the poor dregs of the senior class, who are all scared of the two of us anyway because we fought in the fucking Battles of the Rift? What did I do? I came down *here* to try to fucking cheer *you* up! I'm fucking crying because *I'm* fucking sad." And, annoyingly, she found that she was, indeed, crying. "I'm here because I..."

Eyes wide and face burnished with shame, Ari stepped towards her. "Timi, I'm so sor—"

She turned away, intending to walk out the door, but instead ran directly into Annie. Who wrapped her spindly arms around Timi and kissed her gently on the lips.

It is not too much to say that Timi was already in shock, her own anger singing through her nerves, and so perhaps, when she looked back on it later, Timi thought it wise not to be too surprised that she accepted the kiss, felt its warmth stilling her, and tentatively returned it.

It was when Annie stepped back that a mixture of astonishment, desire, and shame thrilled through her. She looked instinctively to Ari and saw her own feelings spelled out in his expression.

He looked as if someone had kissed and slapped him both at the same time. "I can go..."

Timi felt the urge to howl at him some more, to tell him that he was an idiot, that if he walked out of the door that she would kill him, but Annie was quicker. "I just thought I'd show you what love looks like again," she said.

For the first time in months, something other than images of death and loss rendered Timi speechless. The butterfly heat of Annie's kiss had stolen all power of thought from her. Again she turned to Ari and saw color coming to his cheeks for the first time since the previous spring. He was also speechless.

Annie stepped forward and kissed him too, and he gave a moan as their mouths came together that melted Timi utterly — it could have been sounded from the depths of her own soul.

Timi stood there, dumb, blinking, until Annie stepped back from Ari, leaving him gasping. The blonde girl blinked then too, and twined her arms in front of her. "I sort of lost a boyfriend last June too," she said, very evenly. "Sort of lost two, though Sam only kissed me once and Joe never did seem to be listening when I told him how I felt. But there are two people in this room that I love very much."

Timi and Ari moved towards her.

Night had fallen, and they were arranged, spent, on Ari's enormous bed. A triangle: Timi's head on Ari's stomach, Ari's on Annie's, Annie's tangled hair tickling Timi's belly and the insides of her thighs.

Timi gasped, "Oh, damn."

Ari reached down and stroked her forehead. "What's the matter?"

"We've missed bed-check. Dean Crotchett'll be out for blood." In spite of her anxiety, she let her head melt under his caress, back down on to the flat plane of his stomach.

Ari gave her a smile that — even after all of these hours of shared pleasure — made her whole body blossom. It was that wicked, happy Ari smile that Timi thought she had lost forever. "I, uh..."

"In for a sigh, in for a..." Annie murmured, and Timi found herself wondering how the phrase would end.

"Well, don't be angry — I didn't plan on *this* happening — but when I saw the two of you on the front step, I messaged Chancellor Harrington and Timi's mom, saying that I'd invited the two of you to be my guests here tonight."

"Don't be *angry?*" Timi laughed. "You fucking pervert! You lured two innocent girls here with wicked intent!"

Annie hummed gently, and Timi laughed again.

"You know it wasn't like that," Ari said, and he was smiling still. "I just... The two of you make me *happy*, and no one else does that. Besides," he said, running his fingers down Timi's neck and over one breast, "I'll buy Annie as *innocent*, but you? Based on the working knowledge you've showed us so far..."

"You calling me a *loose woman*, Sundown?" asked Timi, teasing only a little.

"Never," he said, running his fingers lazily over the other breast and along her ribs.

"It's only sex, Ari."

"True," he said, quietly. "But it's very, very nice. And I do..." His face clouded as it had not since early that afternoon. "Can I tell you what happened to Oberon?"

"Of course you can," said Annie. "Would you like to?"

In spite of the fire roaring nearby, Timi shivered.

He nodded. "Yeah. I would. I've never told anyone because... I don't know." He shook his head. "You know I'd tried to... kill him twice, once in the Metaphysics Hall, right after he killed your brothers, Timi, and then again in the Time/Space Hall. And both times it failed, because I just... couldn't do it. You know?"

"Yes, Ari, we remember," Annie said.

"It scared me that you'd tried, and scared me that you'd failed," murmured Timi. She found herself holding on to Annie's head as if it were some fluffy stuffed animal, caressing it for her own comfort.

"Me too." Ari watched her fingers playing in Annie's hair. "When he tricked me into opening the locked room, the portal, I thought I had let him win, and he did too. He was laughing like a maniac when he followed me in there...."

"Yes?" Timi asked. So far as she knew, Ari had never told anyone what had happened in that room. All anyone knew was that Oberon and Ari had gone into the locked room together, and that Ari had emerged with a body that looked nothing like the regal King of Shadows.

"As soon as the door shut behind us, he stopped laughing. The feeling in that room.... It wasn't *happy* or *light*. It was... awesome. That's the only word. It was as if someone had shown me the entire universe, all at once, every atom. The threads connecting every soul to every other. It was the most beautiful and most terrible feeling I'd ever experienced. And I had... a vision."

Timi could see the flickering light of the fire reflected in his eyes.

"It was like I was... It was my parents, yeah, but also Nolicherri and Chancellor Levy, Joe and Jim, TJ and Rue. Sam. Your mum Brigid, Timi." He sighed, his belly rolling beneath Timi's cheek. "And... And you two. And for a second I got scared, because most of the rest were *dead*, you see. But not you. I knew that. I focused on the two of you, and it was like... looking into the sun. But you were smiling. All of you. You were all..." He shook his head, his dark locks flashing across Annie's pale skin. "I looked at you. And I felt so... Jesus. I don't have the words. But I felt *loved*. By every one of you. And it was the most frightening thing I'd ever felt. Then I realized, yes, you did love me, lucky son of a bitch that I am, but that what I was feeling wasn't just *you*, it was inside of me. It was me *feeling* your love. Does that make any fucking sense at all?"

Timi nodded.

"It makes perfect sense," Annie murmured softly. Timi felt her friend's voice humming through her own pelvis.

He looked between the two of them, then sighed. "So then... I looked down. Because Oberon was on his knees, rolled up like ball, moaning. And I knelt down and I... I kissed him. On the top of his head. Like a little boy. And he looked up at me, with those red eyes, and..." Ari's voice had thickened. He was clearly struggling to be able to talk, to finish.

Annie spoke again. "He asked you to kill him?"

Ari nodded, and Timi gasped. "To release him. That's what he said. And I understood him them, or I thought I did. But... he was nothing more than a terrified child who had been running away from something for so long that the flight had taken him over utterly. So I took my wand, and looked him in the eye, and cast the spell." Tears were now streaming down onto Annie's belly, and both girls reached out to touch his face. "He... It was like watching something melt away to reveal a totally different core. It was a man. An old, old man. I picked him up and...."

Ari wept, then, and Timi found herself blanketing herself against his back, kissing his neck and trembling shoulders, embracing him — and Annie, who was gently comforting Ari from the other side. And when his sobs had finally subsided, Ari sighed and said. "When I saw the two of you at my door, today, I remembered that feeling, that certainty of your love, and I wanted to run to you both and hold you, and kiss you and tell you how much I loved you. But I, uh, didn't think you would understand it. Or welcome it."

"Stupid," Timi spluttered — she was crying too, for a change — and she kissed Annie and Ari both.

"Oh," mused Annie, "I don't think it was stupid at all. I rather like the way things have worked out. Don't you?"

Chapter Three

Triptych

Walking out of church, Timi felt an almost foreign sense of well-being; the morning was beautiful, the service had been lovely, and her pussy could still remember the feeling of Ari and hummed gently to itself with the knowledge that it would feel him again soon. Ari, who was shaking hands with Mr. and Mrs. Finneran, whose daughter Rue had been his girlfriend back before.

Timi wished the day could have been free of ghosts. That everyone could have been here. Mom had to deal with the inevitable crisis up at the school, and Mum, Joe, and Jim...

After taking a quick breath, Timi turned and thanked the priest.

"It's good to see to see you, Timi," Father Whyte said, his long face bowed into a smile. "Since your mother's funeral, I haven't seen much of you and yours. Addie, your mother, does come by occasionally of a Sunday, but St. Patrick's doesn't seem quite the same bereft of red heads."

"We've scattered to the winds a bit since... everything that happened," Timi answered, the sense of peace dimming slightly as she searched for understanding in his lined face, and found it. Theodosius Whyte had been a schoolmate of Timi's mother Brigid at the college. As had Annie's father...

Annie. Is she okay?

Two of the parishioners wished Father Whyte a happy Easter, and he nodded to them, smiling.

"So," he continued to Timi in a quiet voice, his grey eyes twinkling, "am I going to be saying the banns for you and young Mr. Sundown any time soon?"

"Oh," Timi spluttered, inwardly cursing her Irish skin. "We haven't quite gotten... to that point..." The thought of how Father Whyte would respond to the question that springs to mind — *If we were to get married, how would our crypto-Buddhist girlfriend figure in to the Catholic ceremony?* — put Timi in one of her least favorite dilemmas: blush or giggle? Given the setting, she focused on swallowing the laughter, and let her skin color as it will.

The good pastor apparently took this for maiden modesty and laughed.

Once Timi and Ari had said goodbye to priest, they walked hand in hand through the village — the smallest of the three towns in Sundown Valley. Timi grinned as Ari took in the quasi-Old World quaintness of Elysian Fields. It occurred to her that, aside from a few of the many funerals the previous year, he may never have actually seen the village itself, the furthest from the main settlement and the college. After all, though he had grown up as she had in Elysium Territory, he'd probably never had a reason to come to this far reach of the magical enclave. She resolved that she and Annie should properly show him the sights before the holiday week was out.

"What was the priest cornering you about?" Ari asked as they strode down the tiny main street towards the green. "Must have been good to turn you so pink."

"Oh," sighed Timi, holding in the smile that wanted to blossom, "he was asking when he could expect to announce our engagement."

Ari's thin eyebrows shot into his hairline. "Our... engagement?"

She grinned. "Yours and mine. I didn't have the heart to tell him just what a mare's nest he was kicking up."

"I guess not," Ari mused, running his hand through his unruly hair. "Timi... How do you feel about that?"

Suddenly she found she can't look at him. Instead, she laughed. "I had dreams of walking up the aisle of St. Patrick's in a white dress since... Well, since before I'd even met you."

She looked over at him, expecting to see him blush, expecting to see him laughing. Expecting at most an embarrassed smirk and a smart comment about how silly they would have looked in wedding clothes at nine and ten. But his face was deeply serious, his brows drawn together, his mouth a thin line. "Don't, Ari. You were supposed to find that silly. I do."

"Why?" he asked. "Why should you? You deserve that, Timi. You deserve the chance to celebrate... to have your dream. I *want* you to have that, I..." He snorts in disgust. "I don't know how."

"Ari." Timi didn't know what to say. Truth be told, she had been so pleased, so relieved to have found what she had with Ari and Annie that it hadn't occurred to her to think past today, past being together with both of them again. Certainly she hadn't thought about what was going to happen after she and Annie left school in June, and if she had, it hadn't been in terms of anything so public or conventional as marriage. As they walked on across the village green, hands coupled, she peered back at him through her bangs.

His face was blank and what passed in him for pale, a look she has come to know well, but which she had hoped she and Annie had banished. Damn. Of *course* Ari would think about this. His deepest, most primal wish was for a family; even if Joe hadn't whispered what Ari had told him, that he'd always hated being an only, that he missed his parents and envied Joe their family (*Mum, Joe...*), she would have known. And all things being equal there was nothing in the world she would rather give: all of her love, every bit of it, and a dozen kids besides.

Well, not quite every bit of it, because of course there is a certain blonde in Weston who could claim every jot as much. "It's funny," Timi muses. "I love you with all of my heart, Ari Sundown. And I love Annie with all of my heart. How is that possible?"

Though his face is still pale, Ari smiles. "When your brothers first started dating Kailey and Karina, you know... I felt really uncomfortable. Left out. Do you know what Jim told me? 'Love isn't a zero-sum game.'"

"What?"

"Well," he says, riffling his hair with his free hand, "as nearly as I could understand, it meant that it wasn't finite. Giving it to one person doesn't mean taking it away from another. One couldn't ever give all of it away. Which was a shock to me, since what did *I* know about love?" He shot her a wink, his impish smile making her heart flutter. Had she inspired that in him? She could only pray so, because if she could make Ari give her that smile on a regular basis, Timi was fairly sure life would never be altogether bad.

Crossing off of the green and back onto the main street, she returns his grin and gave his hand a squeeze. "Did Mom manage to treat you like a person this morning and not one of her Summonings?"

That earned her a full laugh. "No. I think you she's happy to see you..." His face closed off, but it is just for a moment. "Your mom... mum..." he begins, and then looks into her eyes.

She shrugged. "Mom... Dolfy's been very tired, so much to do at school..." She knew, however, that even Ari was perceptive enough to realize that seeing her and Ari together could only make her mother wish that her wife, Timi's birth mother, had been there.

Ari nodded. Then, out of nowhere, he pulled her body to his and kisses her, right there in the middle of the street in Elysian Fields on Easter Sunday for anyone to see, and her nipples blossomed and her blood flowed outward until her skin was singing from ears to ankles, and she felt as if the entire village could see just what this man did to her, and that might be just fine.

He moaned, and it was her turn to laugh. "Clearly I need reinforcements!" she giggled in his ear. "Good thing Annie's waiting for us."

"Timi," he whispered, "I... It was so different, so nice, being with just *you* last night. I missed Annie, but... I didn't, you know? And I just feel..."

"Guilty?" she said, her hand running up the middle of his chest. He nodded, and she can't help but sigh. "I know," she murmured. And they step back from each other.

They were just outside of Fawcett & Sons Apothecary, and through the glass of the door, Timi could feel more than see the hawkish sneer of Sarah Fawcett, her expression clearly broadcasting the message, *Get a room.*

Timi pulled Ari back along towards the road to the west.

As they are clearing the edges of the village, Ari asked, "What has Sarah What'shername got against you, anyway? I mean, she's always treated you and Annie like crap."

"Oh," Timi mutters. "You saw her. Yeah, well, three girls, all the same age, in a tiny town like this, our folks used to get us together all of the time. We home-schooled together for a while, before Annie's mom died. And the thing was.... See, Sarah always hated Annie. Just hated her. And for years she kept trying to get me not to like her either. And then, not long after Annie's mom passed away, and Annie was even... spacier than usual, Sarah turns to me one afternoon, when we're all over at her home, right above the shop there, and says that I need to choose: I can be her friend — Sarah's — or I can keep seeing Annie. And that was it. I walked out and never went back." Timi shakes her head. "Sarah couldn't believe it. And Annie kept telling me to go to her. But I knew where my loyalty lay. And of course, Sarah's the one behind everyone treating her like shit, and..." Timi could feel her anger rising, and she took a deep breath.

"And she's jealous," Ari said quietly. "Because Annie is a war hero, and she's got you, and she's got me, and all Sarah Fawcett has is a string of boyfriends who can't stand her and a face that looks as if one of Poole's nastier experiments went wrong right beneath her nose."

Timi laughed, and now — out as they are passing the base of the Devil's Knob — she pulled *him* in for a long, passionate kiss.

Timi could feel his cock beginning to strain against her stomach, pulsing. An automobile sailed by, and they both looked up, or she would have had her hand down the front of his trousers.

Once the car had disappeared across the Elysium River bridge, Ari whispered into her ear, "Good thing we're getting close to Annie's. Think I'm going to need reinforcements." And he trailed a thumb across one of her nipples — delicious cruelty.

They entered the small clump of houses that marked metropolitan Weston, the tiny, unincorporated non-town between Elysian Fields and Noonday, then meandered up the road that led to Annie's home. Seeing the little house with its surrounding tangle of overgrown apple trees, Timi sighed and mumbled, "I hope..."

Ari squeezed her hand and nodded. Annie hadn't been alone in her family's house since her father died a year before, his blood turned to ink — the Fairy Queen's psychotic sense of humor playing out to the last. Annie had insisted that they leave her alone overnight, her first back in the house since, and they had both agreed, in part because Timi wanted to spend Easter with her mother and barely had the courage to explain Ari to her.

Ari would spend tonight with Annie. And Timi was finding her heart to be far more conflicted about that than she would have expected. Which seemed silly: she and Annie had had so many nights alone this year. And she had had Ari all to herself last night. But in spite of herself she was afraid...

Afraid that Annie and Ari would discover that they didn't need her. That she was superfluous. And Timi had spent most of her life feeling superfluous. Even though she knew this was bullshit, even if they had proved to her, time and again, that they would not forget her. The hardest thing in the world, it seemed, was to trust two people you loved with each other.

Two things landed her back in her body: Ari's hand, dense and warm in hers; and the sight of Annie's figure standing in the doorway.

She was in a red velvet dress that is totally out of character with the day and with Annie herself — low-cut and skin-tight over her lithe body. Her wheaten hair tumbled unbound over a small matching opera cape that hung off-center from her narrow shoulders. A slash of dark red lipstick made Annie's skin look even paler than usual, made her eyes seem almost colorless. Timi hadn't seen Annie wear make-up since they were both seven.

Desire squeezed Timi's middle. Ari's hand spasmed in hers, and she could hear his breath catch; he was as stunned by their lover's appearance as she was, apparently.

"Hello, Timea," Annie breathed. "Hello, Aaron. I've been sorting things." Slowly, tantalizingly, she untied the cape's knot at her throat. "How was church?"

Timi was speechless.

"L-lovely," stuttered Ari. "You c-could have joined us..."

"Oh, I never go to church," Annie sighed, separating the red, silken lengths of the tie and examining them. "My family never did. It all seemed so... silly. My mother used to read from *The Thread of Love* when the day seemed important." She turned and walked inside, loosing one end of the cape. It slipped off the shoulder and down her back, trailing behind her on the floor.

"*The...?*" Timi was transfixed by the sway of Annie's boyish hips beneath the red velvet.

"*Thread of Love.*" Annie dropped the other string, and the cape flopped to the ground. "There are three ways to reach an understanding of the world: Duty, Power or Love. And love is really the nicest, don't you think?" Annie was not looking back, simply gliding forward. One thin arm reached up behind her and slowly pulled down the gown's zipper, revealing Annie's long, white, naked back and high buttocks. She walked right out of the dress, and through the door into her room.

V elvet sounds like what it is, swishing, sliding down over your no-hips. You are wet and hungry, and a year ago you would not have known what this feeling meant, not really, even when you rubbed yourself raw thinking of Joe or of Ari or of Sam or of Timea or of Karina, with her butter-toned skin and the freckles on her nose that you so wanted to taste.

Beer-bottle sea glass…

Nipples tingle as air strikes. Snakebites for breasts you have, tiny nipples swelling between your pinching fingers. That's what Mother always said, that she had snakebites till you were born and then she had apricots. Timea has peaches, ripe and firm and juiced and muscled she is, all of her, square-shouldered as her brothers but small, and so *present*. Agni. *Agnus Dei*. Sacrifice to the Sacrificial. Sufficient unto the day.

Did they understand? People don't understand so often. But Aaron Sundown and Timea O'Danan, they seem to understand so often. So often. Are they?...

There they are. At the door. Flame and shadow. Beer-bottle sea glass, their eyes, brown and green, naught but sand and fire. But they see. They understand.

You see the hunger in their eyes and it unlocks the blaze in your middle, your center. You kneel on your bed, where you were weeping all last night, and you hold your arms out to Timea, to Ari. "I am the ritual, I am the sacrifice, I am the offering, I am the officiant, I am the fire, and I am the oblation."

Ari, his fingers funbling as he zips down Timea's dress, looks serious. Timea smiles, teeth white. As her dress pools at her feet, she says, "Are we supposed to drink you up? Is that the idea?"

"Hmmm." That sounds like a lovely idea. You hold out your arms to them and they come to you, and the ache, the cold of this house evaporates beneath their stinging kisses. He finds one side of your neck and she the other, and your fingers tangle themselves in their hair as you feel the first flutter of faint release at that initial contact. They both smell of the lavender soap that her mother — her *mum* — always concocted, and you wish that you could have been there in that shower, bathing yourself in them, and you fall backwards, pulling their two twined bodies onto you, kissing her flame to life, and her small lips meet yours and you hear Ari groan, his hands dancing over your front, your snakebite breasts, and you feel another shudder, a tiny release, and they can do that, can bring you to bliss over and over and over. Her tongue is so small. You love the feel of it in your mouth, in your ear, on your neck. You want the feel of it on your pearl.

The light flares briefly and time starts again as Ari kneels back, pulling off his shirt, tearing off his trousers, his undies. His him springs out, and you note a new smell as you flop over and slither your way towards their pelves, the rich, tart scent of her on him: they have

fucked already this morning, Eostra's festival, Eostra's bunny, like rab-
bits, and you want to taste him in her, but first...

Her mouth is too small for him, and you know that makes her
sad, that she cannot please him that way, though he clearly does not
mind. But he loves your wide mouth and he whimpers now as you run
your lips over the musty head of him. That first time at Aaron's house,
tasting him and savoring the flavors and the textures, so new, and he
shouted when he came, hot, bitter, earthy taste like the Burn Balm
potion your mother fed you once when you scorched your tongue, and
you had been frightened that you were hurting him, but Timea whispered to you and stroked you, and kissed the overflow off of your chin.
He groans already, hot, but not this time, no, you want to see him in
her, taste him in her, and so, your hands still on his testicles you slide
beneath her, kissing her stomach, leaning her forward so that her hair
sizzles over your own flat chest, her red tangle above you like a Mark
of Life — this way to Heaven. Two small beauty marks line up beneath
her navel like the end stars of the Big Dipper, pointing the way to
Polaris.

One hand looses Ari. Your fingers dance, not quite touching the
pinker-than-yours skin of her ribs, her waist. The fuzz on her bum. She
shivers. Around behind to the split fruit of her, already damp and you
can't stop yourself from pushing up to taste. Yes. Soursweet like green
apple she is, and you can taste his musk on her lips, on her jewel. And
taste. And taste.

Ari is kissing your forehead and her bum, but you don't think he'll
mind, and so you lead him forward by his thick signpost until the tip of
him spreads her fine, pink ruff and Timea gasps into your hip and you
groan to see her quiver as he slowly enters her....

You love to feel Ari inside of you, pressing and stretching. You love
to feel her fine fingers and her tongue moving over you as they are now,
trembling. You love to feel spasms of release in their encircling arms.

But nothing excites you quite as much as being right here, your
nose and mouth and fingers at their point of union, your spit mixing
with his juices and hers to make a single moist libation to pour upon
the flames of your passion, to feed your fire. You drink them in and
they are part of you, and you are not alone.

His *valseuses* tighten as they slide faster and faster along your forehead and your nose. He is close. *Coito ergo...* Timea screams into your
navel, all too soon, and Ari joins her, their thighs spasming on either

side of your face. They each reach release and you drink them in until you are sated. Libation of the gods.

Your mother liked to say that love given leaves more to bestow. She was also fond of quoting the various analogs of the Golden Rule: love thy neighbor as thyself; do unto others as you would have them do unto you; thou art that. As your lovers uncouple slurpily, you rest in the glow of...

Ari's kiss on your *mons veneris*. "I love you."

Timea's lips on your hip. "We missed you."

He rolls you onto your tummy-tum on top of him, and you feel the steam rising from your back. Who knew you had gotten so sweaty? Her fingers find your snakebites even as her mouth continues to explore your spine and you feel yourself blossom with desire.

When his mouth surrounds your pearl, you whimper, and part of it is disappointment because as wonderful and loving as his mouth is, hers is like liquid flame but you can't complain for feeling so good and she will...

As Ari laps at your jewel, Timea's tiny tongue finds your rosebud and...

FUCK

One of your mother's other favorite aphorisms was that time is an illusion. Your father, when tipsy, would inevitably add, "And lunchtime doubly so!" and they would both giggle. But she would encourage you to look at death not as a period, but as a comma, and she would say that, if you were lucky and were paying attention, you would find moments of release, little parentheses in the sentence of your life, when you could stand outside of time. Free. Consumed in the bonfire of eternity.

Release.

Not alone.

Lying on Annie's bed, her long leg draped over one of his shoulders, Timi's head resting on the other, Ari suddenly noticed the pictures. There were so many of them that they took up every square inch of wall space not reserved for bookshelves, the window or the door. There were so many of them that they almost fade out of notice — *did* fade out of notice, since in all of the time that they'd been here, this was the first time Ari had noticed them. Every one was a painting of a couple. Dancing. Kissing. Strolling. A maiden handing a mounted knight a flower and blushing demurely. A pair of women curled around each other like a living *yin-yang*. Ari peered at an ice-skating couple just over Timi's naked back, and the woman winked at him before executing a deft pirouette. Dozens of embraces. Of longing glances.

He kissed Annie's ankle, and she sighed.

If he had imagined what sort of artwork Annie would have decorated her room with, this wouldn't have been it — trees perhaps, or mythic beasts. But not this.

Timi hissed against Ari's shoulder. Something that Annie was doing had gotten her attention. He leaned over and kisses the top of their smaller partner's new-penny head. "Timi?"

"Mmmm?"

"What are those paintings in your bedroom?"

"Mmmm?"

"Those beautiful prints of the paintings of those blonde women..." There were three of them, clustered over Timi's desk. Aside from various stuffed animals, they were the only decoration in her room. Each was staring at the viewer with otherworldly eyes. Each was alone.

"Botticelli," Timi sighed.

"Who?" Ari asked, knowing he wasn't helping her out by running his fingers along her ribs.

"Wizard artist from about six hundred years ago. Painted for mundanes. Mum brought back the prints from Florence about five years back... They're all so.... *Mmmm.*"

Solitary blonde women with eyes that stared out at you from the other side of the universe. From other planes of being. *Changelings...*

"Why?" Timi asked, taking the initiative, nipping at his nipple. "I don't remember — what pictures have you got up in *your* bedroom?"

With a start that was caused in part by an epiphany and in part by her tongue, Ari gasped. "Uh, I don't have any. Never have, any-where."

Annie worked her way languidly up Ari's body in a manner that left him feeling anything but languid. Otherwhere eyes.

"You've got all of those paintings downstairs," Timi mused.

"Yeah, but... I never had anything I'd want to decorate...." Ari gasped as each girl took a nipple in her mouth.

Annie leaned up and gazed at Ari from across the universe. From other planes of being. "If you could decorate your room with any-thing, what would it be?"

Ari grinned, threading his arms around his sun and moon. "That's easy," he said.

And he pulled them both up into a long, satisfying kiss.

Tragedy changes you, but tragedy fades. And each of them helped make it fade for each of the others. Not making it go away. Not obscuring it. Just... making it fade.

Wherever the three of them were, that was home. Wherever the three of them were, that was where they belonged.

Unchanging.

Unchangeling.

Happily ever after.

better than fine

Shannon Meyers

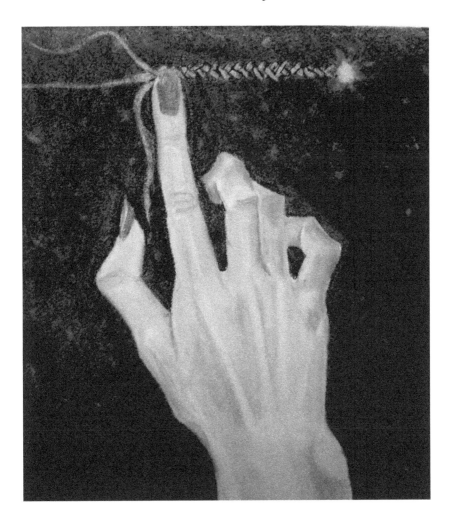

anie kicked another rock in frustration as she walked through the darkened wood. It wasn't like her to be so agitated – she normally had a rather sunny disposition. In fact, her elder sister Mar insisted she was *too* optimistic most of the time.

Not tonight, though.

Tonight Janie allowed herself to be as moody and irritable as Mar usually was.

They were on their annual camping trip to the woods where her parents had met. Both of her parents adored this mountain. Her father was an avid hiker in his youth and her mother had family ties to the area that made them both borderline obsessed with it. Plus, there was the whole, "Your mother saved my life. She was like an angel, performing a miracle," and, "I met my soulmate here," that made it sacred to them.

She tried not to think about how they were "celebrating" their twentieth anniversary in their own cabin at this precise moment.

Janie didn't begrudge them having their own cabin or for their choice of vacation. Her parents truly were soulmates. It was obvious to anyone who saw them. They were wonderful parents too. They deserved the time together.

Under normal circumstances, she would have been ecstatic to share a cabin alone with Mar. But her sister was sixteen and fresh out of her first break-up with the boy she thought was *her* soulmate. Daren absolutely was *not* her soulmate. It was as obvious as the sun in the sky to Janie – Daren was a total dick, truth be told – but Mar was young and too foolish to see it.

Her sobbing into the pillow and ignoring Janie's attempts to cheer her up had driven the younger girl to give up and flee their small cabin for the soothing sounds of the woods.

It wasn't just the crying and drama that had driven her out in a fit of frustration. Janie would normally be able to withstand the storm of teenage angst that Mar was so prone to. She had to admit, if only just to herself, that Janie was disappointed in herself more than anyone else.

Mar had thrown a glass at the wall in a fit of anger and cut her hand. Janie hadn't been able to heal it.

Granted, she'd never been able to do things like that. Healing herself quickly had never been a problem, so she'd maintained hope. She comforted herself by saying "not yet", but she was rapidly approaching thirteen now and still showing no signs of the healing abilities her mother and sister possessed.

Her great-great-grandmother had been a full-fledged witch, like every female ancestor before her, though her power had manifested in the healing arts. Without other magical blood in the family tree, the gift had weakened with the centuries, but most of the women in her maternal line had some predisposition for it. Her mom had become a nurse and healed people the scientific way; she also had a talent for clearing out infection and ensuring the treatments took hold like they should that no amount of science or logic could explain. Mar showed the same abilities.

Janie did not. She had only ever been able to help herself. She couldn't help but wonder what that said about her.

Maybe you're just inherently selfish, she thought.

She was being selfish now, even. She really should have stayed with Mar no matter how much of a nightmare she was being. Soulmates were a big deal for witches. It was well-known by the family that every witch had a soulmate. Even normal teenagers felt like their first love would be the big one; considering she and Mar had their parents' perfect marriage staring them in the face all the time too, it was no wonder Mar was so eager to believe she had found hers.

Daren really was the worst though, Janie reminded herself. *It would have been awful had he been Mar's soulmate.* He was a true example of selfishness, not her.

She was a decent person. Deep down, she knew that. She volunteered on the weekends at the local shelter and soup kitchen, always went out of her way to talk to anyone who looked lonely, and helped people in need to safely cross the street. She did what she could to help others whenever possible, even if it was just offering a smile, but still she couldn't do what the witches in her family were supposed to. Maybe the magic was finally fizzling out, and her daughters would have none.

She felt an uncharacteristic flare of resentment toward Mar. *Daren wasn't her soulmate, but at least she has enough magic to know that she* has *one. I may not even get that.* She angrily dropped herself down onto a fallen log and laid back, trying to glimpse the stars through the canopy of leaves. Maybe if she could see the stars, she'd be able to read the future there.

It was all the more depressing because Mar had never cared about having a soulmate. It was just something that came along with being a witch that she accepted as fact. Janie had always wanted hers though, always admired what her parents had. It had been what she looked forward to most about becoming a witch.

Now that she wasn't, she was uncharacteristically disgruntled that she wouldn't have one. It was unsettling. *Your focus on a soulmate instead of how you could help the world is probably why you don't deserve to be a witch*, she chastised herself.

She needed to let it go or she'd become as bitter toward the world as Mar was naturally. Billions of normal people existed in the world and found love and happiness without one. So what if she couldn't take part in her mother's legacy? She could still help people. That was what mattered. Not a soulmate.

"I don't need a soulmate," she said aloud, trying to convince herself that it was true.

"Maybe you don't need him, child, but he most certainly needs you."

Janie fell off the log in surprise. The disembodied voice was quiet and hoarse, as if little used, but so unexpected that she scrambled back in fear as she searched for the speaker through the darkness.

It took a moment, but then she saw her. It was an old woman, leaning tiredly against a tree not three yards from where Janie sat, head tilted back and looking at the sky as Janie had been moments ago. How she had missed her presence until now, she wasn't sure. Janie could hear her wheezing breaths now that she listened.

Looks could be deceiving, however, so she slid a few feet further away. Keeping her eyes on the woman, she asked, "Who are you?"

"I'm a witch," she said plainly. "Same as you are, my dear."

Janie eyed her with suspicion. It wasn't entirely out of the realm of possibility that she would stumble upon a witch here – plenty of witch lines had descended from the area and frequented it because of the history it held – but how could the woman possibly guess that she was one too? She *wasn't*.

Curiosity got the better of her. She stood and approached the woman. "I'm not a witch, not really," she said.

The woman looked at her then. Her eyes glowed with an odd silver light in the darkness, as if they caught and reflected the moonlight that the thick canopy above them blocked. The light seemed to shine out of them, casting strange shadows over her lined face. There was no denying that Janie was in the presence of a witch now, not with the wave of magic that passed through her as their eyes locked.

"I don't know who you're trying to fool, but it won't work with me. I see you, and I see him. It's my family's specialty, finding and fostering the connections in this world. *You*," she said with emphasis, "most definitely have a witch's bond. Healing, is it not?"

"Yes," Janie heard herself say, her mind in disarray. The witch could see her ability, despite how limited it was. "But I can't heal others, the way my mom and sister can. Only myself."

"Pity," the witch said, though it didn't sound very concerned. "I could use some help. My ankle, you see," she said gesturing to her leg. "Perhaps you could help me the old fashioned way?"

She extended a gnarled hand that Janie took without hesitation. Maybe it was foolish to trust a stranger, even an elderly, injured woman, but she was a witch, and witches could do no harm to others without harming themselves. Unless the old woman was suicidal, Janie had nothing to fear from her. Besides, Janie liked to assume the best in people.

The witch stood with Janie's help and threw a frail arm around her shoulders. Janie supported the older woman's weight and followed her directions without thought, her mind going over their conversation again.

It was several minutes of helping the witch through the wood before she worked through it well enough to form a proper question. "What did you mean? About my soulmate needing me?"

"You misunderstand the concept, little one. It is not he who is your soulmate, but you who are his."

"What?" she asked again, drawing them to a stop so that she could look at the witch properly. It was late, she was emotionally drained, and this old witch had her reeling with the confirmation that she was indeed a witch. She needed more explanation to understand.

The witch seemed unconcerned with their lack of progression and met her gaze steadily. "It is not the witch who receives the soulmate in return for her service, but the man in need and deserving of a witch that does." Her eyes grew brighter, her voice stronger. "I daresay the poor young man is quite in need of your gift."

Janie's heart thudded in her chest as her stomach sank with dread. "But... but I *can't* help him! I don't even know who he is, and I told you, I've only ever been able to help myself!"

The minute that followed seemed to last an eternity as the witch gave her a long searching look. Once more, Janie felt the wave of magic that accompanied it. She felt she might burst with nerves by the time the witch replied.

"I can help with that, if you wish. It may save his life, truth be told." Fear coursed through Janie. It was that bad? She *had* to help him. If the witch was to be believed, that was her purpose. To save him. The witch cut into her thoughts with a warning, all previous weakness lost as she issued her cautions, "Should you choose to accept, it will not be an easy path for you. It will be difficult and full of pain."

"But it will help him?" she asked. Desperation swelled within her at the thought of the boy's suffering. She didn't know him – not yet – but someday she would. *If he survived until then.* The witch had said Janie's help may be what saved him. She couldn't *not* do it. No matter the cost.

Janie woke with a groan of pain. At fourteen, she had grown accustomed to the foreign injuries that resulted from the witch's spell and usually just healed them before going on with her life as if they had never happened. It was uncomfortable and sometimes inconvenient, but she had never once regretted it. Not even in the first moments after the spell, before she fully understood what she'd done and her elbow dislocated without warning. She'd screamed out in pain that first time, but she'd gotten better at hiding her reactions since then.

Well, not enough that she could realistically have friends in the way that most teenagers did. Considering she often woke up in pain with some unexplainable injury, sometimes with blood pouring out across the sheets, she couldn't do sleepovers. Nor could she wear a bathing suit or small pajamas in front of others. Still, they were easy sacrifices to make.

The thought that there was a boy out there who had lived with this kind of abuse, likely for years, without help and without the benefit of magic to fix him, was sobering enough that she never once felt bad for herself or felt the need to complain. If someone were to offer her the opportunity to change her mind and go back, she'd never in a million years consider it.

Besides, she kept enough company with her sister and her books that she never felt lonely. That was enough.

That night was different, though. It was bad. Worse than ever before, she realized as she woke for the second time that night.

The first time she woke, it was to the blinding pain and pounding pulse that resulted from a cracked skull. She healed the bone quickly, if not with extreme difficulty thanks to the excruciating pain, and fallen back to sleep immediately. She must have missed something that first time around, because the room swam around her as she tried to sit up and she vomited over the side of the bed before she could get any further.

A concussion, she thought amidst the dizziness and confusion. Having grown up a nurse's daughter, she could recognize the symptoms. *I've – he's – got a concussion.* She tried to focus, tried to find the swelling to bring down, but she'd let it get too far. Her own mind was too damaged.

She needed help.

Even the nauseating ringing in her ears and frustration at her inability to move her limbs properly couldn't cover up the dread she felt at having to explain what was going on. She'd had plenty of disturbing injuries before, but she'd never failed to handle them on her own. Which meant she'd never told anyone either.

The prospect was more terrifying than the way she fell over when she tried to stand.

The noise drew Mar to her room, however. That was a positive. At least she didn't have to struggle her way out into the hall or risk waking her parents if she stumbled into a wall.

"What the fuck, Janie? I'm trying to sleep and you're –" her words cut off abruptly before Janie felt Mar's hands on her face. At some point, Janie closed her eyes and she had missed the moment of recognition, when Mar realized what happened to her. She knew it must have happened though, thanks to her sister's sharp intake of breath. "What the fuck, Janie?" she asked again, but this time her voice was shocked and panicked instead of angry.

"Concussion," she managed to respond through gritted teeth, trying to hold back the vomit. *Why is Mar insisting on moving my head? It hurts.*

"I know," Mar said. "I know it hurts, but I just have to…"

She trailed off as Janie felt the overwhelming pain fade into nothingness, clarity returning in its place. She took a deep breath in relief as Mar's hands fell away from her face. The contentment was short-lived, as she was greeted by an angry and suspicious sister when she opened her eyes.

She cleared her throat nervously. "Um, thank you?"

Despite all her hopes, Mar didn't accept. She tried again, knowing it was fruitless. "I'm all fixed. You can go back to bed now."

Mar glared at her. In a disturbingly controlled voice that warned of the fury brewing below, she said, "I'll ask *one* more time. *What the fuck, Janie?*"

"It was a concussion," she started.

Her sister raised her hand impatiently, cutting her off. "I'm aware of that. How did you *get it?*"

"I fell out of bed and hit my head. I must not have done a good job healing it," she lied easily. She was accustomed to fibbing these odd instances away. "I didn't notice the concussion until I woke up again."

"*Bullshit*, Janice," she spit, crossing her arms over her chest.

The use of her name meant Mar was serious, but maybe if she pushed the right buttons... "That's what happened, *Marion*. Don't you have a test in the morning? Just go back to bed."

"*Fuck the test*," she said viciously. "You've got bruises on your neck, Janie. *Hand-shaped* bruises. And I know you didn't have them when you went to bed." Worry was replacing the anger in her tone. Mar gripped her hands fiercely. "Talk to me, Janie. I'll help you. I promise."

It was the desperation in her sister's words that broke her. Mar was always a bit rough around the edges, a bit harsh and unforgiving, and seeing her sister let her guard down washed away her own misgivings.

She took a deep breath and then began. "Do you remember Mom and Dad's twentieth anniversary two years ago? That trip we went on?"

She continued at her sister's nod. The words came relatively easily, pouring out as if she'd rehearsed it a thousand times. Perhaps she had; she'd dreamed of that night often enough. Mar kept their hands clasped, but her face remained closed and blank the entire time.

"... so, I agreed, and the witch cast a spell that would bind us."

The silence lasted far too long before Mar spoke. Janie couldn't help cringing when she heard the carefully controlled tone had returned to her sister's voice.

"Let me get this straight," she said slowly. "You meet a strange witch in the woods and help her back to her cabin." She looked away from Janie a moment and shook her head. "Frankly, that sounds *exactly* like the kind of stupid you are, so that's not surprising." Janie didn't take offense, seeing as it seemed Mar was talking more to herself than to Janie. "But then she tells you that your soulmate needs you and you jump at the chance to become a punching bag in his place? That's fucking insane Janie, even for you."

"It's not," Janie insisted, though she kept her tone patient. Mar hadn't exploded and demanded they tell her mother yet. She could handle insults if that was the worst of it.

"Alright. Then explain to me how you getting hurt when he does is supposed to help anyone."

"That's not how the bond works," she explained. "I'm pretty sure I only get the worst of it, when he *needs* the help, and I sort of share it with him. He doesn't hurt as much, and when I heal myself, I heal him too." At Mar's doubtful look, she continued pleadingly, "You don't understand, Mar. I can't heal like you and Mom can, but I *can* help myself, and with the bond, I can help him too."

"I do get it," she replied evenly. Relief began to swell within Janie, but then her sister pulled her hands back and looked away. Her stomach filled with lead at the gesture. She knew what was coming. "But you can't, not really. Look at what happened tonight." She shook her head and looked back at her. *At least Mar looks like she feels guilty,* Janie thought, recognizing the struggle she saw in her sister's eyes. "You have to tell Mom. Maybe she can break it or something."

"*No!*" Janie exclaimed much too loudly for someone who didn't want to draw her parents' attention. It hadn't occurred to her that her mother may try to break the connection. She was more worried that her parents would be angry or disappointed – even worse, that they'd hover over her constantly. "Mar, *please*. I'm telling you, he *needs* this. I know it. I've felt the worst of it. He… I really don't think he'll make it without my help."

"Janie…" Mar's gaze was conflicted, her tone pained. "I can't."

Janie thanked every god she could think of for the slight weakness she saw in her sister. If Mar had fully made up her mind, she never would have stood a chance of stopping her. She pulled at her sister's hands again, squeezing for emphasis. "*Please.* I have to help him. Or else what is the point of all this? Witches help people, Mar. Let me do that. Let me save him." She bit her lip. "Could you imagine Mom having to live with knowing she let Dad die in those woods?"

She knew she'd gone too far when Mar pulled back and straightened up, so that she was looking down at Janie. "This is not the same as that. Mom wasn't hurting herself for Dad. There was never any risk to her." She pulled at her hair and began to pace. "Jesus, Janie. Do you have any idea what could have happened tonight, had I not been here?"

"I'll be more careful," she said quickly, eager to come up with some kind of compromise. "I'll be more careful, check more thoroughly. I'll *practice*. I'll get you if I can't handle it myself, I swear it." Tears had started pouring down her cheeks at some point that she hadn't noticed, and she wiped them away, staring wide-eyed at her sister while she awaited her decision.

Mar bit her lip, mirroring the same worried expression Janie herself had a few moments prior. As much as they looked alike physically, Janie had never thought they resembled one another – their general attitudes and movements were so different – until that moment.

"I believe you Janie, but I won't be here in a few months…" She went back to chewing on her bottom lip, looking dangerously close to breaking the skin, before she stopped and sank down beside Janie on the floor once more and pulled her into a fierce grip. It honestly hurt slightly, but Janie gripped her back just as fiercely.

"Mar?" she asked tentatively.

"I love you. You're batshit crazy, but I love you anyway. I'll help, okay? I don't have to go away to college."

Now Janie pulled back and gave her sister a stern look. "Of course you do! You can't stay behind because of me."

"If you want me to keep quiet, then I need to be able to help you," Mar retorted.

They glared at each other, mirror images with their arms crossed and brows furrowed. Janie relaxed first and blew out a breath. "Can we agree to an impasse right now? Let's just go to bed, and we can talk more in the morning."

Mar agreed. She hesitated for only a moment before kissing Janie's brow and leaving the room without further comment. It didn't escape Janie's notice that she had left the door cracked open, however.

Janie laid down, her heart in turmoil. She felt stuck, torn between wanting to protect the link with her soulmate and not wanting to hold her sister back. Mar should be becoming a doctor, really, but she insisted that nurses had more meaningful interactions with patients and that that was where she wanted to be. Her mother agreed wholeheartedly and wouldn't take issue with Mar going to the local college and becoming a registered nurse, but Janie had argued until Mar agreed to at least get her BSN degree. That hard work might have been for nothing now.

She wanted to deny it, even just to herself, but the truth was that if it came down to it, she'd let Mar make that sacrifice. With every fiber of her being, she *knew* that helping her soulmate was her purpose. It was why she was limited, she reasoned; because he needed her help more than she needed to help anyone else in the world, at least by magic. She'd do anything to keep protecting his life. She wished she could do more.

Closing her eyes, she concentrated on him. It was something she'd done every time he received a bad injury, since the very beginning. He was nameless, faceless, and without a voice; she knew nothing about him. Truthfully, there wasn't any real sense in the exercise, but saying aloud the words of comfort that she wished she could give him made her feel better nonetheless.

"Tonight was a bad one, I know. It seems like there have been a lot of those lately," she said tiredly, thinking of just how many injuries he'd had and how they'd gotten worse. She thought he might have been fighting back, given the broken hands she'd had the other night. She shook away the thoughts, concentrating on him once more. Being sure to insert confidence in her voice, she continued in the gentlest whisper, "It's going to be alright though, one way or another. I'm here, and I'm going to keep helping you no matter what. I promise. Just keep going, okay?" She hesitated only briefly before tacking on pleadingly, "For me. Please. Just keep fighting for me." Pushing back the brief moment of desperation, she pooled all the strength and conviction she could muster and repeated what she told him every time something like this happened, "I'm okay. You're okay. We're going to be fine, I promise."

The sound emanating from the house as Nate approached was loud and obnoxious. Even from where he stood at the base of the long drive, he could hear the cacophony of drunk teens mingling with the bass of some stupid ass pop song. The swarm of chattering kids that bumped into him on their way inside without stopping to apologize were probably drunk already too.

Despite the fact that they partygoers were all probably fairly harmless, Nate found himself frozen to the spot, the frigid temperatures of the end of the year permeating his thin coat and making him shiver. It wasn't that he was *afraid*. He'd faced far worse than this, to be sure. He just didn't like booze, crowds, or loud noises. The party undoubtedly had all three.

He could handle it, though. It wasn't like he had much choice anyway.

He'd had a hard couple of months – really, a hard eighteen years, but who was counting? – and he needed this. Especially since he'd decided to stop street-fighting for money. He'd recently run out of all his winnings and now his options were even fewer and farther between than before.

Sometimes, he still couldn't believe he'd walked away from fighting. It was quick, relatively easy money, especially for him. It made zero sense, but ever since he was fourteen, he'd begun to heal much quicker. Sure, the bruises and cuts he acquired lingered and turned from blacks and blues to purples, greens, and yellows like any other guy in the ring, but he would have sworn that he'd broken a bone or two that miraculously healed overnight. Or taken a blow to the head that should've knocked him on his ass, but he'd recovered from in a few minutes. It made his fighting career a goddamn goldmine.

Yet, he couldn't do it. He'd heard that voice again, the one he always imagined in the worst of times, the sweet feminine tones of a guardian angel that cared about him and begged him not to continue. That told him there was another way. She always sounded so pained when she told him that they were okay – that they'd be fine – that he felt too guilty to continue.

Whatever this magical other way was, he didn't know. He didn't have a high school diploma or any of his identifying documents when he had fled his father's drunken rage and never gone back, and job opportunities were few and far between when you lived like that.

He'd spent weeks damn near freezing and starving to death before he'd found fighting. Hell, he'd watched others succumb to the cold, but it was never him. Not even that particular bitter night when he'd given up his coat to a mother and her young son, wishing that his mother had done the same with him as a child. They'd survived, thank heavens, and so had he. With that voice that never failed to give him hope whispering in his ear all night, he'd somehow managed.

It was probably why he was willing to face starvation again – because that voice, the one that had saved him countless times – had begged him not to. Insane as it was, he couldn't bring himself to let it – her – down.

That didn't mean he didn't need to find another way, however, and this party seemed like the best option at the moment. After all, it wasn't stealing if you were invited to partake in the festivities. So what if it was the result of mistaken identity?

He shook off his misgivings and began making his way inside. What was there to be worried about? He had turned eighteen last week. He wasn't a runaway anymore. It's not like he could be sent back to his shit life or into foster care even if someone called the cops. Not that they would. He'd been invited…sort of.

When he made it through the door, he was greeted with the humid kind of heat that came from too many bodies in a confined area and the smell of liquor in the air. Unpleasant, but everything he expected it to be when one of the local seniors had mistaken him for one of his classmates and handed him a flyer for the New Year's Eve party. No one would notice that he wasn't one of them, which meant it was an easy way to spend the night in a warm place and score a free meal.

He quickly made his way toward the food. It was all junk, really, but he did manage to snag a slice of cold pizza that was missing half the cheese. Looking around the house, he could see that it was a nice, well-appointed place and most of the kids there looked well-off as well. It wasn't surprising that they'd let good food go to waste here.

Unfortunately, his musings also made him realize that the brighter lights of the kitchen showed just how different he was from them. In the darker, louder areas of the house, his beat-up appearance made him look like one of the kids trying to emulate the grunge days, but here it was obvious that he really was just homeless. He quickly grabbed a bottle of water and slipped out the back door, where the only source of light was a fire-pit with a handful of drunk kids mingling about.

From his perch on the outdoor furniture, he had a pretty good view. He could see through the sliding glass door into the kitchen, and, thanks to the house's open floor plan, into the main room beyond. Most of the partygoers were drinking from plastic cups, swaying to music, and chatting in small groups. A smaller number danced obscenely or engaged in dramatic PDA that he had no interest in watching.

Amidst the chaos of spilled drinks and moving bodies, he saw one person moving independently of the rest. She was… cleaning? It was so off that his gaze was drawn to her.

She was small. Her height was probably on the low end of average, but her frame was slight, almost too slight, though her clothes were well-kept. Despite the overwhelming tide of people, her movements were steady as she navigated the crowds picking up bottles and plates as she went. Her hair was a light brown, maybe a dark blonde, but that was about as much as he could tell from his vantage point.

He spent the rest of his time eating peacefully by the fire and watching her. She didn't quite fit in, he noticed – even her attire was different from that of her peers – but she wasn't an outcast either. She stopped and shared a smile or a few words with nearly everyone she came across, yet it didn't seem that she was close to any of them or engaged in any type of meaningful conversations. Most of them she just offered a bottle of water or a snack to before moving on.

Almost unconsciously, he found himself rising and heading back into the kitchen when he saw her enter and accept a video call on her phone. He didn't usually talk to people when he didn't have to, nor did he intend to talk to her now, but he was curious. Maybe he would over-hear something interesting.

Lazily, he walked through the door and leaned against the counter, back to her, pretending to prepare a drink while he listened.

"... having fun." There was something pleasant about her voice. Familiar even, though the way she was shouting made it hard to tell.

He just barely heard the response. "Prove it!"

"Fine!" she yelled back.

The bottle of vodka before him was grabbed by a small pale hand. He turned just in time to see her take a large swallow in full view of the camera. It must have been legit, because she looked like she wanted to hurl and began to cough as soon as it was done.

"*Yes!*" he heard her caller exclaim. She sounded drunk herself. "My work here is done! Have fun, lovely! I'm off to find my New Year's kiss. I expect you to find one too!" He heard the beep as the chat was dis-connected and the girl beside him exhaled heavily.

"Sorry," she said, placing the bottle back before him. He could feel her gaze on him as she spoke – heavy and direct – as if he deserved her full attention. He was surprised by how much it affected him, so much so that he refused to return it. "My older sister is a bit, well, wild, I guess. You know?"

"No," he said tersely.

He wasn't trying to offend her, but he had no intention of actually talking to her when he came inside. In retrospect, it was probably stupid to think that she would have ignored him. He hadn't seen her ignore a single person all night.

He couldn't help looking back at her, however. There was something different about her that made seeing her close up too enticing an opportunity to miss. He caught just a glimpse of tired looking eyes and hazel irises before the lights went dark and someone announced over the speakers that it was less than a minute to the ball drop.

"Shouldn't you be in there? Looking for someone to kiss?" he said, gesturing toward the crowd.

Instead of taking the hint like he hoped she would, she stood taller and met his eye. "Are you volunteering?" she asked boldly.

He gaped at her for a moment, floored by the show of confidence. There was the briefest moment of surprise that flashed across her face, as if she too was stunned by her own actions, but it passed too quickly for him to be sure.

When he didn't answer, she tilted her chin and looked up at him with a smile. "No? Guess I better get out there then." With a small wave, she walked away.

Nate hesitated. She really appeared to be a lovely girl. Kind, caring, and friendly. She was also rather beautiful, in a nontraditional way. There was an openness to her that drew him. She was probably younger than him, but not by enough that he worried it would be morally wrong. Plus, he'd been watching her long enough to know that she couldn't be drunk.

What made up his mind was her parting gesture. Her voice was chipper and the smile sincere, but he could see vulnerability beneath the bravado.

He caught up to her with five seconds to go. She had fled the kitchen, but she was just watching the ball on the screen, not appearing to have been looking for a partner at all.

He tapped her on the shoulder to get her attention. Her eyes widened in surprise when she saw who was standing beside her, but a smile spread across her face almost immediately. He didn't wait for her to ask again.

"Yes. I'm volunteering."

The ball dropped as soon as the words left his mouth, and suddenly she was kissing him.

While he wasn't innocent, he was sure he'd never experienced anything so pleasant in his entire life.

She was the epitome of everything warm, soft, and comforting in this world. It almost felt like a dream, falling into her. Despite having witnessed her take the shot of liquor, there was no trace of it on her breath when she opened her mouth to his. Instead, her tongue was a perfect balance of sweet and fulfilling. He both wanted to spend forever doing this, but was also desperate for more. He assumed he wasn't alone in his feelings, given how she escalated the kiss, using her grip on him to leverage herself closer.

He flinched when her fingers twined in his hair and brushed a particularly sensitive bruise. She pulled back at the action.

He tried to follow instinctively, to let her know without words that he didn't care in the slightest about the brief flash of pain. He'd never had a kiss like that before and wasn't anxious for it to stop, but she stepped back and out of his reach completely.

When he opened his eyes, he was surprised to see that hers were wide with panic, hands up in front of her as if she were afraid of him.

"I'm – I'm sorry," she said, something frantic in her voice. "I can't –". Her voice shook as she cut off and glanced from side to side quickly.

He raised his own hands and took a step back. "It's fine, really. I'm sorry." He didn't think he'd done anything to frighten her. His hands had been firmly on her waist in what most people considered a safe zone. She hadn't seemed to mind until they'd kissed. A kiss she'd initiated.

She swallowed heavily and nodded, standing a bit taller, though her body seemed to vibrate with nerves as she looked around again. A guy carrying three cups bumped into her, startling her for just a moment, before she reached out and took one of the cups and gulped it down as if the alcohol could save her from whatever had spooked her so thoroughly.

The guy tried to protest. Something about how that wasn't meant for her, how he'd paid for it, and she shouldn't have taken it. *It's a party,* Nate thought, *the drinks are free.* He didn't bother saying it aloud though. The guy's words were sloppy, so he pushed him aside without comment, his focus on the girl as she took deep breaths. All night he'd been watching her avoid the liquor here like the plague, with the exception of the shot she took in front of him, and the sudden shift in behavior had him concerned.

"Hey," he said calmly, stepping forward. "It really is alright. Don't freak out."

She didn't back away this time, instead straightening out and plastering a politely pleasant look on her face, all signs of panic gone in an instant. "I'm not," she said confidently. "I'm fine."

It was bizarre to experience the immediate change in her stance and tone. He wasn't sure he'd ever met such a competent liar, and quite frankly surprised that this girl had it in her. By all accounts, she'd seemed the epitome of normal, if a bit uptight, until this point.

"You didn't look it ten seconds ago," he said bluntly.

"Well, I am. I just need some air. It's overwhelming in here, don't you think?" She didn't wait for his response before turning and easily slipping through the crowd toward the kitchen, and, he presumed, out onto the deck.

He rushed to catch up to her, his slightly larger frame requiring him to force his way through the crowd. It was only a minute later that he did, but he could immediately tell something was wrong.

He could only see her back, but from what he could tell, she was just standing there in the open doorway, leaning heavily on the frame and staring at the fire. When he touched her shoulder, she jumped and turned, losing her balance in the process. He reached out and caught her. She wasn't putting much effort into righting herself, however, and he found himself supporting her weight. The biggest concern was that she was giggling.

She shouldn't have been drunk. Especially not this fast, but her eyes had a strange glaze to them that made it clear she was under the influence. How the hell had this happened?

It clicked then, what the guy she'd stolen the drink from meant when he'd said he'd paid for the drink. It must have been some type of drug. The type became clear when she her giggling trailed off and she passed out in his arms.

Fuck.

He wasn't entirely sure what to do now. This girl had clearly been drugged. Even though he hadn't done it, he doubted that she'd remember that if he turned her over to the police. They kissed, after all, in a room full of crowded people. He was eighteen, a stranger to everyone here, and she was probably a minor. It didn't look good. Even he would think that if it weren't him who was in this position.

It would be best if he could get her home quietly, but he didn't even know her name, let alone where she lived. From the interactions he'd witnessed earlier, he doubted she had any real friends who would know either. She'd gotten that call earlier. From her sister, she'd said. Maybe he could call her back?

It took some effort to find her phone without touching her anywhere inappropriate, and even when he did, it required a passcode that he didn't know. *Who uses a passcode instead of a fingerprint these days?* Frustrated, he quickly shoved the thought aside and the phone in his pocket.

What the fuck had he gotten himself into?

He wasn't about to just leave her. She was nice and a decent person too. She cared about others. But now she needed someone to care for her.

He lifted her unconscious body and made his way back into the house and up the stairs. Each room seemed to be occupied and he was about ready to scream at whoever was in the next room to get the fuck out when he stumbled across the guy with the spiked drinks. To his relief, it was just him and a few buddies spread out on the floor, pointing at invisible things. By all appearances, their only intent had been getting themselves high. It didn't change the fact that he had a drugged girl in his arms, but at least he wouldn't have to kill the guy for attempted date-rape.

The guy took one look at him and said, "Told you so, man."

The dipshit was lucky that Nate's hands were full, or he might have punched him in the face anyway. A few moments later, he wasn't so lucky anymore.

Nate had laid her on the bed before finding out the drink was laced with ketamine and then physically throwing the dumbasses from the room. He locked the door behind him, then reevaluated. He didn't want to leave her defenseless, but he also didn't want to hang around and end up getting arrested for something he didn't do. As he watched her measured breaths, he came to a decision.

He'd secure the room and then climb out the window.

He pushed the desk in front of the door as a barricade. It was an old, heavy thing that took a lot of effort to move, so he figured it was as safe as it could get. When he looked at her again, however, he was struck by how small and tired she looked. The bags under her eyes were darker now and her shoulders even more frail-looking without her personality to offset the slightness. Suddenly, protecting her from others didn't seem like enough, not when she was completely helpless like that.

It didn't feel right, leaving her. He needed to be sure she wasn't going to have a bad reaction to the drugs. Resigned, he pulled the desk chair to the side of the bed and settled into place. It felt right.

You're in a warm, safe place, he rationalized to himself. *Of course you're comfortable here.*

He spent the next hours dozing. He slept for about an hour at a time, waking to check on her. When the clock read six in the morning, he figured the greatest risk had passed and that it was a good time to leave. She appeared to be sleeping peacefully now, curled on her side with one arm tucked under the pillow.

Through the profound relief he felt, he almost failed to notice how cute it made her look. He wanted to reach out and push her hair out of her face, but that was stupid. A special kind of stupid, considering that if he woke her and she didn't remember him, she'd probably be terrified.

The thought gave him pause. It would be disconcerting for her to wake up in a barricaded room regardless, he imagined, so he scribbled a quick note that he left beside the bed, alongside her phone, before he slipped out the window and climbed down the side of the house. He stopped briefly in the kitchen to grab something for the road before heading off without anywhere specific in mind.

It was moments like this when Janie hated living with Mar.

True, it had been nice to move into a decent sized apartment with her sister when she'd started school three months ago. After all, she had an entire room to herself and only had to share a bathroom with her sister, unlike ninety percent of the freshman class who were sharing dorms with strangers. Not like Mar had done when she first started at the school.

There was also the benefit of not having to explain any weird cries during the night or the way she sometimes talked to herself.

Mere hours ago, she had considered how lucky she was to live with Mar when her mother had called and her sister pretended Janie was in the shower so that she didn't have to hear her lecture. Without Mar's intervention, Janie would have been feeling like a disappointment the entire time her mother argued that Janie could still become a nurse or a doctor instead of a social worker, even without the aid of magic. Instead, Janie had been on the verge of laughing watching Mar mime their mother's speech word for word. Even after that, when she started in on how Mar should consider coming to work for the research hospital that she worked at herself and extolling the virtues of being able to save those who came to them without any hope, her sister had held strong and refused to leave Janie behind. It was nice to have that kind of support system.

Right now, though, she wanted to curse her sister, who had woken her up, drunk as can be, to rave about what a good time she'd had that night. It wasn't that Janie didn't care, just that she'd prefer to hear it in the morning, over coffee and toast, in tones that would be gentle on Mar's hungover self.

"Man it's good to finally have a night off from the ER. Best fuck of my life," Mar all but shouted.

Janie flinched. That was another thing. Mar was plenty rough around the edges normally, but she was especially crass when drunk.

"That's nice. I'm glad you had a good time. You deserve it," she said politely. Honestly, she didn't understand hookup culture in the slightest, especially not for witches, but she wasn't about to judge Mar. If it made her happy, and she was being safe about it, then Janie would support her.

"Mmhmm," her sister hummed from the other side of the couch, her head leaning against the back lazily. "You should try it sometime. You could do with a little loosening up."

Janie rolled her eyes. "I'm good, thanks."

"Jaannniiieeee," she whined, grabbing onto her arm and shaking her a little bit, all while keeping her head in place. Janie suspected she might have the spins by now. "Come on, what's the point in moving to a college town if you're not going to experience it? It's *fun*. Don't you ever want to do something fun?"

"No," she replied honestly. This had been her life for several years now. Mar had just been too busy with her own life away at school to realize it.

Mar lifted her head – seemingly with great effort, if the grunt she let out was any indication – and squinted at her. "Really? Because all you do is volunteer, study, and hang around the apartment alone. In that order. Sounds like a boring way to live if you ask me."

"Good thing I didn't then, huh?" she replied lightly. She loved Mar, but this was not a conversation she wanted to have again, especially not while Mar was drunk.

"Ugh!" Her head fell back. "You're still on about the soulmate thing, aren't you?"

Truthfully, that *was* what it was really about. Over the last six years, she'd gotten good enough at dealing with the injuries the bond caused covertly enough that she could interact with people normally without concern. They had also reduced in frequency and severity, to the point that Janie hardly worried about them at all. Not like two years ago.

Her sixteenth year had been the worst. She was constantly healing hypothermia and malnutrition as winter settled in. Until she wasn't, and suddenly she was healing fighting injuries – true, repetitive fights, with both offensive and defensive wounds – every single night. Despite how hard it had been, she was grateful Mar hadn't been around to see it, because she was sure that she would have gone to their mother had she been.

It hadn't lasted more than a few weeks, but it had been an exhausting nightmare of epic proportions. So much so that she reached a breaking point and accepted an invitation to a party, one that ended with her waking up trapped in an empty room with just her phone and a note that said, "Ketamine. Don't worry. I made sure no one could get in." She had almost no memory of the night before, save for dark hair and an earth-shattering kiss.

It was possible that memory hadn't even been real, but she was pretty sure it was. The boy whose name she didn't know and face she couldn't remember had definitely existed and she had definitely kissed him, according to eyewitnesses. She was pretty sure the feel of it – the way it felt like every neuron in her brain and body, all the way down to her toes, had fired simultaneously – was real. And that was dangerous.

Even if it hadn't been, she decided that romance was too risky. She had a soulmate, and she wasn't about to get caught up romantically with someone else only to break his heart. Or hers.

"Jesus, Janie," Mar said in exasperation, taking her silence as confirmation. "He doesn't even know you exist! It's not like he's waiting around for you either."

"I don't care. I don't mind waiting, Mar. It'll be worth it," she replied with conviction.

It was true. All that mattered was that she helped him. Plus, it wasn't like she wasn't going about her life, getting her degree, and helping others. That was all she wanted out of life. To make a difference.

Mar eyed her doubtfully, but didn't argue, instead choosing another tactic. "Nothing wrong with getting in a little practice in the meantime though. Right?"

Janie's face twisted at the lewd gesture her sister made and pushed her over the edge.

"And that is my limit," she said cheerfully, rising from the couch and giving a brief wave.

"Aw, come on! One and done! It's great!" Mar called as Janie retreated.

"Goodnight, Marion. Don't forget to drink some water."

She just caught the sight of Mar flipping her off as she closed her bedroom door and laid down. She quickly drifted off once more, into a peaceful slumber where no nosy sisters questioned her sex life. It was much shorter than she anticipated.

"*Fucking – fuck – shit – agh!*" Janie screamed, curling up in pain. At first it felt like she'd been hit in the gut by a car, but then she felt the pain concentrate on a single area. Furthermore, the sleeves of her shirt immediately became soaked in blood as her arms clamped around her middle.

The fact that she was swearing in pain was a testament to how bad the situation was – Janie never swore – and Mar should have come running at the sound. It was then that she remembered how drunk Mar had been when she'd gotten home earlier and she began to panic. She could feel the effect of the blood loss already. She focused on stemming it as best she could, but she needed Mar's help if she wanted either of them to live.

With as much force as she could muster, she yelled, "Mar!" *Please don't let her be too drunk to have heard that*, she prayed.

She'd never felt so relieved in all her life as she did when she heard her sister's muffled voice and staggering footsteps coming down the hall toward her room. Just like she had done the first time Mar had helped her like this, she closed her eyes and avoided her sister's reaction to the nightmare she was walking in on. She knew this one was worse.

The slew of curses that Mar unleashed included some that Janie had never heard before, but was rather impressed by. It was odd how in that moment, when she could actually be dying for a man she didn't even know, that she would find humor in her sister's choice of words. Or maybe it wasn't that odd. She wouldn't be the first terrified person to become hysterical.

After ten agonizing minutes of struggling to focus both their combined efforts on fixing her, Janie could finally breathe again. Albeit, both of them were sweating fiercely and breathing heavily.

It was Mar who spoke first, through gasping breaths. "A fucking gunshot wound. That was... a fucking gunshot wound." Her voice rose as she pinned Janie with an outraged look. "What did I fucking tell you? This is insane!" She pushed herself up and began pacing, the scene all too reminiscent of the first time they'd done this. Except worse. So much worse. Mar was covered in blood as she continued viciously. "Who the fuck even is this guy? A fucking gang-banger?"

"Stop it," Janie cut in, though her voice came out weaker than she had hoped. "He's not....he's clearly had a hard life. Cut him some slack."

"*You've* had a hard life," her sister retorted angrily, "because of him." She pulled at her hair. "Do you realize how fucked up this is? It was one thing when you were kids. I could understand that. But you're fucking adults now. He's responsible for whatever happens."

"You don't know that," Janie argued. "We don't know anything about him. He could be younger than me."

"You're right. We don't know anything. Which is why he could be some terrible sleazebag who isn't worth waiting around for."

"He's not," Janie said, her own anger starting to rise. He was worth it. She *knew* it. "Look, nothing like this has happened in years. I'm telling you; whatever just happened was not his fault."

Mar looked ready to explode, but she took a deep breath instead. Her fists remained clenched at her sides as she took another, and then another, before she finally relaxed. Her eyes were cold and piercing, but Janie knew it was just her fear and worry at play. Finally she said, "Fine. Live with your delusions. But I'm switching to day shift. You're no longer allowed to be alone at night."

Janie resisted the urge to roll her eyes. She wasn't a child. The blood that covered her sister's hands and arms prevented her from feeling any true resentment, however. If the situation were reversed, Janie would insist upon no less herself.

"Deal," she agreed readily. After what just happened, it would be nice to have help close by should she need it.

"Good," Mar said. She looked down at the mess she was before looking at Janie carefully. "I'll run you a bath. You shouldn't stand just yet."

She left before Janie could thank her. For all that Mar could be abrasive, she really was an amazing big sister. She'd have to find a way to thank her. Something big.

She tabled that thought for the moment though, and focused on her soulmate once more and partook in her ritual of reaching out to him. "You really had me worried tonight. I hope you're alright now, that you're stable, if not completely alright. And not too terrified. It's alright if you are. I am too. You're strong though, aren't you? Good too. I know you are..." She trailed off, wondering why that was. She couldn't explain it even to herself, other than the fact she felt it deep in her bones a certainty that he was determined to spread good in the world to spite all the bad he'd had thrown at him in life. "You've had a hard life, but I promise I'm trying to protect you. I'm sorry you keep suffering, but I swear I'll always fix whatever I can."

Mar caught her talking to him when she came back in the room, but she had the grace not to say anything. She simply pursed her lips and helped an aching Janie into the tub. Embarrassing as it was, Janie had to ask her sister to help her wash. It just hurt too much to move still. Mar compiled, but her brow furrowed. It wasn't a surprise when she voiced her concerns after helping Janie into bed.

"You're not better, Janie," Mar said. She was clearly worried, but accusation tinged her tone.

"I'm aware of that, thank you," she replied, avoiding the unasked question.

"What's going on?" Her tone got sharper. "Has this happened before?"

"No." Janie herself was starting to worry. Her previous experiences had sucked, but she'd always been healed with relative ease. She let her magic reach out, trying to sense any damage, but everything seemed fine. She tried not to let her own worry show as she asked, "Can you sense anything?"

Mar came forward, placing her hands on Janie's side and closing her eyes. Her face grew more and more pinched as her hands roamed,

looking for anything they might have missed. "Something is off…
slightly out of place, maybe? But there's nothing there."

"Oh no," Janie groaned.

"*What?*" Mar demanded.

"You said it was a gunshot," she said carefully. "Was there an exit
wound?"

"An exit wound?" She asked, before recognition hit and her expression turned furious. "Are you fucking kidding me?! You mean to tell
me the bullet is stuck and you're fucked until he gets it fixed?"

"Sounds about right," she admitted.

It actually had happened once before. He'd been cut by something,
a large gash on the inside of her forearm that she'd had to hastily patch
up before either of them could bleed out, but part of it wouldn't heal
over. The cut had been jagged and rough. She assumed a piece of whatever he'd been cut with was stuck in the wound, and she couldn't heal
it properly until he removed it.

That was unfortunate. It appeared she was going to be confined to
bed for a while. She just counted herself lucky that she wasn't expected
to do nursing clinicals any time soon.

Mar must have been following her train of thought. After a breath,
she said, "Guess it's a good thing they offer the social work classes
online, huh?"

She closed her eyes against the overwhelming worry and defeat
that threatened, instead focusing all her thoughts on *him* and the fact
that he was alive.

"I'm okay. You're okay. We're going to be fine, I promise," she
breathed on a whisper, clinging fiercely to that one truth she believed
above all else.

Nate was at the hospital of all places when he received his first major
injury since his miraculous recovery following being medically discharged from the army.

After leaving that New Year's Eve party, he'd all but run into a
recruiter who took one look at him and knew Nate was in desperate
need of the opportunities the military could provide him. It didn't take

much convincing at all. One conversation later and Nate's future didn't look so bleak anymore.

His career had been short-lived.

He'd been shot while on active duty, the bullet somehow managing to pierce his torso and lodge against his spine in such a way that the military doctors refused to even attempt to touch it. It left him with limited mobility, but he hadn't been paralyzed and the surrounding damage was shockingly minimal, or so they'd said with stunned and confused expressions. They'd kept him only a short while, just to make sure there was no infection, before sending him home with a referral for a research hospital. The only one in the world crazy enough to take on hopeless cases like his.

He'd expected to die on the table, or at least wake up unable to feel most of his body. Instead, he'd come to perfectly healed, with full mobility and without any lingering pain. If he hadn't already been convinced he had a guardian angel, he certainly was after that.

Free from his obligation to the military and in perfect health once more, he'd horsed around in various fields and cities before finally settling on becoming a police officer. His experiences seemed geared toward it, and he wanted to help people in a tangible way. It seemed like a good enough fit in his mind, so he was now studying criminal justice while working security part-time at the university hospital.

Things had been going well since then, and he'd been injury free for the most part, until today. It was only his second day on the job, which he had just been thinking was a pretty easy gig, when some asshole on a bad trip was brought in and started attacking the nurse.

From what he'd seen, she was tough as nails, but she was smaller than her assaulter, and the guy had her by the hair. She'd been hit in the face and was bleeding from a cut on her brow by the time he'd got into the room, but at least the attacker released her when Nate entered. He didn't think it was going to be as difficult as it was to subdue him – the guy was smaller than him and didn't appear to be that strong – but he didn't seem to be feeling any pain in whatever reality he was living in, and Nate's job description said he wasn't supposed to hurt him if he could avoid it.

Somehow, Nate ended up with a back cut up by glass that needed to be removed piece by piece, and one particularly deep one. He had pulled out the largest piece, though the nurse had yelled at him for it immediately. He wasn't worried. Over the years, he'd had plenty of deep wounds like this and never once bled out or needed a transfusion. He was just strange like that. Good luck, maybe. He knew there was someone out there looking out for him.

The resident that cleaned the wounds and patched him up did comment on the amount of blood, however, and insisted there must have been internal bleeding somewhere. Nate tuned them out as they went about their extensive evaluation, overseen by the attending physician, and focused on the whisper of a voice that spoke to him. By the time her voice came to its traditional closing, *"I'm okay. You're okay. We're going to be fine, I promise,"* the doctors had concluded that there wasn't anything major wrong. He wanted to tell them – both the angel and the doctors – that he *knew* that already, but settled for a quick nod directed at the actual people in the room when he was finally allowed to leave the bed they had placed him in.

The first thing he wanted to do was check on the nurse. His own nurse, Allison, was kind enough to tell him that her name was Marion Price and that she was still being kept in a room down the hall from him. He assumed that under normal circumstances she wouldn't have shared the information with him, but she was looking at him like he was some kind of hero when she told him how brave and considerate he was. It made him uncomfortable, so he quickly excused himself and went in search of this Marion Price.

He found her door quickly, but stopped himself from going in when he saw she wasn't alone. Another girl was there with her, wearing a scrub top and jeans. Even with just a quick glance, he could tell they were sisters, which was odd, because he didn't think she had a sister that worked here. And she definitely was related; they looked nearly identical. Both were slight with light brown hair pulled up in messy buns atop their heads. It was really only the general aura surrounding each of them that was different.

In that respect, they were complete opposites. Usually, Marion Price wore an expression best described as resting bitch face. At present, Marion looked fierce, her head bandaged with a scowl on her face and her arms across her chest. He doubted the other girl ever looked anything but kind. Even facing her sister's upset, she was softer, looking mildly exasperated but also concerned. That was all he saw before he stepped aside and leaned against the wall outside the door, deciding that he didn't want to interrupt their conversation.

"I can't believe you're fucking here," he heard. The angry tone made him assume it was Marion who was speaking, because the other girl's stance hadn't seemed nearly antagonistic enough for it to have been her.

He'd seen enough of Marion around to know that she could be a little brusque at times, but was still surprised by how rude she was being. If he had someone that cared enough about him to come check on him, he wouldn't be a dick about it.

"I'm fine now," the other girl said. *What?* "I was all better by the time you got out of the MRI. No harm done."

His confusion as he listened to their conversation quickly morphed into anger and frustration.

"Bullshit. You wouldn't have come if it wasn't bad. And you wouldn't be wearing a scrub top to cover up whatever happened," Marion said accusingly.

"It was just a little bit of blood, really," the girl dismissed.

"You can handle a little bit of blood. What did that fucker do this time?"

"Stop that. Why do you always have to blame him? It's not his fault."

Nate's fists clenched at his sides. It sounded like this girl had been hurt by a guy, one that she was making excuses for, and not for the first time. It was a situation he was all too familiar with after having grown up the way he did.

"Why do *you* always have to act like he had no control over it? At some point, there has to be some kind of accountability."

At least one of them has some sense, he thought. Still, it was annoying that Marion seemed to be allowing it to continue. *Was this their usual routine? The sister allowed herself to be beat up and Marion patched her up before sending her on her way?*

"I just… I don't know. It's just this feeling, alright? But let's not talk about that right now. That's over."

"It's *never* over, Janie. Not really."

"Enough, Mar. Are you going to tell me what happened to you now? All they said was that you were hit by a patient and needed an MRI to rule out a concussion."

Marion ignored her sister – Janie, apparently – and fired back, "You were in bed for three months last time this happened! I'm calling Mom. This has gone on far too long already."

"Don't be dramatic," the girl said lightly. "If you didn't then, we both know you're not going to now." Her voice became teasing, "Besides, I can tell mom about…"

He was distracted from whatever blackmail she had on her sister by Allison walking toward the room. There was no one else in this section of the hall, so he assumed that she was Marion's nurse come to check on her.

"Hey," she said, smiling at him brightly. He did his best to return it. She was nice, but a little too much for his taste. "Did you talk to her yet?"

"No," he said, shaking his head and doing his best to look confused. "Her nurse was in there, so I thought I should wait."

"Her nurse?" she asked, looking around him and into the room. "Oh. That's just Janie. Her sister. We just lent her that scrub top because –." She cut herself off, looking sheepish. "Sorry. Never mind that. It's just Janie, so don't worry about it. Although I do need to check on Mar now, so looks like you'll have to wait a bit longer. See you when I get out?" There was a little too much hope in her voice at the end.

"Maybe," he said, though he smiled to soften the blow.

She looked slightly disappointed, but nodded and knocked on the door before heading inside. The conversation between the sisters cut off abruptly, before he heard Janie start talking again.

"Well, looks like you're busy now. I'm just going to head home. See you later!" She said, sounding relieved to have a reason to escape.

"This isn't over. We will be talking about this when I get home."

"Sounds great!" Janie said with only a hint of sarcasm, turning around to wave goodbye. It meant she wasn't watching when she turned on her way out the door and bumped right into him.

He was larger than her – he had a decent amount of muscle mass these days – and she bounced off his frame. He reached out and caught her before she could fall.

"Hey. Alright there?"

He was honestly worried that she may have been hurt by the collision. After all, it sounded like she'd been injured when she came in. To his surprise, she laughed lightly before looking up at him with amused eyes.

"Fine. Just clumsy it seems." Her eyes were hazel and warm when she looked at him, and he got the feeling that he'd seen them before, though he couldn't quite place them. He'd seen and met a lot of people through his travels, so it was possible that they'd met, but he couldn't say for sure. She carried on without noticing his distraction. "Sorry about that." She gave him a rueful smile. "In my defense, I didn't expect anyone to be waiting outside the door."

"Oh. Yeah. My bad," he replied distractedly. It was driving him a bit crazy that he couldn't place her, so he asked, "Have we met before?"

Her brow furrowed and she looked at him carefully. "I don't *think* so," she said slowly. "It's possible. I do a lot of volunteer work around here, though. Any chance we might have met that way? Where are you from?" He had barely begun to answer her when she started talking again. "Oh! Sorry. I should introduce myself." She stepped back and put out her hand for him to shake. "I'm Janie."

She was a bit all over the place, but in a good way. She was friendly, but not overly-friendly like Allison was. He was surprised to find that he liked her already. It made him all the more interested in what was going on with her. In making sure she was safe.

"Nate," he offered, taking her hand in his. It was warm and soft, but the shake she gave was firm, as if she knew who she was and was comfortable with herself. He approved, but was even more confused by it. It wasn't meek, like he expected from a battered woman. "I'm new to the area, so I don't think I would have seen you around."

"Oh. Well, I don't believe we've met before, but it's nice to meet you now," she said cheerfully with a genuine smile. "Were you waiting to talk to Mar?"

"I was, yeah. But I think I'm going to head home. It was a rough morning around here."

"So I heard, vaguely."

"Did I hear you say you're leaving? Where are you headed?"

She raised a brow at him.

"Sorry," he said, raising his hands in a non-threatening manner. "That sounded better in my head. What I mean is, I'm about to walk home. I could fill you in on the way if we're going in the same direction."

She narrowed her eyes at him, though he thought he saw amusement shining there. "How do I know you're not a stalker?" she asked, though her tone lacked the bite it needed to be serious.

He had to suppress a smile at the directness, even in the form of a joke. "If I was, I'd go into the security office and look up your sister's employee file and get your address from there."

"Who says I live with my sister?" she shot back.

"Generally when two people agree to talk at 'home', it means they share a living space."

"Ohhhh," she drew out, her eyes lighting up. "A stalker and an eavesdropper. The plot thickens."

He couldn't contain the burst of mirthful laughter that escaped him. Luckily she laughed too. It was a light, happy sound that seemed to brighten his mood. He wasn't kidding when he said it had been a rough morning. It made him all the more eager when she accepted his offer.

"Sure," she said with a smile. "And you're right, I do live with Mar."

He hadn't forgotten the reason he wanted to walk her home, however, so he tried to gently probe.

"So, do you go to school here?"

"I do. Second year Social Work major, with intent to start the combined BA/MSW program next year. What about you?"

"First year, studying Criminal Justice. I was in the Army, but got medically discharged."

"Thank you for your service," she said warmly.

He nodded in acknowledgement. It was always a bit strange when people thanked him like that. Mostly, it made him feel guilty, because his one goal in joining up had been saving himself from a future of being homeless or starving to death. Not serving his country. It wasn't something he liked to get into with strangers however.

"I just started working at the hospital in security, which is how I got mixed in with what happened with your sister." He went on to tell her what had happened, skipping over his own injury and focusing on Marion. "... she's pretty tough, isn't she?"

"Ha. You have no idea."

"I haven't been at the hospital long, but I've seen her around. She seems a bit..."

"Abrasive?" Janie offered, though there was fondness in her tone.

He chuckled. "Sure. Let's go with that."

"She's really not that bad. Her bark is..." she hesitated before letting out a small, amused breath. "Well, I was going to say her bark is worse than her bite, but that's really not true."

"So how's that work out living together?" As smoothly as possible he added, "Is it just the two of you?"

It worked. She answered his question readily. "Yeah. It's just us. Mar works a lot – parties a lot too – and isn't home all that often. I almost always am, so it's almost like living alone. Except whenever I start to get bored, Mar pops back home and it's like a tornado of excitement. It's good though."

"You don't go out too?"

"Not really. I told you already, but I like to volunteer. So I do that, study, and spend the rest of my time quietly at home. Mar is always on me about going out, trying to set me up and things like that, but I think that she's exciting enough for the both of us. I have enough fun living vicariously."

"You seem too friendly to be a loner," he said without tact. It just didn't make any sense to him, the difference between what she was telling him and what he'd overheard.

"I'm not a loner. I socialize all the time. Volunteering." Her tone was patient, but he saw her roll her eyes. A part of him wanted to call her on it, if only to see how she'd react, but he didn't get the chance. She stopped and turned, gesturing over her shoulder as she said, "Well, this is me. Thank you for walking me home, Nate. It was nice meeting you."

He wasn't ready for their time to end. He hadn't figured anything out. She wasn't what he had expected at all. He needed more time.

"Would you like to get coffee?" he asked quickly.

She bit her lip, considering for a moment, but shook her head. She gave him a slightly sad smile as she explained, "I'm sorry. I'd like to – you seem really nice, and you're funny too – but I really shouldn't. I don't want you to think – I don't date. At all. It isn't you or anything. But I still don't want you to think that this could go somewhere, because it won't."

"I'm confused," he admitted. She'd thrown too many words at him that took too many jumps for him to follow when he was trying to determine how he was going to get more information on what was going on with her. "I just asked if you wanted to get coffee… not if you wanted to go on a date. I'm not – wasn't – expecting anything."

"Oh," she said, a blush blooming.

"Not that I wouldn't have," he rushed to explain, the thought that he might have hurt her feelings making him far more uncomfortable than it should have, "because I absolutely would be interested, and I might have asked, but now I know, so I won't." He cringed at how ridiculous his rambling sounded.

"Right," she said, pasting a smile on her face. "Now that I've thoroughly embarrassed myself, I'm going to head inside. Thanks for walking me home."

It was with confusion and disappointment that he watched her turn and walk into the building without a backward glance. She didn't seem to be injured as they had walked or talked, and by all accounts seemed healthy and well-adjusted. Relief replaced the worry he'd been carrying around since overhearing the conversation she had with her sister. Maybe there was nothing wrong, and her sister was just overreacting to something. It was possible he'd misunderstood.

That didn't explain the longing he felt as he stared at the closed door. Nor did it explain the little surge of hope when he saw her peek out the second floor curtains at him. Maybe he'd have another chance. He'd certainly try.

Janie shifted nervously in her chair as Mar stared at her appraisingly, brush poised above the palette, as she made her decision.

It was Janie's twenty-first birthday, and she had finally relented and agreed to Mar's plans to celebrate by going out to the bar. By all accounts, it was a rite of passage, especially in the college town they lived in, and it seemed rude to deny her sister the opportunity to get her sloppy drunk like a normal sister would. Plus, Janie owed her sister a lot. More than most. She never let herself forget that.

Besides, it had been a while since she'd had a major incident. She could handle one night of frivolity. Or so she told herself repeatedly as they got ready together that night.

When Mar turned to her make-up bag to swap something out, Janie chanced a look in the mirror. She was surprised to find that she didn't dislike what had been done to her and stood to take a closer look. As far as she could tell, she still looked like herself, just a bit brighter. No crazy liner, shiny eyeshadow, or dark lips in sight.

"It looks great, Mar," she said with a smile. "Thank you." It wasn't a lie, but her nerves made it sound like one.

Her sister let out a sarcastic laugh. "Yeah...no. That gratitude thing may work on other people, but not me. Sit your ass back down in the chair."

Janie let her smile slip. "Really, Mar. I *like* the way I look right now. Can you please let it go?" She bit her lip. "Why don't you focus on making yourself up? That guy you've been eyeing... Jason? He works at the bar, right? Don't you want to look nice for him?"

"Psh. That won't be a problem," Mar dismissed, before narrowing her eyes at her. "We have a problem though. You're being weird. You're *not* doing that weird smile thing you do always do. What's wrong with you?"

Truth be told, it wasn't the make-up that was bothering her. It was what she was about to admit. She twisted her hands before sighing. "I've been thinking about what you said... and you're right. I – I'm going to give it a chance."

Not a day had gone by over the past two months when she hadn't thought about it.

Janie hadn't realized it was a mistake asking Mar about Nate until three days after she'd done it. At first, when her sister texted to say she'd been joining her at the day program Janie was running, she was excited that her sister was out of bed on a Saturday morning at a decent time and apparently not still upset with her. It wasn't until Mar showed up with Nate in tow that she realized what Mar was actually doing.

Her heart fluttered the second she laid eyes on him and saw the somewhat sheepish smile he was giving her. They chatted briefly before she assigned him a task, but as soon as Nate was occupied helping out with some of the youth there, she dragged her sister to the side where they wouldn't be overheard. Arms crossed, she stared at her expectantly.

Mar only smiled. "As proud as I am to have made the great sunshine-and-daisies-Janie give me that look...don't." Her face twisted, but the grimace felt unnatural. For the first time ever, Janie wished she knew how to give the intimidating look her sister always seemed to favor. It was no use, however, as Mar's amusement seemed to grow as she witnessed Janie's attempt. "He's been asking about you, a lot. Had I known the interest was mutual, I would've done this long before now."

A thrill flashed through her at the words, but she tried to beat it back. "I don't know what you're talking about," she deflected. "Besides, if you really thought I was interested, you wouldn't have sprung him on me like this!"

"You really want to tell me you're not interested in that?" Mar challenged, gesturing to where he stood running drills with the teenagers there. "Because I would be all over that if I were you."

Despite herself, Janie shot her sister a quick glare on reflex.

Mar's hands raised in a surrendering gesture, but her smile was smug. "I'm just saying. He's cute, and nice, but also in a 'please don't talk to me' kind of way that's hot. You know?"

Janie did know – mostly. That was the problem. It had been two weeks since he'd walked Janie home, and she'd only seen him in passing – just long enough to wave from across the room – a few times since then. Yet, every single time, her heart raced and she longed to go over and have a real conversation. He was cute, far too cute, and nice. She'd never once gotten the standoffish vibe from him that everyone else seemed to, however.

Which was bad. Because she already liked him far more than she should after a single conversation. She'd never wanted to risk a relationship with anyone so badly. But that seemed foolish.

"He seems to be genuinely interested in you. I don't get the impression that it's just your looks either, because he's never once hit on me."

Janie couldn't contain the laugh as she recalled the conversation they'd had about her sister when he walked her home. "I'm sure that's nothing to do with your personality," she said teasingly.

Mar pretended to glare, but it quickly dropped it in favor of a mischievous smile. "Fair point. Allison is pretty and nice, though, and he never pays any attention to her at all, no matter how hard she tries. So take that."

"Allison can be a little aggressive in her flirtation," Janie said reasonably. "I think some men can find that off-putting."

"I've never seen him ask about anyone other than you."

"He seemed worried when we left the hospital. I think he might have overheard some of our conversation," Janie dismissed.

It was true, after all. He definitely had seemed a little too interested in her life. Where she lived, who she hung out with, and what she did. He wasn't nearly as subtle as he thought. But he seemed harmless enough, not like a stalker. The memory brought a smile to her face.

"Uh huh," Mar said skeptically. "And that smile is because of what exactly?"

"Nothing," Janie replied, putting on her best innocent expression.

Her sister huffed, clearly unconvinced, but allowed it. "Fine. Forget Nate for a second and answer me this: how do you expect to meet this guy if you never put yourself out there?" Mar questioned.

"I..." she trailed off, uncertain how to answer. Everyone else in her family had done it without issue. By circumstance or fate, each witch found their soulmate before they turned thirty by saving his life and claimed to just know. The connection felt different, they claimed, and the couples just fell together effortlessly. "I don't know. I just assumed it would happen when it happened, just like everyone else."

"You're not like everyone else," Mar said pointedly. "And I'm not talking about how your magic is different. I mean how you and him are already connected with your magic. I doubt you'll have that big rescue scene that everyone else gets. That's not how you two operate." She turned back to crowds of kids playing games and began speaking again, as if she wasn't discussing the center of Janie's universe for the last nine years. "Hell, it could've been that guy you kissed. I've never had a kiss like that, and I've had my share of men..."

She kept talking, but Janie couldn't listen anymore. The words felt like being slapped. It was always disconcerting when Mar was serious, but this time it was even more so. Her point was so spot on that Janie felt a chill pass through her as it landed. Dread settled in her chest like a weight, making each breath more difficult than the last.

All this time she'd been waiting around for fate to intervene. What if she'd missed her chance? Her mind flew through countless encounters with men who had looked or otherwise voiced their interest that she had declined. The most recent, and most painful, being Nate. He even had dark hair, just like the boy in her hazy memory of that night.

"Oh. My. God." she said through too quick breathing. "Ohmygod."

A light slap on her cheek drew her out of her panicked spiral and made her suck in a deep breath.

"Geez, Janie. Calm the fuck down," Mar said. "Now look at me. Follow my lead."

She gripped her by the shoulders and breathed with exaggerated movements in a measured rhythm. Janie followed her example, doing her best to sync her breathing with Mar's until it returned to normal. Mar released her grip and gave her a pat on the shoulder.

"Better?" Mar asked. Her tone was challenging, but her gaze worried.

"Yeah. Sorry," she said shakily.

"Good," she said, apparently accepting it as truth. Her tone turned exasperated. "Because you're not even twenty-one. You have years before you have to worry about this shit. Mom didn't meet Dad until she was twenty-five."

"Right," Janie replied more strongly. That was fair. She couldn't think of a single cousin, aunt, or grandmother among the lot that met their soulmate before their twenty-first birthday. She was being silly. She took one more breath before shaking out her hands.

"I was just trying to tell you it couldn't hurt to get into the habit. Starting with talking to Nate."

Her heart fluttered again as she cast a glance in his direction, the wheels in her mind spinning at the prospect, but she tried to keep herself calm outwardly.

There was no denying that she was attracted to him. He was well-built without being overly muscular, and his dark hair contrasted *slightly with his light brown eyes, making them appear to shine a bit brighter than they might have otherwise. There was a tense set to the way he walked and stood, as if he was always on alert, but he still managed to smile at her honestly and make her laugh.*

Being around him actually gave her the urge to flirt. She had desperately wanted to accept his invitation for coffee that day he'd walked her home, which was why she'd turned into such a bumbling fool. She couldn't recall that ever happening before. Usually, she was much more graceful when declining invitations. Then again, no one ever affected her the way he did

All around, his company was... nice. Very nice. Definitely someone whose presence she enjoyed. If she was going to take that step and get out there, start socializing more, then there was no one she would rather do it with.

She could admit that she had a crush, if only to herself. Plenty of people – normal people – had crushes during their lifetimes. Mar had a new one every week. It didn't have to mean anything. So what if she had never allowed herself to have a genuine one before?

"Maybe," she said, trying to sound nonchalant.

"I know you like him. What's the harm?"

Janie had asked herself that question countless times since then. Especially since she'd been seeing a lot of Nate; between him volunteering with her and her showing up at the hospital to visit Mar, it had just kind of happened that they spent at least four days a week in each other's company. Never alone, not like a date, but they interacted enough that she was fairly certain she was half in love with him already, without having even started a relationship. At this point, she really wasn't sure that she actually was holding back. She just hadn't admitted it yet.

What had truly convinced her to give it a try was Mar's most recent hook-up, of all things. He must have still been a bit drunk when he woke up, because he'd mistaken Janie for Mar when he woke in the morning. He walked out of the bathroom and directly up to where Janie was cooking and kissed her hard on the mouth before she'd had a chance to respond. He was an excellent kisser, according to Mar, but Janie felt nothing. There had been shock, but not the slightest stirring of interest within her. It gave her something to consider, and she decided that perhaps her memory from all those years ago truly had been a fluke. It was simply the drugs or a dream, and that meant it wasn't so dangerous after all.

She shook herself from the memories and doubts and returned her attention to her sister.

Mar was wearing a look that made her resemble the cat that got the canary, but she was kind enough not to say anything beyond, "Well, then, we need to get you dressed properly, don't we?"

"I can dress myself, Mar," she responded automatically. They'd been having this argument for years.

"No, you can't, Janie." Her sister pinned her with a slightly exasperated look. "You are many things my dear sister – lovely, kind, intelligent – but fashion-inclined is not one of them."

"Thanks," she replied dryly.

"You know I'm right," her sister insisted, turning back to the closer without waiting for a response. "Let me have my fun. I probably won't get a chance for another twenty-one years."

"As long as you're aware of that fact, then I suppose I can allow it," Janie replied, brightening up. So far, Mar was actually being pretty decent about the whole thing. She had honestly expected more of an "I told you so" speech.

"I was going to do it with or without your permission," her sister's muffled voice now came from inside the closet.

"No. You were not," Janie sang back.

"Yes I was," Mar responded in her own sing-song, before reverting back to her normal voice as she stepped out of the closet, a dress in hand. "Am, in fact."

It was entirely too short. Perhaps Janie had spoken too soon about Mar not giving her a hard time. "That dress screams, 'Take me home', Mar."

"I know." Mar responded. "Isn't it perfect?"

"For you? Absolutely," she deadpanned.

Mar rolled her eyes. "You and Nate have been hanging out for months. It's alright to show off a little, you know." She turned back to the closet, pulling out an equally revealing dress. It was worse actually, in that it was backless and would leave nothing to the imagination. Janie scrunched her nose.

Mar sighed heavily and tossed the dress on the bed. "Fine. I'll be more reasonable." She gave her a hard look and continued in a firm voice, "But you have to dance. No less than three songs."

"Deal!" Janie chirped happily. *Honestly, three is a steal.* She quickly realized that she made a mistake by agreeing so readily when she saw Mar's eyes narrow.

"And I'm buying you three drinks of my choosing that you *will* drink. All of them."

Janie flinched. "Fine."

Mar looked appropriately satisfied by Janie's genuine reluctance and nodded happily to herself before returning to the closet in search of something more reasonable.

Nate sat in the corner of the bar, a beer he wasn't interested in slowly warming in his hand as he waited. He'd chosen the spot specifically because it was dark and loud and the one place he was least likely to garner attention. There was the added benefit that it gave him a clear view of the door, and the only person he wanted to talk to tonight had yet to arrive.

He kept his view settled on the entryway and resisted the urge to bounce his leg, tug at his hair, or otherwise give in to any of his other nervous tells. There was no reason to be nervous.

True, bars weren't really his favorite place to socialize. He didn't really socialize at all, but when he did, he preferred quieter, more private settings. Loud music and alcohol hadn't been his thing at eighteen, and it still wasn't at twenty-three. For all that he'd changed over the years, that hadn't.

Still, there was no place he would rather be. It was Janie Price's twenty-first birthday, and her sister had invited him out to the bar to celebrate with them. It didn't seem like she'd extended the invitation to anyone else at the hospital either; apparently, Janie didn't much care for crowds either. He couldn't suppress the stupid smile that spread across his face at that thought of her.

She seemed like his kind of girl.

Over the past two months, he'd only gotten to know her here and there through their casual interactions. He'd longed to speak to her again just the two of them, but they'd only spent time together grouped in with others, and most of that time was spent actually doing the various volunteer assignments that he signed up for just to have an excuse to be around her. It hadn't stopped him from seeking out and questioning her sister about her, however.

Despite the general air of bitchiness that Mar put off, she was actually quite willing to talk about her sister. As long as a person could withstand her blunt style, she was pretty easy to get along with. Having grown up with a much rougher crowd, Nate had no problem handling her, and had garnered quite a bit of information about her little sister. It mostly boiled down to a few simple things: Janie was kind, good, and fiercely loved by her sister.

Nate considered himself lucky that said sister appeared to like him. If she hadn't, he wouldn't have had the opportunity to get to know Janie at all.

He'd been conscious of the fact that she said she didn't date. That was fine. He didn't really either. It was hard to form solid relationships when you didn't like talking about your past or explaining that you sometimes heard an angel talking to you; not that that had happened in a while, but still, it was something that was important to him.

It didn't change the fact that he felt drawn to her, nor the odd familiarity he felt despite not knowing much about her. He definitely wanted to know her better, though. On a personal level this time and not through stories he heard from her sister. He'd done what he could to be a friend instead of a suitor, and it was enough that she allowed him to orbit around her.

He tried not to think about how pathetic that sounded. *It's just taking it slow. That's all,* he reminded himself for the millionth time.

But then she was there and the thought was quickly lost.

She'd been beautiful every time he'd seen her. Even the first time he'd met her, it had become clear as day when he was no longer worried about her safety that there was something entirely too lovely about the honest kindness in her gaze when she smiled at him. Every time he thought about it, he felt a small thrill of excitement. It felt like she genuinely saw him, and accepted what she saw, when she looked at him. The feeling had only seemed to grow each time their eyes locked.

And she was looking at him now from the doorway of the bar, her gaze locked on him alone as she made her way over with a smile on her face. He felt his own expression mirror hers involuntarily in response as he gave a stupid wave. He couldn't bring himself to regret it when her grin widened and she began bouncing her way toward him, dragging her sister along.

It seemed he'd already given up on playing it cool, because he found himself rising from his dark little corner and meeting her halfway.

It was only when she was nearly upon him that he was able to take her in fully. She wore a dress that was long-sleeved but fitted to her form nicely – different from the jeans and sweaters she normally wore – and she appeared to be wearing make-up, but it was subtle enough that he couldn't be sure. She looked beautiful, of course, but the change from her normal appearance left him flustered. There was something slightly different about her eyes too.

"Nate! Hi!" she greeted enthusiastically, stumbling a little and falling into him.

"Hey. Happy birthday." He caught her happily enough, but still shot her sister a questioning look over her shoulder when Janie didn't immediately pull back. She hadn't ever hugged him, or even touched him for more than a fleeting moment before, and now she was practically cuddling into his embrace.

"We got a head start," Mar said with a shrug, though she looked amused. "I may have overestimated how much she could handle."

"Hey!" Janie yelled, pulling away from him and giving her sister a small shove. "I had nowhere near as much as you! How are you still standing, anyway?"

Mar threw an arm around Janie. "Practice, my dear sister. Lots of practice." She squeezed her a bit tighter as Janie protested. "Maybe we can get you properly trained someday."

Janie laughed as she freed herself and took half a step closer to him. "No thank you. Like you said, don't count on this happening for another twenty-one years."

"Oh! Right! Time to cash in on those drinks! You owe me three!"

"I have a spot at the bar, if you want. I forgot my drink there anyway," Nate cut in, attention fully on Janie.

He was enjoying watching their sisterly interaction, but couldn't suppress the selfish desire to have her focused on him again. He was a bit ashamed to say how happy it made him when she stepped closer to him after escaping her sister's grasp.

She smiled at him, but it was Mar who spoke first. "Perfect! Jason is working the bar tonight. This way, right?"

She took off toward his corner without waiting for a response, which was just as well, because it allowed him to walk at a more sedate pace with Janie.

"Who's Jason?" he asked.

She huffed a laugh. "Mar's flavor of the week?"

He laughed a bit at the term. It wasn't his style, but he'd never met someone so sure of themselves as Mar seemed to be and he wasn't about to judge her. Nor was he going to say anything to insult the sister of a girl he liked so much. He could be plenty idiotic sometimes, but not *that* idiotic.

"Is that why she invited me?" he asked, keeping his tone light to cover up the hope he was sure was leaking through. "To keep you company while she tries to get his attention?"

"Possibly... although she was rather confident that she'd have no trouble with that." She gestured ahead of them. "Looks like she was right."

Sure enough, Mar had half a dozen untouched shots in front of her, as well as several empty glasses, and was leaning over the bar, speaking into the ear of the highly interested looking bartender he'd met earlier. He couldn't help feeling surprised. As outgoing as Mar was, Jason had seemed like a brick wall when Nate had spoken to him, however briefly.

"Mar's got talent," Janie said with a shrug. They were quickly approaching his loud little corner and she raised her voice to the point of shouting. He was regretting his early decision now, as he worried it might make conversation between them much more difficult. That feeling was quickly replaced by a jolt of shock as she yelled, "She's a bit wild, you know?"

He stopped in his tracks, but Janie kept moving, oblivious to the fact that his world was being shaken by a wave of deja vu. She'd always seemed familiar, but as she stepped out of the direct lights of the main area and was cast in the glow of the neon lights of the bar counter, he could finally place her.

She'd filled out in the five years since the first time he saw her, and her hair had darkened by several shades, but it was definitely the girl he met at that party. The one he'd kissed as they rung in the new year. The one he'd watched over all night, who'd been drugged and probably didn't remember him at all. He couldn't believe he'd missed it until now.

She had already reached her sister's side and was looking back at him curiously, one brow raised slightly in question. He automatically resumed walking toward them, thinking it through as quickly as he could.

Clearly, she had no recollection of him. Nor did they have too much interaction aside from that one kiss and a handful of words. It was likely that was a bad memory and they were celebrating tonight, would she really want to talk about it?

And what if Mar didn't know about it? It had been her sister's encouragement that convinced her to drink and led to the chain of events that night. What if he brought it up and Mar got upset? She seemed like the type to go into a guilty rage.

No. It's better not to bring it up.

Or so he convinced himself. There wasn't enough time to second guess his decision either, as Mar shoved a shot in his hand as soon as he arrived.

"I'm ahead of you both, so you'll have to do them together," she said firmly.

He looked at Janie, who gave him a slightly sympathetic look but shrugged, before he turned to Mar. "I don't really drink."

"Perfect. Neither does Janie. You can be on each other's level," she said dismissively.

"Don't you think it would be better if one of us stayed sober?" he asked cautiously. Five minutes ago he might have been willing to take the shot just to make her happy, but with his recovered memory, not having his wits about him while Janie was drinking made him nervous.

"Oh not you, too," Mar said in annoyance. It was only now as she tried to glare at him that he saw the glaze to her eyes and realized that she was probably more far gone than he thought. "You really are per-fect for each other, aren't you?"

"Mar —" Janie tried to interject.

"Come on, Janie! Can't you ever just have fun?"

"I am having fun!"

The pronouncement was another throwback that was borderline painful for Nate to hear and it made him desperate to escape the situa-tion. Without thought he blurted, "Do you want to dance?"

Mar's face immediately turned smug, but Janie looked almost frightened. He tried to backpedal, "Sorry... I —"

"Yes," Janie said strongly. The look in her eyes shifting from fear to determination as she put her drink down and he copied. She cast a quick glance at her sister before looking back at him. "I'd love to."

A new kind of fear rushed through him. This was a bad idea. He wasn't a dancer, and there was no way in hell that his dancing skills were the way to impressing her. He'd made his own grave though, so he offered his hand and led her to the floor.

Luck seemed to be on his side, because Janie was a terrible dancer, even worse than him. It was incredibly endearing to watch, though. Maybe it was the drinks she'd had, but she moved with joyful abandon completely out of time with the music that played over the speaker. The color on her cheeks said she knew it, but the smile that brightened her face further declared that she didn't care.

At one point, their eyes locked, and Nate was hit with a realization. Whatever past they may have had didn't really matter. He hadn't known her back then at all, and he still didn't really now, but he was determined to. One song slid into another until he lost count, lost to the enjoyment of it. The more time he spent with her, the more he wanted to learn everything about her.

The dance floor wasn't the ideal place for that, so when she asked if he was ready to head back to the bar for a drink, he complied.

"Well, if I wasn't convinced you two were soulmates before, that dancing proved it."

He'd entirely forgotten that her sister was even there until her words cut into their conversation. When he looked up, she was sitting on his stool watching them with a gleam in her eye. A small part of him was embarrassed by it, but most of him was too lit from being so close to Janie for so long to care.

Janie didn't share his lack of concern. Her body straightened with tension as she hissed, "*Mar!*"

"Oh relax. I didn't mean it like *that*," she dismissed, waving a sloppy hand.

Clearly she'd been drinking quite a bit in their absence and Nate looked around for the bartender she was interested in, wondering if he'd been supplying her with free drinks. He spotted him a few chairs down, arguing with a customer. The argument was quickly getting heated, and he was beginning to wonder if Jason had been stupid enough to be drinking with Mar.

"Hey," he said, turning back to the girls intending to ask what the deal was with Jason. He was distracted from that train of thought when he saw their heated discussion. He'd never seen Janie so intense before – not that he'd had much opportunity – but it looked so strange on her that he stopped to strain to catch the words.

"... *let it go*. It wasn't him when I was sixteen and there's no reason to think it's him now."

Sixteen? That would have been when...

"I'm just trying to help," Mar insisted. "You said you remembered dark hair. Maybe that's your type. Just try. Don't tell me you don't like him. I know you do."

"I *am* trying, and I *do* like him." Nate felt a pulse of nervous excitement. *She liked him!* It was quickly tempered by the way she paused and bit her lip. He was expecting some qualification that would diminish her feelings, but his happiness soared as she continued, "I actually really like him. It's –"

The conversation was cut off by the sound of shattering glass and all of their attention turned toward the scene on their right. Jason had taken hold of the belligerent drunk and was dragging him to the side door before unceremoniously throwing him out.

"Oh, finally," Mar exhaled, seemingly unperturbed by the whole affair. At his and Janie's matching confused looks she shook her head impatiently. "We don't need to talk about that," she dismissed, bouncing in her seat a bit before turning to him with a look that was far too amused for his liking. "I still want to talk about the dancing."

"Yeah, yeah. I know. I'm not a dancer," he huffed without heat. Having Janie's sister poke fun at his dancing skills wasn't exactly ideal conditions for trying to impress her, but he'd opened the door himself by suggesting it in the first place.

Janie touched his shoulder and smiled at him warmly. "I think you're great."

"You would," Mar laughed. "You can't dance either."

"True," Janie replied good-naturedly, completely unoffended. She turned to him, "Sorry. I probably should have warned you first."

"Don't be. I can honestly say that's the most fun I've ever had on a dance floor." He leaned in a bit, happy when she didn't pull back at all, and added, "Just say the word and we can go back out there whenever you want."

Her cheeks colored, but he considered it a victory that she didn't avert her eyes as she took a step closer and voiced her agreement.

She was in trouble. *Huge, epic trouble,* she thought from below the comfort of Nate's arm. At some point during the last several hours, they'd steadily grown closer until it had ended up slung around her shoulder with hers snaked around his waist. It was bad. Very bad.

A few hours spent in Nate's direct company and she'd crossed the line into being well and truly head over heels for him. It was why she'd never even temporarily entertained daydreams of giving in to the passing attraction she had experienced for various men, because she was afraid of precisely this.

Well, not *precisely* this. This felt different. So much more than she would have ever allowed herself to imagine with anyone, let alone actually feel. She couldn't seem to stop herself with him. Nor did she want to.

It was just past closing time at the bar, and they had just said goodbye to Mar, who was waiting for Jason to finish up so that she could go home with him. Having spent the whole night dancing and chatting, with Janie holding up her end of the bargain and dutifully taking the three disgusting shots Mar had thrust upon her, she was worn out, but happy as she sagged lightly into Nate's side. She wasn't even drunk enough to truly need it. It was just incredibly cozy there. It felt *good.*

She was even more certain now that if anyone was worth the risk, it was him. He'd been the epitome of a perfect date the whole night – paying attention to her, asking her insightful questions, and genuinely being good company – despite the fact that he wasn't technically her date. She added the benefit that she fit against him perfectly to the list as he looked down and smiled at her.

A concentrated wave of his scent hit her as he shifted and she inhaled deeper on reflex, sinking into it, returning his smile with one of her own, a bit more dreamily than she would have liked.

She could blame it on the alcohol if she really, really tried – and conveniently ignored the fact that he had been quick to supply her with water all night – but it was really just him. It was getting harder to deny that fact with every passing second.

His breath was warm and sent a shiver through her when he leaned down to speak in her ear. "Ready?"

She bit her lip to hold back some of the things she wanted to say as she nodded. The largest part of her wanted to say she was ready for anything, while a small part of her was afraid to give in, and even more afraid that she wouldn't be able to resist if they were alone. A vibration against her hip spared her.

Nate's brow furrowed as he pulled away from her and dug his phone out of his pocket. She had to admit she was curious too. As far as she knew, he didn't have many friends or any family he kept up with that would be calling him at this hour. He glanced at the screen before quickly opening it.

"Hello," he said worriedly, stepping away from the bar and the clinking glass. Janie stayed, unsure if she should follow, until he paused and looked for her. When she followed, his attention turned back to his conversation. "Wait, slow down Mrs. Brakely. What's going on?" His expression grew more concerned as he nodded along and responded, "Okay. Yeah. Stay where you are. I'll be there soon."

He heaved a sigh when he hung up, the look he gave her full of regret. "I'm sorry. That was my neighbor. I have to go take care of something."

"Oh." Disappointment washed over her. She really had been having a wonderful night and wasn't quite ready for it to be at an end. Still, she could tell whatever was going on must have been serious, so she smiled. "That's fine. Thank you for coming out tonight. It was surprisingly fun."

"It really was," he said, sounding wistful. The smile he gave didn't quite reach his eyes. "Thank you for inviting me."

He took a half step toward her, extending his arms in invitation. She didn't hesitate to slip into the hug, enjoying it too much to be embarrassed by the way she lingered there with her head on his chest. For a long moment, he made no move to release her either.

When he finally did pull back, it was only enough to allow her to look up at him. His hesitation was as clear in his eyes as his words, "I'm sorry for leaving like this. Will you be alright getting home?"

"I'll be fine. It's not a far walk."

He stiffened. "You can't walk." She wanted to insist that it would be fine, but she held back, knowing Mar would be pissed if she did. It just seemed like such a waste to pay for a ride when it was so close. He was talking again before she could vocalize any of this, "I'll drive you. I just need to stop at my place first, if you don't mind waiting."

"I don't mind," she agreed quickly, eager to spend more time with him. "But it's in the opposite direction. Are you sure?"

"I'm sure," he replied just as quickly. It brought a small smile to her face, but it was short lived as she heard the tension in his voice as he continued, "but we need to go now."

On the ride over, he explained the situation. Mrs. Brakely, the widow next door, called and said that their neighbors had gotten into a fight. She'd heard the shouting, and when she heard the husband storm out of the apartment, she'd gone over to check on the young mother and baby she heard crying. She brought the terrified young woman and infant son back to her apartment, but they were worried the husband was going to come back. She didn't know who else to call.

Nate didn't say what he intended to do, but his white-knuckled grip and tight jaw showed the strain he felt as he discussed it in a flat voice. She'd catalogued enough of his behaviors to guess that his past had been violent, but she didn't think it was the right time to talk about it.

It was with reluctance that she agreed to wait in the car when they arrived – with the doors locked until he returned – and only out of respect for how close to home this situation was for him. Still, she had to bite the inside of her cheek to resist the urge to offer her support. She settled for giving him a small nod and a tight smile as she promised once more not to open the door for anyone but him.

It came as a surprise when her phone buzzed with a message from him less than two minutes later asking her to come upstairs to apartment 2B. Anxious, she grabbed the keys, letting herself into the building and hurrying up the stairs. She was met by an elderly woman trying to soothe a crying baby while Nate and who she assumed was the baby's mother hastily packed as much as they could fit into various bags. She jumped in to help without hesitation. Within minutes, they'd collected what they could and were standing in the parking lot, Nate loading the car while the woman worked to secure the infant seat in the back of it.

Janie watched with the baby in her arms, a warmth growing in her chest despite the horrible circumstances, as Nate finished loading everything they'd managed to pack into his car and then handed the woman his keys. He didn't ask anything of her in return. With more kindness and compassion than she'd ever seen, he convinced her to take it, telling her to get as far as she could and providing her with a list of shelters in the nearest major cities. His car was a "piece of crap that probably cost more in oil changes than it was worth", as he put it, but it was also the only one he had. Yet he signed the title and handed that over too, telling her to put it in her name whenever she was ready.

When the woman tried to reject it, he simply said, "You need to get out, now. If not for you, then for him." When she still hesitated, he added, "Trust me," in a voice that was so earnest it hurt to hear the words.

The sigh of relief he breathed as he watched the car disappear from view was so genuine that it overwhelmed her entirely. She'd known he was a good person, that he was gentle and patient and kind, but this was something else. Her heart swelled, fogging her brain as she let him lead her back toward his apartment, his hand at the small of her back, the warmth spreading from there into a heat that consumed her.

"... sorry I can't give you a ride. I'll pay for the cab…" As his distant words penetrated vaguely, she realized that he was *apologizing*. For not being able to drive her home, because he'd given his car away to help a woman in need. It hit her like lightning, and she snapped as she took the final step onto the landing in front of the door to his apartment complex.

Without hesitation, she turned and kissed him. With her standing a step above him, they were perfectly aligned as she leaned in, the swell of emotions pouring out of her chest and through her lips as she released all the passion, awe, and love she felt for him. Before her heart could even beat again, he was returning it, fingers twined in her hair and palm gentle on her cheek despite the urgency with which he returned the affection.

The kiss was everything. It completely blew away all the overblown dramatic descriptions in her romance novels, warmth and love permeating every fiber of her being and seeping into her bones, while simultaneously lighting her skin like a wire. She felt hot and cool and *alive*.

The moment felt timeless, like the world had stopped around them and they stood in a suspended state of perfection. She could *feel* the love he felt for her pouring out of him the same way it was pouring out of her. It was the single, most wonderful moment she'd ever felt in her life.

It was her worst nightmare.

The kiss brought it all thundering back. It was a stupid decision. She had been right all along that this was dangerous. Gasping, she desperately tried to pull back, but he was holding her.

"Wait," he begged. "Please, just wait. Don't do this again…" The words were lost on her, though. The only thing she could hear was her own broken words in her head.

I'm sorry, she thought to *him*, feeling horrible and torn. She was thinking of Nate too and how she wanted him to keep holding her, even as she tried to pull away. *I'm sorry. I'm sorry. I'm sorry.*

Nate finally put some distance between them, though he kept hold of her shoulders as he stopped to look her in the eye. She could hardly see through the continuous stream of tears that poured and blurred her vision. Still, she tried to look away, her apologetic mantra on loop.

"*Damn it*," he growled. "Will you stop apologizing and just *look* at me?"

That did it. She stared at him, stunned and confused in equal measure. She hadn't said anything aloud. She *knew* it. Her mouth opened and closed – once, twice, three times – but no sound came out. She couldn't think of the right question to form, but he didn't give her a chance.

Nate blew out a breath and released her, stepping back once he seemed sure that he had her attention. He ran a heavy, agitated hand through his hair as he explained gruffly, "I'm sorry. I shouldn't have held you like that. But I couldn't let you run. Not again."

He'd said that before, but she'd been too in her own head to process it. Her voice came out weak and confused as she clung to that one detail and asked, "Again?"

He turned to look at her head on then, a guilty and wary look in his eyes as he admitted, "Again, yeah. I…" He paused and swallowed thickly, before taking her hands slowly, as if he was afraid she was going to pull back again. "That wasn't our first kiss, Janie. We – we've met before. Five years ago, at a New Year's Eve party. And… you kissed me, but then you freaked out and took this guy's drink and –"

The implications hit her hard and fast. He was the guy from when she was sixteen, the one whose kiss had made her terrified to attempt a relationship of any kind for that last five years, the one she didn't remember…and he knew it. He knew who she was.

Betrayal washed over her and she pulled her hands free of his grasp, stepping back quickly. "You *knew*?" Her voice was hard and accusatory, unlike anything she'd ever heard spoken from her own mouth before.

"*No*," he said forcefully. Quieter, but earnestly, he continued, "No. I didn't. It wasn't until tonight, seeing you under the bar lights that I recognized that you were the girl." He laughed, but it was more incredulous than amused. "I don't know how – I spent hours watching you sleep that night, making sure you were going to be okay –"

She cut off his rambling once more, a foreign anxiety making her irritable. "And you didn't think to tell me!?"

He actually flinched, the movement pricking at her conscience. *Calm down*, she told herself.

"I didn't think it mattered. I didn't know you then." Desperation leaked into his tone. "I didn't think you remembered me or anything about that night at all. There didn't seem to be a point in ruining the night by dragging up ancient history. I'll tell you anything you want to know...everything about that night if it will make you feel better."

He's right, she admitted to herself. "That's fair," she said aloud, surprised to see the tension that drained out of him at those two words. She hadn't realized just how upset he'd gotten until that moment.

He wasn't completely at ease yet, she noticed, as he stepped forward with raised hands, as if frightened that she'd bolt again if he got too close. As much as she wanted to fall back into him, she took a step back and leaned against the door, needing the space despite the way her chest constricted at the contorted look on his face.

"I'm sorry," she began.

"*Please*," he cut in, "*please* stop apologizing. I can't handle it. Just – just tell me why. Both times, *you* kissed *me,* but then it's like you panic and I don't – " he cut off, helplessness and confusion all over his features.

Her eyes closed against the sight. She took a deep breath, trying to settle herself, trying to make sense of the mass of confusion that this night had become –

And was promptly thrown forward by the force of the door behind her being slammed open. A drunk stumbled out, but she hardly had time to notice. The impact had sent her forward into Nate. He caught her, but the momentum carried them both backward and down the two steps. She was protected in the cradle of Nate's arms as he fell back, bearing both their weight as his back broke their fall.

The details of the fall and the drunk muttering apologies were lost on Janie, however, all of it immediately becoming irrelevant and paling in comparison to the realization that struck her when Nate's head collided with the pavement and a flash of blood and pain erupted on the back of her skull.

It no longer mattered that she'd backed away from him only a minute ago, that he should be helping her extricate herself from him instead of keeping her close. He took her by the shoulders, pushing her back a little to get a better view and ignoring the pain he felt in favor of making sure she was alright. She winced at the movement, reaching to rub the back of her head. His heart dropped when it came away bloody. The way she stared at the red staining her hand frightened him – like she'd seen something beyond comprehension and was falling into shock.

"Janie?" he questioned, his voice high and cracking with the nerves pulsing through him. No matter the amount of blood he'd seen, it was different when it was someone you loved. When it happened out of nowhere and without warning.

Her wide eyes settled on his, the look there unfathomable to him. Her pupils were dilated and shining with revelation, like the secrets of the universe had been revealed to her and rested there. As if in confirmation, her tone was laced with wonder and disbelief as she said, "You're hurt."

"I'm fine," he dismissed, his worry growing by the second. "But you're not. You're bleeding –"

"I'm bleeding," she interjected, the same wonder in her tone as before as she looked at the blood on her hand again.

If she hadn't just repeated his words, he would have assumed she wasn't listening at all. She reached out and touched his own wound, there was a slight pain at her touch, but he suppressed his desire to flinch. It was all he could do to stay calm. *This wasn't normal.* Despite the bleeding, the door shouldn't have hit her with enough force to cause the damage needed to impact her behavior, and he'd taken the brunt of their fall.

"Are you alright?" he tried again.

Her eyes trained on his again, still swirling with a mix of emotions he couldn't identify. "I'm bleeding," she said again, though the wonder in her tone had given way to something more like euphoria. "You're hurt! And I'm bleeding!" She laughed, a loud joyous sound.

He barely had time to worry about the incongruity of it all before she launched herself forward, her lips colliding with his insistently. The impact knocked his head back to the ground, sending a pain through him that made him flinch, and he felt her flinch as well in his arms. For a moment, he resisted – he needed to be certain she was alright – but she deepened the kiss instead of retreating. The sensation overwhelmed him, and as the pain faded, so did his worry, until nothing but the feeling of her existed.

It was only the sticky feeling of her blood on his fingers as they tangled in her hair that broke him from the haze of intense pleasure that was thrumming through his veins. As gently as he could, he pushed her back. Worriedly, he said, "Seriously, Janie. You're hurt. Just let me take a look."

Warmth and light spread across her features as a huge smile broke out across her face. "It's you," she said, her tone saturated in amazement. "It was always you!" Her laughter bordered on manic as she jumped to her feet. "Come on!" she said, trying to pull him up. He followed suit, rising on his own, but almost lost his balance when she tugged on his hand enthusiastically before he'd fully stood. "I have so much to tell you!"

The happiness surrounding her seemed to cast a glow that made the dark night shine brighter, but his inability to reconcile her swift change in behavior made him too worried to enjoy it. He pulled her to a stop. Worriedly, he took her face between his hands and said, "Please. *Please*, just let me check you, okay?"

She shook her head and pulled back, her smile only continuing to widen. Her expression became so radiant and warm that he wanted to do nothing but bask in the fact that she was looking at him that way. He knew he couldn't though.

Helplessness settled over him as he weighed the options. He could drag her to the hospital if he really needed to, but it felt like it would be crossing a line to force her. He already felt bad about holding onto her earlier. His deliberation died quickly when she leaned in, bracing her hands on his shoulders and brushing a soft kiss against his lips and cheek before whispering, "I'm okay. You're okay. We're going to be fine, I promise."

The whispered words froze him. He'd heard those words countless times in his life, spoken in that exact voice.

Those words had seen him through some of his darkest times. He didn't know how or why, but he was certain they were true. Especially now. Now that he knew they were from her.

She pulled back to look at him. This time his smile mirrored hers when she said, "We're going to be *better* than fine."

This time when their mouths collided, he was sure he could taste the fierce joy she felt on her tongue, her movements impassioned but full of a love that he couldn't refute. Above all else, those feelings won out. He couldn't pull himself away from her to ask the questions he had, particularly not when she wrapped her arms around his neck and leveraged her legs around his waist. The heat from her center, so close with the way her dress lifted, burned him and spurred him into action. He stumbled blindly, consumed by everything that was her, down the hall and into his apartment.

He was hovering over her on the couch by the time reason caught up to him. It was hard, borderline impossible with the feelings she was drawing out of him and the way they were nearly all consuming, but he managed to pull back. He didn't want to do it like this, not with her. Not Janie, the only woman he was sure he'd ever loved.

Looking at her didn't make it any easier, however. The light in her eyes was brighter than he'd ever seen it, her cheeks flushed and her chest rising and falling heavily, pushing her breasts against his chest in a rhythm that resonated through him like the steady beat of a drum. He'd never been more aroused and he almost forgot why he pulled back, until she smiled at him. *She wanted to tell him something.*

"It's fine," she said, slowing in sync with him. He could see in her eyes that she truly meant it, that she felt what he felt.

He felt the truth of it down to his bones when he added, "We have time."

Trailing his nose across her cheek on a path to her neck, kissing lightly where he had been sucking only a moment before, he caught sight of the mark blooming there. It wasn't something he'd normally do – he liked to think he was more considerate than that, but he'd also never been so swept away before – but he felt a foreign pride. She was his now, just as he was hers.

She was smiling that knowing smile when he looked back at her face. There was no need for words. Gently he stood, offering his hand. She took it, rising gracefully and following as he led her to the bedroom, eyes locked with his the entire way.

She didn't display any hint of nerves as she released her grip and turned, pulling her hair over her shoulder to reveal the zipper of her dress with deliberate movements. His own actions were measured and calm, a direct contrast to the frenzy and heat that led them to his apartment.

Both felt right. The raging fire from earlier and smoldering heat they shared now as he slowly slid the zipper down, revealing the pale expanse of her back. He couldn't resist dropping a kiss on the soft skin of her shoulder as he gently freed it from the confines of her dress. He felt her skin prickle beneath his lips, but also felt his own flesh tingling. Experimentally, he reached out and further explored the sensation, unable to differentiate between what he felt himself and what he imagined she was feeling.

When his hands cupped her bare breasts, thumbs grazing her nipples, his tightened in time with hers. His erection throbbing as she arched her back to rub herself against it. They let out identical groans of appreciation.

"Fuck." The oath was shared.

The fire kindling between them burned a bit hotter, but didn't fully ignite. Janie simply turned on her toes, allowing the rest of the fabric to drop to the floor as she spun and pressed her lips to his. The kiss was laden with feeling, but unhurried as she gently undid the buttons of his shirt one by one until she was able to divest him of it entirely, the bare skin of his torso burning everywhere it met hers.

Slowly, he guided her backward until they reached the edge of bed, where he crouched down, trailing his hands down her sides until he reached the place of her underwear. He took a moment to kiss her over the fabric, feeling a thrill as he did so, before pulling the fabric down to her ankles. She stepped out of them without prompting, and he caught her left ankle before she could return it to the floor and guided it over his shoulder.

He'd been distracted by the sight of her, by the budding anticipation of removing all the layers the separated them, but now he needed to see her face. Looking up through his lashes, he was hit by a wave of desire at the intensity with which she watched him. He meant to ask if what they were doing was okay, but looking into her eyes he could hear the words again.

I'm okay. You're okay. We're going to be fine, I promise.

More than that, he heard her newest promise, that they would be better than fine. It obliterated his hesitation and he took that first step, kissing the heated flesh at the apex of her thighs, unable to resist any longer. As he felt *her* pleasure reverberate through *him* with each movement they made from there, he was sure no one had ever been more fine than they were in that moment.

The witch smiled to herself as she looked over all the connections of the world mapped out before her, endless strands that crisscrossed into a web of magnificent colors and patterns. One in particular was braiding itself into a cord before her very eyes. No matter how many times she bore witness to an event of such greatness, it never ceased to fill her with a sense of power and satisfaction. The binding in this case was particularly strong, however, and gave her great personal pleasure.

For every person she came across, there was a weak, transient string that connected the witch to them and faded into nothingness once her work was complete. Sometimes it was as simple as tipping the rock that would send a person sprawling down the hill into another's path, other times she drew their attention with more purpose. She was supposed to come across the girl and connect the pair so that the girl's magic would aid the boy. She did that, but she had added a personal touch, one that stretched the rules in a way that she rarely did.

The string between the bright-eyed girl and bruised boy had already existed when she'd enhanced it, allowing their connection to manifest early in order to spare them from the cruelty of the Fates who had so clearly been eyeing his fading line. She had warned the girl of the worst parts, but not the best.

Not how hope and love were the greatest healers in the universe, nor how they would be able to share that love between them once they found it.

No one, not even the witch herself, could take credit for the blinding connection between the two now, however. The strings of their experiences and feelings wrapped and spun together with ease and precision into a rainbow of colors. They were separate; each belonging to themselves. Yet, their choice to give to each other so wholly wove their souls together too tightly for even the Fates to sever their bond.

The witch's smile spread as she looked forward and saw the boy's protectiveness and admiration, the girl's fierce loyalty and compassion. There would be guilt and horror, followed by forgiveness and amazement, but most of all love. The connection flared like a comet, before fading to a luminescent glow that would please her for years to come.

Real

TheWordsInMyHead

He knows that for a lot of people this place is one of misery, the kind of place you avoid at all costs, but for him, it's always been where he's most comfortable. The linoleum floors and dully painted walls, the fluorescent lights and the always moving action; they bring him a sense of peace. Or maybe that feeling of rightness is just from being on this plain itself.

Taking a deep breath, he relishes the feeling of being back. His absence wasn't long, really as short as he could make it, but that doesn't seem to have mattered. He notes the changes, significant and not, as he walks the familiar halls.

Everything about it makes him feel alive in a way that his home has never been able to. He doesn't do much here, sometimes he helps heal people, they tend to call it miracles, but most of the time, he just Watches. After all, that's what he's been called to do.

Over the years, the practice of Watching has faded away. His people don't care for humans the way they used to. They don't feel the devotion. Once upon a time, it was an honour to have a district to watch over, to be considered the most capable in helping a lesser species. Now though, it is looked upon as a chore. A chore that not only are more and more families reluctant to do, but one that many have decided isn't necessary altogether.

From what he understands, his family's domain is one of the few places that's still actively patrolled. His people, influenced by those in charge, the high council, don't see that value in protecting the weak. They would much rather focus their efforts internally.

There's no efficiency in a society that prioritizes Watching and the council values productivity above all. Everybody in his world does, at least everyone except him.

For his part, he doesn't understand the disinterest, the apathy. There's something about humans that has always intrigued him. They live so fiercely despite their fragility. It's remarkable. Just being around them makes him feel alive, even if all he does is roam the halls, an invisible observer.

Most of the time, he is happy with his life and the path that he's chosen. There's a beauty in Watching those most vulnerable, a power, that he's never found with anything else. Being here, Watching over them, protecting them, it's all he's ever wanted. It's enough, even if it is isolating.

It's never really bothered him that the people he spends his life devoted to can't see him, don't even know that he exists. He doesn't do what he does for them, for their love; he does it for himself. He doesn't need to be seen. At least he didn't until the moment he lay eyes on her.

Soft wavy hair and a slender figure, he desperately wants to know her. More than that though, he desperately wishes that she could know him. There's something different about her, a brightness radiating off her so strong it pushes past the shadow that everyone in this place carries.

She's brilliant and he can't look away.

Over the next few days, he keeps coming back to her, almost unconsciously. He'll be walking through the old building, doing his regular routine and then suddenly, he'll find himself standing outside her door, drawn to her like a moth to a flame.

And then each time, he inevitably ends up inside sitting in the always vacant seat across from her bed, watching her. He loses hours in her quiet little room watching her, the draft from her window and entirely too cheerful painting on her wall becoming familiar to him in a way that the rest of the rooms aren't.

For the most part, all she does is lie there, sleeping or at least pretending to sleep. Sometimes she'll eat, but never quite as much as he thinks maybe she should. Yet, despite the mundanity of her schedule, he never tires of her presence.

It's never been like this before.

He has always had his favourites, people who he'd spend more time watching, who he'd care about a little more, but never to this extent. Normally, it's a fun game for him, learning who a person is slowly, in bits and pieces. An offhand comment from a nurse one day, a journal left open on the nightstand or a touching conversation with a visitor. He always wants to know more about the people who he spends his days Watching, but he's never needed the information quite like this.

With her, it's a thirst, a desperate need he has to quench. He spends hours searching for any little detail that will tell him more about her. Who she is. Where she came from. Anything. Everything.

Yet, there's remarkably little to be discovered. She doesn't have any visitors, there's no journaling; there's no talking at all that he's heard and surprisingly little gossip between the staff about her too. Aside from the nurses who come and check on her and the orderlies who bring her food, it's almost like she doesn't exist to the rest of the world.

There's something comforting about that, the idea that he's not alone in his isolation. Still, it leaves him puzzled; she leaves him puzzled and a little antsy. He wants more, desperately, but to get more, he'd have to break his self-imposed rules.

For a while, he is able to resist the temptation, satisfied with the small things he is able to learn about her. If she's not resting, lying in bed from an exhaustion he can't begin to understand, she's sitting on the window seat. Not that it's really a seat. Realistically, it's nothing more than an insignificant ledge.

In some ways it makes sense, she's small, slight in a way that he now realizes isn't quite natural and other than his chair and her bed there's nowhere to sit other than the ground. Still, it seems like it would be uncomfortable. Yet day after day, he finds her crowded up into the tiny space, starting outside as if she'd be able to transport herself through the bars if only she could will it hard enough.

He also learns that she's abnormally still. She doesn't move or fidget, she doesn't bite her nails or play with her hair. Hours of watching her and he still hasn't discovered her nervous ticks. He's starting to think that maybe she doesn't have any.

Sometimes, just for a moment, he'll think she can see him. There will be a few precious seconds, a couple of heartbeats, where he can feel the burn of her gaze hot on his skin, then her eyes will slide past him, leaving him with nothing but coursing disappointment and a feeling of foolishness.

More days pass and his fascination with her only grows. For every detail that is revealed to him, he wants a dozen more. It's not really surprising then that eventually, inevitably, he breaks.

Sneaking into the medical files is incredibly easy, so easy that it only increases the guilt pulling at his stomach. It's easy to think of the people he Watches as friends despite the one-sidedness of the relationship and this feels like a betrayal. Especially with her involved.

He hesitates with the folder in his hands, indecision weighing heavy on his shoulders, but ultimately, he opens the document. The reality is that as much as he likes to pretend, to live in a fantasy world where this place is his home, it's not and it's never going to be. His role here is to help the people of this world and he can't do that effectively with the information he currently has.

Or at least that's what he tells himself, but it's hard to believe, especially when he reads her full name for the first time and a thrill runs through him.

Elizabeth Fulton.

He skims the details of the file quickly, eager after all this time to learn more.

Birthdate: *April 23, 1998*

Some quick math in his head tells him that she's only 22. He feels a wave of melancholy wash over him. He knows that there's no age limit to suffering, but that still seems remarkably young. He's not even five years older than her based on their standards of time. He shakes his head to remove the lingering sadness and continues reading.

Certain words pop out to him as he goes. *Voluntarily admitted* makes sense with what he has seen about her. She wants to be here, even on the days when she doesn't. He reads a brief summary of what led to her admission, but there's not much to be found. Nothing more than the word *breakdown* stands out.

Further down, he sees that she *has a medical history of antidepressants.* No surprise there, he would bet that most of these files have that detail inscribed in them. And then underneath, that they're considering a possible diagnosis of *schizophrenia.*

He turns the page, excited, but there's nothing more, just pages of charts that he doesn't need to see. Information that he was there to experience firsthand. Looking at it now, it's easy to tell that it's not like the others in the drawer. It's thinner and lighter. He can't help but feel like it was hardly worth the violation.

Everything in the file was things that he could have guessed.

Still, when he turns back to sit in her room, it's not with a discouraged tilt to his head, but rather a stronger resolve to learn about her the way he's always learned about his friends, by Watching.

By all accounts, it's a normal day. He's sitting on the worn chair in her room as has been his custom of late, watching her, when suddenly she looks up at him and doesn't look away.

Their eyes lock together and he's mesmerized. He's seen her photo before, in the information folder he borrowed from the front desk, but it doesn't do her justice in the slightest. For being here, in a place full of death, she has so much life in her. Her eyes are blue as the documentation depicted, but there is much more to them. The colours in them swirl back and forth like the ocean on a warm summer's day and then every once in a while, there's the smallest hint of gold, the sun reflecting on the waves.

He sucks in a startled breath, overwhelmed by what he's seeing, by the possibilities, but then she looks away and he comes crashing back down, sure that whatever it might have been was nothing more than the product of wishful thinking.

Still, there's the fact that she saw him at all. While he might have wondered, might have speculated, he never once thought her being able to see him would actually be the case. It's impossible, or at least he thought it was.

It takes him a moment to register her laboured breathing, so caught up in his own thoughts, but once he does, it's all he can hear. He forces himself to put aside his crisis and focus on hers.

"You're not real. You're not real," she mutters to herself over and over again, voice nothing more than a whisper. "You're a phantom of my mind. A figment. The dark hair, it's from my father. The leather jacket, from my ex. You're always here because I don't want to be alone, but I *am* alone because you're not real."

He takes a step towards her hoping to comfort her in any way possible and then stops himself short. The absolute last thing he wanted to do was hurt her and right now that's what he's doing. She's afraid of him. Or maybe just of what his being here means for her.

For a second, he considers spilling his people's entire history. The long and complicated relationship their people have, whatever the consequences, just to help ease the panic from her movements, but one look at her, curled up into a ball, and he just knows that his tales of other realms is going to do nothing to calm her.

"Okay," he says simply, not sure what else he can do.

She looks up at him, eyes dry despite the whimpers. "Okay?"

"Okay then, I'm not real."

Her beautiful eyes widen in disbelief and then a half manic, half hollow laugh burst from her lips. "Of course, you're not."

He stays there silently watching, locked in place, as a team of nurses rushes in to do what he doesn't have the power to. They surround her, whispering calming words and making soothing motions. He faintly hears one of them ask if she'd like a sedative.

Her eyes flicker over to him again at the question as if checking to see if he's still there. He stays frozen in place, as her eyes scan his form, just as unsure. There're a few terrifying seconds as he waits for confirmation in her eyes, but then her eyes lock onto him again and there's no doubt. For better or worse, he's no longer invisible to this world.

She shakes her head in rejection of the meds, all the while holding his gaze. He can't look away, not that he wants to. This time there's not the same alarm when she looks at him. There's confusion, and disbelief, mixed with the tiniest bit of intrigue, but no panic.

The amount of relief that fills him with that change is only matched by his own confusion and the twinge of hope building in his chest.

Their eyes stay connected until eventually her frantic movements stop and her eyes slowly close in exhaustion.

He's left the hospital countless times since she first arrived, after all, as much as he prefers this place, it's not his home. What he does here is a job like any other, regardless of the enjoyment he finds in it. At the end of the day, he needs to return regularly not only to make his reports, but also because that's where his life is supposed to be.

That doesn't make it any easier though, especially not now. He's walked away from her more than a dozen times without too much hesitation, but this time it's harder. Now there's more to lose if he comes back and too much time has passed. With the way that time moves between the different plains, a year could pass in the minute he's gone.

It's unpredictable and there are no guarantees.

Still, he forces himself to walk towards the dark, subdued and wholly unremarkable painting on the third floor that serves as his passage home when he feels the internal tug to return a few hours after Beth falls asleep. It comes every 24 hours by his world's time standard to allow people like himself, those stationed in other realms, to be aware of the passage of time. Often, he will ignore one or two, content to stay here, but eventually, he always goes, ready to heed the call.

He'll just submit his report, make a quick appearance somewhere public so people can see him and then he'll be back. It will be fine.

With that in mind, he steps up and places his hand on the door, the focal point of the artwork, pushing it further open with the magical touch of his hand. Taking a deep breath, he tries to absorb a final bit of the fragrant earth air before traversing his way up the stairs and through the narrow path connecting the plains. He has to blink his eyes a few times to adjust to the dimness, fighting off a shiver. This place always feels so cold after the vibrancy of the other plain.

Almost unconsciously, he feels his posture stiffen as he makes his way through the crowds, trying to mimic the reflection of those around him. Even though he is fully visible here, he is able to move past people like a ghost. No one smiles at him in greeting or pauses to ask him how he's been, they move straight forward with undeterred purpose.

It's only once he's nearly finished with the report that someone actually speaks to him. From there, it's a bunch of hurried steps and rushed movements until he's standing in front of the high council wondering what happened.

He twists his hands together nervously thinking about a pair of knowing blue eyes that he neglected to include in his report.

"You are stationed at the hospital, correct?" an undistinguishable voice asks from high above him.

"Yes, sir," he responds, his voice as clear and confident as he can make it.

"Our sources tell us that there may be someone you need to look out for, someone dangerous."

He feels a pit form in his stomach. Out of all the things that he had considered while the formalities of the chamber were addressed, the thought of there being a possible threat had never crossed his mind. No one on that plain can even see him, how can there be danger. *Not no one*, a dark voice in his head is quick to remind him.

"It is believed that someone might possess the ability to see you."

A startled gasp falls from his lips. Until a few hours ago, he didn't think that was even possible, but apparently, he had been misinformed.

The thought sends an unusual surge of annoyance through him towards the people sitting tall and proud on the bench above him. If that information had been readily available, he would have known it.

For all their rhetoric on the importance of transparency, it seems that they have not been very forthcoming.

"Have you seen any suspicious behaviour?"

"No."

The answer is out of his mouth with no hesitation. He thinks of her huddled by the window, small and trapped. He thinks of the fear in her eyes and then the wonder. She's not dangerous, not in the slightest. He knows it as truly as he knows anything.

There's a beat of silence, probably much longer in his head than in actuality, and then "Very well, you are free to go. Proceed with caution."

He turns to leave without another word, valiantly trying to ignore the guilt threatening to consume him. Guilt that is only exaggerated by their easy acceptance of his answer.

With no desire to remain here any longer, he quickly makes his way back to the passage. Right now, all he wants is to be back in his chair watching Beth sleep. The reality is that he was going to linger because it's what he is supposed to want to do, not because it's what he wants. There is no one here waiting to see him. He visited with his parents during his last voyage back and they won't be expecting him again, knowing that his preference is the other plain and respecting that affinity even if they don't totally understand it.

Traveling back down the path is like walking into the light; everything within him comes back to life. He knows that for everyone else in his world, the brightness is too much, but for him it's perfect. He feels a smile grace his lips as he pulls open the door, taking his first real breath in what feels like hours. It smells like home.

A wave of relief passes through him when he looks out the window and sees the moon high in the sky; he can't have been gone for more than a few hours. There's an extra bounce of joy in his step as he makes his way through the building and down a couple of floors to get to her room. The excitement that he was so hesitant to feel earlier when she looked at him, now raging without restraint.

The council knew about her which means it wasn't a fluke. Tomorrow when she wakes up, she will still be able to see him. The many wondrous possibilities are racing through his mind when he passes through the entrance to her room and his feet come to a halt. In the blink of an eye, all his hopes come crashing down.

Her bed is empty. Not only empty but cleanly made as though it hadn't been used in days. He feels his heart lodge itself somewhere in his throat. No, it's not possible, it's not. After waiting so long, she's not just going to disappear right when he finds her. The world isn't that cruel.

He looks around helplessly. She can't just be gone. *She can't.* It's unacceptable.

In all the years that he's been watching the place, he's never left the building, never tried, but when he turns back to the bed and doesn't find her magically reappeared, he's ready to try. One way or another, he will find her.

It's only once he's out of the room and a few steps down the hall that the possibility of something more sinister having happened crosses his mind. The council believed her to be dangerous, did something else think so too? In the time he was gone something could have grabbed her and he'd never know.

In the time he was gone someone else from *his* realm could have come and grabbed her and he would never know.

The thoughts spiral aimlessly through his head as the panic mounts. He has to find Beth, whether that's here on this plain, back on his own or somewhere else entirely, but he doesn't know where to start. Or how to start.

For as long as he has been watching over the people of this hospital, guarding them vigilantly, now that the time has come to do something, he's stuck, frozen in panic. There are no plans of action. No plan at all. The thought of losing her is crippling to him. It's not really surprising, but it probably should be.

As much as he would do anything for those he Watches over, he is willing to do *anything* for her with no hesitation. It is foolish and reckless, everything his people despise, but it's who he is when it comes down to it.

So caught up in his worries, he doesn't notice the two figures walking down the hall until they are nearly on top of him.

He looks up and there she is, looking just as she had when he left her a few hours ago, if not a little worse for wear. The shadows under her eyes seem a little darker, her body a little weaker, resting heavily on the nurse walking beside her.

Her eyes settle on him as they pass for one brief moment, just long enough for him to be confident, she can see him before flitting back to the ground.

For a second, he watches her retreating form, needing the extra time to prove to himself that she's real. Satisfied for the moment, he collapses against the nursing station behind him, allowing the solid desk to take his weight. He lets out a tired sigh, his head falls forward to rest on his chest. His heart is still pounding away loud in his ears, but everything is okay. She's okay.

Eventually, he regains his composure, the desire to be near her overriding the instinct to hide away embarrassed. He lifts himself up, ready to move forward, and it's only then that he spots a calendar sitting primly on the desk beside him telling the world that it's March 18.

He looks at it for a long moment, berating himself for his irrationality. It takes him another moment to get over his annoyance and then he is thankful for the information.

It looks like he did miss some time, he checks the clock on the wall, almost 48 hours to be exact. *Not too long in the grand scheme of things* he rationalizes, but then the haunted look in her eyes comes back to him. Hopefully not too long

Whatever he hoped to change with the revelation that she can see him, doesn't. They continue on much the same for the next week, sitting together in companionable silence. As much as he longs for the chance to get to talk with her, to learn about her in a more intimate way, he is happy with this too.

Something happened in the short period he was gone. He's not sure what, all he knows is that the staff come to check on her far more regularly now and as much as he'd like to know more, breaking into her file now feels like a total betrayal in a way that he's not able to reconcile with like last time. She's real now. Or more accurately, he's real now, which means that the rules have changed once again.

Still, he wonders. She's not different, not really, but something about her is. While she still doesn't look at him for longer than a second, and she hasn't made any more attempts to address him, he can tell that she's actively aware of his presence at all times. The thought sends a tingle of anticipation running down his spine that doesn't seem to be disappearing any time soon.

So, he waits, content for her to get more comfortable around him, hoping that someday she will be willing to do more than glance at him out of the corner of her eye. He should have been hoping for so much more, but then again, she always surpasses his expectations.

"I used to pretend that I had been kidnapped," she says unexpectedly one day from her perch on the window seat, "taken from my real family when I was young so that my parents could have the picture-perfect family."

He looks over at her, surprised to hear her talking to him, only to realize that she's staring out the window. Still, he leans forward in his chair in an effort to hear her better. She might not be talking to him, but she's definitely talking knowing he's listening. It's almost like talking to him. Almost.

"It was stupid. I always knew that they were my real parents, I'd seen more than enough evidence to prove it, but still, I pretended. I had everything a child could ever ask for, the big house, the loving parents, the newest toys, but it wasn't enough. I wanted something else, something more." She shakes her head a little like she still can't fathom what her younger self was thinking.

For a second, he waits with bated breath wondering if the unusual moment of sharing is over, but she continues with another shake and a hollow laugh. "It was always treated as a joke, silly Beth up to her antics again, and eventually, I grew out of it… Still, years later, whenever I close my eyes, all I see is the flash of hurt that would cross my Dad's face when I'd claim that my real Dad was coming."

He sits in stunned silence for a while after she finishes, terrified that doing something as simple as moving might break the fragile understanding between them. For a while, he thinks that she might continue, but as the hours' pass, he starts to relax, becoming comfortable with this new normal. Still, he anxiously awaits the next time. He hopes that there will be a next time.

It takes a couple of days, but when she speaks the next time, he is ready for it.

"I should be on the other side of this door," she tells the room quietly late one night from the bed, starting up at the tiled ceiling like maybe it will have all the answers. "Treating people not being treated. After all, that was the plan, one day I'd run this place as my mother did and her father did before her."

After that, it happens more often. He never pries, and she never looks at him as she shares, not that it makes anything she says less meaningful. There doesn't seem to be any rationale to when she does it or what she says, but with each word, he gains a better picture of who she is. Sometimes it's nothing more than an offhand remark, and other times its titbits of information that help him to understand what brought her here.

"When I was 9 years old, I got this new bike."

At this point, he's come to expect the stories, but that doesn't stop a thrill from coursing through him whenever he hears her voice. Weeks later, it should not still be this exciting to learn about her, but it is. With every new detail, his admiration of her grows. She's so special and she doesn't know it.

"It was red and had these sparkly tassels that would flutter in the wind when I'd go really fast. There was this hill not too far from where we lived and it was the best place for going fast. I'd go up and down that hill, over and over. It was always hard getting back up, but the thrill of flying back down was more than worth it. In those few moments, the entire world was nothing but a blur of colours and everything was simple."

He can almost see it, her, a little girl with pigtails in her hair, a bright grin stretched across her face. It's a beautiful image bursting with life so opposite to the one he sees in front of him every day. The spark is still there, of course, the little bit of joyous life that attracted him to her in the first place, sometimes brighter, sometimes dimmer, but always there.

A month later and her little reflections are almost a daily occurrence. They're never long and always completely random, but slowly, he is able to build a clearer picture of who she was, because she always shares details of the past, and through that who she is now.

With every detail thought, every bit of herself that she chooses to share with him, the urge to return the favour grows. He wants to know her, but he also wants her to know him and as she gets more and more comfortable, his reasons for staying silent drift away until all he is left with is a total and all-consuming fear of rejection.

For weeks, he tries to work up the courage to say something, to share his world with her the same way she's showing him her past in tiny glimpses, but every time he tries the words get trapped. After the fifth failed attempt, he decides that he just had to go for it. No more thinking, just doing.

"I remember the first time I came here," he starts suddenly one day with a shaky voice. She hasn't said anything to him today yet and he can't decide if that's better or worse. It means that there's nothing today to compare to what he says, no standard of openness that he'll have to hold himself to, but if this all goes horribly wrong, it will be one less piece of her he gets to experience.

He clears his throat nervously and continues, not daring to look over to see if she's listening. "I must have been very small, much younger than I should have probably been to be allowed to come with my father, but still the memory is as vivid as if it had happened yesterday. Walking around these halls, listening to my father describe the job as his father had to him, I felt a sense of purpose. Someday it was going to be my duty to watch over these people and I relished that fact."

Part of him expects her to ask questions, after all his history should be confusing, but she doesn't say anything. The seconds drag on and turn into minutes. His hands start to sweat, his heart racing so fast he's honestly a little concerned. *What was he thinking?*

And then she starts to speak in the same melodic tone that he's become accustomed to. She doesn't ask questions, instead, she shares her own story, describing the first time that she had to come with her mom to work, how she was forced to wait for hours in the cold lunchroom until her father could come to get her.

He lets out what he hopes is an inaudible sigh of relief. He did it, he talked and she didn't run away. *She didn't run away.*

Slowly, his heart rate starts to calm, but then she surprises him and starts talking again. "I never felt that passion from this place even though I was ready to spend the rest of my life working here. For me, that moment of rightness came from being in my grandmother's attic with a paintbrush in my hand. I must have been young, she died when I was only 6, but I remember it clearly."

He often wonders what she's seeing when she looks off into the distance telling him these stories, but this time he knows. The woman in his head has long grey hair tied up in a bun, Beth's eyes, and a kind smile.

"I remember her vividly. She was a nurse in the war, she would have been the one to run this hospital if it had been a different time. Actually, she probably still would have if it was something she really wanted, but she preferred to spend her time in front of an easel."

He expects that to be the end, it's already far more than she normally shares, but she surpasses his expectations again.

"She was the only one who didn't think I was silly as the kind ones called it, or crazy as the others did. She always told me that I was special."

A few minutes pass as he waits to see if that's the end, but then minutes turn into hours and then even once he's sure, he doesn't say anything back. Part of him wants to, he wants to continue this strange one-sided conversation that they have going with each other and never let it stop, but he holds back. It's already been a lot for today and he's afraid to push too far.

Who he's concerned for, he's not sure. From the glow of the window, she looks lighter than he has ever seen her and a warmth surrounds him that has not abated in the slightest.

Anticipation of the best kind lingers with him throughout the rest of the day. Even if he follows the unspoken rule, he'll get to talk to her again tomorrow.

The next week passes in a blur of excitement, he shares something every day and she does too. Sometimes what she says will relate to what he shares, but she never makes any direct comments, so he doesn't either. It's still strange to him that she hasn't asked anything about his world; if the roles were reversed, he's sure that would have been his first move.

For a while, he thinks that she just must not be interested, it's possible, but then he starts dropping purposeful mentions of his home to see what happens. After all the time he's dedicated to Watching her and learning her mannerisms, it's easy to see the subtle shifts in her body language once he's mostly comfortable looking at her again. She's always listening, he knows that, but whenever he talks about his life, he can tell she's listening just a little bit harder.

He doesn't know why she doesn't just ask, what's holding her back, but ultimately, it doesn't matter because he decides to take away the need to ask. Throwing away all caution, he resolves to tell her his history in the only way he knows how; through a story.

"My father used to tell me stories when I was young, about our world— about both of our worlds. In a time back before the Great Divide, when our people lived together peacefully and there was no need for Watching at all."

Pausing for a second, he looks over to her for the first time since starting to see her reaction. At this point, he can almost always tell right before she speaks, her head lifts up and her shoulders square like she's preparing to be ridiculed for her words.

There's the usual interest tilt of her head, but that detail is quickly overshadowed by the fact that she's looking at him, actually looking at him. The breath stalls in his throat. In the weeks since their eyes connected, he's replayed the moment over and over in his mind, but his memory didn't do her justice.

Time loses meaning as he stares into the wonder of her eyes. He can't look away, can't focus on anything else, trying to memorize as many details of her expression as he can before time runs out. It's only once her lips start to part and the wonder turns to confusion that he returns to himself, remembering with a start that he's supposed to be telling a story.

He clears his throat, strangely out of breath, and continues. "The legend goes that once upon a time my people were tasked with helping the people of this realm, protecting them. And then in exchange, your people offered their friendship sometimes more if the legends are to be believed. We worked together to create great things, marvellous wonders."

This time when he stops, he has an actual, justifiable hope that she'll say something back to him, but when it happens, he's still completely unprepared.

"Are you real?" she asks, voice nothing but a whisper.

He takes a moment to look at her sitting across the room from him with the most open expression he's ever seen on her. She looks hopeful in a way that he relishes. She wants to trust him, to believe in him, but she's still holding back, clinging to the logic of her world.

More than anything he wants to reassure her fears, to tell her that he's as real as everything else in this room, but he holds back. He doesn't know the right answer, the one that doesn't send her running in the opposite direction or retreating back into herself. The one that means he gets to keep her.

"Do you want me to be?"

She takes a moment to answer him, thinking the question over carefully in a way that he so appreciates, once again confirming to him that she is not illogical. She thinks, she understands, maybe more than most. She isn't silly or crazy or any of the things that most people think she is; she's special.

"I don't want to be alone anymore," she confesses, her hands set rigidly straight in her lap, her eyes locked onto him.

It takes him a moment to classify the feeling of warmth that passes through him. Never in his life has he felt more seen before, figuratively, as well as literally. He's always been the odd one out, never quite fitting into the mold that people expect him to. For a long time, he thought that was why he preferred it here, where the isolation was an active choice and not an unfortunate side effect. But it's been a different type of loneliness, one he didn't realize even existed until she walked into his life.

"Me neither," he responds with a shy smile that she returns after a moment of hesitation.

By that first afternoon, they are talking back and forth like it's the most familiar thing in the world, comfortable in their new dynamic as if it wasn't new at all. They don't say much of any importance, both of them choosing by some unspoken pact to keep the dialogue trivial for now, but every little detail feels like it *matters*.

He finds out that she always wanted to have a pet turtle, even though she had dogs. That she used to like to spend hours out in the forest and that she loves the rain.

In return, he tells her about his favourite books, the human ones that he found when he was just learning to read, and how they changed his world. Carefully, he describes the small hidden room at the very top of his family's home where he used to hide out for hours.

Quickly, faster than he ever could have imagined, she becomes his best friend. It's not a term he ever saw himself using, not because such a thing doesn't exist where he's from, but because he never once wanted one. Until she showed up, he thought his life here, Watching over the people of this place was everything he could ever want. He didn't think he could need more and really, he doesn't,

As tempting as it would be to spend all of his time sitting by her bedside, especially now that talking comes easily between them, he still dedicates time to Watching. He still enjoys seeing the other patients, gets the same rush of satisfaction when he sees someone succeed, and the same twinge of disappointment if they fail. He's still as invested in their well-being as he has always been.

In that sense, he takes his duty as a Watcher just as seriously as he always has. He even continues to faithfully report back with at least some regularity despite the concerns that race through his mind whenever he passes through the door.

No, he doesn't need anything else, but he desperately wants more.

Having Beth around adds a new layer of colour to his life, a whole other spectrum of shades that he didn't even know existed. And he thinks that maybe, just maybe, he adds that same kind of vibrancy to hers.

Now when she looks out the window for hours on end, he doesn't sense the same sort of longing in her gaze. She may still want to be out there, but for now, he thinks she's comfortable in here and he can't help but feel like he's played a large part in that shift.

"What should I call you?" she asks him suddenly a few days later, startling him. Aside from her question that sparked that change in their relationship, they have never actually asked each other any direct questions. He may know more about her than anyone else in his life, but all of that information is stuff that she's chosen to share.

It's a change, but one that he wholeheartedly supports even if he doesn't quite know how to answer. He has a name, of course, but it's not one that he's eager to share. Where he's from, there's none of the attachment associated with names that he knows humans have. His name is nothing more than a means of identification.

"Whatever you want," he offers, kind of liking the idea of a new name for this plain. One that has meaning. One that *she* gives him.

"How about Casper?" she asks with a sly grin, the closest he's ever seen to a real smile.

So caught up in the beauty of seeing her happy, it takes him a second to register her comment. "As in Casper, the friendly ghost?" he asks, humour clear in his tone.

"Seems fitting," she answers, biting her lip shyly, but her dancing eyes tell him a different story. For the first time, he believes that she's really, truly, comfortable with him. He's seen it in her movements, in the way that her shoulders relax now when she's talking to him, but it's not until now that he actually has faith that it might be here to stay.

He doesn't say anything, just shakes his head letting out a light-hearted laugh. With every moment he can feel himself falling harder. He should be wary, it's an incredibly dangerous endeavour, but he can't bring himself to care. Sitting here with her looking at him like that, is more than he ever thought to hope for.

The name doesn't end up sticking. There's really no need for her to call him anything when they both operate on the basic assumption that whenever one of them talks the other is listening, but he's still grateful for the question and not just because it opened up a world of possibilities. Every time he thinks about the integration over the next couple of days, he gets a smile on his face.

"**W**hy do you think you can see me?" he asks somewhat hesitantly a few days later. It's a question that has been plaguing him from the moment their eyes first connected and he still hasn't come to any satisfying explanations. He has his theories, of course, ones that are so fetched he should even be considering them, even with the council's seemingly thorough insight into the subject.

She looks up at him like it's the strangest question in the world, filling him with a rush of fear, only to turn back to the project in her lap a second later and answer him without missing another beat. "They think I'm crazy. I probably am."

For a second, he considers arguing with her. The more time he spends with her, the more sure he is that she's not. He leans over a little to see the character she is drawing, further proof that she's not delusional like she thinks.

He tried to ask her about them a few days ago. In fact, it was the first question that he allowed himself to ask. It seemed safe, asking her about the little figurines that litter the pages of her notebook, even if he knows better.

Like with everything else, she hesitated for a moment before answering, almost as if she was unsure what version of the truth she should be giving. She waited so long that he started to worry, to wonder if he'd pushed the boundary of their relatively new friendship too far, too fast.

Just as he was ready to take the question back, to start rambling to fill the suddenly awkward silence, she shook her head like she was coming out of a daze. "They are just something I've always done," she answered with a little shrug, "it's just a hobby. Something I do to help focus my mind…"

She'd bit her lip then, a nervous habit he'd only started to notice over the last couple of days. He knows the tick isn't healthy, isn't good; sometimes he worries that she'll make her lip bleed with how hard she pushes, but still, it's something, some indication that she's alive and for that he's thankful. Those first few weeks, when she would rightly still for hours on end are not something he wants to return.

Still, he doesn't know what to make of her answer. Just as he's noticed the lip-biting habit, he's realized that it normally happens when she's afraid she's said too much.

If he is to understand her actions correctly, both to his original question and to his latest one, she thinks the creatures she doodles, and him as well for that matter, are simply figments of her mind, but he knows they are much more than that. The sketches that line her pages are just like the ones that used to fill his textbooks.

No, she's not crazy, not in the slightest, but he's not sure how to make her believe that.

The reality is, he's scared to push. For as much time as he's spent watching her people, he doesn't know how to interact with them. He has witnessed the changing customs of this place over decades, learned their ways intimately and found comfort in them, but it is all much harder in practice.

Or maybe that's just an excuse. Maybe his anxiety has nothing to do with interacting with her people and everything to do with interacting with *her*. Over the last couple of months, she's become important to him in a way that no one else and nothing else ever has. He doesn't want to say the wrong thing and have her close off again.

He doesn't even know if he *should* say something.

She seems happy, happier than she's been since he met her anyways and who is he to take away that security. If believing that the things she sees aren't actually real helps her then maybe he's better off letting it go. A lot of the creatures he's seen her doodling are harmless, little woodland nymphs that populate this world or plain travellers like him, but there are a few that are dangerous, ones that he grew up being told to fear.

Maybe she's better off not knowing the truth, he rationalizes to himself later that night, trying to make himself believe something that he doesn't want to face. Making her realize the truth would be selfish and he doesn't want to be that kind of a person, especially not with her.

After that, he keeps his thoughts about her supposed sight to himself. They still talk, more than they did before some days even, and he tells himself to be content with what he has. It's already so much more than he ever thought he'd get; he doesn't need to be greedy.

More than anything, he wants her to be happy, really, that's all he needs. And she is, so they both are.

Slowly getting to know each other is an experience that he wouldn't trade away for anything. It doesn't matter that she might not think he's truly there when she's looking at him with her little half-smile that he's getting addicted to, telling him about her life.

As she gets more comfortable around him, her hesitantly begins to fade away and then so does his. He doesn't notice her shoulders tensing before she speaks anymore and the lip-biting regret seems to be lessening too. Now, when they talk to each other, their eyes are able to meet with ease.

Even though their lives have been very different, it's remarkably easy to talk with her. He's slowly realizing that they actually have a lot in common, for as much as their experiences have differed. It's nice, more than nice. It's relaxing and exhilarating at the same time. He's never felt like this before.

For a while, especially once they started talking more freely, he worried that the spark would disappear, that eventually he would learn all there is to know about her and then that would be the end of it; the mystery would be gone and he'd be bored. Yet, it's been over two months since he first saw her and the excitement hasn't dissipated in the slightest. In fact, he'd say it's grown. Every day he wakes up eager to hear her voice.

He knows that he's spending too much time here, that people are going to start to notice, but he can't bring himself to leave, at least not as often as he should. Over and over again, he feels the pangs of the call home, but he ignores them until eventually, they end and he is left, once again, to pass his day with Beth in peace.

The reality is that there's not much to draw him back other than a sense of loyalty to his position and fear. An all-encompassing dread that they will notice exactly why he is spending so much time far from home.

However, as the days pass and they grow closer, that loyalty to his home and the council which he never thought would waver, starts to fade, replaced with a loyalty to her. Still, the fear lingers and then grows. The thought of them watching haunts his movements.

"Why are you here?" Beth asks him late one night, suddenly changing topics.

He jerks up in his seat, the question sounding harsh in the quiet of the room. Normally, he leaves when the nurses call for lights out. He didn't in those first few weeks, or even after he realized she could see him, but after an off-handed comment about how she doesn't like sleeping when he's around, he started to.

Tonight, however, he couldn't work up the will to walk away. When he'd come into her room this evening, there had just been something off, her body language a little stiffer, her words a little more hesitant.

No, he didn't want to leave, but it's not like she really gave him the opportunity to either. Since the moment he walked through the door, she's kept up a steady stream of consciousness, talking about this and that as though she feared what would happen if she stopped.

And she hadn't, not until about 30 minutes ago. Listening to her rhythmic breathing, he'd thought maybe she had fallen asleep, but even then, he made no attempts to leave, the sound too comforting to just walk away from. Part of him had also hoped that his continued presence might help soothe whatever was disturbing her. Maybe he was wrong though.

"I can go," he offers rather reluctantly, still not making any actual move to get out of the chair.

"No!" she says hurriedly and before letting out a disgruntled noise.

Faintly, he wishes that he could turn on the lights without garnering attention. All he has is the light from the hallway shining in faintly through the window in her door and that's barely enough to make out her familiar silhouette lying in bed. Something is coming, he can feel it in the air, and he'd really like to be able to see her expression when the moment comes. After all his time Watching, so much of his ability to perceive emotions comes from seeing her. It's even more true for her.

"Not right now," she clarifies after a moment of contemplation, "why here, why this place?"

He doesn't need to see her face to hear the unasked, *why me?*

Taking a minute, he thinks it over, giving the question the weight it deserves. "I don't know," he finally answers, "it's always been this place for me. There was never any other real option-- I didn't want there to be and I especially don't now. I'm happy here."

She lifts her head to look at him, her blue eyes shining bright. He looks straight back at her, willing the truth of his words to shine through; for her to hear his unspoken, *I'm happy here with you,* just as clearly as he heard her silent plea.

"I just— I don't understand why you'd want to be here, why anyone would want to be here..." she trails off turning away, something a little broken in her voice.

He thinks back to her file all those weeks ago and the word *breakdown* bolded amongst all the medical jargon. For as much as he knows about her, the million random facts that he could share and the memories he could repeat as if they were his own, he doesn't know what happened to bring her here.

It's easy to see now that this conversation isn't random in the slightest, that nothing really is with her. This setting, this moment, was all planned. As much as he may want to see her, she doesn't want to be seen. He understands now that she needs the safety of the darkness to shield her from the pain of the recollection.

"My parents died," she reveals softly, voice shaky. "Not recently or anything, that's the thing."

She pauses and the heaviness in the air grows, "it was nearly five years ago, and I was fine. *I was fine.* Over the years, I've taught myself how to be okay, how to blend in, so that when it happened, I was able to mourn, to grieve and then move on with my life."

For a minute as she talks, it's almost like they are back to the way that they used to be. Talking, sharing, without the pressure of someone's expectations, but then she lets out a shaky breath and it's not. He knows her in a different way now, cares about her in a different way too. Before it was possible for him to sit back and listen to her struggle without interrupting and now, well, now it's not.

"That's horrible," he responds helplessly as the silence grows between them. He's not sure what to say to make this better for her, how to convey his sympathy and support, but he needs to say something.

"I can't imagine what that was like to lose your parents," he pauses for a moment thinking about it. He's not close to his parents, not really; not in the way she was with hers if her recollections are anything to go by. Still, it would be hard for him to lose them, for her it would be... "It would be devastating—"

She lets out a laugh, hollow and crazed, cutting off his verbal thoughts, "you would think, right? Their deaths, the deaths of the two most important people in my life would have been what set me off, but it wasn't. I was fine after they died, really, truly. It was hard for a while, but I moved past it like I knew they would have wanted. I got into med school, everything was okay."

He's confused, perhaps this isn't the story he thought she was telling. Maybe she feels guilty for moving on, she wouldn't be the first person he's seen to feel that way.

"I believe you, you're strong like that and I'm sure that's what they would have wanted for you," he offers, but it's like she can't hear him.

"Everything was okay. I'd gotten so good at ignoring them over the years, I didn't see anything anymore, not really. There was nothing there, exactly like it's supposed to be, but then they were back and they were everywhere, in class, outside, on the bus. There was no escaping. And I tried to ignore them, to tell myself that they weren't real and I succeeded for a while. For a few years, I was able to keep going, to go to class and have friends, to pretend to be normal, but it wasn't like before. They weren't passive anymore, they started to follow me and then I couldn't take it anymore."

She's out of breath when he moves to stand beside her, each one coming into her lungs with a harsh gasp and then falling out with a dramatic rush. Her eyes which he can now see clearly, flicker back and forth across the ceiling, seeing things he can't. He pauses right beside her, he's hands hovering anxiously by his side unsure of what to do.

Then, as if she can sense his closeness, her eyes snap to his, begging him to help her. "I didn't know how to tell what was real anymore, I couldn't tell," she says, her voice a harsh whisper

He doesn't think when he reaches out to place a comforting hand on her shoulder, he doesn't consider all the reasons he's held off from touching her; why he continued to remain resolutely in his chair across the room, despite their growing closeness. All of a sudden, every worry that had passed through his head as he debated pushing the boundaries of what he knows can happen, disappears.

It's instinct, plain and simple.

There's a desperate need within him to make her feel better, to offer her comfort in the only way he can think and that urge overrides all of his lingering fears.

In fact, he only realizes exactly what he's done when his hand makes contact with her skin and a shock passes through him. It's a shock, but not an unpleasant one in the slightest. It travels through his fingertips and up his arm leaving him feeling warm and tingly inside.

He doesn't know if this is normal, this feeling of euphoria, the only time he's ever touched anyone was in an attempt to heal them, but he can't help thinking that it's not. There's something about her, something special to him that makes every interaction feel like so much more.

It's only then that his focus shifts back to her. He takes in her wide eyes staring disbelievingly up at him and all of his insecurities come rushing back. There must be a reason that they are instructed to avoid contact with the people they Watch.

Maybe it's dangerous for them, the thought rips through his mind panicky.

Frantically he pulls his hand away, afraid of what he might have unknowingly done, but he doesn't get far. She reaches out to grab him, her slender fingers closing around his wrist to halt his retreat. There's the same tingle of possibility as before, not quite as strong now that he knows to expect it, but it hums under his skin, a constant buzz of excitement for as long as they remain connected.

Unsure of what to say, he searches her eyes trying to understand what's happening. What he sees is not what he expects, however, gone is the despair from earlier, replaced by wonder.

Slowly, she starts to rub her thumb back and forth across his skin and it's all he can do to keep the sigh of contentment from slipping through his lips. As it is, he just closes his eyes and savours the moment, trying to commit the feeling to memory.

"I can touch you," he hears her say breathlessly a few minutes later.

He opens his eyes; they meet hers instantly and what he sees takes his breath away. They're radiant. Blue and bright. He can still see the shadows of earlier lingering at the edges, but the darkness is surpassed by the shine of excitement.

Quickly, he takes in the rest of her features, she's radiant. There's a flush to her normally pale cheeks, an ease to the tilt of her head, a calmness to her breathing and he notes with relief, a smile on her face. The first true, unrestrained one he's seen. She's just as affected as him.

"I can touch you," she repeats like she needs the extra confirmation.

He nods his head in agreement needing the reassurance as much as her, a matching grin finding its way onto his face.

"You can," he says, pulling his hand back slowly until her fingers, still locked around his arm, meet his hand and he is able to tangle their fingers together. He holds on tight.

That night he falls asleep sitting on the ground beside her bed, her hand still in his which quickly becomes their new normal. Now, instead of sitting on opposite sides of the room and talking, they sit beside each other. Often, she'll have her hand on him in some way, either entwined with his own or resting lightly on his arm or leg. In the few times where that isn't an option and her hands aren't free, she'll stretch her leg so it's touching his or lean over slightly so her shoulder brushes his when she breathes.

It's never much, but there's almost always some point of contact between them, as though the physical contact with him grounds her. Not that he's complaining in the slightest. Being able to touch her, to feel the connection between then manifested in a physical form is a luxury he never thought he'd have. The change to their relationship is exhilarating but it comes with a new perspective and some added responsibility.

He's always known that she struggled, she wouldn't be here if she didn't have some demons lurking within her, he could see it in her movements, in her speech, but he didn't understand. Not the way he does now and it changes the way he sees some of her actions.

Now, he's more aware of her, if that's even possible. He pays closer attention to the way that her eyes dart from place to place when there are other people in the room with them, the way her smile seems forced and her words more practised. They are all characteristics that he has noticed before, but now that he knows the source of them, he finds their presence all the more troubling.

For so long whenever he looked at her all he could see was the bright and beautiful light shining within her, and now he can also see the shadows.

She's always seemed to him to hold the entire spectrum of colours inside her, he shouldn't be so surprised to find out there are greys and blacks mixed in as well. It's something he's always appreciated about her people, their ability to live high and low all the while balancing the life in between. His people don't live like that and he's always thought it was a shame.

There's a beauty in the brokenness of the people he Watches over, but that doesn't make it easy to see that within her.

As days pass and her smiles continue to show up unrestricted around him, he starts to think that his concern is unwarranted. The reality is that his presence seems to be helping her as much as he may fear that it's hurting her.

There's a newfound ease about her, in the way that she moves and the way that she talks. She seems lighter as though her confession to him lifted a heavy weight off of her. And freer too. He gets to see a side of her that he's only caught glimpses of in their time together.

"I love your eyes," she tells him, still focused on her paper, "they're so unique."

He leans over to watch as she carefully shades in the gold of his portrait's eyes, a warmth filling him at the compliment despite the naivety of the assumption. "They actually aren't. Where I'm from, they're very common."

She turns away from the art in front of her to face him more fully. He wills himself not to fidget as she examines him, choosing instead to revel in the burn of her gaze rather than shy away from it.

"Trust me," she says after a moment, "there is nothing common about you in the slightest."

He wants to dismiss her, he's not special, not in the slightest, but something about the confidence in her voice makes him hesitant. He's not used to seeing her like this, and he loves it. He wonders if this is how she would be all the time if she wasn't burdened by seeing a world that no one around her can.

Looking at her again, he notes the gleam of delight in her eyes at the blush that he's sure is covering his face and feels a sense of triumph. He's the one that helped bring that out. No matter what happens, he at least has that.

Maybe with him around, knowledge of other worlds doesn't have to be a burden. Maybe with him by her side, encouraging her and supporting her, she'll be able to be this person all the time.

After that, he still worries, probably more than he should, but that just seems like fair retribution for the weeks he spent oblivious to the pain that she has been carrying around inside of her. His job is to Watch over these people to protect them, to help them and he failed in the moment that counted the most. With the person who, if he's honest with himself, matters the most.

With that in mind, he remains vigilant. He'll enjoy the positive change, but continue to watch closely. He won't fail her again. He'll protect her, even if that means protecting her from himself.

For a while, they go on happily. By all appearances, she seems just as good as or better than she's always been, but he can't shake the worries. He continuously doubts whether he's doing the right thing by staying by her side. Is he just being selfish, putting her in unnecessary danger? Is he hurting her by staying?

It's easy to see the attachment that she is forming to him; the relief on her face when he shows up, the way she relaxes when he is back by her side. He doesn't leave her anymore, not really. At night, he settles on the ground beside her, his hand still firmly encasing hers.

Really, the only time they are separated is when she goes off for therapy sessions.

Every minute with her is a blessing, but all that extra time around her just exasperates his worries.

He takes in the near consent bags under her eyes and the fragility to her frame a few days later and his concern can't be held back any longer.

"You should do what the doctors tell you," he says, his voice so quiet that he's not sure she'll even hear, part of him hopes that she doesn't. Making the suggestion feels like crossing a line with her that he's been so careful not to cross. He doesn't want it to tell her what to do, to even seem like he's telling her what to do, but it's not something he can hold back any longer.

The dynamic between them is built off of trust, but he's always been aware that there's a power imbalance there. He knows more than her, understands what's happening better and because of that, he's always been incredibly wary of abusing the power that he may inevitably have over her. Still, he can't just *not* say anything, not now, knowing all that he knows.

Since she shared her story with him, he's noticed many new things about her, but perhaps the most notable is the little pills that she drops through the bars of the window each morning. The first time it happened, he thought he was seeing things. For as much time as she's always spent sitting on that seat by the window, he never once considered there was an ulterior motive.

The next morning, he watched carefully as she was handed the little container with the pills and then a glass of water. He watched along with the nurse as she swallowed and then as the nurse took the tray away. Then he watched her take the pill out of her mouth and tuck it under her pillow.

He doesn't know how he missed it for so long, but then again, he missed a lot of things.

She hesitates for a moment, it's the first time she's done so in weeks and he can't help but feel like he's failed some test. Still, he pushes on, meeting her questioning gaze steadily. This is too important for him to back down on, even if it ends up costing him her trust.

There must be something in his eyes that convinces her of his earnestness because after a movement, she shifts so she is facing him more fully, grabbing his other hand too and pulling both of them into her lap.

"They want me to take these pills," she tells him, avoiding his eyes and playing with his hands instead.

He nods his head slowly. He knew that and he's got to figure that she knew, he knew as well, which makes him wonder why. Why is she so resistant to taking them? From what he's seen, she's pretty much the ideal patient, she wants to be here, wants to get better so what is he missing?

"I've been around here a long time," he says and then pauses, there's another line here, one he's even more fearful of crossing. He knows, *knows* that there is nothing wrong with her, that everything that she sees is real, but despite what he's tried to do, she still doesn't believe that and until she does, he doesn't know how much help it is.

The reality is that she's struggling, some days worse than others, but every day it's there and he doesn't want that for her. She needs the weight lifted off of her. Still, he doesn't want her to ever think that he thinks there's something wrong with her.

Choosing his words carefully, he continues, "and in all that time, I've only ever seen them try to help people."

He waits anxiously for her to respond, heart hammering away in his chest.

"They'll make you disappear." There are tears in her eyes with the confession which he hurries to wipe away, pulling his hands from hers gently.

"I'm not going anywhere." Even as he says it, he knows that he's making a promise to her that he has no ability to actually keep, but that doesn't stop him from making it. Almost instantly, he can see the change the promise makes, the way the fear disappears.

Not for the first time, he considers trying to heal her, to make her perfect and whole the way she deserves. Maybe if he could do it, that fearful look would disappear. He wants to, but he holds back for the same reasons he always does. There's a limit to how much he can do, especially if he wants to not draw the council's attention.

Instead, he continues to wipe away her tears, thumbs brushing gently over her cheeks, promising over and over that everything will be okay.

It's only later that night as he watches her sleep restlessly across from him that he allows the shame to wash over him. Silently, he berates himself for his selfishness. The truth is that he's scared too, scared that if the council learns about her, he'll be stationed somewhere else. Scared that if by some miracle, he is able to do it without gaining attention and she gets better, she'll stop seeing him.

After that leaving gets even harder. Before he'd just always make sure to time his trips home while he knew she was occupied and hope for the best, but relying on hope alone doesn't seem like an option anymore; not after her confession and his promise.

He may not be able to ensure that he keeps his promise, there are some things he has no control over, but he can make sure that she knows that he'll always do his best. Hours after their conversation, he realized that he shouldn't have told her that he wasn't going anywhere, but rather that he'd always come back.

With that declaration, however, has to come with an explanation, one that he's not entirely sure that she wants to hear.

Still, he readies himself to tell her as he watches the sunrise through the window, knowing that he won't be able to live with himself if one day he goes through the painting and the worst happens; if one day he leaves, only to return and find months having gone by.

It hasn't happened yet, not really, the longest he's missed was that 48 hour period right when she first saw him, but it always could and he can't take that chance. Not with her.

"I shouldn't have told you that I'll always be here," he starts to say to her, the morning light shining through the window and creating striped shadows across them both.

She turns to him, fear and hesitance coating her movements. When she finally faces him, he sees distrust in her eyes and it breaks his heart.

Clearing his throat, he forces himself to continue, finding comfort in the warmth of her hand that she has yet to pull away. "I do leave. You know that I leave…"

He pauses for a moment to see if she'll ask where he goes. He waits for several long seconds hoping that she'll make this easier with her own curiosity, but when she shows no signs of speaking, he keeps going.

"Or at least I think that you do," he rubs his fingers of his free hand together anxiously. He's not good at this, good at taking and he can't help but feel like he's screwing this all up. He refuses to look over at her and see the disappointment, knowing that if he does he'll lose what little nerve he still has.

"Even though I leave, I have to leave, to go... home" the word doesn't feel right, even more so now, but it's all he can think of. Shaking off the hesitation, he continues "I always try to come back as soon as I can. I do come back as soon as I can, but that doesn't always mean that I show up back here when I want to. So far I have, at least for the most part, but it doesn't always work like that."

He chances a glance over at her and sees her listening to him intently, she squeezes his hand reassuringly, giving him enough confidence to continue. "I don't always know what's going to happen so I can't promise to always be here, but I can tell you that I'm always, *always*, trying to get back as quickly as I can."

She stares at him for a few moments and then nods her head in acceptance. "Okay."

"Okay?"

"I know I seem unstable most of the time," she lets out a self-deprecating laugh and then just shakes her head with a sweet smile when he starts to deny her claim, "but I understand. Just because people want to stay doesn't mean that they get to."

He watches her in amazement; he can see the sorrow in her eyes, but through there shines a strength, an acceptance of the grief he knows has shadowed her past and a determination to move forwards. The change in her demeanour from last night to now is remarkable. He doesn't know how she does it, how she continues to pull herself back together.

It would be easy to assume that he's said enough, that she's once again as fine as she appears to be, but he knows her better than that now. Despite the understanding smile and the kindness in her eyes, he can see that the thought of him vanishing still troubles her. There's a crease in her brow and a stiffness to her shoulders.

She needs something more. The reality is that her fear isn't just of losing him, but what his disappearing would represent; that maybe he was never here to begin with. He understands that, but that doesn't really help. Not when he's still uncertain that she believes he's real right now with him sitting in front of her, her skin touching his.

His mind races, trying to think of some way to guarantee that she'll continue to believe in his existence, at least as much as she does now, even if he's gone. When he finally thinks of something, he feels some relief, but it doesn't slow his racing heart in the slightest. He doesn't know if it will do any good, but it can't hurt to try.

"When I travel back," he tells her, "I travel through this painting on the third floor. I don't know if you've ever seen it, it's big, almost the size of the window. Inside there's a door, dark and bold against the backdrop, but that's not the important part. In the bottom corner there's this symbol, like a stretched out star, right where a signature would normally be."

She doesn't seem to be disturbed at the information, if anything, she looks intrigued. Once again, he curses himself for not noticing and sharing sooner.

"What I'll do is whenever I travel back, I'll leave a note with that symbol on it for you. Most to the time it won't matter, you'll probably see me before you see it, but that way at least you'll have—"

He cuts off in surprise when her arms wrap around him, pulling him into a hug. It takes him a second to come out of his daze, the feel of her all around him wiping all thoughts from his head and then he pulls her more firmly into his chest, folding his hands together across her back. She tucks her head into the crook of his neck and all he can smell is her shampoo. She's everywhere, consuming all of his senses and it's overwhelming. It's amazing.

Through it all he struggles to finish his thought, "that way at least you'll have something to hold on to, something to remind you that I'm coming back. And if you ever have doubts you can go look at the painting and see the symbol and know that it all happened. That works, right?"

Holding on tighter, he can feel her nod her head against his chest. "Yes, it's perfect."

"Thank you," she adds on after a moment, burying closer until she's almost in his lap.

They stay like that for hours, silently holding onto each other on the hard floor as though it could be enough to ensure that they never separate. Having her so close fills a need within him that he didn't realize existed, but it also amplifies his worry.

For as tightly as he holds on to her, her grip is twice as desperate. Almost from the moment he saw her, he knew that she was going to matter to him, that he was going to need her more than anyone else, but he thought that it was fine. Back then he thought that he was the only one who could be hurt by such an attachment and that's not the case anymore.

He doesn't know what he's doing with her and it is disconcerting. Most of his life he's been sure, he's known his path and now everything is conflicted.

Blatantly, he wonders if this is what love feels like and if it is, he can't help but feel like the stories all lied. Or not lied, but left out half the experience. It's wonderful, exhilarating and beautiful, everything that they promised, but it's also exhausting and terrifying. Still, he wouldn't trade what he's got with her for anything.

There's a new level of trust between them after that which he relishes, but he also fears. He starts leaving little notes whenever he returns home and it takes a little pressure off of his chest. It's fun too, in a way that he didn't expect. He can say things in his notes, tell her things, that he doesn't have the confidence to say to her face.

Telling her how much he looks forward to seeing her. Explaining how she's brightened up his life.

In a lot of ways, he's living his perfect life, he knows that he should just savour it and he does, each day with her is a blessing, but he also feels an approaching storm. He doesn't know where it's coming from or when it will arrive, but he knows it's coming with a certainty deep within his bones and he can't help but try and brace himself for the fallout.

He doesn't know when he became this person, the one who lives in fear of the worst happening. For a long time, he was optimistic, confident in his ability to help foster a better world here. Now though, he just doesn't know. Everything is uncertain and he's afraid.

134 - into the mystic

Maybe that's the difference; before he had nothing to be afraid of losing and now, he does. Before he had no one waiting for him to come back, no one to care about his movements and now he does. It's a responsibility, but one that he thinks is worth all the anxiety, a million times over.

Every time that she looks at him, touches him, talks to him, it's a rush like nothing else.

One day, his timing doesn't quite line up and he doesn't make it back to her room until the sun has already started to set, hours after he expected to return.

The relief in her eyes, the joy, when he walks into her room is equal parts exhilarating and concerning.

Part of him expects her to be upset that he wasn't here, the rest fears that she might be angry, but she doesn't say anything about his absence. All throughout the night, it hangs over their heads, an uninvited tension filling the room that's never once been there before. He needs her to say something so that he has some way to expel the guilt building up inside of him.

For as much as she seems fine, he doesn't think she is. There's a franticness to the way that she holds on to him, a heaviness to the silence. Or maybe that's all in his head. He doesn't know what to think anymore, hasn't really since her eyes locked on to his.

They go on for the rest of the evening without mentioning it, until right as he's resigned himself to not addressing it, convinced himself that he was merely projecting his own feelings onto her, suddenly she turns to him.

"I miss that when you're not here," she tells him softly like it's a confession that she's not sure she should be making.

At his confused look, she reaches over and stills his fingers that he didn't even realize he was rubbing together. Sheepishly, he meets her eyes and is shocked to see her smiling back at him with fondness. He's had that tick for as long as he can remember and everyone around him has always found it to be extremely annoying. Teachers in the classroom, peers that were supposed to be friends; his parents.

For a long time, he tried to get rid of it and he succeeded for the most part, but it shows up again uninvited whenever he is nervous about something. Now that he thinks about it, he's probably done it a lot around her. She has a tendency to make him nervous.

"You do it whenever you're thinking about something really hard, your eyes will go distant and you'll get a crease between your eyebrows and then if you still haven't solved whatever is troubling you, your fingers will start to twitch."

He feels a rush of warmth spread through him. It's heartening to realise that all along, she's been paying just as much attention to him as he has her.

"It's soothing, just quiet enough that if you're not listening then you might miss it," she continues, "like leaves ruffling in the wind."

She looks embarrassed for a moment like she's said too much, but then he squeezes her hand to get her attention. When she looks at him, at the grin he's sure is on his face, the embarrassment dissolves and they are just left staring at each other with love-sick grins on their faces.

After that, everything between them goes back to normal, or at least what he's new normal is anyways. For a while, her comment does its job and alleviates his worries, but like always, when she drifts off the sleep, they come back with a rampage.

The reality is that he likes the fact that she misses him, it feels a hole in him that existed for a long time before he met her, but that enjoyment also brings guilt. Her attachment to him, because he's nearly certain it's actually an attachment to *him* and not just what he represents, is an amazing thing for him to get to experience, but a terrible one for her.

She shouldn't need anyone, he's sure that she hasn't in the past, and he can't help but feel like his selfish want to have her in his life is pulling some of that strength that he so admires, out of her. There's a line between what's good for her and what's good for him that has always existed, but now it's moved so many times that he doesn't know how to re-establish it. Or even how to find it.

He's lost. It should be troubling, but because he's lost with her, it's incredibly easy to just push his worries away.

For as much as she seems better, he worries all the same. It seems ridiculous, until one day when the warmth of the season hits the building hard and he realizes that his concern is justified in every sense.

They are sitting on the ground as they have taken to doing, next to the window trying to get even a hint of a breeze coming through the tiny opening. She has her sketchbook in her lap, nearly filled, working on her latest project while he watches when a line of red on her arm grabs his attention.

It takes him a moment to understand what he's seeing and then a wave of horror washes over him. He thought it was probably a bit of a pen, he could tease her about being a classic messy artist, or maybe a paper cut, but not that, not there.

His understanding of the world starts to slide out from him. Logically, he knows that he can't know everything about her, even with how close they are, it hasn't even been a full year, but he would have thought he'd known about that.

Thinking back to the early days, before he knew that she could see him, he tries to remember her file. A suicide attempt should have been in there, but try as he might, he can't get the memory to focus. He can't really get the present to focus either. All around him, the room is spinning.

For the first time, he finally understands what the rest of his people mean when they say that this plain is too much, too bright.

Trying to find something to hold on to, he turns to look at her and that brings everything back into focus. Unaware of his discovery, she has continued to work away, shading in the edges of her picture with the careful precision he's come to expect from her.

He takes her in, sitting there beside him contently, trying to reconcile the brightness he sees in her with how darkness he now knows for certain she's got within.

"What are these?" he asks softly, tracing the rough red ridge on her wrist.

Frantically, she pulls her arm away from him. It's the only time she's ever recoiled away from his touch and he can't help but feel the sting of the move even though he knows it has nothing to do with him.

"They're nothing," she says moving away from him, pulling at the sleeves she had unconsciously pushed up.

Normally, he doesn't push her, knows that despite whatever place he might hold in her life and in her heart, he doesn't have the right to demand answers from her. That's normal how he feels, but even with her skin now covered, he can still see the marks. They're burned into his mind, confirmation of all his worst fears.

He can't let this go.

"They aren't," he tells her emphatically, moving towards her slowly, careful to keep all traces of pity and judgment from his tone.

She shakes her head, her back still to him in shame or regret, he's not sure. They stay like that for a moment until with a deep breath, she turns back to face him, determination in her movements.

"They are old," she tells him. "From a long time ago, back before I figured out how to get a handle on it all. I'm good now, I promise."

"You don't have to worry," she adds on, coming towards him and then taking his hand. Not for the first time, he marvels at the picture their hands make together. The contrast of her pale skin against his tanned. The perfect way her small hand fits into his. The way his long fingers are able to enclose around her hand completely.

His heart breaks at the thought of her worrying about him. After everything, that's her focus.

He can see it clearly now, what he has to do. She deserves whatever relief he might be able to give her. And he needs it too. He's barely hung on these last few weeks wondering what could happen and now that he knows, well, there's nothing else he can do.

"Would you like me to try and heal you?" he asks knowing that she needs to make the choice, knowing that he can't just do it in the middle of the night without her knowledge.

"Can you?" she responds, scepticism colouring her voice.

"I don't know," he tells her, trying to be as honest as possible, "I don't even really think there's anything *to* be fixed— but if you're okay with it, I'd like to try."

She thinks it over for a minute which he is glad for even if it makes his nerves skyrocket, before eventually nodding her head in acceptance. "What do you have to do?"

"Just," he steps closer to her and grabs both of her arms where the scars mark her skin, using them as a tethering point. He feels the warmth spread through him as always, but this time it's different; this time there's no need for him to hold back. For so long, he held off of touching her because he didn't want to accidentally do anything to her, to inadvertently heal her, but now that's exactly what he wants to happen.

He looks into her eyes, hesitating for some unexplainable reason and there, shining back at him is an unwavering trust. Within an instant, his reservations disappear. This is what he's supposed to do. Maybe this was his purpose all along.

Closing his eyes, he focuses on the power within him, gathers it into a ball ready to pass into her. Then he shifts his focus to her, letting the feel of her skin and the sound of her breathing guide him as he searches for the darkness that he knows lingers within her.

Over the years, he's done this process hundreds of times, far more often than the council would like, but then again, he's always been a little too attached to the people he Watches.

Yet it's nothing like what he feels for her.

He searches and searches, expelling wave after wave of energy into her until his head starts to spin, but it's no use. He may be able to heal the physical, but it's not her body that's broken. A dark part of him argues that there's nothing wrong to be fixed. It's the people here that are the problem.

"Did it work?" she asks him, her voice a mixture of hesitance and hope, once he steps away from her.

He keeps his eyes closed for a moment not wanting her to see the disappointment in them. It was always going to cost him something to try that, he had just thought that the cost would be more than worth the reward of seeing her at peace. Now though, he can't help but feel like he made the biggest mistake and she doesn't need to see that dejectedness within him.

Taking another second, he forces himself to pull it together, regrets aren't going to help either of them now.

When he opens his eyes, she's the first thing he sees. He studies her, the curve of her jaw, the shape of her nose, the brightness of her eyes, and peace washes over him. Whatever time they have had together is a blessing that he's not going to tarnish with regret.

"I don't know," he tells her and it's the truth. Whatever he might think now, he poured a lot of power into her, and it could make a difference. He hopes that it makes a difference. "We'll just have to wait and see."

They pass the rest of the day just like they always do, with her curled up against him, them whispering randomness back and forth to each other. Occasionally, she will pause and look at him strangely, like she can tell that something is not right, but then she'll continue on without another thought. Part of him hopes that she doesn't realize what's coming, but the rest of him knows that she's just kind enough not to push.

Even though no part of him wants to go, when the familiar tugging comes a few hours later, relentless in its ferocity, he forces himself to untangle their limbs and get out of the bed. The minute that he decided to try and help her, he knew that this would be the consequence.

He knows that the council monitors for influxes of power, that they track even the most mundane of healings. With the amount of energy he just gave off, they are going to know that something is up and the absolute last thing he wants is for one of them to come here. To come to her.

He stops at the edge of the bed to look at her, just in case it's the last time that he ever gets to see her. She shifts a little in her sleep, her nose twitching like she is disturbed by his absence.

For several long minutes, he watches her, needing to see her settled again before he can muster the will to walk away. She lets out a content sigh turning to press her face into the part of the pillow where his head was just resting.

He lets out a matching sigh, it's time to go. He knows it's time to go, but still, he can make his feet move. More than anything, he wants to crawl back in with her, to forget his world and her world and create one just for the two of them.

If it was within his power, he's sure he would, but at last, it's not.

Reaching over to grab her notebook and a pen, he flips to one of the final pages, taking the time he knows he doesn't have to look at all the pictures as he goes. Despite the lingering, he still doesn't know what to say when he finally reaches an empty page.

He stands there, his pen hovering over the blank page for far too long. There are so many things that he'd like to tell her, too many for the time he's got left.

In the end, he scribbles down the one thing that his heart has wanted to say for a while now, *I will always love you.*

Adding his mark to the end, closes the book, and replaces it on the nightstand. He doesn't allow himself to linger on the words, the temptation of saying more, of writing and writing and never stopping too high to resist for long.

Instead, his focus shifts back to her again. He really should go.

Just one more minute.

Giving in to his recklessness again, far too aware that this could be the end, he leans down and presses his lips to her forehead. The same pulse of warmth that goes through him whenever they touch happens, but amplified. That little hint of what could be is everything he dreamed it might be and so much more.

It's both exhilarating and excruciating. He wants so much more than this one-sided goodbye with her.

"I really hope I get to come back to you," he whispers into her hair and then he turns and walks away, knowing that if he stops for one final look, he'll never actually leave.

"**Y**ou're spending too much time in the other realm."

Even though he knows it's coming, he can't help but wince when the stern reprimand reaches him. Really, he should hope that his sporadic returns are the reason there was a guard waiting at the end of the passage to escort him here, but it's hard to have any sort of positivity.

The greyish tones of this world seem more oppressive than ever and all of his hope was left in that hospital room with Beth. Still, he knows that he needs to make an effort, if not for himself then at least for her. If he can keep the focus on his actions and away from her then he owes it to her to try.

"Sir, with all due respect, it's my family's sacred duty to watch over that hospital. I'm only doing my job."

He tries to keep his voice polite, to mimic the speech patterns and posture of the people around him, but the attempt falls flat. After so much time in the human world, interacting with Beth, the mannerisms sit awkwardly on him. Not that the discomfort is new. He's never fit in here, he just used to be better at pretending he did.

"You're too emotionally invested! You need to take a step back," one of them responds, ignoring his answer altogether.

"I am fine," he responds, trying to remain calm, "it has been busy, I will make sure that my check-ins are more regular, my reports more detailed."

"Don't make the mistake in thinking that we don't know about Elizabeth," another one remarks pointedly.

He can almost feel the blood draining from his face. It's all of his worst fears coming true. Desperately, he tries to calm his frantic heartbeat; just because they know of her doesn't mean that they know everything. He has to believe that if they knew more, he would have been pulled back here months ago.

"Somehow that girl has managed to suck you under her spell," he hears one of them say with disgust.

"It's not surprising," is the not successfully hushed response, "they are a manipulating species and he's barely more than a boy."

"Their emotionality has undoubtedly rubbed off on him. Did you see that reaction?"

He has to physically bite his lip to stop himself from responding. He knows that they are just a bunch of foolish men, unwilling to look past their own understanding of things to perhaps see something different, but that doesn't stop him from wanting to change their minds. She's not this person that they seem to think she is and it pains him to let their bias stand unopposed.

"You are not to go back."

The commandment rings out loud against the grumblings of the group, stopping his thoughts in their tracks.

With that, they say the one thing that he didn't want to hear, but with it, he's got nothing else left to lose and there's a freedom in that.

"And what if I do?" he asks heatedly. He's not this person, not really, but they have pushed him into a corner and now he needs to find a way out.

Sitting at the centre of the ledge above him, the man levels him with a piercing stare, "if you do, don't expect to be coming back."

The threat is clear, one more trip through the painting and that's it, no return trip. He's never heard of this happening before, someone facing banishment. Maybe it's unprecedented. It probably is, he's never met anyone like him, anyone who didn't feel at home here.

Silence fills the room, an uneasy tension passing through the people around him. Up above he can see them all looking down on him with solemn faces. The one who made the comments about Beth eyes him with a self-satisfied grin.

All around him people wait with bated breath for him to repent, to declare his love for his people and promise his unwavering devotion. They all think the answer should be obvious and it is, just not in the way that they expect.

Turning on his heel, he walks away without a backward glance.

Let them seal the passage behind him, he doesn't care. At this point, he'd happily take a life with Beth, any life, over going back to the one he had before he met her. He'll walk the world an invisible ghost to everyone else as long as she's waiting to welcome him home.

By all accounts, it ended up being a simple trip back, in and out, just like he's done countless times since he met her, but life is not that easy and the world, neither world, is fair.

The moment that he walks through the door, he can tell that something is off. Desperately, he tries to stop his panic from building as he walks over to the small window in the corner of the room. Even though it's dark, he can see the bare branches of the trees outside shining in the moonlight.

And it's not just the leafless trees. The ground is cold, dead, barren in a way that is nearly opposite to the budding summer that was just starting to take shape when he left. In a few moments for him, a matter of hours, everything has changed.

He's lost months, if not years.

With his heart hammering in his chest, he traverses the familiar path to her room. God, he hopes it's still her room. And he doesn't. The thought of her still here after so long sends a stab of pain through him so intense that he has to stop and catch his breath.

He pauses a few steps from her door, unable to take the final leap. He wants her there. He doesn't want her there. It's an internal fight that he's had more than once since he's met her. What he wants for himself in conflict with what he wants for her.

Maybe if she's in there, the two objectives don't need to be at war anymore.

The thought sends enough hope through him that he's able to take the remaining step, but then he stops, not even a full step into the room when he spots her lying on the bed.

His heart stops with relief, with despair.

"Beth," he breathes out a mixture of relief and horror knocking the air out of him. If he thought that she looked fragile before, it's nothing compared to how she appears now. Her hair is limp, the little fullness to her face gone and then, when she turns to face him and there's a blankness to her beautiful eyes that he'd never thought he'd see.

For as intently as she's looking at him, it's almost like she's seeing through him. It sends a shiver down his spine.

"Beth," he repeats more purposefully this time. Taking another step and then another into the room, he continues, waiting and praying for a moment of recognition. "It's me."

"You're really here?" she asks hesitantly.

"Yes," he tells her, voice breaking, "I'm here and I'm not going anywhere."

Looking at her now, it's hard to see the woman he knows, he loves, but he's determined to find her again. She's in there. She has to be.

"You disappeared," she tells him in an eerily monotone voice.

"I am so sorry," he says rushing up to her bed and kneeling beside it. He wants to take her hand, but he stops himself unsure of what her reaction might be. "I didn't— I'm so sorry."

"You left," she says again and then her voice cracks, "and you didn't come back."

"I know," he responds, resting his forehead against the bed to hide the glassiness of his eyes, the guilt, the brokenness.

He stays in that position, overcome by grief and guilt, until a gentle hand on the side of his face draws his attention. He looks over at her, hesitantly, terrified of what he might see, but he need not have worried. There's a spark there, just a tiny hint of life, but it's all he needs to latch on.

"I'm sorry— it's, how long has it been?" he asks with an internal wince. "It's only been a few hours for me… not that it matters, I know. I just don't know how to— did you get my note?"

Watching her try to process it all, he forces himself to stop. After a minute that feels like forever, she starts to nod. "But I didn't think it was real. They convinced me it wasn't real."

Even as his heart breaks at the thought, he focuses on the logic of it all. "Remember the symbol? The painting?"

She shakes her head dismissively. "That symbol used to be all over my grandma's studio and that painting was created by her great, great grandfather. I made it all up. It was a conveniently placed idea to feed my delusions."

Ignoring the implications of that piece of information for the moment, he keeps his focus on her. More than anything he wants to grab her hand and never let go, but he waits. She's been waiting for who knows how long and now he can too.

"I didn't know," he says softly, trying to come up with some other way to prove himself to her, "but I'm here, I promise. And Beth, this time I'm not going anywhere."

She stares at him, her eyes telling him that she wants to believe in him, but she's scared. He nods his head slowly, a, what he hopes is a comforting smile, sliding onto his face. It's fine, he's gained her trust once before, he can do it again.

He'll do it a thousand times over for her.

Slowly, the hesitance starts to fade away, allowing the brightness in her eyes to shine through more clearly. His smile comes more easily. He's here with her, that's all he needs.

"Hey! What are you doing in here? You're not allowed!" the familiar figure of her nurse yells barging into the room.

He looks over at Beth questioningly and then back to the nurse who's looking at him pointedly.

"Me?" he questions hesitantly looking between the two women. For her part, Beth looks just as confused as he feels.

"Who else?" the nurse asks looking at him like he's an idiot, but he couldn't care less. She can see him.

He hears an astonished gasp from beside him and then,

"You're real."

SaSha Shutland

LegendDairy

The wooden chairs were uncomfortable. It wasn't a wonder that the children in the waiting room with their mothers would not sit still. It would have been smart to have toys or something to occupy them instead of just a few rows of chairs to run around and crawl under. Their mothers had apparently given up attempting to make them behave. And why shouldn't they have? She'd been sitting here for thirty minutes at least, and the poor dears had been here for God knows how long before she'd arrived with Thomas.

Oh, Thomas.

Her poor husband.

He was the real reason they were sitting here waiting for the doctor.

He'd been so eager to start a family and pass on his name to a son. So overwhelmingly eager that he'd progressed their relationship entirely too quickly, and she'd done nothing to stop it. Nor had she told him anything of her past.

To be fair though, he hadn't asked.

To Thomas, she was just a shop girl who came to the old world from America because she had romantic notions of coming to Britain and falling in love with the architecture and history, not to mention the lovely manners and accents of the gentleman that occupied the country. Thomas had certain ideas of what America was like and had told her many times what a brave and correct choice she'd made in leaving it behind.

It was all very quick; their courtship.

He'd come into the shop on a Tuesday looking for a replacement tie pin and asked her to accompany him for a stroll the day after.

Less than two weeks later he'd asked for her hand.

His family didn't think anything of it; indeed, his mother was delighted he'd settled down at the 'ripe old age' of thirty-one. And there he'd been with his fiancée that he'd only known for twelve days, then a twenty-five-year-old brunette with a slim waist, childbearing hips and fresh a face with an American accent and a history they knew nothing of.

But what did that matter when they had plans of her being nothing but a housewife and mother?

Sasha Toften, nee Shutland, had been gifted with this comfortable life and was now feeling emotionally ambivalent about how it might come crashing down around her after this appointment.

Any other woman in her situation might be anxiously wringing her hands, terrified that her husband might find out the reason. Other women in her predicament would be planning on running out that door to the street, never be seen from again.

There was a very good chance that Thomas would use the belt on once he found out the truth. There was an even greater chance that he would divorce her and leave her penniless.

She'd been penniless before and dealt with it.

And she'd been beaten before too.

Brooklyn, New York 1895

"Sasha" Meredith whispered harshly. "Sasha, wake up." She shook her awake.

"What?" Sasha didn't open her eyes. It was the middle of the night. She and her sister were warm in their shared twin bed and she'd been having a nice dream that had made her forget what night this was.

Sharing was their only option for comfort, not only because the bed-to-children ratio in the house had a higher number on the children side but also because the temperature dipped dramatically at night and they required another body in order to keep them warm.

Sasha was about to close her eyes again and ignore her big sister, then she heard it.

Their father had finally come home. It was payday after all, and no payday would be complete without him coming home stinking drunk and either beating his children, getting overly enthusiastic about 'keeping his woman in line' or, if they were really lucky, he'd stumble in the door, yell a bit and then pass out on the floor.

Mother didn't do much to stand up for herself, or for her children.

Meredith and Sasha were the oldest, then there was Terrance, Lincoln, Madeline, Keith and little Diana.

The boys bore the brunt of father's brutality. The girls were mostly just the clean-up crew. They'd sew together the ripped clothing, wipe off the blood from flesh and various surfaces and bandage up what they could. It was their entire job in life to clean-up after him and their little brothers.

And it was all going to change for the worse. Lately father had been giving Meredith and she these... looks.

It was similar to a look he had on his face when their mother had just had her washing day. She was a beautiful woman, probably could have had any man she wanted when she was younger and before she'd borne seven children and gotten rather soft in several places. Sasha most resembled her with the thick wavy brunette hair and healthy cheeks. Her breasts had come in as well and seemed to keep getting bigger. Meredith on the other hand, while herself quite pretty, had dark blonde, pin-straight hair and a lanky form; her legs were ridiculously long.

At sixteen and fifteen years of age they were both aware that it was just a matter of time before they had to leave, but neither had any prospects that looked appealing. They'd been inseparable since Sasha could remember, and she couldn't bear the thought of being away from her. They were each other's rock, the person they turned to when they needed someone to lean on. If Meredith left Sasha would follow.

Which was something they'd talked about in a more impending way lately.

There wouldn't be an ideal situation for them to run away to, but they didn't want to wait for the worst to happen either.

"Where is she!?" Fathers drunken voice slurred loudly through the thin walls.

The two sisters sucked in a breath. Their mother would have been in the bed in the front room, where she'd always slept as soon as the children were in bed. Which meant that 'she' was referring to Meredith.

This was it. This was what their mother had warned them about. Men had needs and their father was no different. He was their provider, what happened inside the walls of their home was entirely up to him and there was nothing they could do about it. Apparently that he was their father would not stop him from eventually trying to take either of them by force.

They'd been horrified when they'd been informed of this 'fact of life'. It made their worlds tilt. And it was because of that that they'd been planning their escape. There was no money earned between them for this escape. But they had a plan.

They'd made sure the shelves in the kitchen were stocked, the clothes for all the children had been darned and any other supplies or necessities were available. But a cache had been hidden carefully under their bed for this moment.

Their brothers and sisters would not starve for the month it took until the next payday.

It had been agreed; when their father came for one of them, the other was going to attack. Together they would steal his purse and run. That was the plan.

They'd thought it all out and knew what was going to happen; He was going to come at Meredith and order Sasha out. Sasha would take the frying pan from under the mattress and hit him on the back of the head. He'd be knocked unconscious and they'd quickly dress, gather up their satchels and leave with his coin purse.

His clomping footsteps drew closer and Sasha's heart began pounding erratically as she felt down between the wall and the mattress grabbing onto the steel handle of the pan, her breathing becoming forced.

This was it.

In the ten seconds that it was taking their falling-down drunk father to barge into their room they'd managed to only sit up and wait. Meredith was clutching Sasha's hand, her nails digging into her skin.

The door flew open and knocked against the table behind it. Baby Diana had woken up in the front room and was crying loudly, something that Sasha wanted to do herself if only her terror would let her. It was dark in the room. Their candle had been blown out hours ago, and the light spilling in from the main room wasn't doing any more than casting shadows.

That may have been the reason why he'd grabbed for her instead. Perchance he had not known that it was Meredith that he was throwing to the floor and his second eldest he was pinning to the bed. Or maybe that was his plan all along. Sasha was the one that looked like their mother after all, and perhaps that was his type.

Her instinct to fight and kick out wasn't doing anything to stop her large and strong father from carrying on as he pleased. She may as well have been swatting at flies instead of striking with all her might, frying pan forgotten.

He growled at her squirming and managed to roll her over onto her stomach. She still waved her arms and legs about frantically trying to escape him and crying out in the struggle for Meredith to do something. But where was Meredith? She should have been fighting their father off her, as she had been prepared to do for her.

A cool breeze hit her upper thighs as her night gown was pulled up and was aggressively poked near her bum. She cried out for him to stop. She cried out for Meredith, for her mother. Again, she was poked, this time closer to her sex.

The third time he found his target and shoved himself inside her while she screamed at the pain that ripped through her. She kept screaming while he thrust inside her, each time hurting just as much as the first.

CLANG

His movements stopped and his heavy weight crushed her into the mattress.

Sasha tried to roll over and get him off her. She struggled to get to the corner of the bed and wrap her arms around her knees, ensuring that no part of her was touching any part of him. Tears rolled down her face and she looked up at her mother, her eyes having adjusted to the faint light.

Mother stood there with a cast iron pan in her hand looking down at her husband. The expression on her face was too hard to read in the shadows.

Meredith was still on the floor clutching her knees to her chest.

"Why didn't you stop him?!" Sasha cried out accusingly, noticing how she was just sitting there.

"I couldn't!" Meredith cried back.

"You could have tried. Why didn't you try?" It was what Sasha had been prepared to do for her, now her innocence was gone. She'd been violated by her father. She was a ruined woman now.

"You have to leave. Both of you." Their mother said in a calm and stern voice. "You need to be gone by the time he comes 'round." she knelt down and fished out the rucksacks from where they were hidden and shoved them at each of her daughters. "Clean yourself up and go."

Meredith snapped out of it and grabbed Sasha's hand, pulling her off the bed and into the sitting room.

"Mama?" Madeline asked in her sleep from where she lay beside baby Diana in the main room. Diana was quiet now with Madeline's arms soothing her.

"Back to bed. Your father's just fallen asleep in Mere and Sasha's room."

"What about you?" Meredith asked their mother in a whisper.

"What about me what?" she asked harshly. "You knocked your father over the head to get him off your sister. You think he's going to ask questions about that?" she went to the water bin and wet a cloth handing it to Sasha.

Sasha looked down at the cloth and back up at her mother in confusion.

"Wipe yourself." she ordered.

Flinching, Sasha lifted her gown and gently brought it between her legs. It was tender down there, but it didn't hurt anymore. She brought the cloth back and was a little shocked by the blood she saw. It wasn't her time, so it must have been a result of what just happened.

"You're a woman now, and you two need to leave and take care of each other." she took the cloth, tossing it in a bucket, and went to pull down some of their clothes from the line strung up by where the fire had been burning in the afternoon. She tossed the clothes at them.

"How did you know we were-" Sasha started.

"You girls don't talk as quietly as you think you do." she said softly. "Take it." she held out her hand to Meredith with their father's coin purse between her fingers. "I've kept a little bit for an emergency, but you two take the rest and get somewhere far away from here." Even in the darkness Sasha could see the lines of her mother's face draw deeper. "And don't ever find yourselves in trouble with a man like him. You'll never be able to get yourselves together after that." she warned them against her own experience.

Sasha shivered as she pulled her night gown over her head and put on her best clothes. These were the ones that her mother had insisted needed to be washed that morning. She really had known that it would all happen tonight.

"What about. . . ?" she looked over at her sisters in their bed.

"They'll find their own way when they're old enough," she told them sadly.

Meredith leaned forward and gave her mother a kiss, but not Sasha. She couldn't help thinking her mother hadn't acted soon enough. She simply nodded and pulled the strap of her bag tighter.

The sisters huddled as close together as they could heading to the train station. New York City was not a safe place for two young ladies to be out on their own in the middle of the night. They had enough money for a ticket for each of them to go anywhere the rail would take them. And there were opportunities for everyone in the West.

They'd made it to the station with-out more than a few lewd hollers from drunks and waited out at the station until the ticket booth opened. The whole time they waited Sasha couldn't say anything to her sister. They had promised each other that they weren't going to let their father take away their virginity. Meredith had frozen, she would have just sat there on the floor the whole time and wouldn't have moved again until he was done. Sasha couldn't even look at her.

At morning light, the booth opened, and they purchased two tickets to the Pacific Northwest. If they were going to get as far away from New York as possible, they'd go all the way to Seattle. They'd find work as scullery's or laundry girls.

Anything.

LONDON, ENGLAND 1909

A child bumped into Sasha as she was caught up wondering how Meredith might be fairing now. Her sister had a husband the last time she'd heard from her, but they hadn't been in contact for years now.

"Sorry." The little boy replied automatically.

"David. Come here please," his mother called.

Sasha gave his mother an understanding smile and Thomas patted her leg twice from his seat beside her and turned back to his paper.

"Mister and Misses Thomas Toften?" A nurse called out from the doors leading to the doctors' offices and examination rooms.

Sasha held up a hand to signify they were there and ready, then they both stood to walk solemnly towards her to be led to what would possibly the end of Sasha's life here in Britain.

The nurse was a matronly looking woman. Stern but kind with a sizable bottom and bosom. No doubt capable of both restraining and comforting the children this doctor treated.

They were led into a tasteless and cold examination room. Why Thomas had to accompany her she didn't understand. It was supposedly some kind of civilized society thing, but woman treating woman in privacy would have been much preferred. Instead she was stuck with a male doctor. The only kind there were.

If she could have a mid-wife examine her then she might be able to explain to her. She couldn't explain this to a man. A man wouldn't understand. Sasha herself didn't understand the last bit of what happened to her, nor would anyone else except for those women that… fixed her situation.

She could already picture what was going to happen here;

The doctor was going to come in, shake hands with Thomas. Thomas was going to explain their reason for coming in then she'd get up on the table, that one with the straps looking like they were made from former belts and used to restrain children or uncooperative wives down. Then the doctor was going to take one look up her dress at her lady parts and see her whole history there.

"Everything will be alright darling," Thomas told her kindly. He had worried that it might be him that was the problem. Not out loud, but she could see it in his written on his face. Checking him out for any sort of defect would have shamed him though.

"You don't know that," Sasha said looking down at the floor. The sight of the table disturbed her. It was like a torture implement more than a medicinal one. Most medicinal implements could be used for torture, but that table looked particularly sadistic.

She wouldn't give them any reason to restrain her though. She was too upset with herself for allowing it to go this far with-out telling Thomas the reason. This farce she had exemplified as the type of woman her husband wanted as a wife had gone on too long.

She knew why they couldn't conceive; she didn't need a doctor to tell her. Thomas didn't though, and she'd hoped he never would need to know.

He was desperate for a child, and when they first married she thought that maybe there was still a chance. Maybe it had been long enough that her body had healed itself, or the magic had run out. Maybe the doctor wouldn't see anything odd down there and she could carry on pretending to be this person longer.

Possibly forever?

Or maybe the doctor would be able to tell that the reason she couldn't conceive was because of all of the attempts to prevent herself from conceiving before Thomas came along.

Whether Thomas had known he wasn't her first, they hadn't discussed.

He was rather rigid in bed, and a proper Englishman that didn't talk about such things because it wasn't polite. When they'd lain together for the first time on their wedding night it had been so perfunctory. They both undressed, lay on the bed and he lay over her and spilled his seed after only a few moments.

Every time since had been relatively the same thing. After two years she still hadn't told him that there were more enjoyable ways to have sex. It would probably shatter this glass house lifestyle he had made for them.

She was fond of Thomas, but she wasn't in love with him. They worked together as man and wife. She'd come to understand his expectations for her role in his life and fulfill her duties to his standards.

All save for one.

SEATTLE, WASHINGTON, 1897

"There would be more opportunities there." Sasha argued with Meredith for the umpteenth time.

"It is so far! And so... wild. It could be dangerous." Meredith argued back.

"We've gone farther before. There are more opportunities there than there are in San Francisco." Sasha rolled her eyes.

Since news of the Yukon Goldrush had reached Seattle the two of them had played with the idea. Sasha was willing to move to Skagway, or even all the way to Dawson City. They were in Seattle still; it would just be a matter of jumping on a boat and going up there.

Meredith on the other hand was more interested in heading south to the warmth of Southern California.

There was currently a massive influx of gullible and eager men flocking to Seattle as a stop-over or a starting off point on the way north to try and strike it rich.

Seattle had been the means to an end where the sisters had managed to make a go of things. Meaning when they arrived on the train two years ago, they'd found their way to an inn and managed to source out employment. Sasha worked in the laundry of a hotel and Meredith was hired on as a nanny to a well to do family. They shared a room at a boarding house and were getting by just fine until now.

Meredith was loving her work with the babes and had been courted by a man for a few months, but he had broken it off with her and left town with-out so much as a promise to write.

Sasha had allowed a few men to take her on a date here and there. The idea of finding a husband was still a ridiculous notion to her after her violent deflowering. She'd been traumatized by it at first, but then curious about it; about men in general and their needs. None of her dates progressed into much more than a few chaste kisses. She was too hesitant to do more than a bit of exploratory fondling, but felt it was more due to worry of word getting out as opposed to moral reasons.

Now that Meredith was unattached it was the perfect time to leave.

But they couldn't come to an agreement on where to go.

"If we go to San Francisco we'll just be pickpocketed and find ourselves destitute." Sasha had been relayed stories about what was going on down there, and it was getting increasingly unruly by the day. "In the north there are more and more opportunities and you could find yourself a husband out of one of the men that strike gold before they come back south."

Meredith twisted her tightly drawn lips to and fro going over that. She was still hoping to settle down with a nice big house and have a few children. Watching over two babies had just made her yearn for it more. "It could be really dangerous for two single girls to head up there unaccompanied."

"Well this time I'll keep my grip on the frying pan." Sasha narrowed her eyes. She hadn't let her forget it.

"Sasha." Meredith closed her eyes, eyebrows knit together and sighed.

Sasha looked away and started unnecessarily cleaning up their room. It was already as clean as it was going to get. She'd been regularly sneaking their sheets and clothes into her work to clean them. They probably had cleaner laundry that the people they worked for, they certainly had cleaner belongings than the other boarders in the house.

The two of them had settled into a nice content life here in Seattle, but this was too good an opportunity. Meredith's two babes were heading into governess territory and since the S.S. Portland had come into the harbor the town had nearly tripled with visitors. Everyone was going north.

If they didn't head up with the first wave, then there would be nothing left up there.

Sasha didn't want to strike it rich herself, she wanted to work herself ragged in the boom and then come back south with enough to support herself for a few years to come. And she wanted Meredith to come with her. They could split the cost of boarding, they would be sharing in expenses, clothes, and even beds. She may have pushed the guilt when it came to what happened with their father, but she still needed her big sister.

Their current boarding costs were about to skyrocket as well. People were letting out closet space as bedrooms for $5 a night. Once their month was up in eight days, they could only imagine how much this room with two twin beds was going to wind up costing them. Four more mattresses could easily be wedged in here and each let for $100 a week probably.

"It would cost us a fortune to get a ticket on one of the steamers, and that isn't accounting for all the supplies we'd be required to take with us." Meredith was still pointing out the issues.

"Not if we get hired on by one of the men going up there." Sasha pointed out.

"What. You want to just go down to the docks and offer ourselves up? Like prostitutes?" she scrunched her face up in pain and distaste at the thought.

Sasha rolled her eyes and scoffed at her sister's narrow-minded thinking. "There are men travelling with their wives. Businessmen who have legitimate postings that we could fill."

"This is really risky." Meredith intimated.

"So was coming to Seattle in the first place. Face it, Meredith, we can't afford to live here anymore."

"There are opportunities here too." Meredith whined. She'd been in such a cozy position for so long that she'd gotten soft and complacent.

They could have tried for extra employment on the side of their current postings with all the businesses popping up all over Pioneer Square, but there were enough people already vying for those jobs.

Sasha had found that people were creatures of habit. Their landlady had never been outside of Seattle and to her Sasha and Meredith were exotic being from New York. The girl across the hall from them was exotic too in that sense and she was only from Portland.

Also, how many working women were heading north with all these prospectors?

Sasha really believed that they had a shot at a once in a lifetime opportunity here. The first round of prospectors had only just come back. If she and Mere didn't get on one of the first ships heading north, then they were going to be shit out of luck.

"Mere-" Sasha started, dragging out her name.

Five days later was when the next ship was going to leave, and Sasha went down to the dock and spoke to a few of the deck hands and the ships cook. The ships cook was a sweaty large balding man with a tough look about him. He hadn't been convinced she would be able to stand straight on a sea faring ship, let alone be of any use to him.

She showed him though; a sailing line had been thrown by where they'd been standing from a small passenger boat. Before a dock worker could come over, she'd taken hold of it and done a Cleat Hitch with-out a thought. Standing back in front of the Cook she told him she and her sister would work for passage and would smell much better than any man he could hire.

In the end the cook agreed to hire them, but not for free passage, they each had to pay him $25 and had the promise of working them-selves to the bone starting three days before the ship was even due to leave port.

They bundled up their clothes and sold off a lot of their meager possessions they'd collected over the years and reported to their bunk on the ship.

They had a small room with one bunk bed that they had to share with two other men that also worked for the Cook. The men showed no sign of discomfort, or interest, with their presence. Meredith was weary at first, but as they all worked themselves ragged and in shifts there was rarely opportunity on their two-week journey to worry about propriety.

And that ship was where Sasha met Floyd.

Working in the scullery had been consuming all but one of her waking hours, and that one hour she managed to get to herself she would go up onto the deck and try to get some sunshine on her skin. There were plenty of men about on the deck and a few trussed-up women that looked rather out of place among the hard fabrics and flannel surrounding them.

She'd seen Floyd on the deck every time she went up there. His brilliant blue eyes made all the brighter in comparison to his brown and curly hair and trimmed beard. They'd made eye contact a few times but said nothing to each other until the fourth day of the journey.

He'd been leaning on the railing and looking off towards the shoreline when she approached him, his broad shoulders beckoning her over to stand beside him. There was a magnetism he possessed that had her drawn to him and couldn't resist any more.

"Now I know you aren't going up there to be prospecting. So, it must be a husband you're hoping to get from the Klondike." This was the first think he said to her. He hadn't taken his eyes off the shoreline, but it had been as though he was looking straight at her.

"Are those my only two options? Pick-axe or ball and chain?" she countered.

He turned his eyes to her then. He gave her a good looking over and she stepped back from the rail to allow him to take in her form entirely with a challenging smile and an outwards gesture of her arms.

"What other reason could there be for you to head on up there? Isn't exactly a forgiving place we're headed to." There was a small tug on the corner of his mouth.

Her spine straightened. "That's fine by me. I'm not exactly a forgiving sort of girl." He gave no more than a nod in response and looked back out at the shoreline. "There wasn't going to be anything left back in Seattle, nor anywhere else in the west. Figured if I headed north now then I had a chance of beating out the crowds for a job. Any job."

"Whorin' ain't ideal." he stated offhand.

"Not what I'm planning on, but I'll do what I have to do and see where things lead." she told him honestly.

Sasha watched as his jaw clenched at her answer. She wasn't going to lie, becoming a whore in the Rush might be something that she would wind up resorting to, but it'd be a last resort. There were legitimate ways to make an income and she'd find them. Her and Meredith.

She and Floyd wound up standing beside each other every day when she managed to steal away to the deck. They would generally do nothing more than stand beside each other, but she had managed to find out that he had been working in the Nebraska Timber industry before getting on this ship. He was hired by an aristocratic brat that thought he was going to strike it rich, at least have his men to strike it rich for him. Floyd saw the possibility of working up a nest egg from the Gold Rush, just like she did.

On the last anticipated day of the journey Floyd followed in behind her after her daily dose of sunshine, down into the bowels of the ship. They came to a stop at the bottom of the second level, where the scullery would be found.

"We might not see each other in the chaos tomorrow." Sasha pointed out, trying to keep her tone light. "I hope your prospecting is… fruitful." she searched for the right word.

Floyd reached his hand out and tucked a lock of her hair between his fingers to give it a twirl. He stared at it for a beat before casting his eyes up to lock on hers. They looked so dark with only the light from a single porthole on the opposite side of the stairs provided. The thought that she might never see him again was causing a sensation in her chest she'd never felt before.

"When you get to where you're goin'," he started, taking a step closer to her so the fabric of their clothes gently brushed together. "You do what you got to do. But you be smart about it, yeah?"

He said this to her with such an earnest tenderness that she felt she might melt into a puddle at his feet. "I will," she promised. "And you watch your back. Build your nest egg, then get back home and be safe." she whispered, her gaze darting down to his lips and back up to his eyes.

He leaned down and she held her breath, eyes slipping closed and puckered her lips in anticipation of his own to accept what she was offered. The tickle of his beard came against her chin. His nose rubbed softly against her own.

But their moment was lost by the sound of pounding footsteps coming down the stairwell, causing them both to pull back. They separated enough for the man descending the stairs to pass between them.

Sasha allowed herself a regretful sigh as she took in what might be the last look at him before giving him a quick kiss on the cheek, turning back get to work and to prepare the lunchtime meal.

By the time they reached Dyea Sasha took charge. She hauled Meredith behind her and headed straight for the inn closest to the harbor, making sure that they were the first ones off the ship while the eager prospectors still aboard were triple checking they hadn't left any of their precious belongings behind.

She rushed right up to the man working at the inn and said they were looking for a job, any job. And told him that he was about to be overrun with more clients than he would be able to handle, but she and Meredith would be able to handle them.

The proprietor was impressed with her brazen attitude, not so much her sisters quiet and meek demeanor though and set them to work. Meredith was sequestered to the kitchen, and Sasha was given the position of a chambermaid. He seemed sure that Sasha would be able to deal with the unwanted advances that had driven several of his girls to seek employment elsewhere.

The Pullen House Inn continued to keep the girls in room and board, and in coin, for months.

Many prospectors had tents set up along the water, but as winter settled in and the town truly experienced the boom from the Klondike there was never a shortage of work for Sasha and Meredith. There was a dairy attached to the Inn and they had to learn how to deal with that on the go.

Sasha's world view had never been through rose colored glasses, particularly after 'the incident' but she hadn't felt like a girl closely linked to morality for the years since it happened. She hadn't told Meredith, Meredith wouldn't have been able to stand knowing, she still went to church on Sundays. And if Mere was working during service, she'd go after.

Sasha didn't. See, Sunday's left several prospectors feeling a little sinful, and Sasha turned a profit off that.

Prostitution in these parts was on the rise. Able women had accompanied their husbands north only to watch them perish and needed to find a way to support themselves. A lot of those women weren't nearly as young and pretty as Sasha.

She'd been curious about men in Seattle, but in Dyea they were in town for only a night and then gone the next. Here her curiosities could be answered discretely with-out word spreading.

Rooms at The Pullen House were $1.25 a night for a single, and for a dollar extra she'd make it so particular men understood just how good a sleep they could get for their stay. She'd polished a few Johnson's with her hand, bared her breasts and even used her mouth on a few of the better-looking men provided they'd had a bath. She'd squirrelled away a fair amount of coin in the few months she'd been there. It helped to close her eyes and imagine that each interaction had been between she and Floyd, that they had managed to prolong that moment they shared, and it had become something much much more.

All was going well until Jefferson Randolph "Soapy" Smith the Second showed up with his gang.

LONDON, ENGLAND 1909

"Mr. Toften," the doctor came in and shook Thomas's hand and nodded at Sasha. He pulled out his notepad. "Now then. What can I help you with today?" he looked only at Thomas with his pencil ready over his paper.

"My wife and I are having trouble conceiving." Thomas answered. Sasha could hear how uncomfortable he was saying that out loud. By telling the doctor he was admitting to a fault, faults were not something to be discussed, only prestige and accomplishments.

"I see," the doctor nodded and scribbled. "And how long have you been trying?"

"Two years."

"Hmm." The doctor scribbled and looked over Sasha with a scrutinizing gaze. No doubt taking in age, weight, and health. He nodded. "And how often are you trying?" he asked Thomas directly again.

"At least once a week." Thomas' shoulder gave an involuntary shrug, a sure sign of his discomfort.

Sasha was listening, but also staring at a spot on the wall. It was slightly discolored, the paint around it was lighter, like it had been scrubbed at with ammonia to try and remove something unsettling.

"There are certain times that you needn't try, but others that you should try more often than that in a woman's," he cleared his throat. "Cycle." he said distastefully.

If she hadn't been forcing herself for so long to play the role of decent and God-fearing woman, she would have scowled and made a face at the man. Instead she managed to shift to portray discomfort with the topic and let them think that the pink coming to her cheeks was due to embarrassment instead of anger.

This man was a medical practitioner and he clearly thought that the woman's menstrual cycle was disgusting. She already knew all about these things. She'd learned to read and had gone over the material relating to it. She was now a pretty educated for a woman, and for someone with her upbringing, and had been able to figure it all out. That and she'd learned a lot from other women. If it wasn't for this 'cycle' that the doctor was making a face about then none of them would be there.

"You needn't bother during her bleeding times, nor for a week after." the doctor assured Thomas.

Thomas in turn relaxed slightly at that information. Sasha could have told him that, but then she'd have to tell him how she knew. He hadn't looked forward to 'fulfilling his husbandly duty' when she was bleeding. She hadn't particularly enjoyed sex then either as it required her to be extra aggressive with the laundry the next day.

"How often then?" Thomas asked.

"At least every other day." the doctor said regretfully. "There have been a few studies done. None released to the public of course, only in the medical community. But these studies have shown that there is really a three- or four-day period that is ideal."

Thomas sighed and brought a hand to his face. His facade was cracking. "I just don't understand how some of these vagrants on the street have so many children. One right after the other, and yet." he cast his hands out with wide fingers at a loss.

The doctor rested his notebook on his lap. "I understand your frustration. I believe it is simply due to upbringing. The more well to do families simply have less children, and generally a harder time conceiving."

Sasha wanted to laugh in his face. She couldn't tell if he was being serious or not. He had to have known it was simply because those 'vagrants' as he called them had one pastime, and it was that pastime that caused all those babies. Meanwhile Thomas preferred their pastimes to be garden parties and reading, or chess and billiards with the boys.

"Now, this part may be rather uncomfortable for you both, but Mrs. Toften, I will need to examine you. Just to rule out any... abnormalities." Finally, the doctor's gaze was on her properly.

"Of course. We understood that it was a possibility." Thomas answered for her.

Sasha looked at Thomas, then over to the doctor before her eyes rested on the torture table.

This was it.

Her eyes cast down she stood and wearily went over to place her bottom against the end of the table.

The doctor pulled a partition over to create some facade of privacy, so her husband didn't have to watch this. Thomas didn't look at her down there when they were in bed together, he certainly wasn't going to 'examine' right alongside the doctor.

The doctor pulled a small stool over and indicated for her to hop up on the table. Sasha steeled herself and slid off her shoes before she pulled down her knickerbockers and stockings from under her dress skirt then awkwardly shifted herself back on the table. She lay back and bent her knees, jumping at the gentle touch of the doctor telling her that she had to spread her legs in order for him to get a good long look at her privates.

Sasha rested her head back and looked up at the ceiling, shivering as he began to probe her.

"Hmm," the doctor made the noise curiously after a moment. She could picture his head leaning this way and that, trying to make sense of what he was seeing.

DYEA, ALASKA 1898

Soapy Smith was a con artist and a gangster. He was taking over the towns of Skagway and Dyea with his men running a scam about 'prize soap'. He was selling soap that one had the chance of finding a gold nugget in, and they did exist, but he only sold them to members of his gang, thus his moniker.

He'd also taken a shine to Meredith.

Sasha was weary of his men, and warned Meredith against him, but he was promising her the world and she was lapping up the attention from such a 'prestigious' man. It didn't matter that he was nineteen years her senior.

Truth be told that wasn't so out of sorts around here.

It also didn't matter to Meredith that he was probably going to be arrested and killed at any moment, she was too pleased with his infatuation in her and wasn't thinking things through properly. Soapy invited her to be his girl and move down to Skagway with him. He was opening up Jeff Smith Parlor, named after himself, and Meredith wanted to go with him.

Sasha wasn't having any of it. If she moved down to Skagway with Meredith and Soapy she'd be a tag along. She wasn't a tag along. Meredith and she had several arguments about it, and it culminated in Meredith simply turning heal and following Soapy.

Sasha was content to stay in Dyea by herself. She was older and wiser now. She had real life experience and a good thing going where she was and didn't need a man to look after her, especially when that man wasn't even her man.

Few letters had passed between she and Meredith over the next two months, but it looked like Mere had a comfortable situation set up for her, and Sasha was still making a good amount of money where she was. With the arrival of more ships and men the unrest in the mountains and on the trails began. Bodies began to find their way back to Dyea to be sent home on these ships. And when given the opportunity Sasha would head down to the building by the docks to see if she might recognize any of them.

The people settled in Dyea were slightly starved for entertainment, so coming down to the building by the docks and seeing who of the prospectors had passed away was what they did when there was a break in the day.

Sasha made sure to come down once a week and check their faces. She recognized a few of them, but none were the face she worried over the most. It wasn't out of a twisted sense of curiosity; it was to make sure none of them were Floyd. She was rather embarrassed with herself over how she'd romanticized their liaisons on the ship. She hadn't been able to pin down what it was about him that made him stand out in her mind the way he did, but whatever it was, she was desperate to see him again and hoped it wouldn't be because he was dead in this dock house.

His was the face that she'd had so many pleasant dreams about. Dreams of working a property in Nebraska alongside him, telling her to do what she had to do to assist him when he would come into their house with an inexplicable gash on the front of his shirt showing off the toned and sweaty chest beneath. He would say such wonderful words to her before she would seize the fabric in both her hands and rip it the rest of the way off of him.

Those dreams came to her regularly and she would wake desperate for him to be twixt her legs but having to compromise with a pillow and her own fingers.

She dreamed of him so vividly and often, and imagined his face on some of the men she'd earned extra coin off of that when she was walking back from her check of the bodies and another was being carried in she thought she was just imagining things again.

The one of the men carrying the new body into the building resembled Floyd quite a bit and it was so easy to superimpose his eyes onto that face. The hair and beard could have easily been what he would have looked like after so many months in the wilderness. His frame too would have slimmed down to that size after so long on rations.

This mans eyes locked on hers as they grew closer and she froze in shock. It was him. This was Floyd.

The grim expression he had been wearing relaxed into one of pleasant surprise. A smile almost appeared on his face. "Sasha." he barely whispered, but it carried to her ears as though it were a booming declaration that had her heart expanding to twice the size and warmth spreading to her cheeks that shouldn't be possible in this spring cold.

She stood still as he passed her and remained in her spot until he came back out to stand in front of her. He was as close as he had been those months ago on the ship when they bid each other farewell.

"Floyd." she breathed out his name, not bothering to reign in the emotion her voice was carrying.

"You're still here." he looked gaunt and in desperate need of some hygienic care. But he was here. She could have reached out and touched him.

"You're still alive." she smiled up at him. "How. Did you." The questions of whether he struck gold, or if he was heading back south and everything in between were lost in the overwhelming joy of seeing him again.

He shook his head, his eyes never leaving hers. "That was my boss I just carried in. The fool thought he could manage giving the hard labor a shot and fell down a ravine. We didn't strike anything." he relayed sadly. "Now I'm stuck until someone else hires me on."

He was stuck there. In her town. All sorts of rendezvous scenarios came to her mind of nursing him back to health and bathing him, trimming his hair and beard so he would look presentable and capable for the next rich man looking for hands. "I'm at the Pullen House." she blurted out. "There's a room with a bath available. Do you. Have you found somewhere to stay yet?"

He shook his head again in despondence. "We have a tent. I can't afford-"

"I can." she stepped forward, so they were nearly pressed up against each other. "Please. Let me."

"I can't take your hard earned-"

"Yes, you can. Please." she begged. "I've been... worried. About you." It was irrational. They didn't know each other, but he was here, and she was here. They could spend time together. Alone.

His eyes softened even further, though his tight shoulders remained as stoic as she remembered, and he nodded. Her chest heaved with pleasure and she finally caught him taking a look at her bosom, it sent a tingle of excitement down her spine.

"I have to get a few things done first," he told her softly.

Sasha nodded eagerly. "I'll go and secure the room for you. And make sure the bath is warm."

He sucked in a breath at the promise of a warm bath and regarded her a moment longer before turning back to his companion and she spun on her heel back to the Pullen House to get his room prepared.

There was still work to be done with the rest of the rooms and in the kitchen. With each task she smiled her way through completing it, knowing that right then Floyd was in the same building as her and was luxuriating in some well-earned self-care. She sent up some whisky and food with one of the runners and counted down with mounting antic- ipation for the end of dinner service.

When the last of the plates came back, she cleared them off and tucked a few bread rolls into her apron before heading straight for his room.

He answered after the first knock, opening the door just enough for her to slip in before she closed it behind her and stood before him. He smelled so sweet now and was clean wearing a trimmed beard and mustache.

"Your hair is still long." she smiled and reached up to tug gently at one of his locks, twirling it in her fingers. She was feeling slightly shy and shaky. It wasn't something she'd felt with any of the other men she'd had experiences with. It felt nice.

He reached for the doorknob and turned the latch before wrapping an arm around her and pulling her flush up against him. She wove her other hand into his hair and their lips finally met. His were chapped but right. Their mouths devoured each other in a desperate dance of longing. She had to gasp in breath at each movement, as did he.

Sasha tugged at his clothes, then to the ties on her own desperate for more of him. Floyd pulled back to yank her dress down over her shoulders, so she stood in only her slip before him. She reached forward and undid his buckle, yanking his trousers down as well while he pulled his shirt over his head.

The months of small rations that had shown in his face was even more evident in the greyish sallow skin he bore, but that didn't stop her lust for him. They kicked their clothes out of the way as they made for the bed, mouths still feverously kissing and hands wandering.

She lay back on the bed and he came on top of her, pulling up at the cloth of her slip. "Be gentle with me." she pleaded in a moan as his lips had begun trailing down to her breast.

Floyd pulled back to look at her in alarm. "Are you? You haven't?"

She looked down at him, biting her lip and shaking her head. "I had my maidenhood stolen from me, but that was years ago. And I haven't been touched since."

His eyes darkened and she felt his member twitch against the inside of her thigh. "I may not be able to please you at first, but I promise I'll be gentle." he raised himself up to take her lips with his again and she felt the pressure between her legs.

It was different this time. He had caused her to grow wet there and as he slid inside it was a pleasurable pain that made her sigh with desire as he filled her completely. When he withdrew slightly and thrust forward again, they both groaned. He repeated the movement again and again, gripping her thigh and her back arched with the delicious feelings he was eliciting throughout her entire being.

The headboard knocked against the wall in time with his thrusts, but it wasn't long before he let out a long groan and his thrusts turned into rutting movements culminating in his resting his full weight on hers.

With a sigh he withdrew his member and came to lay beside her, pulling her close. "If you'll let me, I'll be able to do that again and try to give you the same reaction."

She had brought about that finish he'd experienced in herself a few times and hoped he spoke truth. It was only a moment however before his breathing turned to snores. She didn't mind. He was still here beside her with his arm wrapped possessively around her middle. She tucked herself against him even closer and closed her eyes to enjoy his warmth.

It could only have been a few hours later when his shifting awoke her. His hand travelled beneath her slip and along her side encouraging her to take it off. The candle had burned out and the room was completely dark. She pulled the slip off over her head and felt his head lower to her chest. Somehow being able to feel him against her, but not see, made the sensations of his touch amplify. He cupped her breast with one hand and kissed the other, spending time appreciating her bosom before his hand travelled between her legs. She rocked against his fingers wantonly and enjoyed the noise he made at discovering her warm and wet for him.

He mounted her once more and she felt how ready he was to take her against her triangle of curls for only a moment before he entered her again.

This time he did last longer. Long enough for she herself to get to the point of having the waves of crashing and all-encompassing pleasure take over her body that were so much more than what she'd been able to give herself. He followed right after, again turning his thrusts into smaller movements and resting fully on top of her.

"Now how is it you've been doing so well for yourself here?" he whispered after coming back beside her.

Her body came back down to earth and she turned to face him and told him unabashedly what she'd done for extra coin. She told him how her sister had run off with Soapy and how she'd been careful. But most importantly she told him how she'd dreamed of seeing him again.

He listened to her tale and his gentle touches to her side and breast didn't hesitate once during her telling of the nefarious doings she'd taken part in. Then it was his turn to tell her about what he'd needed to do in order to stay alive, including making the choice to end a life of a man who would have taken he and a few other men over the side of a mountain to their death had his line not been cut. He'd also lain with a prostitute in Dawson City where it was legal, a thank you from his now deceased proprietor for all the men in his employ for getting them to that point.

They talked into the night and made love once more before she heard the grandfather clock chime five times and she regretfully found her clothes and made her way back to her room.

The next morning was when her whole life came crashing down.

Ben Parker returned. He was a prospector that had headed into the Klondike months previously and had come back having struck gold.

Ben had made a pass at her in the parlor of The Pullen House, right in front of the U.S. Marshall. He'd propositioned her, offering to pay again for certain services in a State where prostitution was illegal, and the U.S. Marshall was in Soapy Smith's pocket.

Soapy wasn't too happy with her trying to stop Meredith leaving with him.

It only took one smug look from the Marshall before Sasha rushed back to her room and retrieved her satchel and tossed all her belongings into it, her coin purse she tucked under her dress before pushing open the window and climbing out. She was halfway through it when a pair of strong hands came under her arms and scream nearly escaped her lips before Floyd hushed her.

Tears of worry were falling down her cheeks when he righted her in the snow. "What am I going to do? I can't escape on a ship, there won't be one for two days!" she clutched at his jacket desperately.

He gripped her shoulders. "Go to Dawson." he told her with wide eyes. "If you can't pay him off?" she shook her head no. He was in Soapy's pocket and Soapy had more coin than she. "Then go where it's legal."

"But," she searched for the right words. "You." Was all she managed.

He searched her face before pulling her into a hard kiss. "I need to stay. You need to go. Get to Dawson City, I'll wind up there eventually. And remember. Do what you have to do." He told her importantly.

With a dumb nod she pulled up her hood and made her way for the trail that went around the men policing the wagon route for the trail through the pass, not looking back.

Dawson City was the most northernly town that she could have possibly settled in, and the most outrageous.

Chorus girls, unabashed brothels and general unlawful merriment. Except it was lawful here. It didn't have much in the way of law enforcement and there were several things one could get away with in this little edge of the earth.

Sasha found employment as a chorus girl herself. As one of nearly 30,000 people that flooded into this small area, she had little choice as to opportunities for an eighteen-year-old woman if she wanted to keep herself on the road to being self-sustaining. She found work as a seamstress as well, but that work was occasional.

She'd grown accustomed to her routine, generally just doing what she could to earn money and hoping that Floyd would appear before her like he had done before. It was only a few months before the offer from the Klondike Roadhouse came her way.

She'd been cutting up a block of ice behind the dance hall when she was approached. A woman with a pickax in hand wasn't exactly an uncommon sight around these parts. A woman maybe, there was maybe one woman to every forty men, but those women usually had a pickax. To any southerners right off the boat she sure must have looked a sight with her can-can dress pulled up high enough on one side to see her garter, bright red lipstick on her face, hair piled high and swinging a pick ax at the block of ice for the barman in her boots.

Joseph Nickel's was the proprietor of the Klondike Roadhouse and he was recruiting new girls. New prostitutes was what that meant. Girls didn't last too long around this environment, they either married themselves off to the men who struck rich or bought a one-way ticket into the Yukon River, in part because of the cold and depressing winter months and in part because they believed they'd sold their souls when they took up as a working girl.

Well, Joseph had four rooms in his brothel and only two girls.

Being a chorus girl was exhausting. Being a prostitute, particularly in a roadhouse, that would be a hell of a lot easier. See, there were certain class systems in these parts when it came to whoring. Roadhouses were at the top. That was for the classiest of whore's, the ones that were regularly allowed access to baths. Warm baths too. Then there were the cigar shops where the girls weren't quite as pretty and weren't anywhere near as clean.

Then there was the Hutches. Those were usually the native girls. The men had to be too long in the wilderness and running shy of coin if they were desperate enough to go to the Hutches.

Sasha hadn't spoken to any of the Native women yet. She'd been curious about them, but they were from a whole other world than she. Her work kept her plenty busy and she was near ready to throw in the towel when Joseph Nickel came along offering her prime placement as a whore in his establishment and all the niceties that came along with it.

Her mind drifted back to Floyd and her only proper experience with sex. It had been lovely, she felt like she'd given a piece of herself to him that night and hadn't done anything with a man since to save her-self for him. A fantasy had built up in her head of him coming for her.

But fantasy wasn't going to keep her warm at night with a full belly.

She got herself drunk her first night she worked for the Nickel's. It was really Amelia Nickel that ran the roadhouse, her husband Joseph was just the front man that tended the bar and tossed out the drunks. And apparently it was his job to proposition the new working girls.

Amelia gave Sasha a good looking over, going so far as to lead her into the bathing room and watch her strip down and bath herself while she asked her questions. It was an uncomfortable situation for Sasha to find herself in but understood the necessity. If Sasha couldn't strip down for Amelia, then she might not for any John that came along either.

She drank three successive shots of whiskey before heading into her new room. It was excessive comfort this room. There was a proper mattress and the bed was big enough for three girls to fit. There was a washing bin and pitcher on the bureau that was meant for cleaning herself up after.

The smaller bowl and sponge beside it were something else entirely.

She'd heard all kinds of stories about how these prostitutes kept themselves from getting 'in trouble', no doubt the success rate of these attempts played a part in the number of girls that found themselves floating face down. This here was known to be the most reliable. She had to take that sponge, soak up a good amount of the Lysol and push it up inside her as far in as it would go.

Sasha stripped down to her uniform, meaning a short lace slip that Amelia had handed her, and took the sponge, sopped up the Lysol and spread her legs, bearing down and awkwardly pushing it up into her-self. It continued to feel strange when she stood up and squirmed as it shifted around as it settled inside her.

She didn't have much time to get used to it though. The heavy foot-falls of the first John along the wood boards outside her room some-how echoed through her body and could be heard over all the ruckus going on down in the main parlor area. As they drew nearer, she moved back away from the door and towards the bed.

She'd had to plaster a smile on her face as a chorus girl, it was how they got the tips. This wouldn't be any different. No matter how ner-vous she was. Some of these men that came through could be brutes, but some were okay to look at. Just had that air of desperation around them.

The door opened and Amelia stuck her head in to check if Sasha was ready, then pushed the door open further and gestured for the John to head in. Sasha couldn't help really smiling at the man presented to her.

He was an eager looking boy really. He couldn't be much older than Sasha herself, and must have been brand new to the Klondike because he still had a softness about him.

Sasha came forward to him and nodded at Amelia in thanks. The woman had to have been starting her off with something easy and she was quite appreciative. Sasha gently pulled at the boy's jacket to slide it down over his shoulders. It fell to the floor and his britches were the next to be removed, his trousers falling to the floor with-out their anchor holding them up. They both giggled at that and she found herself feeling ready to do this. He stripped off the rest of his kit and she walked herself back to the bed, bringing him with her.

After that night she'd had men that were gentle with her, some that were rough, and some that liked to do things that she demanded they pay her extra for otherwise they could take it up with Joseph Nickel and find themselves missing a finger.

It got easier and easier to do the job over time. She and the other girls built up a comradery over their meals, laughing over some of the john's and some of the rather silly things they asked the girls to do for them. More often than not the men just wanted a decent fuck, but sometimes they asked for the girls to call them things or act a certain way.

The other girls told her how to make the men finish sooner by putting her finger up their bum. It had been something she'd found disgusting at first, but after a few drawn out sessions it had become her salvation. She'd even had a few regulars that she looked forward to being with. Two in particular enjoyed making her finish and working her over until she got there.

By the time spring had arrived Sasha was wondering how much longer she would have to keep this up. She had a lot of coin now, enough to get back south and set herself up with a nice house and rent out some rooms to keep herself solvent.

Maybe find her way to Nebraska and try and find out what had happened to Floyd. He could have been dead, or maybe he'd been one of the lucky ones that struck gold and had kept a good chunk of it for himself. Either way, she couldn't help closing her eyes sometimes when she was with her men and imagining it was him instead.

But all that got shot to hell when she missed her monthly.

Amelia had kept track of the girls bleeding times. When she missed her second monthly Amelia pulled her aside and told her her options. There was a trick with a coat hanger that could land her at the doctors, or she could try and figure out how it was the native girls dealt with it.

"What do you mean?" Sasha asked incredulously. She hadn't heard anything about the hutch girls having a way to get rid of a baby.

"Ever notice how many native babies are born round here?" Amelia raised an eyebrow at her. "Just last month that one from the blue hutch three back was clearly showing, then one day," she gestured with a straight palm facing her belly and made a sweeping motion. "Nothin'. There's another one showin now that's two down from the blue one. I can promise you that a week from now, she'll be flat as well." she made a cocky face at her and turned away to get back to her business.

Sasha stared after her. She didn't want a baby now. She didn't know who the father might be, and she'd been barely able to keep accountable for herself. A baby couldn't happen.

So, she begged off her work to deal with the problem. If that native whore was going to be getting rid of her baby soon, then Sasha needed to keep tabs on her to figure out how.

For two days she watched out the window of the Nickle's second floor for movement on the hutch before one bright evening another native woman went to the hutch and collected the one in trouble.

They were going to do something about it.

Sasha scrambled to leave the Roadhouse and catch up to them. She followed them as they made their way up the hill closest to the city. She tried to remain as quiet as possible as she trailed behind them. It took a full hour before the two women got to where they were going. It was going on eleven at night and had gotten properly dark out finally.

There were other native women at the crest of the hill when she got there. They were doing a dance in a circle holding onto some kind of crude musical instruments. It was an odd sight to behold, but then after a few minutes of watching their ritual the skies opened up and the green lights of the Aurora Borealis joined them in their dance.

She was completely mesmerized as the Hutch girl she'd been watching became visible in the middle of the group, her robe removed to reveal her pregnant belly. The lights that were dancing around the other women converged on the one in the middle, surrounding her until she was nothing but a ball of dancing bright green light. The women danced faster and began making music with their mouths and hands, clapping and snapping their fingers. All at once they stopped and thrust their hands towards the sky and the light around the middle woman shot back up to the sky. She rose up to the sky herself for a moment, a light emanating from inside her swirled around and then the light shot straight up her belly and out her mouth right before she fell to a crouched position.

Her companions came forward to aid her. Two of them each took one of her arms and brought her to her feet, no longer pregnant.

It was magic. But it was too beautiful to have been anything like what the church talked about. There was no evil to it, save for the baby now missing from the womb of the naked woman.

With the singing stopped and the lights no longer dancing around the women, Sasha stepped forward from the bushes. The sound of her foot snapping a twig had three of the native girls snapping their heads in her direction and looking feral.

Sasha gulped, but continued forward slowly. "How?" she pointed to the woman that the others had to hold up now and were covering back over with a robe. "How make baby gone?" she said as simply as she hoped they would understand.

A few of the women exchanged looks and spoke to each other in that language of theirs, several sounding argumentative. Gesturing in ways that indicated they might be looking to kill her to stop her from telling anyone what she'd seen, others pointing at her belly and guessing why she was asking.

She stepped forward once more with a look of desperation. "I not tell." she shook her head. "I need," her hand went to clutch at her belly, and she shook her head again.

"We speak English." one of the women growled. "You don't care to know our language. We know yours."

"Oh." Sasha sagged with relief. It had been ignorant of her to assume they didn't speak her language. "Then please. Tell me what I have to do," she pleaded. "I can't have this baby."

"This ritual isn't for you," one of them spat. "We shouldn't have allowed it to happen for her." she said pointing at the weak one now sitting on the ground again in her robe. "She gave the baby up to the ancestors, and now she will have to live with that for the rest of her life."

"Never again will she carry," another woman stepped forward. "It is a last resort, and it is a sacred ritual that you should never have been witness to. Use your white people methods." she scowled.

"Fall down the stairs," one offered.

"Drown in the river," another suggested.

"Poke yourself with a rusty wire."

They were all converging on her, but she fought not to display how much they scared her. If they were going to kill her then they would, nothing she could say to them would stop them. She'd heard of what the Native Americans had done. Scalping or tying her to a horse. Well, she didn't see any knives on them, nor was there a horse around.

"Please. Please help me. I'll give you money!" she offered. "I don't care if I can't ever get pregnant again."

The one that looked to be in charge of the others said something in their native tongue that had the eyebrows raising in interest on the others. One of the others had the starting of an evil smile come to her face and answered her with a verbal reply and a nod.

"Okay Sasha." the woman in charge said.

Sasha gave a start hearing her own name from one of their lips. They knew who she was, but she couldn't name a single one of them.

"We will perform the ritual again. But we don't want your money."

"What. What do you want?" she asked, her worry now apparent in her voice.

"The fire brigade is refusing to work right now. You promise to burn down the Nickle's saloon and leave town immediately after, we'll get your baby gone tonight."

"That. That could burn down the whole town!" she said in shock. There had been two fires the previous year set by the same ditsy whore. She'd been driven out of town and they'd finally put a fire brigade in place, but now they were on strike. "Why would you want to burn down the town? It provides for you."

"We provide for ourselves. Just like we did before you people came here." one of them stepped forward and told her forcefully.

Sasha thought quickly over her options. Had they offered the same thing to Belle Mitchell? Belle was the whore who set the last two fires. But Sasha hadn't heard anything about her getting herself in trouble.

"Okay." she nodded. She had enough coin that she could leave now and be comfortable. And she certainly couldn't have this baby.

"Okay." the one in charge nodded back. "Just know," she warned. "You don't follow through and we will kill you."

One of them came behind her and began to untie the knots on her dress. She nodded dumbly and pushed aside any feelings of modesty at being stripped in front of all these women. She closed her eyes and focused on breathing.

It was the end of April and the air bit at her skin as it was exposed. She relied on the woman undressing her to guide her through what was expected of her while the music and chanting started up again. Step by step she came to stand in the middle of them all, fighting not to grasp for the hand of the helper woman as she left her standing there alone and joined the others.

Sasha shivered as she opened her eyes again and saw all the women dancing around her. She raised her eyes to the sky, expecting to see the green dancing Aurora Borealis as she had before, but there was nothing, just the black and stars.

She closed her eyes again and thought about what it would look like to give the foreign entity inside her to the ancestors of the native people. Of how she didn't want it. Of how it would look and feel to have it removed from her in the way she'd seen it happen for the other girl.

She brought to mind how the light had come down and tickled around the other girls skin, caressing her in a way before seeping into her until she glowed with it, and raising up in the air gently before her head tilted back and the light shot out through her mouth.

It wasn't until a hand grasped her under her arm and heaved her to her feet that she realized it hadn't been her imagination showing her this, it had happened. And she was entirely exhausted.

"What? How. I didn't even." she sighed, not able to articulate her confusion.

"That took a long time." the woman shook her head. "We'll get you back down into town. You get some sleep, but when morning comes you better follow through on your promise."

Sasha looked up to the sky again in her half-hooded eyes. There was no trace of the green lights. She didn't know if it had worked properly, or been real, but it was now full night. It was as though she'd been in a trance for hours and had lost all sense of time.

They did get her back to the saloon, and she walked on shaky feet to her room, locking the door and falling into bed, asleep in an instant.

Come morning time she was bleeding. The relief she felt at the sight of the blood between her thighs was immense and as she cleaned herself up, she replayed the previous evening in her head.

It had worked.

And she had promised.

Before she could psyche herself out of it, Sasha packed up her belongings into a large satchel, determined to do it. She lit her candle and placed it under her bed before leaving the room and heading downstairs to the kitchen to fill up any space left in her bag with food and getting the hell out of there.

By the time the alarm bells of the Nickle's Saloon went off Sasha was already on the river boat, crossing to the other side for her journey back down along the Yukon River with the caravan of prospectors heading south.

In each stop over on her way she asked around about a prospector named Floyd, but no one she'd met had known of him. By the time she reached Whitehorse she'd heard of the devastation the fire she'd started had caused. It was larger than either one that Belle Mitchell had been responsible for, but at least no lives had been lost.

She herself was at a loss though, about what to do and where to go. Travel was pretty easy at this time of year. The sun was getting warmer, staying up in the sky longer, but the ground was still frozen, so crossings and roads were easily navigable.

A letter had found her a few months back from her sister. It seemed Meredith had found herself a man, not one of Soapy's gang either. There was a man that struck gold that took her away from Soapy before he's been shot and this man had taken her away to Edmonton, Alberta which is where Sasha was now. Meredith wanted Sasha to come and move to Edmonton too. She was a married woman now and knew of a respectable, well-off man that Sasha could marry.

Sasha never met up with Meredith though. She passed right through Edmonton, but she couldn't face her sister after all she'd done. She couldn't tell her, and if she saw her, she'd be compelled to tell her.

Instead she continued south, all the way to Boston, and then all the way over to England. Again, she'd talked her way into a job in the scullery aboard a ship for cheaper passage.

She was tired and burnt out when she arrived in Portsmouth, England. A train ride to London was the first chance she'd had to properly put her feet up and wonder what the hell she was going to do when she got to London.

But then she found a room to let, and a job as a shop girl, and then Thomas.

Poor sweet Thomas, who just wanted a simple life with his wife and child.

A child she couldn't give him and couldn't tell him why.

LONDON, ENGLAND 1909

"**W**ell," the doctor said with finality. "You can get yourself dressed." He told her pushing back from his short stool between her legs and standing up.

Her knees came together, and she lowered her thighs to rest on the table before sitting up and doing her best not to give him a bewildered look. He'd barely examined her at all. There had been no mention of any previous Lysol use, or some sort of magical green remnant from the native ancestors.

Nothing. He said absolutely nothing about it.

Maybe there was nothing down there showing any signs of that? It had been several years after all. Perhaps any residual effects of her previous contraceptive use weren't obvious to the naked eye, even from that vantage point.

The magic though, well that had gone into her and come out her mouth, so maybe there was nothing to see down there. Perhaps he couldn't tell that she'd been pregnant once before?

She got down from the table and pulled her knickers and stockings up once he'd stepped around the partition, then took her previous seat beside her husband who looked rather uncomfortable now.

"Alright then," the doctor started. "Everything with your wife looks fine. Her body is still young enough and there was a healthy amount of-" he paused and wrinkled his nose with a glance to Sasha. "You should keep trying as you have been, perhaps more often in the week after her bleeding."

"Alright." Thomas shifted before standing and reaching his hand out to shake the doctors, but then pulled back once he remembered where the doctor's hand had just been and chose a polite nod instead. "I will take your advice under advisement." he opened the door and held it for her to go through first.

Sasha was trying to figure out what she should do. Could she live with this? Should she let Thomas suffer thinking that one day she would miraculously be able to give him a child when she knew she couldn't? And how would she be able to tell him why she couldn't have children with out telling him everything else? If she told him she had been a whore he'd divorce her, if she told him about the magic, he'd send her to the asylum, and if she told him about intentionally burning down a town in the Yukon she'd be sent to jail.

Maybe...

Maybe she could keep it all to herself. Maybe she could just stay and make him happy some other way, like teaching him how to be a good lover. And maybe then he would enjoy sex, and they could be man and wife the way she'd dreamed she and Floyd might have one day.

"Darling," Thomas started when they were readying for bed that night. "It's the week after your. You've."

'Bled.' she finished for him in her head.

He was so uncomfortable with their relations. She looked over him carefully. He was a good-looking man; he had a nice body, and would no doubt be capable of being a good lover. She'd been pretending to be a good little wife for too long.

Being in Dyea and Dawson City had been freeing. Even being in Seattle. Because she'd been herself. Herself was a curious woman that enjoyed being with a man. Thomas couldn't get his baby, and she was never going to get Floyd. It was time to make a compromise.

"Thomas," she cut him off, turning from boudoir to stand in front of him. "If the way we've been doing this hasn't been working, then I want to try something."

He gave her a confused and hesitant look as she sauntered over to him, slowly stripping off her clothes as she went. He didn't move as her dress fell to the floor, nor as her fingers worked the buttons of his shirt open. He did however suck in a breath when she quickly undid his trousers and plunged her hand inside to stroke him to life.

She wasn't in her bedroom anymore. She was back in the Nickle's Saloon and Floyd had come to find her. And she was going to teach him all the new tricks she'd learned to please him. Starting by getting down on her knees.

A Tree of Life

Arden Wiles

Chapter One

A Child of Ice

Eira Galatea was a fair child. Her pale skin was almost translucent, nearly appearing blue, especially when she was in the sun. Not that she saw the sun much living in the coldest part of the world where clouds covered the lands, bringing a constant snow with them. Eira loved to dance through the snow, not noticing the sting of the cold as others around her seemed to. She had once turned completely blue from being out during the biggest ice storm their land had ever seen, but Eira never felt the pain, and never suffered from the frostbite that plagued the villagers.

She was not a vain child, but she had enjoyed using her talents to her advantage. She would dream of the heaviest snows and when she awoke in her pitch black room at noon, the snow would be piled high above the windows and doors of every room outside her home. Her mother would scold her, and somehow her mother would part the clouds and the sun melted the snow before nightfall.

Eira worshipped her mother; she was the most beautiful person Eira had ever seen. She had an ageless face with round eyes that were the brightest blue Eira knew, matched only by the ice reflecting the midday sky on a rare sunny day. Her long raven locks curled gently as her hair waterfalled down her long neck and back and Eira would brush her fingers through it for comfort as a child.

As Eira grew older, her sparse neighbors often said she looked just like her mother, which made Eira gawf. She did not think she was nearly as wonderful as her mother. She felt much less appealing, with her lanky limbs and invisible curves. Her mother could turn every head towards her as she walked with effortless grace through their tiny town, while Eira would stumble along the jutting stony path.

Eira had only ever known living in the small snowy mountain town, but she knew from the looks of the villagers that her mother had not always lived there. The whispers would follow them as they shopped in the town square, or skated across the lake, really any activity, had troubled Eira since she was a young girl. Her mother had done her best to shield Eira from their stares and harsh words, but Eira still heard the rumors in the wind, on the water, and in each snowflake she touched.

One day, she noticed how frail her mother was rapidly growing. Her ribs could be counted through her skin, and it was astonishing to Eira that the skin could stand up to the bones, and that she was not yet a skeleton. Her veins stood out, an icy blue, against her paper white skin, and her hair started to gray, until it was entirely white. Eira started to believe her mother was turning into snow. Nevertheless, her mother still taught her at home, as far away from the village as they could survive. Her mother taught her the basics of life: how to read, how to write, the numbers, but also several languages. The most useful thing her mother ever taught her was how to keep the Darkness away.

Nightmares had plagued Eira since she was an infant. Her first memories consisted of dark shadows and demons clawing their way through her brain, it was these that she believed were draining her mother's energy, causing her to become the frail woman she was. Once Eira told her mother of these dreams, her mother taught her the Ways. Eira did not know how her mother had come to learn the Ways, but she did and said Eira could too.

Eira studied old books, with yellowing paper and ancient languages written in timeless black ink. She would repeat the words over and over until she knew every word in every book by memory. As she would fall asleep, she would chant over herself, sending any Dark Spirits away from her home. Her mother had begun to get better as Eira drove the Dark away. Until Eira had uncovered the Book of Xeo.

The young girl had studied every book but one in their small library. Her mother had kept it behind a solid block of ice, or she thought it was her mother. She had begged her mother to let her read the book, but she never as allowed to touch the ice, or to look at the book. One day, while her mother was away to the village, the Book of Xeo began to call her.

"Eira," she heard a small voice whisper.

"*Mama!*" she shouted with joy, "you're back already!" She ran towards the sound of the voice. Only to be met with an empty library. "*Mama?*" she called again.

"Eira, blessed be," she heard the voice say again. This time, she could tell it did not belong to her mother, but to a more ancient being that had a hoarse and raspy voice, as if it had just awakened from a deep slumber. She hesitated by the door of the library. The voice felt familiar to her, though, she couldn't place where she knew it from. She tried to leave, feeling a Dark One present, but she was unable to move.

"Eira, come here my child," the voice spoke to her. She felt magic wash over her and her feet moved on their own accord, against her will. She was pushed from behind out of the doorway to the library, and the door slammed shut behind her. She heard the door of the cottage open and slam shut, meaning her mother was home. Eira tried to turn and warn her mother to leave, but she could not move, nor could she speak. Magic pulsed from the Book of Xeo, which melted the block of ice it was encased in. The book began to shake and flipped open to a page.

"Read," the voice commanded Eira. She went to the book and began to chant the words inscribed on the snowy pages. Snowflakes developed from the moisture in the air and swarmed about her, sticking to her eyelashes, making it difficult to see. She continued on, compelled by the ancient voice. Once she finished the page, the magic was released from her and the aged voice sighed. The words had disappeared from the page but were inscribed in Eira's mind. She closed her eyes and saw the words imprinted and glowing. Her mother threw the door to their humble library open, waking Eira out of her trance, and saw Eira with the book.

"*Mo leanbh*, what have you done?" her mother cried.

It was the last thing Eira ever heard her mother say. The room had erupted with ice crystals that cut through the books shredding the pages, none coming in contact with Eira, but one had pierced her mother's throat. The magic in the room subsided and Eira rushed to her mother's side.

The ice cut threw her mother's frail skin, but no blood came with it. Instead, the ice seemed to settle in her neck, choking out any words she tried to utter.

She had survived but could no longer speak, so she could not practice the Ways, nor could she teach them to Eira. With all the books destroyed, including the Book of Xeo, Eira had to only rely on her own memory to keep the Dark Ones away, but she could only remember the frozen words inscribed on her brain. Her nightmares came back with a vengeance and crept into her days as well. Her mother grew wearier and weaker, before she died.

Eira was devastated but didn't know what to do. She couldn't bear to live in the once happy home, now swarming with Dark Ones, her mother's lifeless body laid out respectfully on her bed in her eternal slumber. She couldn't go to the village, but she couldn't stay there either.

Packing the essential clothing and items she thought she might need, she half-filled a rather large rucksack and completed her pack with food and water. She set out to head to the remote mountain tops that surrounded her village. Not long after she reached the base of the mountain, she was stopped by the vision before her of a woman coming towards her. Eira was hesitant, as the woman approached her it became apparent that she wasn't simply a vision. She was real.

She was not from any nearby village, that much was obvious. Her furs did not come from any local beasts, and she did not look like anyone Eira had ever seen before. Her dark curly hair was pulled back away from her round face. Her skin looked as if it had been darkened from years in the sun, but that the woman had once been fairer. Her eyes glowed, and Eira could not place what color the large eyes truly were.

"Blessed be," the woman finally spoke to her, once she was about twenty paces away from where Eira stood. Eira was confused at the greeting, she had never heard the strange tongue that the woman in front of her was speaking. However, the language was not completely foreign to her, she felt a memory prick in the back of her mind, but try as she may Eira could not recall where she had heard it before.

Stepping away from the woman, Eira began to move the snow around them, widening the distance between herself and the woman. The woman's eyes grew wide in fear, or perhaps surprise, as she saw the snow move. Suddenly, the woman knelt down and placed her hands deep beneath the snow, vines sprouting from where her hands were and traveling up her arms. Eira stopped the movement of the snow, shocked by the vines. She had never seen plants grow in the mountains. The woman stood, the conjured vines snapping and shriveling back beneath the snow, smirking at the shock plastered upon Eira's face. She held her hands up to her mouth and moved her lips against them, speaking soundlessly. She looked up and met Eira's icy stare, but still Eira could not tell what color the woman's eyes were.

"I am Rowan. I have traveled far, on behalf of Nature itself. I have something for you," the woman, Rowan's voice rang out clearly, as if she were standing next to Eira, and the tongue was immediately familiar and recognizable to Eira. *This must have been caused by the muttering, a spell*, Eira thought to herself.

Intrigue and curiosity plagued Eira, and not knowing how to communicate with the stranger, she slowly walked forward towards her.

Rowan stood tall and strong as Eira approached and when she was an arm's length away, she lifted one of her furs to reveal the leather satchel tied around her body. She slowly reached into it, bringing out a linen package. She held it out to Eira, signaling for the girl to take it from her. Trustingly, Eira did so, and unwrapped the simple linens to reveal a single ice crystal.

To Rowan, it was just that, a plain ice crystal that had led the way to the Arctic One, but to Eira, the ice crystal was rusted with blood, the blood of her mother. She dropped the package, as if burned by the sight of the crystal, and the blood disappeared once the linens had left her hands. Rowan started to bend over to take the linens back, assuming she had the wrong person, but Eira had reached the crystal before Rowan, and as she touched it, the ice became blindingly bright.

Rowan smiled at Eira as the light emitting from the crystal dimmed down. "Blessed be, Arctic One, you are the one I've been searching for."

Eira had no inkling what Rowan meant by 'Arctic One,' Eira had never heard that term in her life, and she did not have the faintest idea why the woman before her would have sought her out. Eira decided to try speaking, not knowing if Rowan would understand her. "I am Eira Galatea, I have lived here my whole life. Why were you seeking me?" she asked, hesitation and doubt creeping into her words.

"Eira," Rowan began, smiling at her name, "that is a beautiful name, and a proper Nature one at that. I can tell you have been trained, at least partially, you know how to use your gifts. I need your help." Rowan stretched her hand out towards Eira. With great hesitation, Eira took her glove-clad hand, the black leather a stark contrast to the pale translucent skin of her own bare hand.

Rowan smiled and led Eira back down the path she had taken up the mountain. They came upon Eira's cottage, and Eira was shocked to see it freshly painted and undestroyed from the ice and snow that had plagued it before, and not at all in the location it had been. Rowan stepped to the door with such familiarity, Eira was confused; how could this stranger know her home? Watching the maneuvers Rowan carefully performed to open the doors drew harsh memories to the front of Eira's raging thoughts.

"*Mamai?*" Eira questioned, breathlessly.

Chapter Two

A Woman of Nature

The cool air whisked past her, bringing fallen leaves in its wake. She pulled her cloak tighter around her, shuddering from the breeze. She stared angrily at the fallen leaves, hating their meaning. There was still so much to accomplish, and she was running out of time. She hurried forward, looking around her at the darkening sky. Twilight was looming, and the night spirits would soon be out, meaning more danger than she had anticipated.

She approached the small brick cottage, with its slanted roofing. Bringing both hands together, as if praying, she quickly jutted them out, sending a strong gust of wind flying at the cottage door. The door swung open with an unexpected slowness. It should have been blown off its hinges by the blast of air; instead, it creaked open, revealing its vacancy. The woman was not deterred, she hustled through the door, and shut it hard behind her.

As the woman entered, the cottage began to shake. The shaking increased with such vigor, every window and brick within its walls rattling so hard that it was surprising the cottage still stood. Until suddenly it stopped, and the cottage had vanished from its spot in the woods, leaving no trace that it had ever stood.

Rowan stepped out of the cottage into the sunlit fields, a place as familiar to her as her childhood home had once been. The clearing was encircled by the tallest trees Rowan ever saw in all her travels. The Spirits here were happy and flourished in the constant sunlight; she had never seen night fall in this place. The flowers by her feet had already begun to fade in color and were beginning to slowly droop, as if they were dozing.

She brushed her hands to rid the soot that the shaking had rained down upon her. Conjuring the wind, she thoroughly dusted off the dirt and grime from her clothing and hair. She had grown accustomed to it from her trips here, but still did not like the soot. Reaching down and stroking a sad dahlia, she muttered a spell to strengthen its roots. As she pulled back, it followed her hand and stood up for only a second before falling farther than it had been before. She frowned and looked around the field, taking note of the changing leaves. She was disheartened at their reddening and browning but was relieved to see that they had not yet fallen, she may have more time than she thought.

She set out to the edge of the clearing and placed both her palms flat against a tree, almost as if enveloping it in a hug. The tree hummed at her presence and she grew warm from the motion. She closed her eyes at the bright light that grew and opened them to see another woman standing there.

"Willow, it's been too long," she greeted the woman.

Willow's dark skin still flickered with the fading light that had brought her out of her slumber from the tree. She towered over Rowan, her head almost reaching the treetops, but Rowan knew Willow could control her form and had chosen to stay much taller than herself. Tears were streaming down her face, looking like sap flowing from a spigot. She looked around the clearing and stared forlornly into the forest. Her dark eyes, as dark as the pupils set within the black irises, shone, the sun glaring off the water of her tears. Her green tendrils draped like curls from her head, covering her naked form. Rowan wished to reach out and push her hair away from her body, but she kept her hands strapped to her sides and pushed her desire down as she saw the woman choking on her tears. Her full lips, darker even than her skin, quivered with the sobs racking her body.

"Why have you brought them here?" she asked Rowan scornfully. Rowan's face showed her confusion, she had come alone, she always had. Rowan shook her head and began to speak before Willow put up a hand to stop her. "You did not sense the Dark Spirits watching you. Mother Gaia was not guarding your travels this time Rowan, you have brought the frost with you."

"No, Willow, this is why I have woken you. I did not bring this frost; it has been seeping into all of Nature for months. I fear we will feel the Boreal here once more. Mother Gaia has fallen asleep. You must have felt her slumber?" Rowan had grown more frightened. Surely Nature had felt what was befalling them as they were the most affected.

"I worry you have spent too much time away from here," Willow whispered, brushing her hand across Rowan's face, pushing her dark hair aside. "Darling, it has been too long since you have woken me." It wasn't a question, but Rowan could hear the silent, unspoken why, sitting upon Willow's lips. Rowan twisted her face out of Willow's gentle grasp.

"The Spirits have grown frantic and they cannot fall back asleep once they are awake. I didn't want to risk you until I had to," Rowan answered, knowing that Willow would not appreciate such human emotions. Spirits didn't understand humans as well as they did Nature. Nature reacted and survived, humans felt too much, and Willow sometimes wished she could impose more Nature into Rowan, then she'd make a rightful leader of Nature. Even so, when Rowan looked at the giantess with such tenderness and familiarity, it stung Willow's wooden heart.

"That is not for you to decide. If what you say is true and the great Gaia has fallen into her slumber once more, I do not worry about us Spirits falling back asleep, I fear we will stay asleep," she spoke blankly, without inflection or emotion. Rowan knew she was using Nature to defend against the human in her. Willow reached a hand to Rowan, who pushed her away.

"I have to go back. I only wished to see if the frost had set in here," Rowan lied through her teeth. They both knew Rowan had needed to check to make sure Willow could wake up. Rowan quickly enveloped Willow in a hug but walked away before Willow could return it. Rowan headed towards the cottage, away from Willow's roots, and out of her reach.

"Rowan!" Willow's voice boomed, stopping Rowan in her tracks. Rowan turned and caught the leaf Willow had blown into the wind.

She opened her hand and read what Willow had written on the leaf. She looked up in shock, but in her place stood a strong willow tree, its weeping branches nearly touching the ground; Willow had gone back to sleep. She looked back at the leaf, not truly believing what she had written, knowing Nature could not survive it. *Let it freeze.*

Nimue was the oldest and wisest of all the Spirits. She had been born before Time or Earth had been formed; in fact, she had had a hand in their creation. She had played Fate, bending him to her will, but she had never met Rowan, Queen of the Wiccans, before now. *At least,* Nimue thought to herself, *not when I looked like this.* Of course, Nimue knew that Rowan was not truly a queen, nor was she a Wicca. The word for what Rowan and the others could do did not exist. They were born with their abilities, which they honed with practice. They could converse with Nature and materialize its Spirits. No matter what their name may be, Rowan was their chosen leader. She was the strongest and most powerful, and she was also the least manipulated by the Dark. *She is a worthy queen of the ladies*, Nimue thought proudly.

Rowan approached Nimue's door at the Witching Hour. *What a brave girl,* Nimue thought wryly. The Wiccans had not been traveling outside the sunlight for centuries, and Rowan had not been alive in the Dark Times. Nimue opened the door before Rowan even had a chance to knock, leaning easily against the frame, in nothing but a silken robe. Rowan trampled in, and opened her mouth to speak, but Nimue was quick and first to speak.

"Blessed be, Rowan," Nimue spoke darkly, inflicting power behind the words, causing the other girl to narrow her eyes.

Rowan didn't question how the old Spirit knew her name, Nimue knew all. Instead, she stuck her hand out, barely bothering with niceties as she thrust the leaf into Nimue's hand. "Blessed be, Nimue," Rowan whispered back. She looked pointedly at the leaf she had given Nimue, growing more urgent the longer Nimue took. "Not all of us are immortal now, *Memory*, you'd be good to make haste," Rowan spoke, using ancient words only Nimue could comprehend. She flinched at the true meaning of her name but had to bend to the will of the speaker. It had been centuries since she had heard the name spoken aloud. She didn't ponder how Rowan had known it, the girl was close with Nature, and Nature did not forget.

"As you wish, *Tree*, but it would behoove you to stay awhile," Rowan similarly flinched at the ancient power in Nimue's voice, but sat down stiffly. "Speaking of trees, how is Nature doing? I felt Gaia doze off just last week. Is Willow awake?" she asked numbly. Rowan knew Nimue was not on the side of Nature, nor was she on the side of the Dark, Wiccans, or humans. Nimue had been completely self-serving since her inception, and Rowan knew she would choose the winning side each time.

Nimue walked slowly about the small sitting area. Rowan's eyes followed her, not daring to look away at the room she was in. Nimue couldn't help but smirk, the girl was smart; several objects in the room were bewitched and would hold the viewer for eternity. After some time, Nimue finally looked down at the leaf in her hand and cackled.

She continued to roar with laughter as she saw Rowan grow more worried. Fate was a funny man.

"And freeze it shall," she said, crumbling the leaf and blowing its brown pieces into the fire. Rowan stared at it frighteningly, seeing a girl appear within the flames. Looking to Nimue, she saw the same shock mirrored on the Wise One's face. Nimue spoke with her power once more, "it would do you good, *Tree*, to find the One who controls the Cold."

R owan had only moved her childhood cottage to one place outside the clearing. She had rested for several days in preparation for the strain the journey to the remote ice would place on her. Since she had never been to the location, and it would be the farthest she ever traveled, the journey was sure to test her abilities. She had filled her cottage with much needed supplies, stocking its old wooden shelves with food. Nimue had instructed her on where to go, and who it was she would be looking for. Nimue's Fire Spirit had spat out the ashes of the leaf that Nimue flicked her hand at lazily, transforming the ashes into a single ice shard. This ice shard that would glow when given to the Arctic One, and Rowan had tied it in linen and then wrapped it in black fur, taking great care not to cut herself with it.

On the day of her journey, she did not dress in her usual linens, instead, she chose dark leathers and furs to keep her warm, but still grounded with Nature. She took a small Fire Spirit, given to her from Nimue, and placed it in her hearth to light her journey there and back. She made sure to send any Dark Spirits away before placing her hands together as if in prayer and shooting a burst of air at the door. She entered the cottage and once again ensured the Dark was warded against. She laid out the ice shard and began chanting, channeling all of her energy into finding the Arctic One. The cottage began its typical shaking and trembling, before flying through the air with Rowan in tow. Rowan kept her hands out and eyes closed while she continued chanting, guiding the cottage to where the Arctic One would be. She landed with a soft thud, puffs of snow billowing out from underneath her. She sent the Wind all about the cottage, ridding any dust, including any on herself. She rewrapped the ice shard and placed it safely in a leather satchel bound to her body. She took a small portion of the Fire Spirit and provisions for a day's journey and set out to find Eira Galatea, the One who could control the Cold.

Chapter Three

A Deal of Pain

Rowan turned around, confused by her own native tongue coming from the young girl. As she met the eyes of Eira, she finally noticed the sapphire orbs reflecting her own. She felt dread fill her stomach, joining the confusion growing there.

"We have to leave," Rowan said decidedly. Firmly grasping Eira's arm, she led her into the cottage, and turning away from the snow-covered mountains.

Rowan released her hold on Eira's arm and watched as the girl sat down, ever so careful and hesitant. Preparing the cottage to travel as quickly as she could, Rowan kept a watchful eye over Eira. The young girl had curled in upon herself, pulling her knees to her chest and tucking her head down. Her hair spilled over her small legs and hid her face from Rowan's view. Unsure of herself, Rowan returned to her task at hand and focused on sending them back to Willow's clearing. She muttered her chants, mindful of the distraught girl hunched in the corner. She kept her eyes open, being so associated with the journey it did not require immense concentration and she was instead studying Eira as the cottage began its tremors. The girl seemed unbothered by the shaking, and Rowan wondered how familiar Eira was with this magic.

They landed soundly on the edge of the clearing, and at last, Eira raised her head, her eyes puffed and rimmed with red. Rowan started towards her, but Eira was up and at the door before Rowan had reached her. Rowan ached to help the girl, though she was unsure of her role in this; she longed for answers as to what was happening and was eager to confer with Willow. Following Eira out the door, she stopped short at the sight before her.

The trees were barren, their leaves had been dropped to the ground and were now covered by inches of ice and snow. Stepping forward, she flinched at the sickening crunch of the earth beneath her as the ice and leaves broke. Panic flooding her senses, she rushed toward the great tree at the other end of the clearing and saw the long weeping branches once filled with narrow willow leaves now replaced with hard, cold icicles. The clouds above cast a dull grey over the entire scape, adding an eeriness to the scene. The air was thick and heavy. There wasn't any wind to blow away the small crystalline ice structures hanging in the air. It appeared the world had frozen solid in an instant. She wrapped her arms around the broad trunk pressing her body against the tree. She scrunched her eyes closed against the tears that threatened to fall as the silence of the clearing grew to an almost deafening roar. Rowan squeezed the trunk impossibly tighter, softly murmuring a spell, pulsing her own magic into Willow, willing the dryad to awake from her frozen wooden slumber.

Sensing, rather than hearing, Eira behind her, she still held fast to the tree. Eira set a cold gentle hand upon Rowan's shoulder, and the touch seemed to wake her out of her stupor. Rowan instantly dropped her arms from Willow's base and stood there dejectedly.

Trying to remain hopeful, against all odds, she was reminded of Willow's final message to her, *let it freeze*. Rowan had brought the Arctic One here to help them save Nature, she hadn't ever imagined that Willow had meant for the clearing to freeze over. She had assumed the message was to find Eira, but now her intentions seemed laden with deceit. Had Willow known about this child, had she known it was Rowan's daughter? Rowan tried to recall ever learning the ways of skipping time, but she had not been taught. When learning to move the cottage, her teacher, the old Queen, had only instructed on the intricacies of skipping space, on how to land exactly where someone wanted; she had never spoken of landing *when* one wanted.

Rowan felt inexplicably lost, she grieved for Willow, not knowing if she, or anyone of Nature, could survive a freezing such as this, even herself. The longer she stood in the frozen tundra once full of sunlight and life, the more her power seemed to drain. Without the roots of Nature fueling her, she was sure to wither away as well.

The ice seemed to cut through every branch, each blade of grass, and even the tiniest stems of all the plants. She feared for the Spirits held within the flora, and the terror threatened to overtake her. She felt Eira's hand on her shoulder tighten, and finally looked over to meet the icy eyes that were almost identical to her own.

Waves of sadness overtook Rowan and she could not contain herself any longer. Tears broke out now flowing heavily and freely down her paling face. The frigid air threatened to freeze the tears, but Rowan did not succumb to the typical shivers. She felt a heat spread through her, erupting from Eira's nimble fingers pressing into her shoulder.

Staring into her piercing blue eyes, she saw a strength deep within Eira masked by a great tragedy.

They headed back to the cottage as the clouds above began to darken, night descending upon the clearing. If the frost could come, Rowan feared that the Dark Spirits would not be far behind. The cottage did not seem nearly as cozy or homey - to Rowan or Eira - as it once had; nevertheless, this was both of their homes, though Rowan did not know when it had become Eira's. Sitting upon the plush dark cushions of a small sofa in the open room, Rowan felt Eira grasp her hand tightly. She still had not taken her gloves off, and Eira's hands looked to be completely blue. Rowan tried to sense Eira's feelings but was blocked.

"Who taught you the Ways?" Rowan questioned, deciding to speak freely. She could only assess that Eira had been magicking Rowan out of her mind.

"My *Mamaí,* sorry, my moth-"

"I know what *Mamaí* means," Rowan interrupted Eira, smiling slightly at the fond name. "That language, that is not the tongue of the village. Where are you from?" Rowan continued her interrogation.

"I have only ever known the village, but *Mamaí* was not from there. The townsfolk would whisper when we came down, we looked too different," Eira said, looking down at her fingers twiddling anxiously.

Rowan removed her hand from Eira's and slipped her hide gloves off to reveal pale skin, nearly the same shade as the young girl's. Softly, Rowan cupped Eira's face and turned it towards her own, studying the delicate and pale features. The villagers all had strong jaws, dark eyes, and firm, wind burnt skin. Rowan questioned why some future, or past - she wasn't entirely sure how she was skipping time - self had taken her to a place where Eira would be even more on the outskirts of society.

"I am sorry, this must have been difficult. Did your mother," Rowan could not bring herself to utter her native tongue, "ever tell you where she was from?" she questioned, releasing her tender hold on Eira. Rowan was only slightly hopeful that Eira would say something different than the answer she dreaded.

"She was from an old country," Eira began. Rowan's heart dropped as she continued on, "it was destroyed long ago by a horrible fire carried on the wind."

Rowan knew exactly how that fire and wind had destroyed the land, leaving it desolate. The Dark Spirits had played their tricks, and

Rowan had pushed them away, blowing the blaze to the fields. Only a magicked clearing had survived, the clearing where the dryads had flooded, sealing off the outside world, encasing their pristine world. Rowan had to seek the counsel of the old Queen just to magic a way in, but it had all been worth it to see Willow.

Shaking herself out of her memories, she slightly nodded at Eira's worried look in understanding. Rowan couldn't imagine that Eira's mother, well that meant her, but she couldn't imagine any parent would have detailed that horrific and terrible fire.

"Who was your father?" Rowan finally asked the question that had haunted her since she had suspected that Eira could be her daughter.

Eira seemed surprised by the question, "I never knew my father. I never even thought to ask about him, honestly. *Mamaí* was enough. Better than enough, she was everything to me." Sadness crept into Eira's voice. The start of tears made her eyes resemble the waves of the ocean, a storm threatening to brew.

Rowan was as surprised by Eira's answer as the other girl had been by the initial question. Unsure of herself, Rowan did not ask the question she truly wanted to know, where was Eira's mother? She feared she knew the answer for Eira to have been alone on the mountains and the melancholy that was present.

"We can't be certain that you are my mother, even if I called you *Mamaí*, you just looked so much like her when you opened the cottage doors," Eira cut through Rowan's swimming thoughts. Rowan gave her a small, sad smile, but she did not entirely believe what Eira had said, and Rowan had a lingering thought that maybe Eira was trying to convince herself more so than Rowan.

"This was the cottage I grew up in, long ago, in an old forgotten country, that was destroyed by a great fire carried across the whole land by a fierce wind," Rowan spoke, watching the realization cross Eira's face as she had confirmed that she most likely was Eira's *Mamaí*. "*Mo leanbh*," Rowan began, gently running her hands through the ends of Eira's dark waves of hair, so matching her own that was pulled back away from her face, "I am sorry. I didn't mean to come to you like this. In fact, I'm sorry, I did not recognize you, nor can I tell you who your father is. I have not yet had the chance to meet a man I love," Rowan admitted to Eira.

"Where do you live?" Eira asked abruptly. Sensing Rowan's confusion at the question, she further explained, "I mean, you moved the cottage, and it was not ruined by the snow, where have you been?" she finished, genuine curiosity written plainly across her face.

"With my people. Us two are not the only ones trained in the Ways. There are many of us, and we live together, but only women can perform the Ways, so I have never met a man who has interested me in any way," Rowan answered Eira's question, though Rowan did not fully explain that she had fallen in love with a dryad and that she would never love a human man. Looking at Eira, Rowan questioned whether she could save Willow, and if she failed, whether or not that would push her into the arms of another.

"Can you take me there?" Eira asked, breaking Rowan out of her reprieve. Rowan shook her head, saddened by the news she would have to share with Eira.

"If the clearing, the truest form of Nature, is frozen, I cannot risk the others by taking this frost to them. I have been chosen to be their leader, and I will lead them properly, maintaining their safety," Rowan said, firmly, truly believing that she was choosing the safest decision for everyone: her people, Eira, and herself. As Eira's face fell, Rowan was quick to add, "I'm sure you will see it one day, only time will tell." This seemed to cheer the child up slightly. Rowan led her mind wander to the ladies. The others would want to help, and Rowan didn't want them to see Nature in this state, it would only frighten them. *No,* Rowan thought soundly, *I have to seek Nimue.* She spoke this aloud to Eira.

"Nimue?" Eira asked

"Ah," Rowan started, "it seems I did not train you in all of the Ways. Nimue is the Spirit of-"

"Memory, yes, I know," Eira interrupted. "I thought she was not to be trusted?" she finished, her voice raising at the end, as if it were a question.

Rowan's eyebrows shot up in astonishment, but she pondered the meaning. "You may be right. We cannot always trust our memories, though I don't know about Nimue. She is not on any one side, she is for herself, but I think she is our only chance at thawing Nature. She led me to you," Rowan said, remembering the night that was not so long ago for Rowan, though she had no clue how much time had truly passed since she visited Nimue to find the answer to Willow's command.

Rowan decided to rest in preparation for the journey. Moving the cottage so many times in such a short amount of time was taking its toll, not only on her magic, but also on her physical well-being. Eira took to her former room but found none of her previous belongings there. She was grateful that she had packed most of everything, including items she held dear that had belonged to her mother. Gently, she pulled a pale pink silken blanket from her pack, she clutched it tightly against her face and chest. Eira had the blanket since she was a child. It had been given to her mother, Eira smiled at the story her mother had told her about it.

"For the coming baby," an elderly woman had croaked to a young and frightened pregnant woman that had hiked down to the village from the mountains, alone. No one had seen her go up there, but everyone had noticed when she first came to their small town.

Eira had kept it close by her whole life, never sleeping without it tucked close to her side.

As she went about the room taking in the foreign setting, Eira set up a makeshift bed out of pillows and blankets Rowan had in an old chest Eira did not recognize. She realized this was Rowan's home more so than it was hers. Softly closing the door, she laid down, gripping the blankets tight around her, keeping the silken one closest to her heart. She knew the air was cold, but she was still unaffected by it.

Restlessly, she tossed and turned the whole night, feeling the Dark Ones lurking just beyond the barriers Rowan had set up. She longed to go to her mother's room and crawl into bed with her, but Eira knew that woman in there, Rowan, may look like her mother, but she did not act like her. It felt as if someone had taken over her mother's body but left a different soul within it. Eira was sure she could trust Rowan, she had sensed as much from her, but she thought that perhaps it was her mother's long-lost sister.

Yes, Eira thought to herself, letting out the breath she hadn't realized she was holding in, *she must be related to* Mamaí, *but she is not her.* These thoughts eased some of the tension and anxiety Eira had kept pent up, and she was able to sleep peacefully, if only for a few hours.

In the other room, Rowan slept soundlessly, until she was awoken by the inches of snow piling on the end of her bed. Her shivers shook her out of her slumber, and she sat up, frozen to the bone. She saw the snow floating down from the ceiling, but there were no holes or gaps in the roof. She arose out of her bed and wrapped a large crocheted blanket around herself. She went to the Fire Spirit still burning in the hearth, instantly feeling the warmth seep into her. Glancing about, she saw the Dark Ones peering through the windows, but the Ways held them at bay. Pulling the afghan tighter around herself, she looked towards the closed door down the hall, noticing a thick layer of ice forming.

Rowan couldn't help but laugh at Fate, he had granted her an Arctic One after she had burned an entire country; the irony was not lost on her, but what a funny man Fate must think he is. Rowan raised her hands to her mouth and quietly spoke a spell over them. She watched as they glowed ever so slightly orange, and then reached into the fireplace, pulling out the Spirit. Holding it close to herself, she walked down the short hallway, the ice melting away. Once the door was able, she opened it and saw the young girl laying on the haphazard pillows and blankets on the floor. Rowan felt a pang of sadness run through her. She had forgotten to magick Eira a proper bed.

Vanishing the Fire Spirit back to the hearth with a small flick of her hand, dismissing the glow from her hands as well. She carefully studied the girl. She couldn't have been more than fourteen, and Rowan thought that may have been pushing it. Eira was tossing in her sleep, snow piling up the more restless the girl became. Gently, Rowan eased herself to her knees next to Eira's dark curls, so matching her own. She ran a hand through them, noting how Eira relaxed at the motion and the snow then stopped falling. Rowan felt a strange pride that she was able to calm the girl. Mindlessly, she continued to stroke the girl's hair, letting the tendrils pull through her fingers. Rowan couldn't help but let her mind run free as she considered Eira's parentage. Rowan had always been surrounded by women, ever since she left her old country and joined the ladies of Nature. Her frequent trips to the clearing had led her to fall in love with the most beautiful creature she had ever seen, the dryad Willow. Rowan would never forget the day she met Willow.

Chapter Four

A Meeting of Lovers

Rowan had been nervous, the old Queen had been pushing her harder, making her jump further than ever before, but Rowan had finally succeeded. They landed with a resounding thud, dust billowing from the cottage. Triumphantly, Rowan exited the cottage with her head held high. Stepping out, she took in her surroundings. Huge trees towered over her, dwarfing Rowan and the Queen. Beneath their feet, flowers moved to avoid being trampled, and grass billowed. She had barely taken two steps out of the cottage before she saw her.

The most beautiful woman stood directly across the clearing. She stood taller than any human Rowan had ever seen. *She isn't human*, Rowan thought, suddenly realizing the woman looked just like a tree. Her hair fell down her nearly naked body, covering her breasts, but it wasn't truly hair, it was a multitude of fine branches covered by long and thin forest green leaves. The green was made even more prominent by her dark skin that looked to be composed of dark willow bark. Her nimble limbs moved gracefully as she twirled in the sun, dancing with the other dryads. Rowan hardly noticed any others, eyes fixed only on her.

The dryad moved elegantly in the most stunning display Rowan had ever had a privilege to lay eyes on. It was obvious to Rowan that she was leading the dance. At the center of it, she moved and others gravitated towards her, the rhythm ebbing and flowing in tandem with her. Her energy radiated, the allure overpowering Rowan's senses, and desire pooled deep within her.

Rowan started to make her way towards the woman but was stopped by a hand on her shoulder. She turned to see the Queen shaking her head at her. A blush flamed her cheeks, embarrassed at her loss of control by the dryad.

"You cannot approach them directly. You must be invited in," the Queen said disapprovingly in the strict manner Rowan had slowly grown accustomed to after their many journeys together.

Rowan nodded downheartedly, hating the scoldings that had been coming with increasing frequency. The more she worked with the Queen, the harsher the Queen became, and the more despondent

Rowan was. Her magic grew stronger though she felt the stress tearing her apart. She had glamored her features to mask the unrest that was painted on her face each day.

Staring at the delicate petals of the flowers near her feet, Rowan was oblivious to the dryad strutting towards them until she saw a dark hand gently grab her chin and raise her face. Rowan felt electricity course through her body at the touch of the woman's hand on her face and she couldn't help but let out a sharp gasp. Despite the appearance that the dryad's skin was made of the bark of a tree, the hand felt like satin as her lengthy fingers brushed her neck. The deep blush flooded Rowan's scarcely tanned skin, returning with a vengeance and easily showing due to her light complexion. The dryad's onyx eyes sparkled as they met Rowan's sapphire orbs and a beautiful smile painted her features. Rowan realized the woman was not nearly as tall now; instead, she stood even to Rowan, their eyes meeting seamlessly. Her ringlets of fronds still canopied her body from Rowan's glance, though Rowan was careful not to stare at the woman studiously watching her, as much as she longed to take in the breathtaking features before her.

The Queen broke Rowan out of her trance, "Willow," she addressed the dryad, bowing slightly. Rowan began to follow suit but was stopped by the hand still on her chin. The Queen raised out of her bow, ignoring Rowan's flustered state and Willow's smirk at being the cause of it. Willow nodded her regards back at the Queen.

"Queen of the Wiccans, you grace Nature with your presence. And you have brought someone along," Willow stated, staring at Rowan the entire time, curiosity burning in her charcoal eyes.

"We are not Wicc-"

"You are Wiccan enough," Willow interrupted the Queen, hesitantly stripping her eyes from Rowan's own, "and before you continue on to say you are not a Queen, you are a lady in charge, and I've even heard your students are referring to you as a Queen. You've grown to like it," Willow stated frankly. Her smirk grew as she teased the old Queen.

Rowan was confused by the term '*Wiccan*', she hadn't realized there was a name to what they were, only that they knew the Ways. She regarded what was said about the Queen, discovering that she did not know any other name to call the woman who had been her teacher for months now.

The Queen seemed flustered, though Rowan could not ascertain why. "You know why I am here. I do not have time to dawdle," she said. Rowan recalled that the Queen hated the games of Nature and their disregard to time, as they were not affected by it nearly as much as humans were.

Willow slowly lowered her hand from Rowan's face, tracing the outline of her neck, over her shoulder, dragging the end of her fingertips down the entirety of her arm. An almost unbearable burning heat traveled where Willow's fingertips danced on Rowan's pale skin. Rowan was sure that blisters would form from the coals that lived within those fingers. Shivers racked Rowan's body at the ghosting caress and her eyelashes fluttered shut, her breath becoming ragged. As the fingertips left her skin, an ice replaced that fire and she opened her blue eyes, now darkened to an indigo by desire. As she opened them, she saw humor dancing in Willow's obsidian orbs, and a playful grin pulling at the corners of her plump russet lips.

"What is your name, Wicca?" Willow questioned, genuine intrigue decorating her features.

Rowan opened her mouth, willing to comply with anything Willow asked of her, but before she could begin to speak, the Queen interjected. "She is not any of your concern."

Anger flared in Willow's eyes, and Rowan imagined flames erupted in the coal eyes, though, she wasn't sure how imaginary the fire was. Willow faced the Queen and leaned forward. She placed her hands on the woman's shoulders and pulled her closer, raised slightly on the end of her toes, Willow whispered directly into the Queen's ears, so Rowan could not hear what was said. Fear appeared to course through the Queen, a shudder closely following, before her olive skin paled drastically. She nodded when Willow withdrew.

Turning to face Rowan, Willow smiled in encouragement. "What is your name?" she repeated.

"I am Rowan," she said, her voice sounding more confident than Rowan felt. She was grateful that she did not betray the quaking she felt at being calculated by both Willow and the Queen. Willow beamed, and Rowan's heart melted at the sight of the most magnificent and stunning smile she had ever seen. Her own lips upturned on their own merit and she mirrored the brilliant smile. The Queen was not as happy.

"My apologies," the Queen whispered sadly and pulled Rowan away, "one moment." Willow inclined her head in approval before

Rowan was forced to look away from the dazzling view of Willow's grin, at the Queen's insistent grip on her.

"Yes, my Queen?" Rowan asked.

"I cannot stay here or with you any longer. You must complete your journey and I am not a part of it," the Queen said candidly and bluntly. Rowan was taken aback but knew better than to argue with the Queen. "You will stay in the clearing until Willow has instructed you to leave, then you will return to the Ladies of the Ways. You will be their leader."

That was the last Rowan ever saw of the Queen. She had walked into the dense forest surrounding them, and Rowan had remained to learn more of Nature.

Rowan returned to the clearing to see Willow dancing once more. This time, she let herself be taken over by the music made from the gentle breeze blowing through the leaves. Dryads surrounded them, singing along in an indecipherable language.

"Rowan!" Willow called out, grinning widely as she approached. Rowan quickened her pace and was enveloped by outstretched arms.

She swung her body to the beat of the song, the mood changing as other dryads drifted away.

"Where are they going?" Rowan asked. Willow seemed surprised, and looked around to see what Rowan was referring to.

"The magical hour is upon us," Willow responded, as if the answer were obvious.

"I'm confused," Rowan stated plainly. "The sun is not yet setting. How can it be the witching hour?"

Willow let out a chuckle. "You are so human, it's charming. We have never seen darkness before. The sun always shines, we know not of a witching hour, only of a *magical* hour," she said, emphasizing the word magical.

The bewilderment was painted on Rowan's face, the puzzlement in her shining blue orbs.

Willow reached out a hand, and Rowan happily took it. Drawing Rowan's body tight against her own, Willow pushed Rowan's hand down her body. Rowan closed her eyes as she felt the supple and smooth skin beneath her palm.

"I'll show you what magical hour is," Willow breathed seductively into Rowan's ear, sending shivers down her spine.

With her eyes still closed, Rowan felt Willow's plush lips pressing against her skin, sending shocks through her. She sighed as each kiss moistened her skin, and shivered as the wind cooled the heat left behind. Willow made her way to Rowan's own lips and pressed hers against them. The kiss was unlike anything Rowan had ever felt. It was like lightning had struck and caused a forest fire, the heat unmanageable and destroying all the dead foliage within Rowan. She felt alive.

Willow began to pull back, but Rowan's body finally responded, and her hands went to cup Willow's face, holding her to her own. Her lips moved frantically, trying to soak it all in. They kissed as if it was their last night to be together, even though it was their first.

During her many weeks with Willow, she fell even more in love with the dryad, and had come to truly appreciate the magical hours they shared. They spent every waking moment together and slept embracing one another beneath the constant sunshine that shone above the treetops.

212 — into the mystic

Chapter Five

A Journey of Memories

Eira stirred under Rowan's hand, waking Rowan out of her reverie. Eira blinked her eyes open, noticing the puddles around them.

"I'm sorry, when I have nightmares, I can't control my Ways," she apologized meekly.

"*Mo leanbh*," Rowan said softly, still stroking Eira's hair, "it is not your fault. We have a hard enough time controlling the Ways awake, we cannot expect our unconscious to comply, just yet."

"*Mama'i* would say that to me," Eira said, sadness creeping into her words.

Rowan stopped her motions through Eira's hair, realizing it was making the young girl worse. Standing, Rowan reached a hand down to Eira. The girl took it hesitantly, and Rowan pulled her to her feet and led her down the hallway. Eira looked frighteningly at the Dark Ones encroaching on the cottage.

"The only way to master the Ways, is to practice the Ways. Place your hands together, like this," Rowan instructed Eira, demonstrating to her how to place her hands in a prayer fashion, against her chest. "Good. Now, repeat after me," and Rowan led Eira through warding the cottage and pushing the Dark Ones away.

"I did it!" Eira exclaimed after the Ways were complete. She beamed with pride and Rowan couldn't help but feel overjoyed for the girl.

"Yes, you did. Watch closely, I'm going to move the cottage, and you should learn how." Rowan proceeded to go through the now familiar routine and transported the cottage.

Nimue jumped at the knocking on her door. It had been ages since anyone visited her; they just didn't want to remember anymore. Slowly, she made her way to the heavy wooden door, aged and decaying by the frost that had passed. She opened it without looking and was shocked to see the old Queen of the Wiccans, now thought long dead.

"Rowan?" she gasped, "how can it be?"

The woman, Rowan, looked identical to the night long ago when the Great Frost had begun. Even to Nimue, it seemed impossible that the girl was before her.

"Nimue?" Rowan questioned. Nimue nodded in response, unsurprised that this Rowan would not recognize the decrepit woman before her. "What happened?" The woman asked her, though Nimue could not answer her, she was just as confused.

"Well, you should come in, standing out in the cold won't do you any good," Nimue said, stepping aside to let Rowan enter. Nimue was even more shocked when a young girl, nearly identical to Rowan stepped in, close to Rowan's side. As she began to shut the door, she saw that the ground they had been standing on was devoid of all ice; in fact, the grass was beginning to poke out again.

"Who are you?" she questioned the child, who could not have been older than fourteen, practically a babe compared to Nimue.

"This is the Arctic One," Rowan answered for her. At the same time, the girl spoke.

"Eira." Rowan grimaced at the girl's word, knowing Nimue would be able to read more deeply into the name.

"*Snow?*" Nimue asked in an ancient language, magic washed over Eira as she did. Nimue welcomed the knowledge, letting the true name sink into her, reading the girl's short memories. In them, she saw Rowan, though she looked nearly as aged as Nimue was now. She shuddered as the Book of Xeo called out to the child and erased The Ways from her, embedding the Frost into her heart and soul. She felt the hurt within the girl as her mother died, and the even worse pain of seeing Rowan, a woman who did not recognize her, but appeared to be her own mother. Deeper, she sensed a powerful life force strengthening the girl, though Nimue was blocked from reading any farther. Nimue hadn't a clue who had placed the obstacle, but she sensed Nature was at work. As she opened her eyes, Nimue saw Rowan kneeling beside the girl, holding Eira to her chest, tears rolled down the child's face from reliving the memories with Nimue.

"*Tree,*" Nimue spoke in the same language she had used previously with Eira, Rowan reluctantly met the old woman's eyes, and Nimue was flooded with her memories, though she knew she had seen them long before. Flashes of an old Queen danced in her head, mingled with flares of passionate kisses and intimate desires which ignited her soul. A vast sense of protection and pride flooded her as she saw the child, *mo leanbh,* accurately perform the Ways, casting aside the Dark Ones. As Nimue fluttered her eyes open, she realized a block had been put in Rowan's memory, by Nimue herself. Decidedly, she removed the obtrusive device, and she watched as realization dawned on Rowan's face.

"My Queen?" asked Rowan, dazed at the realization. Nimue proudly nodded her head.

"You wouldn't agree to be my apprentice any other way. It wasn't even my idea, it was Willow's," Nimue answered the questions Rowan had not yet asked.

"Willow? I hadn't met her then," pain rushed over Rowan's face, as Nimue recalled their most recent journey to the clearing.

"Ah, you silly girl," Nimue admonished her, "you have been there so many times, you are lucky Willow can remember you, with all your skipping. I don't think you've ever been there linearly. Each time you move that cottage, you are moving the space around you, yes. But you are also moving the time, it's a simple word you add in each time." Nimue knew from Rowan's memories that she had been the one to teach her that extra word, but Rowan had not remembered the original incantation, instead, she defaulted to moving space and time. Quiet enveloped them as Rowan pondered Nimue's words.

Eira was the first to break the silence. "How is she moving space and time? I thought we moved the cottage?"

"Oh, what a sweet naïve child," Nimue said, belittling affection in her tone, which Rowan did not appreciate. "The cottage has never moved, it is still standing in its original form, on the edge of an old country, long burnt away," she said, shooting a pointed look at Rowan. "The owner of that cottage simply moves the space around it to arrive at the location they want. As a matter of fact, that owner moved it accidentally the first time, landing at Nature's purest place. They took in the scared child, and Willow cared for the girl, only a young sapling at the time herself, until the girl's powers were too much for any of them to help with. They called me to take away the painful memories, and I took the girl to the ladies of the Ways, the Wiccans, and they had me be their Queen for a time, to train the girl, as none of them could reel in her powers. Willow told me that when the girl was finally able to come back to Nature and speak her true name, then she could control the Ways and I could return to what I do best, memories."

Rowan's face had continuously grown pale at Nimue's explanation, memories haunted the edges of her mind, clawing their way to the forefront, but each time, Rowan felt herself push them away, almost as a reflex. Rowan had known all of this, but she had chosen to keep it all pushed aside.

"Nimue," Rowan finally spoke, her voice barely audible, "what happened?" She asked again.

Understanding Rowan's meek question, she began the story. "It has been many ages now since you came to me clutching a leaf with Willow's scratchy handwriting." Rowan turned her nose up at the small insult, but Nimue didn't seem to care. "The message was not only to find the Arctic One, but to also prepare ourselves for the Great Frost that would come if you had not. You never returned, though I can see now that you did, it was just not the right time. Nature could not withstand the cold, and the ladies who protect could no longer draw their powers from Nature, as I'm sure you have noticed," she directed towards Rowan, who nodded in agreement. "The Wiccans couldn't survive without Nature, nor could Nature survive without its ladies, especially without its Queen. Since you never returned to choose the next leader, the ladies fell into chaos, forgetting the Ways. The Dark Ones set in, taking the energy from everything. I was forbidden from going to aid Nature, Willow would not allow it. She said I had to remain here, because you would come back. My own magic has depleted just warding this place from the Dark Ones. I have aged, which I have not done in some eons. Though the rate of aging seems to have increased," she said, her eyes scanning her own body dejectedly. "The Great Frost has set in, and you have returned with the Arctic One. Though, I do have to ask, are you actually her mother?" Nimue finished, leaving her question hanging amongst the three women.

Rowan let the past sink into her. She felt wholly responsible for what had happened, since she could not fully control *when* she landed. She contemplated Nimue's question, though she felt that they both knew the answer.

Meeting Nimue's eyes, she nodded her head in affirmation, gravely, not remembering the child's birth, or knowing the father. Nimue softly nodded back, in as comforting a fashion as she could manage.

Eira was looking at her feet on the floor, refusing to meet either woman's eyes. Inaudibly, she muttered, but Nimue had been carefully watching the child, and not much could escape the old woman, especially in her own home.

"You have to stop the Frost from coming, though I believe if we get to the right time, I can help with that," Eira seemed shocked that she had been heard. She hadn't meant to ask what her role was aloud.

Nimue gave a pointed look to Rowan. "Do you think you could concentrate enough to go back to the correct time?" she asked, the old Queen's attitude apparent in her words.

Rowan stood, pulling her shoulders back proudly. "When shall we go back?"

"The day before you came to visit me. However, I am not sure if that would have been immediately after you received Willow's message. I sense that she knows more about this than even I do," Nimue said, the latter mainly to herself. Slowly raising herself to her feet, Nimue walked over to Rowan, grabbing the girl in a fierce hug. "We have lost so much, though I fear you may lose more. Blessed be, Rowan." She pulled back, tears brimming in her ancient eyes.

Rowan was taken aback by the sudden display of affection by the rigid woman, and Nimue had pulled away before Rowan could respond. Almost out of habit, she returned the saying, "Blessed be, Nimue."

"Eira?" Nimue said, her voice raising at the end, almost like a question, "You'll know how to find me when the time comes."

Eira only nodded, Rowan was unsure of what Nimue meant, but thought it better not to question the elder woman.

Leaving Nimue's house, Rowan and Eira made their trek back to the cottage, both silent at the many revelations Nimue had unloaded on to them. Both felt as if they were carrying the weight of the world. They entered the stony cottage, and Rowan began the incantation to move. Not only did she concentrate on the picturesque clearing of Nature's perfect form, but also the time, the day she went to see Nimue on the peripheral of her mind. Eira paid close attention, noting the additional word spoken to move time as well. Eira could clearly remember her mother aiding her in the Ways and the many spells she had memorized. It seemed her memories could be trusted after all.

Rowan was anxious as she exited the cottage, truly afraid of what she could find there. Stepping out, she barely contained herself from sprinting across the open field, painted with blooming flowers and sprouting seedlings. Straight ahead, Willow, as beautiful as ever, danced in the sunlight.

As if Willow could sense Rowan's presence, the most bewitching smile erupted over her face, joy sparkling in her eyes as they met

Rowan's. Relief pooled in Rowan's entire body, followed closely by the immense love she felt for the dryad. In the back of her mind, she could not ever imagine loving a man quite the way she loved Willow, leaving the question unanswered as to who could be Eira's father.

Willow gracefully strutted over, meeting Rowan halfway. She had chosen to be the shorter today, Rowan's favorite. Pulling her tight against her own body, Rowan cradled Willow's head close to her breasts, placing a kiss amongst the swirling tendrils of jade hair, a leaf tickling her face as she did. She breathed deeply, trying desperately to flood all of her senses with Willow.

"My love, you were just here yesterday, to what do I owe the pleasure?" Willow asked, wholesome jubilation illustrated across her features.

Rowan racked her fuzzy memories to recall the day Willow was referring to, and her thoughts must have been displayed clearly on her face, because Willow's own smile fell as she watched Rowan.

"Ah, you've done it again, haven't you?" she asked, and Rowan was staunchly reminded of every time Willow had asked that very same question, always puzzling Rowan, until now.

"I'm so sorry, Willow," Rowan apologized, "I never realized I was skipping time." She brushed the ringlets out of Willow's face and caressed her face gently. "Oh, how much hurt I must have caused you."

At her apology, Willow's face evolved, comprehension replacing the sadness. "You know?"

"Yes, I have found the Arctic One. I have been to Nimue, the old Queen, and I have traveled through many centuries. I had to save you," Rowan quickly explained, knowing that Willow had knowledge that was beyond her own. Tears brewed in Willow's eyes as she reached up to hold Rowan's face, enclosing her pale face with her own dark palms. Rowan reveled in the silken fingers spreading over her cheeks, emotion threatening to overtake her as she was overwhelmed with love for Willow.

"You won't save me," Willow whispered, sadness swimming in her voice.

Dread filled Rowan, had she indeed failed?

"You'll save her," Willow continued, pulling away and motioning to the young girl that stood marveling in the sights around her.

Rowan's heart flipped in her chest, pain rippling out through her body. She had never been more conflicted. Willow had outright said she wouldn't be saved, but they would save Eira, who would save Nature.

"Won't the child save you?" Rowan whispered, aware of all the plants listening to them.

Willow began to answer, but she stopped herself. "Eira?" She called out to the girl. Looking up, she smiled. Rowan realized with a pang; it was one of the first real smiles she had seen on the girl's face. Willow gestured for her to come over, and she complied, though the walk was slow, as Eira was taking in all of her surroundings.

Rowan was aware of how truly amazing this place was, especially for one who had grown up smothered in snow and ice; Eira never would have glimpsed a fraction of this flora. Eira's sapphire doe eyes glimmered in the sunshine, her skin appeared ivory and iridescent, refracting the sunlight and finally losing the blue hue. She radiated warmth and appeared genuinely happy. Rowan struggled with why she had been in the mountains in the first place.

Eira came to a stop in front of Willow, taking in her figure, which may have seemed strange to someone not familiar with dryads, but Eira did well to hide any shock. Willow gave the girl a friendly smile.

"Eira, I have a task for you," Willow started, ignoring the anxious glare Rowan was shooting at her. Willow continued when Eira nodded, causing Willow's smile to widen. "I need you to go to the edge of those trees," she gestured to the grand weeping willow, her own home, "and ward off the Dark Ones and the frost, can you see them creeping in?" she asked, and Rowan watched as Eira's eyes grew at the sight of the impending ice crystals cutting into the tree.

"I'll try my best," Eira responded.

"That's all we need, child," Willow reassured her.

They watched as Eira went over to the tree and wrapped her arms around it, just like Rowan would. Willow smirked at Rowan's astonishment at the identical movements but grabbed her hand and led her away from the clearing, in the opposite direction Eira had gone.

"That should take her a bit," Willow said, watching Rowan closely.

"Do you know who she is?" Rowan asked suddenly.

"Yes. She is you," Willow began, changing course at Rowan's frightened state. "And she is not. You humans are too complex. Plants are simpler."

"Until they aren't," Rowan teased the dryad.

"Until they aren't," agreed Willow. "She is your offspring, genetically the same, but there is a different spirit in her. Can you sense it?" Her voice dropped at the end, making the question nearly inaudible.

Rowan stood very still, eyes shut, magicking her mind through the trees, back across the clearing, and into the spirit of the child. Eira was unaware, this was not the same as Nimue's magic, she would not have to feel a thing. Rowan pawed through, but when her eyes flickered open, there was only confusion.

"I only sense Nature," admitted Rowan.

"Who's Nature?" Willow let the question slip out.

Rowan shook her head, not allowing the thought to take root. It couldn't be, it *can't* be.

"Rowan, my love." Willow stepped towards her, reading the pain crossing her face as plain as the sun crossed the sky. "You knew this would happen; you've always known."

Rowan evaded Willow's outstretched hand. She tried to stop the memories flooding her, but she couldn't.

Chapter Six

A Measure of Love

The stars had twinkled over their heads. They had left the clearing, going away to their own private oasis, a place where Willow was finally able to see the moon and stars. Their limbs were entangled, sweat still glistening in the moonlight. Rowan watched as Willow's chest heaved from exertion, matching her own. The close proximity caused Rowan's heartbeat to thunder in her ears. She could just barely hear Willow's soothing breaths over the waves coursing through her veins. Their scents were thick in the air and Willow's arousal struck Rowan's nostrils, reigniting the waning passion in Rowan, but it was stopped as she met Willow's eyes. Sorrow pooled in the obsidian orbs, and stout tears cascaded down her smooth cheeks.

"Willow? What is the matter?" Rowan questioned, terrified to her core that she had done something to hurt the woman she loved.

Willow let out a sad chuckle, wiping away the tears that were readily replaced. "I am only thinking. The stars tell me too much."

"What do they say?" Rowan asked, mindlessly stroking a pattern on Willow's arm.

"You should read them. Tell me what they say," instructed Willow, knowing Rowan's training would have included the ancient magic.

Reluctantly turning away, Rowan stared at the stars above until her vision blurred at the edges. Scenes began to play, displaying the future. Rowan saw Willow, stuck in her tree, ice seeping into the trunk and destroying the very being of her. She saw all of Nature, frozen solid, without anyway to unfreeze. The ladies of Nature laid dead, unable to protect themselves from the Dark Ones that lurked constantly. Rowan did not see herself anywhere, nor did she sense any living creature. The Frost had consumed it all.

Tears now freely pouring down her own face, she opened her blue eyes to meet Willow's black ones, matching her own only in the despair they held.

"Willow, everyone will be gone. The air is already growing colder. It's coming now, isn't it?" Rowan finally spoke.

"Yes," Willow bleakly responded. Silence flooded them, even the surrounding flora and fauna were quiet, heavy with the impending future.

"I know how to stop it," whispered Willow, sitting up and turning her back to Rowan.

"Then we must," Rowan said decidedly.

"The idea will upset you," uttered Willow, still not facing Rowan.

"You cannot speak for me," Rowan said, hurt by Willow pushing her away.

Willow turned at this, hearing the pain in Rowan's voice. "I know you. I know every part of you. Your body.," Willow said, so much passion inflected in her voice, Rowan couldn't help but shiver. "I know every inch of your mind. I know you will not like it."

"I may surprise you," tried Rowan, conscious that Willow was most likely correct.

"There is a child, born of Nature and a Wiccan, who will be able to control the cold. She can stop the Frost and the Dark Ones," explained Willow.

"This doesn't sound too bad. What else aren't you telling me?" Rowan implored.

"It will be our child," murmured Willow, almost unwilling to tell Rowan.

"How can a dryad have a Wiccan child?" continued Rowan.

"You would carry the child. She would be human, with the soul of Nature."

"The soul?" Rowan asked. Willow refused to meet Rowan's eyes, and realization dawned upon her. No Willow, I won't let you," argued Rowan. "You can't sacrifice yourself." Desperation poured out of Rowan.

"We must.," Willow responded, desolate at Rowan's distress. "You know we must."

"When?" demanded Rowan.

"You said so yourself, the air is growing colder." Willow trailed off.

"Now? You expect me to do this now?" Rowan's voice raised, nearly to a shout.

"You can visit me whenever; you can skip time. I will always be with you," insisted Willow.

"It won't be the same, you will be a fragment of my memory. I can't love you how I do now. I can't be with you," cried Rowan.

"You will still love me. You will get to love a child. We must, Rowan. I can't allow Nature to be gone, for all the Wiccans to be gone. We cannot let the Darkness win," declared Willow.

Rowan sat defeated. She knew Willow was right, in more ways one. She did not like this idea, but it was entirely necessary.

"The child can stop the Frost?" Rowan ensured.

"She'll have help." Willow tried to reassure her.

"I don't want to know this. I want to raise her without this depression," said Rowan, determination setting in.

"Nimue said you would. She has a small fruit, when eaten, it erases what the mind deems too heavy for the heart. You can eat it whenever you want," offered Willow.

"Where will you go?" asked Rowan.

"I am not sure. The tree will remain, and my spirit, the Nature of my being, will be in the child. I think that is all I am," she said softly.

"You are so much more," Rowan stated, never surer of herself. She grabbed Willow's face, pulling it to her own. She rested her forehead against the dryad's, not realizing that tears were streaking paths on her pale face.

Wiping away her tears; Willow gently kissed Rowan. Tears still swimming down her face Rowan returned the kiss with a fiery passion that now ignited her soul.

Willow let out a tiny gas gasp and Rowan took the opportunity to bring her to slip her tongue between Willow's lips claiming her mouth as her own. Willow happily obliged and let Rowan take the lead, laying back on their flower petal bed. Willow's head was caught by Rowan's hand before it could hit the ground and being as gentle as she could, she laid her down, falling onto Willow.

Gasps of breath escaped them both, soft moans following suit. Rowan ran her hands over Willow's entire body, wanting to commit every detail to memory. One hand came to rest on Willow's supple breast, and Rowan rolled the tip between her fingers, eliciting the most beautiful sound from Willow. Rowan moaned in response, and ground her hips against Willow's, desperate for contact. Willow widened her legs, and one of Rowan's thighs came to land between them. Raising her hips, Willow thrust against the contact, urging for more. Rowan was more than accommodating and started to kiss down Willow's body. She stopped at her breasts, kissing and suckling on the mounds, only furthering Willow's growing need and deepening her own desire.

Continuing, Rowan ran her tongue along Willow's soft skin down to the place Rowan most desired to taste. She leaned back, taking in the delicate folds and sensitive nub that begged to be savored. Rowan licked her own lips in anticipation. Meeting Willow's eyes, she saw the dryad bite her supple lip, and Rowan couldn't stop herself if she had wanted to.

Flicking her tongue out, she ran it along the entirety of Willow's folds, memorizing each crevice within them. She persisted with these movements, adding pressure as she reached the peak. Willow's head was thrown back, her lithe fingers entangled in Rowan's silky waves, keeping her head in place, though Rowan wouldn't want to leave. Rowan added her fingers, stroking Willow, and entered her. She moved her fingers inside of Willow, feeling her walls tighten. Willow's hips bucked against Rowan's hand, urging her fingers deeper and raising her face. Their eyes met and Rowan saw the hunger dwelling. Rowan quickened her pace with her hand, and she watched as Willow came undone.

It was one of the most magnificent sights. Willow's eyes rolled back, her mouth agape and her chest heaved from labored breaths. Each breath came out as a moan, the volume rising to a crescendo as Willow reached her peak. Her tension snapped and her body caved, falling back to the ground causing petals to flow out. As her breathing returned to normal, Rowan climbed her way back up to hold her body as close to hers as allowed, barely leaving any room between them.

Squeezing Willow, Rowan felt slow tears rolling off Willow's face onto her chest. She held back the sobs that threatened to take over. The future weighed heavy on them both, the impending task hanging over their head. Neither dared to kill the silence that stalled every creature. A short distance from their secluded area, the dryads had stopped singing in the sunshine, their dances halted.

"Darling, the stars are moving faster," Willow whispered, though it sounded like shouting in the quiet reprieve of the night. The world awakened with Willow's words, the crickets chirping, the leaves rustling. Rowan still held her breath, longing for the silence again.

"I'm not ready," Rowan finally murmured back, misery seeping into her voice. She buried her face in Willow's tendrils, which tickled her lips. Rowan clutched Willow close to herself, relishing in the feeling.

"No one is ever ready to let go," said Willow, "I don't believe I am quite ready to leave, if that's what I'm doing. Though, I don't think I am. I will be here," she spoke, looking around. "And I will be with the dryads. And I will be with you," she finished, caressing her hand along Rowan's cheek.

Rowan placed her hand over Willow's own that laid upon her cheek. "Forever?" she asked.

"And ever," Willow responded with a finality.

Rowan tried to prepare herself, but when the time arrived, she still felt as if it were too sudden. They had stayed together wrapped up in each other, as long as they could, but Willow was right, time kept moving, and the cold was creeping in. No matter how soon the child was born, they would still need to age, to learn, and to master their abilities. Rowan worried they would be too late, though Willow assured her.

"Time is easily malleable," Willow told Rowan when she voiced these concerns. "Wiccans have been manipulating time as long as they have been protecting Nature." And Rowan believed her, fully and wholly. She had to, in order to move forward and to raise the child, to protect all of Nature, not just the one piece she loved.

But the time finally came. It hadn't been decided upon officially, but both felt it. Rowan secured the fruit from Nimue within her cottage, memorizing its location, knowing she would seek it out if it was necessary. They left their sanctuary together, walking hand in hand. Leaving the clearing behind them, they walked out of the moonlight towards the sunshine. As they walked, the sunrise followed them, painting the sky with burning oranges, bright pinks mixing with the bluest sky that matched Rowan's eyes brimming with tears. The sky turned from black to blue the further they walked. Rowan kept her eyes on Willow's only staring at the depths of her ebony pools, reflecting the stars and moon disappearing.

Willow stopped them both once they reached the edge of the field, next to her towering tree she called home. She turned, facing Rowan. She held both of Rowan's hands in her own, looking into one another's eyes. The vast blue sea met the infinite night sky in their eyes. Leaning forward, Willow captured Rowan's lips with her own. Rowan returned the kiss, both trying to convey the love without speaking, it felt too heavy for words.

They finally parted, both failing at keeping the tears at bay. Standing under the weeping branches of the grand willow tree, Willow brought Rowan over to the wide trunk. Together, they placed their palms against the tree, allowing both their souls, the very essence of their being, to enter the tree.

Their souls wound about each other, interlacing and tangling together. Each action became paralleled and mirrored, everything they did in tandem. They breathed each other in, taking every ounce into each other, becoming one, as if their parts were destined to be together. Their essences mixed, ebbing and flowing together and apart, until finally, Willow placed every fiber and piece of herself into Rowan, making two into one completely.

Rowan's soul left the tree, and she stood beneath the branches alone. She felt full inside her body, the weight of Willow's life filling her to the brim. Closing her eyes, Rowan set out to find Willow inside herself, but she couldn't. She dropped to her knees, breaking down as deep sobs wracked her body. She pulled her arms tight around her body, desperately trying to hold herself in one piece.

Minutes, or perhaps hours, passed, and Rowan's tears subsided. She stood and went to the cottage, searching out the plant Nimue had provided. Eating it, she felt her sadness ease, the most painful memories escaping.

Crying, Rowan's thoughts returned to the present. Willow stood before her, studying the pain displayed on Rowan's features. She reached out and placed her palm gently against Rowan's pale face, her nimble fingers cupping her chin and reaching around her neck. Her thumb rubbed gentle circles around Rowan's rosy lips.

"What now?" questioned Rowan, tears still freely flowing. She leaned into Willow's touch, savoring the feeling so much more now that she had relived the loss.

"The time has not yet approached, you're a bit early, my love," Willow answered. "All the better. Eira can do this, and you can help."

"Help? What can I do?" Rowan intrigued.

"She will need strength, both physically and emotionally. You are her mother, she trusts you," responded Willow.

Rowan met Willow's eyes, with a tear-stained face and drying eyes. "You are her mother, too," Rowan retorted.

This seemed to amaze Willow. "Yes, I do suppose I am," she pondered. "Although," she continued. "I do not believe I could provide anything of substance to the child, she holds my soul. You are the only one who could bolster me."

Before Rowan could consider this, Eira approached them, the Dark Ones gone, and the frost with them. She looked utterly pleased with herself, and pride surged through Rowan. She knew then, she would help Eira conquer all, no matter the consequences.

Rowan turned to Willow, determination filling her eyes. "Where do we go?"

Chapter Seven

A Power of All

Rowan set out with Eira, bundled in the same furs and leathers she had worn when the two had first met. Unaffected by the cold, Eira's skin was almost hidden by the surrounding snow. They ventured to the highest peak of their land, right by where the cottage had been when Eira left. Rowan felt as if her powers were depleting just by being in the tundra, whereas Eira flourished. The girl was prancing, skipping and swaying as they climbed, powered by the thickening ice and snow.

The wind blew a great gust, causing Rowan to pull her clothes tighter around her. Ahead of her, Eira closed her eyes, arms spread, soaking in the frigid air. With the wind, came flecks of snow that stuck to the ends of Eira's dark locks. Each speck that touched Rowan seemed to absorb more of her essence, draining her energy.

They approached the summit of the heavy snow-laden mountain tops. A small plateau stretched before them. Eira seemed to thrive with the feet of ice beneath their feet and Rowan had never felt more drained nor emptier. Her life seemed to edge away the longer they stood upon the sleet, Nature buried beneath the snow packed ground, with it, Rowan's connection to her powers.

She hadn't heard Eira's question, nor realized the child was speaking to her until the girl laid a gentle hand on her arm.

"*Mamaí?*" asked Eira, worry spilling from her lips.

"Do not fret, *mo leanbh*, you must focus," reassured Rowan, though she did not quite believe herself. She began to instruct Eira on how to proceed. "Place your hands as deep in the snow as you can. Feel for the source of the ice, for its fingers stretching out and choking the roots of Nature. Can you sense it?" The young girl nodded in affirmation. Rowan continued. "Good. Now pull it back. Bring it into yourself, as if you are the tree and the ice is your roots."

Sweat glistened on the child's head, exertion apparent. Rowan stepped close to the girl, placing her hands on the small shoulders before her. Closing her own eyes, she pulled in a deep breath, and concentrated on the Nature that dwelled beneath the thick layers of ice. Eira's tension began to ease, the child was better able to pull her own power from within. Rowan could just barely sense Nature flourishing in the sun, many miles away in the pristine clearing.

Rowan reached further still, trying to grab hold of something tangible. She yearned for the calming presence of Willow but stumbled when the painful memories resurfaced. Beneath her hands, Eira lost her grip at Rowan's mishap, and the ice expanded once more.

The girl broke down in tears, ashamed that she had just made it all much worse.

"No, no, *mo leanbh*. You're doing it. We can do this," Rowan tried to say it as convincingly as she could, though her own weakness made her voice sound small and meek on the grand mountaintop.

Eira cried out in pain, the ice had begun creeping into her, crackling inside bursting her vessels. Her hands were as hard as stones, and as blue as the sea. Seeing this, Rowan grew more determined, and pushed aside her own worries, concentrating on filtering her power to Eira.

The ice crept forward, but Eira felt rejuvenated with Rowan's hands pressing into her shoulders, urging her on. Clenching her fists, grasping the earth beneath her, she shut out everything focusing only on the cold.

It swirled in her veins; the very essence of ice was *her*. Eira remembered the passages she had read from the Book of Xeo. In her deepest memories, as if it had been hidden from her, laid the answer.

"*Gread leat,*" Eira's voice boomed out. The ice retreated from the earth and encircled Rowan and Eira.

The cold cut through Rowan's thick leathers, chilling her to the bones and making her blood stand still. Eira stood and turned to face Rowan.

"You cannot claim my *Mamaí* for yourself. *Imithe,*" she commanded, and a great shriek rang out and the ice stood still.

Rowan let out a breath she hadn't realized had been held, and the world shattered around them. The Frost crackled beneath their feet, sprouts shot out, awakened from their frozen slumber.

"I am so proud, *mo leanbh*. You did it," Rowan praised Eira, and Eira could barely stop the tears of relief as she was pulled into a tight hug.

Eira landed the old cottage, or rather, the world stopped moving around her. Years of trembling had worn down the bricks. She opened the beaten down wooden door and stepped out onto the plush grass. The dahlias, lilies of the valley, and daffodils moved away from her impending and foot as she walked across to the edge where the heavy forest encircled the open field. They huffed in anger at the effort, causing Eira to smirk at the dramatic dryads within them.

She walked purposefully to the towering tree, with its broad trunk wider than her outstretched arms. Its branches hung low, some of the leaves tickling the grass beneath. Once she was covered by the weeping leaves, Eira knelt by the bottom of the trunk. She placed her hands against the earth, feeling the thrumming of life all around her, but sensing the emptiness from the willow tree. Eira let her tears run free and bowed her head, resting her forehead against the rough, black bark of the massive trunk.

Pressing a gentle kiss to the tree, she spoke softly. "Thank you, *Mamaí*."

The Witch of the Margins

deadwoodpecker

CHAPTER ONE

I t stormed over most of the kingdom the day Nerissa learned of the princess's curse – her *other* curse. The rain spattered against the stone walls of the forgotten lighthouse and the howls of the wind were louder than the low cries from the white and crimson cormorants that made their home here. Nerissa could *hear* the storm perfectly well, but the enchantments that protected the peninsula from the elements didn't allow a single raindrop inside. It was warm, cozy even, and Nerissa allowed herself a moment of contentment as she sat on a low stone wall overlooking a private, secluded cove. She was somewhat far from her lighthouse today, having wandered to the ruins of what had once been a stately manor.

One of her cormorants chose that moment to arrow in; water sluiced from its wings and dripped cold water onto Nerissa. It gave a rather human-like cry, dropped a crimson feather with a lock of hair twined around it in her lap, then waited, head cocked and wings pumping, for a reply.

"Well, well, well," said Nerissa. "They have not yet forgotten me after all. Would that they had." Then, shrugging, she made to set the feather aside. She took little interest in the comings and goings of the kingdom; there were much more interesting things to concern herself with: the tides changing their patterns due to interference from the ladies of the moon, the seasons growing cooler decade by decade, the storms – such as the one building over ocean right now as she watched – bringing smells Nerissa had never before tasted on the wind. These things were enough and more to occupy her. What need was there to obsess over the humans?

The cormorant bridled and screeched again.

Nerissa brought the gift closer to her, studying it carefully. *Not a gift*, she reminded herself. *A summons.* The cormorants liked humans less than she did. Years had passed since the last time a seabird had brought her a similar message and even longer years since Nerissa deigned to reply. Never had one of her companions demanded she pay attention to one of them.

Years and years.

Her fingertips brushed over the pale strands.

The hair was so pale a blonde it was almost white. There was very little variation in the color of human hair and skin. The gods had made the creatures from dust and mud. As true creatures of the earth, their coloring reflected that from the deepest brown to the palest cream. Only their eyes could reflect the colors of sea and sky. The whiteness of the lock of hair before her was not a surprise; this was in the normal range of human color. It was the hints of blue and purple that surprised her to her core. She brought it up to her face and inhaled deeply the scent of brine.

"The princess is here," Nerissa said. It was unnecessary. Her eyes lifted to the cormorant. There was an imperious tilt to its head, and its beak snapped open and closed. The cormorant knew perfectly well who it was who summoned Nerissa for aid.

She looked out to the sea again. The problem that had vexed her for months now receded in importance. A rogue wave barreled against the cliff, splashing both her and the hovering cormorant. Neither one reacted and the wave slunk back into the sea, ignored.

There was a small grey apron draped over a low table. In the pocket were two wands made of driftwood and ambergris; Nerissa drew them, feeling them grow heated in her hands. When they were hot and smelled of bonfires, sand, and sea, Nerissa painted three sigils in the sky in front of her. It parted like a curtain. Before, the peninsula had looked deserted of anything but the lighthouse, the cliffs, and the cormorants. Nerissa reminded it that there had once been a road here before she'd hidden it with enchantments.

It's more of a path, Nerissa corrected herself. She followed it. It was more moss than cobblestone, but she still followed its spiraling path. It led down the hill behind the lighthouse. Rain began to fall: the storm Nerissa had been watching became one she experienced. Drops of water arrowed onto her shoulders and a cold wind blew her skirts around her legs.

"Oh, it's you!" The bright, cheerful voice halted Nerissa in her tracks.

The princess stepped out from under a sheltering tree just at the edge of Nerissa's domain. With the rain and wet smearing the forest and road together, she looked as though she were standing against a painted backdrop. It had been a long journey from the city and she looked the worse for it, having been out in the storm. Her simple, capped-sleeved dress clung to her, revealing all of her curves, and her pale hair hung in damp strands over her bodice.

There was a parasol in her hand. It was ruined by rain and wind, and must not have been much protection even before the elements had got to it: it was a gauzy, lacy thing. Despite the fact it was little more than a rag hanging from a stick, the princess still held it as an umbrella. Water drops glistened at the ends of the long, dark lashes that framed her eyes – her slightly too wide, slightly too blue eyes.

And yet for all that she looked miserable, the expression with which she greeted Nerissa was that of open, genuine warmth. Looking at her, Nerissa felt a pang of hurt deep inside.

"—much younger than I expected! The way people tell it, I thought you must be an old crone! Oh, I do hope that isn't rude. I always worry I've been rude, but it's only *after* something has come flying out of my mouth. And I've come to ask you a favor! Please tell me I haven't insulted you!"

Her gushing speech gave Nerissa enough time to catch her breath.

"I am not insulted," Nerissa told her.

"I haven't forgotten the formal request," the princess assured her. Then, drawing herself up to her full height, she said: "I ask sea and sky and stone to grant me leave to make my request. Hear me, my lady, and be merciful."

There was a small area that blended the boundaries between Nerissa's domain and the human world. It was a deliberate mix of magic and mundane. It was in these marginal spaces – the space between sea, sky, and earth – that Nerissa thrived. A sapphire cormorant stood atop a cairn – to the untrained eye, it appeared real enough to be about to take flight. It took a moment to realize it, too, was made of stone. It was a place created precisely for a human supplicant to ask a favor of a witch. It was a border place. Nerissa watched, back straight, as the magical nature of this border place distracted and entranced the princess.

"Oh, this is lovely!" she said, trailing a finger over the cormorant statue. "Did you make this?"

"I did," said Nerissa.

"I shouldn't have spoken again." The princess looked up at her, stricken. "I've interrupted the ritual. It's just they didn't tell me how *beautiful* it would be here."

A decision was made in between one heartbeat and the next.

Nerissa shifted to the side. "Come closer," she invited.

The princess crossed the boundary with the ease of a delicate summer wind. Magic chimed in Nerissa's ears and she could feel the princess — she could feel *her*. Her presence had a scent to it. There were flowers that grew in undersea caverns. They gave off light and had a sweet, unforgettable scent. No human would ever smell them. But Nerissa caught the scent in the princess's hair and on her skin and gave a shiver of delight.

As the princess drew closer, the raindrops grew fat and slow, and formed a pattern in the air. There were dangers to entering a witch's domain, and this was one of them: Nerissa read the princess's name — her true name — in water and light: *Meri*.

"Is this *too* close, my lady?" Meri asked.

"No," said Nerissa. "Pardon the pause, I was distracted a moment."

Relief fluttered in the back of wide blue eyes. "I didn't know if you would allow my kind in," she said. Her arm brushed Nerissa's. "I had to try, though, I had to come see if you could help." A desperate little smile flitted across her face. "It's tradition, you see, for one of my kind to seek out a witch."

A chill ran up Nerissa's spine, smothering the delight. It was unbelievable to her that what had once been a terrible, cruel choice had become a *tradition*. But Nerissa did not want to invite that kind of darkness here. She did not want to think of *her*. Instead, she asked: "Do they call me a witch, then?"

Blue eyes widened. There were tiny flecks of white in them, Nerissa noticed; hints of white caps on the waves. "I... if that word is an insult to you, I apologize," said Meri. "It is said in the city that you have... magic. And I'm *sorry*, I shouldn't have said it so bluntly. That was crude. I'm often crude, you see, I try not to be, but—"

"Who has called you crude?" Nerissa asked. There was a sharp crack of a whip in her tone.

There was a pause. "No one," Meri said. "No one has said it. But I..."

The wind whipped her hair around her face. The churning sea sprayed them with icy water. Nerissa waited, but it seemed the other woman's words had evaporated. Taking advantage of the lull, she raised her driftwood wands again. With a soft murmur, the enchantments sank down once more on the peninsula. The wind died. The ice turned to mist.

"It will be more comfortable inside," Nerissa said.

"You're inviting me inside?" Meri asked. There was sudden unease in the question. "They said you might not even see me. They said I might wait for hours or even days. Oh, I didn't expect you to be so kind!"

"Do I have a reputation as a cruel witch? Is that what the people of the city say of me?" Nerissa asked. Tilting her head, she considered Meri, whose cheeks turned a delicate shade of pink.

"Oh, no!" Meri said. Her fingers clasped together in front of her chest. "No! I implore you, please don't think it. It was simply — oh, I have gone and *muddled* everything again. They say you are *busy*."

"It is true that I do not often make myself available to them," Nerissa said. True amusement bubbled up inside her. "I suppose that might seem cruel to those who wish for magical solutions to their problems." The newer generations did not realize it was an act of mercy for a witch to not take interest in their small, short lives.

"I... yes," said Meri.

"Will you come inside to discuss what you have journeyed here to ask of me?" Nerissa asked. Her gaze remained steady on Meri's face, watching different emotions wash over it. One of these was fear but it was determination that finally won.

"If you will tell me why you have allowed me inside so readily," Meri said. "Not only inside a few steps. Everyone told me it would be just a few steps... but you've encased me in your enchantments and invited me into your *home*. My lady... why?"

"Ah, you have not forgotten the old stories about witches, have you?" Nerissa asked.

"I have not," said Meri.

"No harm will come to you while you are my guest," Nerissa promised her. The scarlet cormorant that was her companion let out a loud screech. "I have invited you into my home because I know who you are. And I am curious."

"You know who I am?"

"Indeed, mermaid," Nerissa said. "I ask once more: will you come inside?"

Meri cast a look behind her. It was a fleeting look, as though she needed one more glance at the path behind her to give her courage to step onto the path before her. When the wide blue eyes again met Nerissa's, desperation lurked in them. Nerissa's heart was a slow thud in her chest as she awaited Meri's decision. A hint of crimson moved in the corner of her eye: the cormorant, too, was waiting.

"I would be delighted, my lady," Meri said finally. The words were small but bravely spoken.

"Well done," said Nerissa, permitting herself a small smile.

When she turned to head back up the path to the lighthouse, Nerissa's enchantments whispered in her ear. *This is one who has lived through a transformation*, they told her. *Her humanity is a lie… she is a creature of water and salt, not earth.* Little motes of magic swirled like tiny stars in her vision all desperately trying to capture her attention. But Nerissa knew all of this and her hand was in constant motion, quelling the magic and pacifying it with sigils she drew in the air.

"What… what are those stars?" Meri asked when they were halfway up the path.

"It is my magic warning me that you are not what you seem," Nerissa said calmly.

"Is that how you knew?" Meri asked. "Am I allowed to ask that? Ignore my blunder if I am not, I *am* sorry—"

"I will let you know if you overstep," Nerissa told her. "You need not offer me an apology again until I demand it of you." Then she turned back toward the lighthouse. "As it happens, I knew who you were the moment I saw your message."

As she could not see Meri's face, she didn't know if this frightened her or not. Meri would know better than most that to have the attention of a witch – whether benevolent or not – was not in anyone's best interest. Humans were short-lived creatures with little capacity for magic. Most who were touched with it had even shorter lives than usual. There was always a price for magic. Always. And witches were the ones who collected the debt other creatures incurred.

Always.

But Meri did not need to fear Nerissa. Long ago, when a mermaid first dreamed of having legs, the price to be paid for such a transformation was terrible. It had been a new path forged for those first mermaids. Now the magic was gentler and more benign. The price to be paid was not as total as it once was – something Nerissa knew all too well. Whatever the price had been, Meri had already paid it. There was no debt for Nerissa to collect. Her interest in her was as a curiosity.

Nerissa held that curiosity in as she led Meri into the lighthouse. There was a small kitchen and sitting room on the first floor. A half wall made of stone separated the two. Meri perched on a chair in the sitting room while Nerissa set about making tea. It took her a moment to remember the steps. The kettle was filled with water and set over a newborn fire. Nerissa almost added the tea leaves before a memory of doing this long ago nudged her: *You have to wait for the water to boil.* Once that was sorted, and everything was done in its proper order, Nerissa took two chipped tea cups to the sitting room.

Meri was quiet and still and clearly still frightened. But she took the tea Nerissa gave her, even though her fingers trembled to do so.

"Was it love?" Nerissa asked. The abrupt words fell like stones in the quiet.

Those wide blue eyes flew upward. "Love?" Meri asked, as though she had never heard of such a thing before. "You mean why I am human now?"

Nerissa waved her hand. Of course that was what she had meant.

"It wasn't love," Meri said. She dipped her finger in the tea and stirred it. Nerissa's lips twitched. "My father and his father made a trade deal. The kingdom's ships will be the only ones allowed in my father's territory. In return, my father will have first pick of the opals harvested in the mountains beyond the city." Her shoulders lifted in a shrug. "In the old stories, it is always love, isn't it?"

"Until others saw ways it could benefit them," said Nerissa. It had only taken four hundred or so years. "But there is a price to be paid, still, even when others make these decisions for you. Or was the price leaving everyone behind in order to transform into a strange new creature?"

"The price!" The words tumbled out of Meri's mouth. Red washed over her cheeks and a storm grew in her eyes. "The price! I have a little sister whom I will never see again. I am told that even if she is right in front of me, my eyes will slide right by her." Anger and despair entwined in her tone. "Not that I have seen anyone from home at all in the two years I have been human."

Nerissa raised her eyebrow. "Did you expect to?"

"I – no," Meri said. "I just didn't expect it to be so lonely."

Curiosity stirred in her. "Is that why you have come to me? To ease your loneliness?"

Meri shook her head, then set her tea cup down. The storm in her eyes receded, and Nerissa suspected that the princess hadn't had any intention of hinting at her loneliness. "No, I would never be so silly as to bother a witch over loneliness. They say I am silly, but I am not *that* silly." She took a deep breath and squared her shoulders. "No. I came to you because – because I think my body is wrong."

Both of Nerissa's eyebrows raised at that. Then she looked Meri over. What, exactly, did she mean by her body being wrong? Her hair was drying into frothy, lovely curls that framed a face that was almost impossibly lovely: sharp nose, wide eyes, skin like cream. There was a poignance to her loveliness, to be sure; there was a wistfulness in the cant of her eyes and the quirk of her lips. The way Meri held herself spoke of sorrow, at odds with the fresh, tumbling way the words came out of her mouth.

The rest of her body was as lovely as her face. High, full breasts filled her bodice. Her waist was narrow, her hips a gentle curve, and her legs long. There was not a single thing wrong that Nerissa could see, but the despair in Meri's eyes was real.

"Is it an illness?" Nerissa asked. "Something I cannot see?"

Meri shook her head. Paused. Then nodded. "You have to understand that mermaids are different from humans."

"I understand that very well," said Nerissa.

Meri blew out a breath. "We don't have – there was so much *pain* the first month after my transformation." Tea sloshed over the rim of her chipped cup. "I learned I wasn't to mention it, they said it was unmentionable. That to discuss it is crude. Even the prince was shocked when I brought it up. But no one *warned* me I was to bleed every month. I didn't know."

Fingernails cut into Nerissa's palms. "No one warned you the ways in which a woman's body is subject to the tides? To the moon herself?"

Meri looked at her, lips falling open. "Subject to the tides…" she muttered. "I… no. No one mentioned this until one of the older serving women taught me how to catch the blood in rags. I thought something had gone wrong with the new body." Then, with visible effort, she calmed. "But I got used to it."

Nerissa leaned forward. "Your menses are not why you have sought me out?"

"No," she said, shaking her head. "I learned this is normal. It comes, often enough, with much pain."

Nerissa did not smile at the sudden indignation, but it took an effort.

"I learned that I couldn't speak of such things without accusations of being crude," said Meri.

"Humans are far too squeamish," agreed Nerissa.

"This… it has to do with…" Meri bit her lip and cut herself off. "The prince and I… we have shared a bed in the times when I'm not bleeding. The activity there… excites him greatly. I *know* they excite him greatly. He's very stirred by them and wishes to – *I'm sorry* – surely this must be one of the unmentionable things—"

"The prince has the human urge to have intercourse," Nerissa interrupted calmly. "It has many names, so it is hardly unmentionable. He wants to make love to you, copulate with you, and fuck you."

A glimmer of humor sparked in Meri's eyes, adding a depth to her sudden relief. "*Yes*," she said with great feeling. "All of those things. I thought it was something done on their festival days, such as when we jumped over the embers to celebrate fertility. Then when he hinted it was an activity he wanted to do more often, I thought once a moon was proper." Her hands spread in a gesture of pure bewilderment. Her eyes were even wider. "Last we discussed it, he indicated he wanted to do it far more often. As often as he can, he says, as often as his body is ready for it." The storm grew in her eyes. "His body is *always* ready for it. It is *always* pointing straight toward me – not always, but sometimes even just minutes after he has – has—"

"After he has found his completion," Nerissa said. "It is often the way of men." Cocking her head, she looked at the miserable princess before her. "You do not enjoy the activities with him?"

The storm broke. Meri put her face in her hands and wept. Words tumbled out of her mouth in a tangle. Nerissa grabbed the thread of it and tried to follow. "—wish wish wish I did – he says I ought to enjoy it more. He is greatly angered when I refuse him." Wet blue eyes looked up at her. "But just last night he looked up at me and asked why a former mermaid was so damn dry!"

Nerissa blinked.

"And then I thought – I discovered something – I wondered… I thought perhaps there is something wrong about this body," said Meri, gesturing at herself. "So I thought to come to you. I thought to ask if there was a price I paid without knowing I paid it, and…" Her voice trailed off into silence.

And to see if I could fix it for her.

Her fingers tightened on the tea cup. Nerissa could read Meri's thoughts as easily as though they were glowing sigils etched in the air. No enchantments were necessary to read her. Hope and despair peered out at Nerissa from Meri's eyes: despair because she was a new wife in a new body, subject to the demands of an inconsiderate husband; and hope because of anyone in the kingdom, Meri had cause to believe in magic.

"I will need to examine your body," Nerissa told her.

A shoulder lifted in a shrug. "This is fine with me," she said. "I'm not shy with this body. The servants, they – well. I'm not shy."

"If I find a cause for why you do not enjoy the marital bed, there may not be a simple solution," Nerissa warned.

Meri just looked at her.

"There will be a price," said Nerissa. Gooseflesh erupted on her arms at the thought and her driftwood wands grew warm. The wands were as eager to collect a debt as they always were. "There is always a price, Meri."

"I know there is," said Meri. "I'll pay it. I just… I want to be happy. I want this body to be happy. I even want my husband the prince to be *happy*." She swallowed. "Will you *please* help me?"

"Yes," said Nerissa. "I will."

Gratitude suffused Meri's features. Her head canted to the side, her lips parted, and her eyes widened enough that the light filtering through the small windows in the lighthouse struck them. It looked as though sunlight struck the water. Her words of thanks were hardly even necessary, not when her expression said everything for her.

"Well, then," said Nerissa. "Take off your clothes so I can see what the problem might be."

Meri shot to her feet. "Oh," she said. "But I'll need help, is that all right? A maidservant always helps me undress. I haven't got the reach for all those buttons…"

"I will help," said Nerissa. A shiver went over her body. It was the second time she'd agreed to help Meri. If she agreed a third time, she had to do it no matter what it cost her to do so. *Guard your tongue*, Nerissa warned herself.

Now that Meri's dress was dry, Nerissa realized it was deceptively simple. True, the high waist, short sleeves capped with lace, and snug fit had little in common with the ostentatious fashion Nerissa remembered from the last time she'd taken a peek at the human world. But hundred buttons that trailed up Meri's spine were made of real pearls and the fabric itself had an intricate, embroidered pattern made from actual silver thread.

"The humans used to wear skirts decorated with peacock feathers and all other manner of things," said Nerissa. She began with the top button and worked downward. Her fingers slipped against the silky pearls when she tried to do it with speed. So she slowed down and undid the buttons with deliberate slowness. "Their skirts were so large, the human women had to enter through the doors sideways."

"I've seen some of that in paintings around the palace," said Meri. "Her Majesty the Queen, my husband the prince's grandmother, wore a skirt so full the artist could not paint it within the frame. He says it's what he remembers best of her. The volume of her skirts, and how he used to hide in them without her knowing."

Nerissa's hands stilled. "She's dead? The old king's wife?"

Meri turned slightly, revealing the crisp perfection of her profile. "For quite some time now."

Absorbing this, Nerissa continued at her task. More words washed over her, as Meri had taken her surprise as interest. Nerissa was not so much interested as she was surprised she'd missed – or had forgotten – the death of a queen. *You've spent more time with the larger magics and forgot there is an entire kingdom down the road,* Nerissa thought. Not that it bothered her she didn't make herself available to the humans. But the strong walls of her enchantments were higher and more impenetrable than she'd thought...

By the time Nerissa pulled herself out of her thoughts, the back of Meri's dress gaped open. The pale white expanse of her back was revealed bit by bit. What intrigued Nerissa the most wasn't the creaminess of her skin or her slim lines, but the tiny shadows that gathered at the base of her spine. More subtle than freckles, they hinted at the scales that used to there in Meri's prior life. For a long, breathless moment, Nerissa couldn't look away from them, wondering what color they'd been. Then—

She wrenched herself away. "You may disrobe now," said Nerissa. "I have undone your buttons."

Meri nodded and stepped away. In moments, she was naked and facing Nerissa.

Her clothed body had been lovely enough to break a heart. Naked, she was lovely enough to give a goddess cause for jealousy. Her breasts swelled like creamy waves, and were capped by nipples the color of a rose at dusk. The curve of her waist complemented the swell of her breast and the flare of her hips. And there, at her center, a triangle of glossy pale hair drew the eye.

Taking in a deep breath, Nerissa looked her fill. Her own nipples tightened and tingled and grew more sensitive to the rough fabric she wore.

"Is it true?" The fearful tone in Meri's voice was the shock of cold water. Nerissa's gaze flew to her, wondering how it was possible gossip lived that long.

Blinking, Nerissa just looked at her.

"Am I wrong?" Meri asked.

Ah. Meri's own predicament.

"I have not yet discovered that," said Nerissa. "I will need you to recline and spread your legs for me."

"I can do that," Meri said in a rush. "I can do that, and you can tell me if I – what I – if there is anything you can do." There was no hint of hesitation as she took her place on the sofa and spread her legs wide apart for Nerissa.

The cushions behind Meri were a dark enough contrast to make her seem even paler. Nerissa's eyes were drawn first to the delicate bones that connect her upper thigh to her center. They lingered there; the memory of scales was present there as well and Nerissa had a sudden, striking curiosity: would she be able to *feel* them? Was the memory tactile as well? It was a moment before she looked away, looked at Meri's most intimate parts.

Though her legs were spread wide, her folds were shy and closed. There was only a tiny hint of her inner, more sensitive folds. As though reading Nerissa's mind, Meri reached down and spread herself with her fingers. Then she was wide open, and revealing her center to be as delicately pink as the inside of a conch shell. Everything was in order; everything had been perfectly crafted; everything was exquisitely lovely.

Everything was perfect, except for the lack of one tiny thing.

"Ah," said Nerissa. "Ah, yes, I see."

Meri's eyes widened with distress. "What is it?"

Nerissa cast a quick look around the room, eyes landing inadvertently on the heap of Meri's dress. The mass of pearl buttons curved like a sea serpent. "Your instincts were correct," she said, perching on the sofa next to Meri's hip. The former mermaid's legs were still open and Nerissa did not need the further distraction. "A human woman has a marvelous little organ that provides her pleasure during intimacy equal to that which human men feel. You mentioned your husband the prince finds pleasure in your arms?"

"Yes, he does, quite a lot," said Meri, with a small grimace, plucking at the fabric of the sofa with slim, nervous fingers. "The first time, I thought something dreadful had happened. I thought he was getting a rapid sort of illness. I thought something had gone horribly wrong."

"There is no greater physical pleasure than what is created from intimate acts," said Nerissa. "There is a small pearl hidden in a woman's secret places. It is the source of her pleasure. And yours is missing."

"*Missing?*" Meri's legs shut with a snap that echoed the snap in her voice.

"Or perhaps too well hidden," Nerissa allowed.

"So there's nothing you can do," Meri said. She shoved scrambled to her feet, seeming not to care when her bare breast brushed Nerissa's cheek. "I am cursed in this new life. I ought to have known I would be forced to pay and pay for a decision I was not even one to make. First the memory of a sister I had – what if I loved her?" Color blazed in her cheeks. "And now I've attempted to make another bargain with a witch! What a fool I was! I am not even—" Meri's angry tumble of words had the same energy as a swift-moving river.

"Meri," Nerissa murmured.

Meri stopped, eyes reflecting enough light on the water that Nerissa had to look away. This time, the rushing river of words were an apology. "Oh, lords of the deep, I am *sorry*. That was *unforgivable*—"

"I told you not to give me another apology until I ask for one," Nerissa said. There were worse things implied about witches and half of them were true. It was good for Meri to be at least a little wary. Setting that aside, Nerissa tilted her head. "Did you assume I would no longer try to help you?"

Meri's mouth opened and closed several times. "I thought for a moment… there was somewhat in your face that made it seem like it would be impossible."

"No," said Nerissa. "I hope not, at least. It will be more difficult to help you should your pearl be missing as opposed to just… hidden."

Meri looked away and out the window toward the sea. "My sisters and I – the sisters I remember, at least – we used to collect pearls, you know, as material for our playthings. We had millions of them by the time I... left. They let me bring them all with me, to remember them by, and I took them." She gestured down at her dress. "They are so valuable here, it is hard to believe. But I suppose the most valuable one of all is the one I'm missing?"

Nerissa did not answer for a long moment. The long, clean lines of Meri's naked body had distracted her. The weak light illuminated her, making the small shadows on her spine, her bottom, and her thighs even more apparent. It took several breaths before Nerissa remembered she ought to answer. "Oh, yes," she said. "It is a pearl of great worth."

"Is it every mermaid who has been deprived of this?" Meri demanded. "A mermaid! Deprived of a pearl. The irony of it... it has the scent of a magical curse."

"It is not every mermaid," Nerissa said. Her touch on Meri's shoulder was gentle and easy. "It is not every transformation."

"Then why is it *me*?"

"This I cannot answer for you," said Nerissa.

Meri whirled. Her pale hair whipped Nerissa. The air between them crackled with an energy similar to the storm outside. There was a fresh, sharp scent in the air, and quiet thunder offered Nerissa a warning. "Will you help me?"

There were dangers to a witch agreeing to help without limits offered. An agreement, thrice spoken, was unbreakable.

"Yes," said Nerissa. "I will help."

CHAPTER TWO

There was a tremor in the ground beneath her feet. The sleeping
earth responded to a witch's unfettered promise with a murmur
of earth and stone. Nerissa's bones vibrated; there was a moment
of pure fear – *what had she done?* – before she forced that thought out of
her head. What was done was done. There was nothing Nerissa could
do about that.

Meri sank into a crouch, arms outspread, and eyes impossibly wide.
"What was that?" she said. "The earth *moved*, what's happened—"

"The slumbering earth moves at times," Nerissa said. There was
something about Meri's panic that steadied her. Warmth infused her
tone. "It happens more often here, out on the peninsula; you must not
be alarmed."

The tense line of Meri's shoulders eased. "I… did not know it did
that. Oh! Yes, I did. One of the servants told me… that's why one of
the large bridges in the city has got a great crack in it… the earth shook
it apart." Blinking rapidly, the former mermaid collected herself. Nerissa did not want to spoil her sudden calm by telling her that it had not
been an earthquake that had shaken the Bridge of Whispers apart.

"Do not be alarmed," Nerissa repeated.

"I won't," said Meri. She shook her head. "I'm not. Not anymore.
I just fear that… it has been quite the adjustment becoming human."

"I know," said Nerissa. "But let us focus our minds back on your…
problem. I will need some of your blood."

Meri gave her a quick, sharp look. "My blood?"

"I need to know if this indeed was a price you paid in order to
become human or if it really was a true afterthought," said Nerissa. "In
your blood flows the memory of the magic worked in you. I will need
to read it."

A tiny grimace flickered over Meri's face.

"I want to help you," said Nerissa. *I have to help you.*

"It's just that I've heard stories of what – what witches can do with
blood," Meri said. Her arms folded across her chest and she hunched in
on herself. "You could – you could do… all manner of things."

Nerissa could only imagine the stories told under the sea about
what witches could and could not do. The witches who walked the
earth and breathed the air may be more vicious in nature and deed than

those who made the sea their home, but there was an inexorable cold-
ness to the latter. She was sure the merfolk told all manner of stories of
those who wielded the unforgiving tide of magic against them.

"I have promised to help you, Meri," Nerissa said. "I will not use
your blood for any purpose other than to taste your memory. This I
swear."

"I… all right," Meri said.

A small nick was all it took. Nerissa used the knife she kept on the
hearth for small, private rituals, and she pressed it against the skin of
Meri's upper arm hard enough to draw out a bright red drop of blood.
It beaded on the edge of the knife.

"Show me the price," Nerissa commanded it.

For a moment, Meri's reflection ghosted across it; a moment later,
Nerissa flicked out her tongue and licked it.

> *Brine.*
> *Blood.*
> *"If you choose to forget me, you'll miss me less, won't you?" It was
> a little girl's voice, sweet and lilting. "I think you should choose that."*
> *Nerissa fought to open her eyes. It was more than water that
> pressed down on her; it was blood: Meri's blood. Through it, she
> could see two mermaids. They were both young, but one was hardly
> an adolescent. Both their fins were long and flowing and comprised of
> scales the same color as one another's. More than just sisters, Nerissa
> realized. Kindred souls.*
> *"Thalassa! I don't want to forget you!" Meri cried out. "I don't
> want to leave you at all…"*
> *"Father says you don't have a choice," said Thalassa. "I don't
> know why you've got to be the one to give something up, though, not
> when it's Father making you do this."*
> *"I know," Meri said. "I know. Oh, Thalassa… you see forgetting
> you as the best price, but I see it as the worst…"*
> *There were flashes of light flickering through the water and blood,
> now. Sobs as loud as thunder echoed in Nerissa's ears, driving her
> to her knees. Lightning stirred the sea to boiling. A witch – he had
> a man's face and chest, and the long, flowing tentacles of a squid
> – shouted words and sigils blazed whenever he spoke. Meri's body
> writhed in front of her. She'd been chained to a stone slab and her
> movements threatened to break the links and free herself…*
> *She wouldn't, though. Nerissa already knew how this ended.*
> *A merman and a human watched. Strong sigils of enchantment pro-
> tected them and allowed them to watch the magical transformation
> taking place before them. Nerissa moved to stand closer to them. The*

*merman must be Meri's father, but the man... he was old. Much too
old to be Meri's young husband.*

"It was well thought, this bargain," said the merman.

*"You will have all the opals you could desire," said the human. His
eyes were dark and cold. "And my grandson gains a fine wife."*

"And the trade winds," said the merman.

*"Yes, the merchants will thank me," said the human. There was lit-
tle interest writ in his tone; his entire being focused intently on Meri.*

*There was something about him Nerissa did not like. There was a
circlet over his brow, dark bags under his eyes, and heavy jowls. He
was old but not ugly... except for a glint in his eye that grew larger
the longer he watched Meri stripped of her tail. Triumph wed with
distaste and Nerissa's skin crawled...*

*His face twisted with disgust and Nerissa glanced over at Meri: her
long fin was gone, in its place were two legs.*

"Remember what I told you," the human said to the witch.

"I remember," said the witch. "I told you I will do what I can."

"What is this about?" the merman asked.

*"There is a part of a human woman's body that I have asked the
witch to neglect adding," the human said coldly. "It is none of your
concern."*

"But what is it?" the merman persisted.

*"It is a non-essential, inconsequential thing that plagues women,"
said the human. "It makes them emotional, hysterical. It is the direct
cause of poor decisions. Your daughter need not be plagued with it."*

*Lightning stirred the water. Meri arched her back on the stone slab
to which she was tied and screamed her sister's name. "Thalassa!
THALASSA!"*

"She will not miss it," said the human.

*Wrong, Nerissa thought fiercely. If only she could effect change...
there was a smirk playing across the human's face. It made him ugly.
Nerissa wanted to carve a similar smile just under his chin...*

It took a moment for Nerissa to realize the memory had released
her. The contempt and desire to do violence was nearly impossible to
shake off. Fingernails bit into her palm as she clenched her fists. It
would not take much enchantments at all to focus the malevolence of
her thoughts and send them winging toward the old king.

"—need to sit?" Meri's anxious voice cut into Nerissa's thoughts.

"Sit?" Nerissa said blankly.

"You look quite, quite pale," said Meri.

"I... no," said Nerissa. Bit by bit, the malice of her own thoughts
released her. The king was safe from having stroke this night. Clarity

returned. "What I learned from your memory and from what I know of transformations of the magnitude as what you experienced… it is inconclusive."

"Inconclusive?" Meri said. "How so?"

"Transformations are… they are all or nothing," said Nerissa. "They take who you were – your deepest self and *change* it into something else." It was much more complicated than that. "It is as though…" Her thoughts fixated on what Meri would know, what she would connect with. "You are the water. Your body is the space it fills. Your body was changed from mermaid to human… but the witch didn't create every part of your new body. He simply… changed the shape of the space you fill. So he shouldn't have been able to do any such small things." He shouldn't have been able to… and yet it was a fact that Meri's pearl was missing.

"I don't understand," Meri said, biting her lip.

"I know," said Nerissa. "And *I* don't understand what has happened to the pearl that ought to have been yours." *I will do what I can,* the witch had said. Had he cursed her somehow, after the transformation? "I will need to do some research. I will need time to discover what has happened."

"Books and things?" Meri asked hesitantly.

"And things," agreed Nerissa.

First, she helped Meri dress. Her fingers flitted over the buttons and all the while she looked at their reflection in the window. Meri's hair, so blonde it was nearly white, contrasted sharply with Nerissa's, which was as dark as a crow's wing. It was impossible to take her eyes off the reflection so Nerissa didn't try.

"If you find yourself bored, there is a book upon the mantel that I think might interest you," said Nerissa, once half of the tiny pearls were buttoned. Long ago, a winter of boredom had Nerissa deciding to create a book that would tell her the story that would echo her soul. In the way of witches, favors were traded for favors. A quill was dipped in the ichor of a muse in return for the eggs of an albino hippocampus. The paper was crafted from the bark of one of the trees of the Western Isles – this she'd paid for with an entire storm she'd coaxed into a bottle. And all of this was bound together with a sigil gifted to her by the titan queen, the one whose gift was generation.

More than three decades had gone into crafting it and it ought to occupy the mermaid for the few hours it would take Nerissa to conduct her research.

A few minutes later, alone, Nerissa went to her workroom.

The place where Nerissa performed most of her magic and created most of her enchantments was not properly located in the lighthouse – rather it was under it. She closed the door to her sitting room, crossed her kitchen, and opened the door that led to a tiny stone staircase that twisted downward. This small cellar was where she kept most of her food and wine... it also led to her private spaces. Nerissa pricked the tip of her finger, drew the rune of revealing on the stone wall at the back. It dissolved into motes of light, which swirled and blinked around her like a curtain made of stars. Sparks clung to her as she walked through it.

Over the course of several decades, Nerissa had used magic to create a network of caverns woven through the cliffs that edged her peninsula. The largest of these was where she kept her books. Sigils of warmth and protection had been wrought in the stone; none of her collections would be ruined by damp or cold. And her jewel-colored cormorant servants stood sentinel against any brave rodents that might find their way here – their short lives further shortened by talons of stone and magic.

She could hear stone wings scraping against each other. The further she went down the secret stair, the louder they grew. The cormorants were restless tonight. Nerissa wondered if they were aware enough to know there was a mermaid-turned-human in the house... or if they somehow sensed Nerissa had just made a binding promise. The cavern that housed her workroom was quite large, but still, magical artifacts had found their way out here, sitting on the steps, hanging on the walls or from the ceiling, and another screech from a cormorant had Nerissa nearly tripping over a tiny cabinet filled with fire-rose seeds.

It was then she became aware of the strange pattern to the beat of her heart and had to pause, arms outstretched to brace herself against the wall, and head down.

Breathe. Draw in the calm of the deep.

But it had been foolish – so *foolish* – for her to do what she had done. Offering Meri help, saying it *thrice*, not placing limits. She was so *foolish.*

Opposite her was an oval mirror, bolted to the stone. It was framed with rune-inscribed moonstones. They were hammered flat and melted into the reflective surface. At first it only revealed Nerissa – pale and wide-eyed. But this, a gift from the Ladies of the Moon for favors done, was no ordinary mirror. Then, the face of it shimmered and waved. A full moon appeared, shining bright on a sheltered cove. Two figures were revealed in the moonlight; they were entwined together, moving sinuously, and there was no way to tell where one ended and the other began.

Blackness descended as she squeezed her eyes shut. Her mind chanted a denial; her heartbeat sped up. *You fool. You fool.* The mirror revealed the hidden thoughts of whoever looked into it. Her mind was on that beach. Meri had stirred these memories.

This is why you promised to help her, Nerissa told herself as the panic began to recede. *It all goes back to Dianora.*

With that thought, she forced herself down the stairs, taking care not to look into the mirror again. Her chest still tight, she – *silently* – cursed the gift from the Ladies of the Moon. What need did Nerissa have of such a thing? A part of her – the best part of her – would always be on that isolated beach with Dianora.

Now more than ever.

Dianora was closer in her thoughts today than she had been for decades. It was Meri, it was *this* cursed mermaid, who was dredging her up from her rest. It was *this* curse that made Nerissa ache over the other.

Calm, she ordered. *Calm.* She drew the rune for calm over her breast. Then again. And a third time. It was only then that she felt calm enough to walk down the last few stairs that led to her workroom, where she could begin to do as she promised Meri.

It took a few moments, but her skin felt normal again and her breathing steadied. It helped to allow her eyes to rove over her workroom; the intimacy with which she knew each object steadied her. Her driftwood table held a half-carved cormorant – it needed a few days carving and a new moon so Nerissa could harvest the soul of a drowned fisherman. A bowl of powdered sulfur sat next to it with a long knife resting over it. More than half the table was taken up by a huge basin. In it, was a perfectly replicated tide pool, and she used it to watch over the creatures who lived in the blurred margin between sea and shore.

The waves calmed her as they always did. After a few minutes of watching them, Nerissa's pulse was steady, and her heartbeat was within a normal boundary. It was then that she lifted her eyes to the small shelf that hung over a narrow arch. Beyond it, Nerissa could see her library, packed with shelves and filled with more books than anyone could read in six lifetimes.

Nerissa had read them all.

But now was not the time to browse and get lost in the stacks. Instead of stepping through the arch, she looked above it, to the shelf where her cormorants sat. Each one was a different color, as bright as possible, except her oldest servant, whose paint was nearly entirely worn off. They pecked at each other, rustled their feathers, creating a cacophony of sound, until the plain cormorant snapped at the others. It was him she eyed before bringing her fingers to her mouth and whistled.

"Attend me," she ordered.

The restless stone cormorants stopped moving at once.

"Mistress," croaked out the plain cormorant. It was the only one given the power to speak. It had been a mistake to do so, and Nerissa had made sure the others were mute.

"You are to seek books for me, my librarians," she said.

"Mistress, what would you have us seek?" it asked.

"I need information on curses of a sexual nature," Nerissa told him. "Limit your findings to that which affects only females."

"As you desire," said the cormorant. His wings gave a mighty flap – the stone made a terrible grating sound – and he tumbled down off his perch. A moment later, the rest of the cormorants did the same, and Nerissa retreated from them and their loud sounds, and moved to stand next to her whale.

She brushed her hand across one of the ribs. Her body had nearly assimilated the compulsions and a half-formed thought tugged at her. Among other things, ambergris was a powerful aphrodisiac, if she—

A slim book dropped onto her head and tumbled to the floor.

Blinking, Nerissa stooped to pick it up, and brushed her thumb across the cover.

> *Bile and sweat crashed down on her.*
> *"What do you want from us?" A man in a friar's robe shouted these words. He stood in the center of a monastery library. His arms*

stretched out as though to protect the books from the army of mountain trolls that poured into the room.

A mountain troll grunted. The brave friar's head was hewn from his shoulders. Blood splattered—

Nerissa came back to herself, shaking, staring incredulously down at the book she held in her hands. The blood on it was old and dry... and yet it had drawn Nerissa into a memory. *Perhaps he had a spark of magic in him,* she thought. *Or perhaps he was the keeper of that particular monastery's lore.* Nerissa knew that she'd been the one to send the mountain trolls, yet could not remember what it was she'd needed from them – a bit of lore? a fairy tale? a map?

Let's see what the brave friar died for, Nerissa thought.

The book was well worn and fell open in her hands to a page somewhere in the middle.

Her legs were open and her center dripped with witch's honey. "My lord, I've been cursed!" she sobbed. "Only your staff can break the curse!"

But he held himself back from her. She was beautiful enough: glossy dark curls framed a pale face. Wide eyes begged for his mercy. His gaze fell on her bosom: it heaved as though he touched them, and their tips tightened into hard points. And, further down, she was so glossy and swollen, flushed and ready. His hand went to his robes and unfastened them.

Nerissa slammed the book shut with a roll of her eyes. Stories of that sort of explicit sexuality had enjoyed a period of immense popularity. The more salacious the better. A frown knit between her brows. They were illegal now. The old king, the same one who had decided Meri did not need to experience sexual pleasure, had outlawed them as one of his first royal decrees. Anyone caught reading them would have their dominant hand chopped off at the wrist. Anyone caught writing them were beheaded so their "base and diseased thoughts could no longer escape".

Her finger tapped against the driftwood table as she repressed a shudder. The way the old king had stared at Meri...

There was a grating of wings and a great clatter. Her cormorant dropped a book the size of a dinghy onto the floor; it was so heavy the shelves rattled and a jar of newt eggs nearly toppled over. Nerissa caught it, and peered over at the book the cormorant brought for her: her increasingly malevolent thoughts of the old king wafted away.

Nerissa opened it with a grunt of effort and found it full of etchings. An artist, or several of them, had compiled depictions of cursed witches, their legs open wide. Nerissa flipped through it: a tentacle emerged from a vagina on one page, a thick forest of trees in place of pubic hair on another, and a snapping set of teeth growing out of the labia on a third. Nerissa flipped that one quickly, and the scent of cayenne pepper wafted up. *Genitalia cursed to smell of strong spice*, it read along the outer edge.

With a sigh, Nerissa hefted it closed.

She found the answer in the third book the plain cormorant sent to her. Her heart had stuttered quicker when she flipped to the table of contents and found a concise list of curses – and, more importantly, their counter-curses. They were helpfully grouped in categories. Nerissa trailed her finger down the page, reading quickly, until she finally came to a section labeled "pleasure". Ignoring the curses that made witches insatiable, she found the section she needed and flipped to it.

No more than a few candlemarks later, Nerissa returned to the lighthouse proper. After the cold of her workroom, stepping into the cozy sitting room with the fire in its hearth and a beautiful woman standing at the window, it was almost shockingly warm. The sensation of sinking into a warm bath was so strong and so encompassing that it took Nerissa much to long to realize Meri was silent.

"I think I have—"

"I worried you weren't coming back," Meri said in a flat tone. There was tension in the line of her shoulders and she held herself much too rigid. Nerissa's stomach sank. "I worried that you would just – just disappear and I would have to find my way out of this storm."

It was then that Nerissa noticed the storm that had been threatening for the last week had arrived. Rain slanted against the windows. It ought to be mid-afternoon, but it looked dark as midnight. In her bones, Nerissa could hear the wind howling its fury over the sea. Lightning illuminated strange shapes in the sky.

"We are safe here," Nerissa said. "I—"

"I have not seen such a storm on land," Meri said. "There were a few times in the sea… I remember very little of what it felt like to transition from mermaid to human. But it felt like this." Finally, she looked back at Nerissa, who was experiencing regret at having left the mermaid alone with her own thoughts for so long. There was bleak despair in those impossible eyes. "I wondered what would happen if I stepped out into the storm? Would magic take hold of me and return me to my prior state?"

"Unlikely," Nerissa said tartly. "More likely, you would be driven up against the lighthouse and knock yourself senseless."

Meri's lips parted.

"Now, attend," said Nerissa. "I have chased down two likely reasons for your dilemma. One is a better option than the other, of course." When the bleak expression remained, Nerissa heaved an internal sigh, and reached out to brush her fingers down Meri's arm. Her skin was cool to the touch, as though her thoughts had kept her from experiencing the warmth of the room. "But both are things I am able to fix."

Pray that it be so.

Meri's lips quivered. "I... thank you. Thank you." Her head cocked. "You're awfully kind, did you know? Our witches under the sea aren't nearly so kind... or perhaps their reputation for cruelty is undeserved."

"I doubt that it is undeserved," Nerissa said dryly.

"Is it that earth witches are kinder, then?" Meri asked.

"Hardly," said Nerissa. "Earth witches are violent and inexorable."

"But—"

Nerissa reached into the pocket of her jerkin and pulled out the bottle of potion she had prepared. "I will be happy to answer your questions later," she said. "However, I advise that we set aside the conversation on the differing natures of witches until after we have dealt with your pearl."

"You're right," said Meri. Her head bobbed and she bit her lip. "I'm – I'm sorry. I do hate being alone and to be quite honest, after I read a bit from your book – it was a dark little story, I'm afraid – and it kept prodding me to remember what it was like. The scales on my fin were scraped off and—"

Nerissa had no idea why Meri's soul had needed to remind her of the violent transition she had gone through. But Nerissa needed her to focus on pleasure rather than pain. "Meri," she said firmly. "I need you take three deep breaths."

"Three breaths? But—"

"Close your eyes," Nerissa commanded. "Close your eyes and take three deep breaths. Focus on the scent in the air. Think of that."

"But I—"

"What does it smell like?"

Nerissa's hand was still on Meri's upper arm. She *felt* when Meri relaxed.

Meri took a great many more than just three breaths. This was perfectly fine with Nerissa; she needed a perfectly calm mermaid, not one who was a step away from fracturing. Minutes passed. The storm raged on, but it no longer had Meri in its grip. A small, private smile stretched across her face.

"What do I smell?" Meri asked finally. "When I was small, my father took us nearly to shore. It was so different there – mostly we stayed in the depths. Father was very traditional, you see. But once we went to shore; we were close enough to hear the waves crashing against rocks and water rushing up onto the sand. There was this sweet, sweet scent. Brine and… I've since tasted honey. I didn't know what it was called. But I could smell it… taste it on the waves. It was honey. It's honey. I can smell it here."

Nerissa took a quick step back.

Meri's eyes blinked open. "I wonder if that's why Father chose to use me as his bargaining chip. He told me it was unseemly to talk about the shore so. My sisters, they always loved the scent of the flowers that grow deep in the undersea caverns – and they do have a marvelous scent. But I always loved honey best. Oh, goodness, listen to me prattle on!"

"It is fine," Nerissa said after a pause. "You are less afraid now."

"I am," admitted Meri. "It's a good trick, that. I'll have to remember it." She stooped slightly and peered more closely at Nerissa. "Your cheeks are flushed, is it an illness? Are you all right?"

"It is warm in here, that is all," said Nerissa. "Thank you for your concern."

"I am always chilled," said Meri. "It drives my husband the prince to distraction. I always want to sleep under blankets. I didn't know heat could make you flush like that."

"Speaking of sleep," Nerissa said, slightly desperate. Once more, she brandished the bottle of potion. This time, Meri took notice of it. "I have devised a way to ascertain the true nature of your dilemma. I will need to walk into your dreams."

"My dreams?" Meri said. Her mouth formed a small oval. "I confess, I did not know witches could do this, my lady!"

"I can," said Nerissa. Dreams existed in one of the margins of the world. In between sleep and waking, Nerissa was allowed to walk there. "I swear to you, I mean no harm."

"I – I'm – I do believe that, truly," said Meri. "What do I have to do?"

"You will need to take a sip of this and recline on the sofa," Nerissa instructed. She passed the potion to Meri, who eyed it thoughtfully for half a moment, then obeyed.

It took less than thirty seconds for the mermaid to fall asleep.

Nerissa watched her for a few minutes – *just to be sure she was actually asleep* – and so saw all the small changes that transformed her face as she slipped from waking to sleeping. The faint lines over her brow smoothed, her lips slackened, and her eyes went still behind her lids. She started off on her back, but made a small sound and turned to her side, pillowing her head on her arm.

I'm always a bit chilled, she'd said.

Nerissa draped a soft, thick blanket over her.

It took a few moments of preparation. She threw a fistful of dried lavender into the fire, causing the flames to take on a purple hue. Once the sent filled the air, she drew her driftwood wands and traced a few symbols in the air: dreams, purpose, togetherness… Then, with practiced movements, she spread ambergris in a line over Meri's brow and then her own. She took a sip of the potion, set it to the side, and stretched out on the floor.

Pushing the sounds of the storm out of her awareness, Nerissa focused on Meri's deep, even breaths. She matched her own breathing to the sound of Meri's. Her heart slowed. *In and out, in and out.*

The potion worked as it was meant to. It was a slow sinking into sleep — too fast, and Nerissa might break through Meri's dream in such a way that it would become a nightmare. No, it needed to be slow and easy. Meri's deep, even breathing lulled Nerissa and drew her inward.

But not to rest.

Stepping from her own dream into Meri's was as walking through a cobweb or a bubble made from viscous liquid. The boundary sought to stop her. Nerissa's own dreams gave a half-hearted attempt to keep her, but gave up once Nerissa stepped over a threshold as invisible and strong as the one that separated her domain from the human kingdom.

"Come find me!" said a bright little mermaid. Her two front teeth were missing and her smile was wide and bright as Meri's. The eyes were different, though: there were grey and blue in equal measure. The next moment, she disappeared in a burst of squid ink.

The little sister Meri lost, Nerissa realized. *That was Thalassa, haunting the outer edges of Meri's dreams.* The magic had stolen Meri's memories of the small one, Neri knew. It was the price Meri had been forced to pay in order to secure her father's trade deal. In dreams, Meri knew what she was missing. Even now, so far away from the center of the dream, Nerissa could hear muffled sobs.

Ignoring the pang in her stomach, Nerissa drew her wands and touched their tips together. Ambergris formed between the two as swiftly as a spider made its web and nearly as gracefully. Drawing the wands apart, it formed a thin barrier. Gently, Nerissa blew on it, creating a bubble of pure desire. Heat licked up Nerissa: her nipples tightened and wetness gathered between her legs. The effects of ambergris made her own pearl throb.

The effect on Meri's dream was much more subtle.

The sobbing stopped and there was the sound of a breath being drawn. The bubble bobbed in the air and Nerissa followed it through a landscape that flickered and changed. She swam through a bright channel between underwater stalactites, then she walked down a forest path, then she splashed in a tide pool, her mermaid tail translucent with two human legs inside it.

It grew warmer and brighter until she came around a corner, opened an ornate door, and found Meri herself naked on a bed. "Oh, it's you!" Her voice chimed. She reclined on her elbows and her legs were spread casually. Instead of a triangle of pale hair between her thighs, iridescent scales caught the odd, impossible light of the dream.

"Let us see what you have to work with, my dear," said Nerissa.

"I'll do anything, my lady," said Meri, eager. Her knees widened. "Anything."

"It is dangerous to offer a witch *anything,*" said Nerissa.

Meri's smile did not change. "It's a dream. Where is the danger?"

Nerissa drew closer, choosing not to answer Meri's question. Here in the dream was a peculiar intimacy; she felt freer and so, after a brief hesitation, she brushed her thumb across the bright scales between Meri's legs. "I will need to see this woman part of you," she said.

"Oh! Yes, of course," said Meri. "How silly. Am I even sillier in a dream? It seems I must be."

"Relax," Nerissa ordered.

Meri's thighs trembled and a moment later the scales shimmered and evaporated, revealing her center. It was just as lovely as it had been in the light of day. The shadows were longer and drew the eye to Meri's folds, the small, sensitive folds of skin that protected it. Nerissa drew a finger along the edge of it as Meri watched, eyes bright and curious.

"Does the prince caress you?" Nerissa asked.

"Not often," said Meri. "Though I do believe he likes this part of me best of all." She did not give any sign of discomfort that Nerissa touched her most private flesh. "When he comes to my rooms, this is what he wants to touch."

Nerissa dipped her eyes down to where Meri's pearl ought to be but was not. There was no hood covering a shy pearl, which should be the center of Meri's pleasure. It was a flat, pink space as smooth as the inside of a shell. Pressing down on it with her thumb, she said, "Tell me a moment — if any — that you have enjoyed with your husband."

"I enjoy... I enjoy the kissing. I enjoy his kisses. He used to kiss me for quite a while before he would climb atop me," said Meri. She said this as though it were a recitation. There was no reaction from her body.

Nerissa winced. This did not bode well. Still, she pressed on with both words and thumb. "Does he play with your nipples? They are very sensitive. Have you found yourself growing... restless when he kisses them and touches them?"

"No," said Meri.

"That is bad news—"

"But he can't because I decorate them," said Meri. "I paint them with rouge and such. It's a tradition where I am from — from the sea."

"That is still done?" Nerissa asked, shocked. She looked at Meri's nipples — they were slightly darker than usual. The dream blurred for a moment and paint stroked onto them with an unseen hand, swirling color around them that enhanced the shape and gave them a shadowy sort of mystery all at once. She squirmed, the combination of ambergris and the sheer loveliness making her pearl throb at her center.

"It fades in and out of custom but I have always loved it," said Meri. "You know an awful lot about mermaids, don't you? You know an awful lot about everything."

"Yes," said Nerissa. "I have lived a long life." Their conversation edged toward territory Nerissa did not want to explore with Meri. "You have said you enjoy his kisses, has he kissed you at your center?"

"No," said Meri. A flicker of knowledge lightened the depths of her eyes. "He has not. I asked him once… a few weeks ago. He enjoys it well enough if he puts his member in *my* mouth… but no. He says he is the prince and he doesn't perform acts of service."

"He would say that," muttered Nerissa.

Meri sank back onto the bed. "He seemed shocked I asked. There was an interrogation, of sorts, and his member became soft and withdrawn. He demanded how I would know of such a thing."

"It stands to reason that if it can be done for a man, it can be done for a woman," said Nerissa. "I suppose this thought did not cross his mind?" *The fool,* she added silently. "You have more intelligence than that."

Meri was shaking her head. "I don't believe I would have thought of it on my own. In fact, I saw my serving girls at it."

Nerissa blinked.

"One night I couldn't sleep… there was music, I think, drifting through the open window. It was making me miss my family and the sea. When I got up to close the window, I heard cries coming from where they sleep – it's a little room just off mine and the door is always held open."

There was a tiny, tiny pulse under Nerissa's thumb. *Perhaps you imagined it,* she thought in the next moment. It had been so tiny… "What happened?"

"I worried one of them was sad and fearful I would find out about it," said Meri. "I went to the door and – there they were. One was on her back on her pallet. It was she who was crying out."

The flutter was unmistakable this time.

"Why was she crying out?"

"The other girl, her friend, was kissing her quite thoroughly," said Meri, squirming. "At first I thought it was pain, but then she cried out, 'don't stop!' and her hands were in the other girl's hair. The sky was so clear, and the moon was shining down on them. One girl kept kissing the other at her center until she seemed to experience the same crisis my husband the prince does."

The pulse under her thumb was subtle but steady.

"So it *is* there."

"My pearl?" Meri said, sitting up. "You found it? I am no longer cursed?"

"Not yet," said Nerissa. "I have some few things to do." With her fingernail, she drew a sigil for pleasure just over where she had felt the small thrum of Meri's desire. It glowed silver and sank into her flesh.

"Oh!" said Meri. "Oh, that felt... that felt different." When Nerissa looked up at her, her lips were still parted in an o shape. A halo of light — rosy with ambergris — had appeared around her head.

It was difficult to maintain dignity. Not only had the ambergris suffused Meri's dream with desire, but even without it the former mermaid was lovely beyond imagination. That look on her face — that look that was as much surprise as it was pleasure — Nerissa could gaze on that the rest of the century and never tire. Her breasts were heavy and her pearl throbbed as Nerissa struggled to hold her private thoughts to herself.

It's the ambergris, Nerissa chanted to herself. But the longer Nerissa remained in Meri's dream, the more difficult it was to remain composed. It was with shaking fingers that she drew a second sigil — the one that would connect dreams to desire — and watched it, too sink into Meri's flesh.

"That is all I can do for the moment," said Nerissa.

"But what *did* you do?" Meri asked. "I felt something, didn't I?" Her head bobbed on her neck as she looked around at the landscape her dreaming mind had created. "I *feel* something."

"This is promising," Nerissa managed. "I must go — I cannot remain — when you wake, come find me."

Then she fled. It was desire that tried to keep her in Meri's dream and it was desire that had her turning corners and finding herself in the center of it all, where naked Meri held court. It seemed to take an age before the ambergris began to lighten. Nerissa's heart slowed, her breath steadied, and the labyrinth became an easy path through a damp forest of seaweed. Flecks of water dropped on her as the seaweed stirred in an unseen wind.

Nerissa was so distracted by the force of the desire she felt that she barely paused at the margin between Meri's dream and her own sleeping mind. Her only warning was the subtle chill that wrapped around her as a dead lover's cold embrace.

It started lovely, of course. Her nightmares of Dianora always did. How could they not? But for the last ten minutes of Dianora's life, every moment Nerissa had spent with her had been lovely.

"Of course it is the same as the hair on my head!" The red head was now more woman than girl. She was as casual with her nudity as she was with her words. She was splayed out on a rock, legs open. "They are meant to match."

"It is beautiful," said the mermaid, who was almost completely out of the water. Her fin was a dazzling sapphire in the sunlight. "May I touch it?"

The girl sat up onto her elbows. "Well... yes. You may touch it. But you ought to know that it is not the... same as me touching your fin."

"Not the same?" the mermaid asked. She'd been out of the water so long, her long, plentiful hair was nearly dry. "How is it different?"

"I do not know why, but it feels wonderful when I touch it," said the girl. "It feels... it is special. If I touch it long enough, there is a sudden burst." She clasped hands with the mermaid and brought it between her legs. "I can teach you, if you want to learn."

That day, the mermaid learned the difference. The memory lingered here in the secret cove, while the mermaid touched the girl between her legs, petting the fiery hair there, and discovering other, hidden treasures. Soft, low cries came out of her mouth. "Nothing has ever felt so wonderful," she said.

The dream changed in an instant. A sigil was torn into tender flesh. Both mermaid and girl were screaming corpses—

Nerissa scrambled to look away—

The corpse's eyes opened. *"Your fault,"* it said in a sibilant whisper. "Your curse gave me no choice. *Your* curse."

"No," said Nerissa. It took every ounce of willpower she contained but she turned her back on the memory. Her mind chanted a denial while Nerissa sank down into her coldest thoughts. Her body was waking; ruthless, Nerissa forced herself away from her own dream. *I do not have time to remember you. I do not want to remember you.*

But as Nerissa's eyes flickered open, it was not the cozy sitting room she saw. It was the stateroom of a ship built long ago. A twisted body lay on the floor, and another on the bed. There was so much blood. It covered everything. It turned the world red.

Nerissa pressed the heel of her hand against her eyes. The echoes of Nerissa's own curse swirled around her, suffocating her. *Forget about it,* she ordered herself. *Forget it. It is over and done. It was over and done centuries ago. The curse no longer binds you. It cannot. It cannot hurt you.*

It will not hurt Meri.

CHAPTER THREE

There was no time to sleep that night. It took minutes of Nerissa employing the breathing exercise she taught Meri to calm herself of both the despair of her nightmare and the eroticism of Meri's dream. It was a relief to leave the slumbering mermaid on her sofa – she would sleep until dawn, Nerissa imagined – and escape to her workroom.

It was an actual sketch that Nerissa worked over, muttering to herself, trying to perfect the likeness of Meri's center, drawing lines with assurance, and erasing them with a shake of her head. Long hours passed under the blue flame and it was not until dawn that Nerissa finally happened upon a solution. Bleary-eyed, she stared at the tide pool contained in her tub, watching the slow dance of the starfish, the darting quicksilver fish, and the gentle motion of the anemones. Her mind drifted to when she was young and curious — lifetimes ago — and how she and her sisters would stick their fingers in the anemones and feel the gentle suction—

"That's it!"

Her voice was rusty with lack of use. Her thought were as quick as the darting fish as it all came together for her. Her sketch of Meri was pushed to the side as she reached for the materials she would need to create an instrument of gentle suction, one that would coax Meri's pearl to the surface. Relief — warm, powerful relief — surged through Nerissa. It stayed with her as she created the instrument out of clay and carved the sigils and runes it would require. When she was done, she pressed it to her arm, and felt it pull gently at her skin. It felt like it was suckling at her—

A vivid image of Meri splayed out before her rose up in her mind's eyes. Instead of using the instrument she had just created, Nerissa used her mouth, suckling at that pristine flesh—

"None of that," Nerissa murmured.

By the time dawn came, Nerissa had finished, and was in the kitchen preparing a meal for the both of them. She'd heard stirring from the sitting room for some time; when Meri stumbled in with tousled hair and bleary eyes, Nerissa was waiting for her. The chairs around the small wooden table were mismatched and had been carved by Nerissa's own hands. Meri chose the one with the high back and carvings of delicate flowers all along the armrests.

"Would you like some tea?" Nerissa asked.

"Please," Meri croaked.

"How do you feel?" Nerissa asked. She pointed her driftwood wand at the stove and watched light blue flames erupt under the kettle.

Meri did not answer for over a minute. "I had the strangest of dreams," she finally said as she slumped to the side. Nerissa stole a glance at her. Strands of her pale hair clung to her cheek and sitting like this, Meri looked more human than she had yesterday.

"Nightmares?" Nerissa asked.

Her head wobbled back and forth. "No, I don't think so. You were in them. You told me you would be, but it surprised me. I don't remember what happened, they're just *impressions*. I was so cold, and then you were there… and suddenly it was warm. *Warm*," she repeated. Wonder suffused her tone. "I felt *warm*. And then you left but I *think* I kept dreaming of you." She sat upright, blinking. "That book you gave me yesterday! That story was in there, too, I think. That's when I got *cold* again. Don't you find that story a tad… disturbing?"

"I have never been disturbed by a story found in those pages," said Nerissa. Meri would have to be content with farm fare: all she had were eggs, cheese, and toast. She brought them to the table and served her. "Careful, it's still hot," she cautioned, as she took her own seat. "About that book… it is a magical one; it tells the story our soul needs to know." She picked up her tea and blew on it. A spicy citrus scent wafted up from the cup. "I have opened it up many a time and never found the same story twice."

Meri's face fell back into sleepy lines. She picked up her fork and stared at it as though she had never seen one before. "I wonder why it was my soul needed to know that."

Curiosity flickered in Nerissa, and her fingers tightened on her teacup. Then, just as quickly, she forced herself to relax. Nurturing Meri's body enough to allow it to feel true pleasure was going to be intimate enough; Nerissa did not want to further impose on her. Instead of allowing the question on the tip of her tongue to escape, Nerissa forced herself to remain quiet. She did not eat, but sat, patient, as Meri had her breakfast. It was not until Meri laid her fork down and sat back that Nerissa spoke again.

"I will need to keep you another day or so," said Nerissa.

Meri's eyes flickered to hers. "A day? Just a day?"

Nerissa tilted her head. "Did you want to stay longer?" she asked. Then, leaning forward: "*Can* you stay for another day? I never thought to ask what the old king thinks of you alone with a witch."

Meri gave her a long look. "Interesting that you mention the old king and not my husband the prince," she said. "It seems everyone knows that it is not just the two of us in our marriage, but the shadow of the king is always there. Is this a human custom? To form an odd triad?"

"No," said Nerissa. "It is not common. It happens, as I understand it. And the old king has been monarch for quite some time. Power like that… it is pervasive."

"As it happens, I was encouraged to seek understanding as to why I was not conceiving a child," said Meri. "It was decided that I must approach the witch – I mean, I was told I must approach you and ask if there was aught you could do to help."

A laugh bubbled out of Nerissa before she could stop it. It was so clear in her mind: the old king and the prince, sending Meri to the peninsula and to her; neither one of them would want to pay the price for any magic performed on their behalf. As with everything, they made Meri bear the brunt of it. But in one small way, Meri had not allowed them to take complete control. Not one mention of a child had passed Meri's lips until this moment. The more Nerissa thought how outraged the king and his progeny would be the more she laughed.

"The servants laugh at me as well."

It was the accusation in Meri's tone that made Nerissa finally quit.

"I do apologize," she said. "You misunderstand. I do not laugh at you. I laugh at the old king and his – his grandson." Nerissa nearly called him a fool, but she did not know how fond Meri was of her husband the prince. "They have an entire kingdom of riches, and yet they seek to make you pay the price at every turn."

Roses bloomed on her cheeks and she ducked her head.

"And yet you did not do as they bade you to," Nerissa said. She could not keep the smile off of her face. "You may have been maneuvered here, by them, but you asked me a question of your own choosing. I *approve.*"

There was a long silence. "You look so different when you smile," Meri said. "It is as though the clouds broke and the sun came out."

Nerissa drew in a deep breath and let it out slowly. A flicker in Meri's eyes told Nerissa that the observation had been a charming, though clumsy, deflection. *I do approve*, she said silently. She picked up her cup and saluted Meri with it, allowing a small smile to remain. *I understand you do not wish to discuss what you worry might be a betrayal. But I approve of it, betrayal or no.*

Meri tucked a strand of pale hair behind her cheek.

"Have you finished your breakfast? Do you wish to begin?" Nerissa asked. Her smile widened. "I have no intention of helping you to conceive, but only to help you find pleasure in your own body. Is that sufficient?"

There was a darkness in Meri's eyes. They were suddenly more tinted with grey and Nerissa realized she was *worried*.

"Meri," Nerissa said. "I have promised to help you. Only you. Not the old king. Not your prince. No one will ever know what happens in this lighthouse. No one will ever discover what you have truly asked me for."

"Do you – will you promise me?"

"I promise," said Nerissa. Heat washed over her; this was another way to help Meri. It was easy enough to do; if Nerissa never set eyes on the old king and his heir, she would be perfectly content. What mattered at the moment was Meri's comfort, especially considering the intimacies Nerissa was going to require of her.

"Should we – do we – are we to get started now?" Meri asked.

"Yes," said Nerissa.

"I'll need help with the buttons again—"

"Not here, Meri," said Nerissa. "Not here in the kitchen. And – I do believe we should find a bed. The more comfortable you are, the better."

Meri kept up a nervous chatter as Nerissa led her out to the hallway, opened a door, and revealed a winding stair that led to the upper levels of the lighthouse. It had been Nerissa's home for centuries; once the daze and shock of becoming what she had become wore off enough that she no longer wandered the coasts of the continent, she had found her way back here. It was here that she had put down roots and carved a space for herself.

And after all this time, this was the first time she had ever shared it with someone. Her infrequent visitors had been kept to the standing stones outside. A rare handful had been allowed in her sitting room.

Three hearth witches had once visited and Nerissa had fed them in her kitchen. But no one had ever seen her bedroom.

The significance was a weight pressing her shoulders down. When they reached the third floor, which was an entirely open space, it made her silent.

"Oh, this is lovely!" Meri cried.

Nerissa had salvaged what she could of the glass that the sea gave up. Her walls were made of windows. The glass was all different kinds: stained and clear, old and new. It showed a view of the cliffs and sea around them that Nerissa did not think could be replicated elsewhere. Still, it was her own work, and warmth spread over her at Meri's open, unfettered delight.

"It is still raining," Nerissa said, feeling a pang of regret. "You ought to see it at sunset on a clear day. It is lovely."

"It's lovely *now*," Meri said. She'd pressed a hand against the glass. "It reminds me of the sea... somehow you've captured the sea. The rain just adds to the beauty of it." The fervor in her tone made Nerissa's heart hitch. "Oh, it is *lovely*." She turned to Nerissa. "Have you done an enchantment on this as well? Am I seeing the view I need to see? Because – because I..."

"No enchantment, other than getting all this glass up here in one piece," said Nerissa. She looked at her wall with a more discerning eye. Never before had she thought the kaleidoscope of colors as the sea, but now it was obvious. "I am glad you like it."

"I suppose we should get started," said Meri. "But I just don't want to look away. How is it so colorful when it is barely light outside? There are places in the ocean, you know, where if you look up, you can see exactly this: tides of color swirling above you, echoing the sun. I didn't know I *missed* that."

"You can continue to look while I help you undress," Nerissa offered. The longing Meri had for home was so recognizable that a sharp pain shot through her stomach. It was not simply the sea that Meri longed for, Nerissa knew. It was the bright, familiar splash of color. It was the scent of sea flowers in the caverns. It was the luminescence found in secret corners; the gentle sway of life; the brush of seaweed against hand and fin. So Nerissa was exceedingly gentle as she undressed the mermaid, who would probably never lose the sadness.

"All those buttons," Meri murmured. "All of my pearls."

Nerissa's hands stilled at the last row. "Are you ready?" she asked.

It was a surprise to Nerissa that when Meri turned to her, her eyes were a clear blue – and dry. *I ought not to have expected tears,* Nerissa thought. Not everyone cried as they mourned what they had lost. But still, the hint of steel in those wide, wide eyes surprised her.

"I'm ready," said Meri.

Again, Meri displayed no modesty as she climbed onto the bed. For a moment, Nerissa had the absurd urge to change the color of her bedclothes — the colors weren't perfectly suited for Meri. It could be better.

"Attend," Nerissa said in a low voice.

"Do I need to do something else?" Meri asked.

"I spoke to myself," said Nerissa. Meri was not splayed totally open as she had been, but she held a natural position that revealed the pale hair between her thighs and a hint of shyly closed folds. It was difficult to look away.

"Is this difficult for you?" Meri asked. Her knees snapped shut and she sat up. A flush spread across her cheeks. "I'm so sorry! I ought to have known I—"

"What did I say about apologizing?" Nerissa said, amused.

"But *still* — oh the servants are right. My husband's sister is right. I am always forgetting that you land-dwellers are so modest and—"

"I am not a human, I am a witch," said Nerissa.

Meri wobbled her hand. "An *earth* witch."

Nerissa did not correct her. "I am not uncomfortable with helping you, Meri," she said instead. "But I feel I ought to warn you that I — this will be very intimate. As intimate as the moments you've had in bed with the old king's grandson." She took out the instrument she had made out of clay, embroidered silk, and sigils. "I do not wish for *you* to be uncomfortable."

The look Meri gave her was both direct and filled with a shadowed emotion Nerissa could not name. The air grew heated; a scent sprung up between them — it was the scent of the world just after lightning struck nearby. Clearing her throat, she tugged on her neckline. Her jerkin was suddenly too tight. Her movements were jerky as she got onto the bed with Meri and withdrew the instrument she had crafted.

"I have to touch you," said Nerissa. It took all of her willpower to keep her tone light.

"All right," said Meri.

The space between her legs widened and Nerissa settled between them. The pale strands of hair at Meri's center provided a fine privacy screen. Her fingertips brushed through it, and then she was spreading her open. She whispered a word and the instrument in her hand warmed. Very gently, she placed the tip of it – the part that looked a bit like a flower with plush, folded petals – against where Meri's pearl ought to be. Nerissa issued another command, and the petals unfurled and latched on.

Meri dragged in a breath.

"Does that hurt?" Nerissa asked sharply. "It should not hurt."

"No, it… it feels *strange*," said Meri. "I would not call it *pain*."

"Do you want me to continue?"

"Please," said Meri. She swallowed and added: "Can you tell me what it is *doing*, thought?"

And so while the instrument did what it was built to do, Nerissa explained. "You remember that I entered your dreams and did a magical working in them. I discovered then that your pearl was not *missing* – I was nearly positive the sea witch could not deliberately leave anything missing. Transformations are *total*. But your pearl is not where pearls are generally to be found, that could not be denied." Meri was squirming slightly, and Nerissa placed a hand on her hip to hold her still. "Try not to move, I want to be sure it's latched on properly. When I entered your dreams, I discovered that the pearl is not missing, it is hidden. So I crafted this instrument to – to bring it to the surface."

"Now I've a seal in mind, poking his head above the water," said Meri.

"Physically, yes," said Nerissa. "But the further we go along, the more… stirred you will be." Her thumb was stroking the outer edge of Meri's folds; as soon as Nerissa realized what she was doing, she stopped. And cleared her throat. "It was just as well that you were able to – stirred you so I knew it was hidden, not just—"

"The memory of the serving girls *stirred* me?" Meri asked, incredulous.

Their eyes tangled together.

"It did," Nerissa said. Something fluttered within her chest. Through all the talk about the prince and his member, it was the memory of watching two women that had stirred Meri's hidden desire. A pulse beat between her legs.

"Not the prince," Meri said, tone flat. "I am unsurprised. I suppose it isn't *terrible* with him, but it is too hard. Too rough. Being inside someone else's passion like that is as though being caught in a rogue current and battered against the rocks. Kissing is the easiest part of it." There was a glimmer in her eyes, like sunlight peaceful waters. "And I suppose what the serving girls were doing was kissing.

Heat crept up Nerissa's neck and she ducked her head, clearing her throat, and shoving images out of her head. To help with that, she began to speak very quickly and at great length. More explanations flowed from her; she described the sigils she used, the runes she'd carved, and even the provenance of the clay. Her heartbeat was a quick drum in her chest, though, since no matter how much Nerissa talked about the smallest details, she could not escape the intimacy of what she was doing. It was nearly a relief, a few minutes later, when the instrument released itself from Meri's flesh.

"Is it done?" Meri asked, looking down her body, brow creased. "I confess I don't feel much different."

"You—"

"Perhaps I'm a bit too eager," said Meri. "That story... there was a mermaid in it who enjoyed having a human body quite a bit, and—"

Nerissa moved away from her, blood a sudden thunder in her ears. "Remember I said that this would take some time?" she asked. "We do not want to do this all at once, but want to maintain a gentler pace." *Now I am the one who is rambling.* "We will wait an hour or so before we resume." With deft motions, she tossed a blanket over the mermaid, told her she ought to get some rest, and fled. Down the stairs she went, down to her kitchen, into her cellar, and down the secret stairs she'd hollowed out from the cliff. As she passed it, the moonstone mirror showed her pale, frightened face.

For a brief, dizzy moment, Nerissa stood in her workroom and felt a stranger in it. Her centuries drifted away and she was fresh and new and so very out of place.

Dianora.

The name whispered through her and she felt it in the sudden tremor in her fingers. Her eyes fluttered closed and she was no longer in her workroom, but in another time and place. The water around her was warm, and there was taste and smell on the current that Nerissa knew now was the smell of mead, but then it had enchanted her, made her curious... made her foolish.

Two small girls, both from different worlds, meeting at a beach after a shipwreck. Dianora, with her bright hair the color of fire. The last time Nerissa has seen it, it was the color of blood spilled.

Centuries later, and a whisper of Dianora's memory nearly brought Nerissa to her knees. Her hair, spilling down her back, her bright blue eyes... later, the way her lips had tasted of salt and sunshine. All the stolen hours they'd had together over the years came back at once.

Desperate, Nerissa looked at the conch shell. It gave off a gentle light, and it was this she latched onto during the storm of her past. After she had created the instrument that would help Meri, she would exact the gentlest of prices from the mermaid: her memories of the time spent with Nerissa on the shrouded peninsula. It would keep her safe. It would protect her, the forgetting would. The old king would not be able to pry any secrets out of Meri — how could he, if the secrets were safely housed in a shell?

And Meri would be safe from Nerissa's own curse...

Nerissa's grip tightened until the wood bit into her palms. Cold skittered up her spine and she was aware of a hum in the room. The knife... it was hidden in the wall and kept in a box, and yet... she could feel the cold that pulsed from it, and could hear its hum. Her teeth clenched. *Do not be afraid,* a musical voice whispered. Dianora reached for her across the centuries. *Do not be so afraid.*

There was tenderness and desire in Nerissa's thoughts for Meri — it was dangerous for Nerissa to *care* so much. Dianora of all people ought to know as much. Look at what Nerissa had brought about...

Remember, you are no longer under the curse. You are the witch now.

Clarity returned bit by bit. There was a long, dizzy moment as Nerissa sought her bearings. It was the safe, familiar enchantments of her workroom that steadied her and gave her surer ground to stand on. The tide moved in its basin, unconcerned with Nerissa's state. The conch shell glowed. A cloud formed over her table, warning sign of yet another storm heading toward the peninsula. Quiet sounds of lingering magic showed Nerissa the path.

When she brushed her thumb over the conch shell, which was ready to house a few of Meri's memories, her balance was restored.

Now she no longer trembled like a leaf, she managed a more sedate pace up the stairs. In the kitchen, she prepared a light lunch for Meri, toiling over it, still not quite ready to return to her bedroom. Instead, she finished up her tray and wandered into the sitting room. Curiosity pulled at her. What story had the book told her? Meri had been disturbed and yet…

Nerissa gave into her impulse, drew a rune in the air above the book – still laying on the settee where Meri had left it – opened it to the first page and began to read.

> *As our grandparents taught us, there are secret coves and beaches, and these are the places where you may walk along the shore and see a mermaid sitting atop a rock. She will be combing her long hair and perhaps you may even hear the silver bell of her voice ringing out over the waves. "Go at dawn or dusk," our grandparents told us, "the sea folk are shy, but they do like to let their hair dry in order to comb it." And we listened to them because we knew their age had granted them wisdom.*
>
> *It is not just dawn and dusk or the need to comb their hair that brings a mermaid to shore. A young girl realized to her everlasting delight that mermaids cannot resist the scent of honey. Her uncle was the king, but her parents had been out of favor with him since she was born, and they refused to give her to the palace to raise. So the young girl ran wild along the coves and cliffs, and it was on one of these occasions that she came upon an enchanting sight: a mermaid splashing in a pool of mead.*
>
> *"There was a shipwreck!" cried the mermaid. "I pulled the casks to shore and now I'm having a lovely bath!"*
>
> *The little girl was so charmed by the mermaid that she climbed as close to her as she could. They were near the same age, and neither were afraid of the other. It was the beginning of a friendship that grew stronger with every season that passed.*
>
> *"I worry about you being gone so longer every day," both sets of mothers would say, one in a large manor on the hill, and the other deep under the sea.*
>
> *And both fathers would say, gruffly: "I hope you keep your safety in mind."*
>
> *It was only the sea witch who knew of the friendship between human and mermaid, as she knew many secrets. They drifted to her on the currents of the sea and she caught them in her nets. The seasons passed, as did the years, and only the witch knew how deep and abiding was the love between them.*
>
> *One day, the king and his sons were struck down. The next day, the human girl – now a princess, of course – and her family left the manor by the sea. The father was now the king of all the land, and her mother the queen. Her small brother was the Crown Prince. Their fortunes changed overnight.*

"Why do you cry so?" the king demanded of his daughter. "You are now a princess. You will have everything you could want."

"I will not have the sea," she said.

Her grief was ever-present. Tears slid down her face at her father's coronation and then her mother's. The court whispered about her, as she would begin to cry at the oddest things. She grieved every day until her family decided it was madness that held her in its grip and that was what made her so sick to be away from that manor by the sea.

"Arrange a marriage for her," the queen said at last. "Let her be distracted. Let her tend to husband and children. There is naught else we can do."

Thus the king set his mind on finding an appropriate husband for the princess.

It was the first day of spring when the mermaid walked out of the river where the princess was having a picnic with the younger lords and ladies of the court. Her legs were new and wobbly and the soles of her feet were cut on the rocks. Despite this, it took little time to find her. The princess sat under a tree, embroidery in hand, speaking to no one. She looked up and was so struck by the sight of the mermaid walking toward her that she felt as though struck by lightning. What else could that grip around her heart be? How could her mermaid be standing there in front of her? The lords and ladies of the court were forgotten.

The princess drew the mermaid up into the palace and into her room.

"You have legs? You have legs! How is it you can be here?"

The princess said this over and over again. Her madness was shock and delight mingled together. Her attention was fixed now not on tears, but on the mermaid and her impossible legs. She took to running her hands over and between them, touching smooth flesh instead of scales. After a time, she cried again, this time from sharp-edged joy.

"When you disappeared—"

"I know you thought I left you. I would never leave you. Not willingly."

"I was distraught," said the mermaid. "I thought you gone from this world. I waited and waited for you, every day, until my mother and father took to sending my sister along with me whenever I left home. I could not come to the surface then..."

"But how are you here?" the princess implored.

The sea witch had come to the mermaid. She had known where the mermaid's heart was, and that it was not in or of the sea. There was an old fear of witches; there were dark stories told of murderous currents and poison waters. It took some time before the mermaid *would listen to the witch. But when she did... the witch showed her the princess through one of her mirrors; the mermaid saw how sad she looked. It was then she made a bargain with the sea witch for her legs.*

"What price did you pay?" the princess whispered at the end of the telling.

"It does not matter," said the mermaid. "I would pay and pay again three times as much."

The princess was so filled with joy that the mermaid had been returned to her, she decided not to peer into this miracle. She announced that she had taken on the mermaid as her new hand-maiden and companion.

If the king and queen had reservations of the princess clasping to someone of unknown birth, they held their tongues. The princess was so much happier now; they told themselves it was because she had been lonely for friendship. Now she had a devoted companion. Every lord and lady in the court noticed a difference: the sad princess they had known was gone; now it was joy that radiated from her.

The king was so distracted by his daughter's refound happiness that he quite forgot that he had arranged a marriage for her. A kingdom some distance away across the water had a prince of marriageable age. He would bring with him gold and livestock, fifty archers and ten knights. This foreign prince was desirable in every way, and when the king got around to remembering him, he told his daughter this.

To his shock, the princess's protest to her upcoming marriage was bitter and full of rage. There was no desire in her to marry. When he argued that of course she wanted to marry, of course she wanted to have a family and raise them here at the palace, she flung at him words she would never take back.

"You have become like the king you were estranged from," she told him. "You let us be free when we lived in our manor by the sea. Now you hold us prisoner in this gilded palace."

"Oh, you and that manor!" the king thundered at his daughter. "You will never return there. Never! I will tear it down if I have to."

After these words, even the mermaid could not calm the princess. It was not until very late that night, when silence fell over the palace, that the princess realized the mermaid was pale and shaken.

"Oh, and even if he does force me to marry, it will change nothing," said the princess, anxious to reassure. "You will still be my hand-maiden. We will never be able to live in our manor just the two of us. But marriage or not, I will still be yours."

The mermaid sat up, shivering in the cold air. "It is my fault."

The princess laughed. "How can it possibly be your fault?"

The light of the moon fell upon the mermaid's face; she looked as though carved from marble. "My curse," she said finally, with great misery. "I fear this is my curse."

"Your curse?"

"My bargain. With the sea witch."

"Your – what has that to do with my father arranging a marriage for me?"

The mermaid told her, in halting words and whispers, that as the price to be paid for such transformational magic, the sea witch had given her something of a riddle. "Your bond is one of love, and it is love you will choose again and again."

"But that is not terrible!"

"The one you love will not have freedom to choose," said the mermaid. "Bonds of love will not hold up to bonds of power."

The princess was quiet after that until near sunrise. Many things ran through her head, not least of which was a surprising amount of anger at her mermaid. This curse of hers did not seem a curse upon the mermaid but upon the princess herself. Her curse was that she had no power to choose...

"It is not any different now than it was when my father suddenly became king," said the princess. The birds were singing outside their window. There was a space between them in the bed that had not once existed since the moment the mermaid had walked out of the river. "I had no choice in the matter of leaving the manor or leaving you. Perhaps you did not cause this. Perhaps the witch simply told you the truth of what our companionship will be. Marriage to a prince aside, I would never be allowed the choice to marry you."

"I see," said the mermaid. "You may be right."

But in the weeks leading up to the wedding, the mermaid was fretful. The princess made her many promises, and these would cheer the mermaid for a time. But then her spirits would sag. It grew worse when the prince came. Tall and handsome, his crown shone in the sunlight. The ladies of the court fell in love with an immediacy that made them swoon. The lords were jealous of his erect carriage and the riches he brought.

"He matters nothing to me," said the princess.

"You will be bonded to him," said the mermaid.

"I am bonded to you in a way I will never be to him," said the princess.

She kept every single one of her promises. Her handmaiden was not to be separated from her. Even when they took a honeymoon voyage in the handsome ship the prince brought, her handmaiden would go with her. The prince agreed to all of the terms; if he found them odd, he did not say a word.

"I do not like him," the mermaid said the night before the wedding. "He is made of hard flint. It does not bode well that you will be bonded to him."

"I do not wish to speak of him tonight," said the weary princess. "This is the last time we may share a bed for a little while. Come, my mermaid, let us make the most of it."

The mermaid hated each moment of the wedding and looked away when the new husband and wife lifted a glass together and shared it. His eyes were cold and the color of flint. The fact the princess did not have the gift of choice reverberated through her bones and made her new legs weak in the knee. Should the prince not heed any of the princess's wishes, the princess would not have a choice in the matter. There was nothing the mermaid could do.

The thoughts consumed her. The honeymoon was to begin right after the ceremony. The princess gave her one last glance, a stoic grimace, then disappeared belowdecks to the stateroom she would share with her new husband: the prince to whom she was bonded. The mermaid stayed on deck, watching the water, and feeling the weight of her choice to become human.

What if the prince ordered her away from the princess? The mermaid would be trapped as a human... trapped in a new form and without her love.

"There is nothing I can do," whispered the mermaid. Her words drifted over the water.

The sea witch had been waiting for her.

Her head breached the waves and she stared at the mermaid as though staring into her soul.

"What has brought you here?" Terror gripped the mermaid.

"I am here to ask if you wish to be let free from our bargain," said the witch. "You stand here on the deck of your love's wedding ship. It must hurt, knowing what intimacies are occurring in the stateroom of this ship."

"It does not."

"Do not lie to me," said the witch.

Then she offered the mermaid another bargain. A small knife, made of coldest black flipped upward and onto the deck at the mermaid's feet. Trembling, the mermaid kicked at it. But, as though it were made of heaviest stone, it refused to budge. Should the mermaid kill with this knife, the bond would be broken. The mermaid could return to her home, her true home under the sea, where her family missed her. The witch showed her a hint of them on the waves, showing how they grieved for her.

"I could not kill my love," said the mermaid.

The witch scoffed at her.

It was then that a terrible scream tore the night in two. A ghastly smile spread across the witch's face as the mermaid – without thinking or planning it – plucked up the small knife from where it lay at her

*feet. It was the princess, screaming out in terror and pain. It surged
across the water as the witch laughed and the mermaid ran.*
No one ever found what was left of that handsome ship.

Nerissa's eyes fluttered closed. Old, old pain clamped around her.
The story was near enough to true to have fangs and claws that sank
into old wounds. There was only one thing she could do: she ignored
them, closed her eyes, and breathed in deeply and evenly. After she'd
woken after her transformation, alone, in the middle of the sea, she had
been the wreckage of a soul. She remembered her lessons from that
time: deep, even breaths. Carefully, she drew herself back. The memories faded. In her mind's eye, Dianora's image turned away.

Nerissa retreated to the margin between thought and memory.

It had been centuries, and yet still so fresh.

Meri is a different mermaid with a different curse. The cool voice of reason
found her there in that boundary. Nerissa's shoulders loosened. "It was
just a story," she rasped out. Her voice strengthened as she used it. The
pain let go its grip. Here, in these margins, Nerissa had *power.* "Begone
from me," she murmured. "Begone from me." With forced gentleness,
she shut the book. Dianora's image faded and Meri's open smile greeted
her.

It was then Nerissa realized that this… this was the last sign she
needed that her plan to use Meri's memories as the price she would pay
for Nerissa's help was a good one. It freed her from the last, clinging
bits of memory, and her gaze turned toward the stairs where the mermaid awaited her.

*You are a witch. These curses are gone and forgotten. And even if some vestige of
them still remain, they need not touch Meri. Enjoy the moments you have, and then…*

Let her forget.

It was this idea, that Nerissa could erase any danger from Meri's
thoughts, that lifted her spirits. A smile – which would have been
impossible a minute ago – lifted her lips. She fairly floated across the
floor of her sitting room and to the stairs. Yes. This was freedom to do
the best by Meri. She would restore the pearl to the mermaid. Nerissa
would give her all the help she needed… and then she would send her
safely home.

Nerissa would *indulge* her.

And then she would say goodbye.

CHAPTER FOUR

"Well, hello again, my lady. You left very suddenly," said Meri. Her gown draped down her arms, revealing her breasts. The dusky roses of her nipples contrasted against the fabric. "I felt that despite your reassurances, you *are* uncomfortable. It's unfair to you—"

"I am not uncomfortable," said Nerissa, briefly disoriented. "I am a witch."

"Are witches born with different emotions than mermaids? Than humans?" Meri asked.

It was meant to be a rhetorical question, but Nerissa seized on it. "I can count on one hand how many were born to be witches, and that is a mystery none of us have been able to solve. Most of us had a similar... transformation as you did."

Meri's gown fell to the floor. "You did? You were transformed, too?"

"Yes," said Nerissa. "As far as I know, we still have the same emotions we had in our first lives. Are you not so different from who you were as a mermaid?" She made a sweeping gesture toward the bed. "I am not immeasurably different from who I was when I was born. The same desires are still within me. But Meri... I was born long, long ago. Centuries ago." There was a sudden, swift lump in her throat. "I have spent much of your lifetime here, alone, but for the cormorants. I am having to... adjust to not being alone."

Meri's lips parted. "I didn't realize that," she said. Nerissa, who had just realized Meri's lips were precisely the same pink as her nipples, barely heard her.

She was so lovely. Every bit of her was perfectly formed. It had been so long since Nerissa had seen anything so beautiful.

"*You* think *I'm* beautiful?"

Startled, Nerissa caught Meri's eye. The mermaid gaped at her. It was then that Nerissa realized Meri was nearly always in motion; it was not until now, when her face was so still and frozen, that she realized how expressive Meri was. "Yes, of course I think you are beautiful," said Nerissa. When she gestured toward the bed again, Meri complied.

Nerissa peered between Meri's spread thighs. Was it her imagination, or were the folds slightly rosier than they had been? And more open? The flesh where Meri's pearl out to be was pale, still, though, and when she brought her instrument up to it, it latched on eagerly. This time, she was quiet. Meri was sitting up on her elbows — Nerissa could *feel* the weight of her gaze — but neither one said a word. After some time, the instrument fell away again.

"Oh!" said Nerissa. "It is working already!" There was a tiny silvery mark exactly where Meri's pearl should be. It formed the shape of the sigil of pleasure, and it was faintly luminescent. Pride surged through her and she tossed Meri a fierce grin. "It is only a matter of time before your pearl comes out of hiding." Without even realizing it, she'd pressed her finger against the sigil — and so she felt it when Meri quivered beneath her.

It was a subtle quiver, but there was no mistaking what it was.

What it meant.

Nerissa dropped her eyes and her hand, cleared her throat, and sat back.

"Last time it just felt something was pulling at me," said Meri. She crossed her legs and bounced her foot. "It didn't *hurt*, exactly, but it felt... not like this." Her hands slid down her stomach. "It felt... warm. Like the dream."

"It will become more sensitive the longer we do this," said Nerissa.

Her lips quivered into a smile.

This time, as they waited for Meri's body to adjust, Nerissa stayed in the room. It was mostly quiet, and she stood at the window. The colors blurred her view of the peninsula, but she could see the pounding sea swirling just beyond the cliffs. It was at this time that Nerissa gave herself a private admonishment. Her age was counted in centuries yet she acted like a callow girl. It had been silly of her to run away.

The next two times Nerissa used the instrument, she was careful to lock her own desires away. Meri's private flesh blossomed more and more but Nerissa did her best to ignore it. No more stroking her folds, no more brushing her thumb against the sigil at the top of her slit that was now beginning to give off a subtle light.

Her composure cracked after lunch.

Meri was in her now familiar sprawl, and Nerissa was between her legs. The instrument had not even touched Meri, but her folds were dewy with moisture. Unable to help herself, Nerissa took in a breath. The scent of Meri's arousal was heady and unmistakable. *But the instrument has not gone near her for an hour,* Nerissa thought. Over an hour, really, considering how long it had taken to heat the stew for her. And yet...

"What are you thinking about?" Nerissa asked.

"Thinking?" asked Meri. "I wasn't thinking much of anything. Except... you have beautiful hair, you know. It looks pure black but there are hints of blue and even purple. I thought perhaps it was the window, you know, all that stained glass reflecting in your hair. But I was watching you in the kitchen, and it was still there."

"You were thinking about my hair," Nerissa said. Her breathing deepened.

"It's up right now, but it was down in the dream," said Meri. "I was thinking how it looked swirling around you, all black and blue and purple. You were close enough that I could see all the subtle color. You're close enough right now." Her eyelids lowered and pink blossomed in her cheeks. "It reminds me of what it feels like to be warm."

Nerissa's nipples tightened.

Then Meri reached out and brushed her fingers in Nerissa's hair. Little tingles of pleasure accompanied the touch, spreading out like ripples. Carved sticks of driftwood held Nerissa's hair in place, and Meri tugged them out. Nerissa's hair – long and dark and now free – tumbled down like a heavy curtain. Pale, slim fingers threaded through it.

When she sighed, it felt like a prayer.

Of course, when she pressed the instrument against the faintly glowing sigil, it was different. With Meri's hands in her hair, it was impossible to remain aloof. Another sigh, this one more apology than prayer, and then Nerissa stroked Meri's folds. They bloomed further under her touch and the dew spread, coating Meri's center and Nerissa's fingers with wetness. By the time the instrument fell away, signaling it was done for the moment, Meri's scent had flooded her senses.

Nerissa shifted the instrument out of the way and grazed the sigil with the tip of her finger. At the same moment Nerissa felt a distinct, hard knot, Meri gave a low whimper. Meri's pearl was still hidden under a layer of flesh, but it was close enough to the surface that Nerissa could *feel* it. This much she said to Meri as she drew back.

Meri's hands were no longer in her hair, but were stroking across her stomach. The mermaid was quite stirred, Nerissa thought, with no small amount of pride. At the moment, Nerissa did not think it possible for her to experience fulfillment... but her dusky rose nipples had tightened into buds, the muscles in her stomach quivered, and there was a gleam in her eye.

"That was it, wasn't it?" Meri said. "That *was* my pearl. You were right. My, I feel so…"

"As I said, the more we do this, the more stirred you will become," said Nerissa. Instead of moving off the bed and redoing her hair, she reclined just a foot away from where Meri sprawled.

Meri rolled to face her. "It feels so good. Your hands on me…"

"Did it concern you?" Nerissa asked.

"The opposite," said Meri.

"I am not your husband," Nerissa pointed out.

"The *prince*," said Meri with curious emphasis. "The prince would not know how to be gentle like that. I am *glad* you are not the prince."

Nerissa brushed her thumb along Meri's brow, where a crease had appeared at the mention of her husband. "We do not have to speak of him," she said. "There are many things under the sun and sky that we can discuss."

A smile tilted the corners of Meri's lips. "Like pearls?"

"Indeed," said Nerissa.

"I *am* curious," said Meri.

"This is fine with me," said Nerissa.

"Does it *look* like a pearl, though?" Meri asked.

Nerissa thought about it. "In truth, they are all fairly unique. Some are large, some small. Everyone is different."

"May I see yours?"

The question was so direct and so *private* that Nerissa breathed in a deep breath. Letting it out, she thought of all the ways she could appease the mermaid's curiosity. Surely there were etchings in her library that could show her uncursed feminine centers. Her cormorants would hardly need to search, would they? She could also suggest Meri wait until her own pearl was entirely visible. All she would need was a bit of dexterity and a mirror…

"Yes, you may see mine," Nerissa said instead.

The jerkin and undergown Nerissa wore were not nearly as complicated as the gown Meri had arrived in. There were no buttons. It was easy to undo the laces. And yet, the whole time, Nerissa was exceedingly, achingly aware that with every bit of clothing she took off, she crossed another boundary. It slowed her movements, made her more cautious, and by the time she lifted her undergown over her head, her hands were shaking.

"Your breasts are bigger than mine," said Meri.

"I think just slightly," said Nerissa.

"You look barely as old as one of the prince's sisters," said Meri.

"I look as I did when I became a witch," said Nerissa. The conversation eased her, though, and she was quick to return to the bed. Meri's gaze was avid on her. That scent – the smell of the earth just after lightning has struck it – rose between them again, mingling with the lingering scent of Meri's arousal. Added to it was Nerissa's own.

Meri did not seem to be any hurry to examine Nerissa's center. Instead, she kept up a commentary about Nerissa's body, ranging from how her nipples were pale and pretty, to the slimness of her waist. At one point, she spread Nerissa's hair over her breast and made a throaty humming sound that sent a wave of heat to Nerissa's center.

"And these!"

Warm, smooth fingers swept up Nerissa's hip. "My hips?" Nerissa asked, amused.

"No!" said Meri. "This little pattern… these dappled shadows. It looks like scales!"

"Perhaps they do," said Nerissa.

Meri's hand lingered there, playing over the marks on Nerissa – the ones that matched the marks Meri had on the base of her spine. When Meri did not make a further remark about it, Nerissa decided she did not know or suspect that they were a remnant from Nerissa's *first* transformation. After another murmur, Meri moved to kneel in front of her.

Nerissa spread her legs for her.

A featherlight touch high on her inner thigh made her muscles jump.

Meri drew back. "Am I allowed to touch?"

"You may," said Nerissa.

Small touches continued to tease her. The mermaid was in no hurry to see Nerissa's pearl, it seemed. Instead, her hands swept up and down her thighs. Nerissa aged another century before the barest tip of a finger caressed the outer edges of her folds.

Meri moved to lay between her thighs.

Warm breath washed over Nerissa's center, and then Meri nuzzled her. "You smell so good," the mermaid told her. "Did I mention to you that I smelled sweet water, once, when my family ventured near the shore? I've thought about it while I've been here, but I don't know if I ever spoke of it."

"I... you did," said Nerissa, who was trying not to push her hips forward. But the desire to be *touched* was so strong... it had been so *long*. "You did mention that—"

Meri looked up at her, her eyes glittering. "I can smell that same sweetness. It smelled of you." She leaned forward and breathed in deeply. Nerissa moaned low in her throat. "You smell so good, my lady."

Then gentle fingers separated Nerissa's folds and stroked them. The ripples of pleasure spreading through her body became waves of pleasure, responding to the nearness of Meri and the way she was touching her. Gentle hands stroked her, pet her, opened her, and explored her. The mermaid played with Nerissa with an exquisiteness that bordered on torture. With every brush of her fingers, the pleasure surged higher.

And then—

"I think I've found it," said Meri. "I think I've found your pearl."

Nerissa's hips canted forward when the mermaid touched her. A low moan slipped out from her. "Oh yes," she said in a voice not quite her own. "Oh, yes, there it is."

"This is it?" Meri asked. A hint of laughter lurked in her tone. Her finger worked over the small nub, rubbing it... nudging it.

"Yes," said Nerissa, after a long moment trying to absorb the pleasure moving through her.

"It's very small," said Meri. "It's nearly covered, I almost didn't find it, but there it was, peeking out at me. And... it's pulsing? Is that your heartbeat?"

"Yes, that is likely," said Nerissa.

"It's very small," said Meri.

Then she pulled away.

Nerissa's eyes lifted to Meri's. Her heart, already racing, skipped a beat. Her body, already stirred, tightened further. There it was, in Meri's eyes – and unmistakable glimmer of pleasure. And not just in her eyes. Want and desire had done their subtle alterations to that lovely face: her lips were glossy and parted, pink brushed across her cheekbones, and... her eyes spoke of it most of all. There was a cord between them, Nerissa realized, and it was drawn taut. Desire pulsed between them, the scent of lightning and honey. She felt it in the tingle of her nipples and the steady throb between her thighs.

It was inevitable that she lean forward, draw the mermaid close to her, and kiss her on those sweet, parted lips.

When Meri stiffened in surprise, Nerissa pulled back. "Was that not permissible?"

"Oh, no, I was just... surprised," said Meri.

Then she fairly threw herself into Nerissa's arms. Their breasts pressed up against each other. Heat radiated from Meri, and Nerissa held on as tight as she could and kissed her. Meri's tongue slipped into her mouth, and Nerissa moaned against her. It was glorious, this, all her senses were alive, dancing a sailor's jig, spinning around. Meri was in her arms, her tongue was in her mouth, and it had been centuries since Nerissa had felt so alive. Not since Dianora—

Dianora.

Meri made a small sound when Nerissa pulled away.

"I do not want you to feel buffeted around by the waves of passion," said Nerissa, as an explanation.

"I did not feel buffeted around," said Meri. "I feel quite nice, to be honest. Warm. Warm and restless."

"We still have some way to go with your pearl," said Nerissa. When she moved up the bed, the mermaid followed her. With a sigh, she settled onto her sighed and wrapped her arms around Meri, keeping her still. "I think you should rest and reflect on what you feel. It will make it all the easier when it comes time to use the instrument again."

As the mermaid quieted, Nerissa closed her eyes. It was no surprise to her that Dianora's image sprang up immediately in her mind's eye. She had felt so close today. When she breathed in, it surprised her that it was Meri's scent she smelled, not Dianora's perfume. The passion had been similar – at the same time, it had not.

Nerissa wanted more – so much more.

Meri's restlessness transferred over to her. A few minutes of attempting to get comfortable, and Nerissa left the bed.

"You're leaving again?"

"*We* are leaving," said Nerissa. Meri blinked at her. Then her gaze swept up and down Nerissa's naked body. "We are going upstairs. I wish to show you the lantern room."

"In the storm?" Meri asked. Though she sounded unsure, she too got off the bed. Nerissa opened the chest at the end of her bed, and tossed the mermaid a blanket.

"Wrap that around yourself," Nerissa said, as she did the same with a sheet. But the mermaid had a point about the storm. After promising Meri she would be back in a moment, Nerissa went down to the sitting room and retrieved Meri's parasol. "I know that no one thought to tell you that a parasol is not appropriate for a true storm. See how dainty the lacing is here? The wind was strong enough yesterday it surely ripped it to shreds within an hour."

"Within minutes," Meri admitted. "Why bring it up, then, if it so useless?"

Nerissa retrieved one of her driftwood wands. "I am a witch," she said. "I can make it strong." And she did just that, drawing runes for strength over the shredded white lace. The damage reversed itself; the parasol bloomed outward, full and lovely and intricately made. The runes glowed; lines of quicksilver were absorbed into the lace. Once satisfied, she looked back at Meri, whose eyes were wide and stunned.

"Now will serve you better than any umbrella of mortal design," said Nerissa.

"I... thank you," said Meri. She took the parasol from Nerissa's outstretched hands. "Is it just witches who can use those – those – whatever it was that was just shining?"

"No," said Nerissa. She took Meri's hand and laced her fingers through hers. She led Meri along the curve of her window, toward a small alcove where an archway led to another curved stair. "Witches are but one class of beings – mortal and otherwise – who can use runes and sigils to effect magical change. The gods, such as the lords of the deep... part of their power involves the creation of such runes and sigils. They are symbols of both natural and unnatural forces in the world: tides and currents, storms and waves, fertility and barrenness... everything has a symbol. Humans can use the runes, but they will only know the common ones. Priests and priestesses..." Her voice trailed off when she looked back, and saw Meri's eyes had glazed over. "I do apologize, that was not the easy sort of answer you were expecting, was it?"

"I'm afraid I didn't follow all of that," Meri admitted.

"Just know that witches have an... intercessory sort of role between the gods and the humans. While a mortal could transcribe what runes he knew onto this parasol and have somewhat a similar effect, though no mortal could do it so swiftly or so easily. Magic is... think of water trying to fit itself inside a small vessel. Mortals do not have the capacity to use very much of it. Their bodies simply cannot hold enough of it to do anything large."

"But witches do," said Meri.

"There are certain circumstances in which mortals are transformed into witches," said Nerissa. "The transformation requires a mortal to be hollowed out, filled with magic... their – our – mortality is burned away and we become capable of handling... more."

"Like transforming mermaids into human," said Meri. Her palm was slightly damp.

"Exactly that," said Nerissa. "Now come, let me show you the lantern room." She fisted her other hand in her sheet, holding it up over her ankles, and led the way. The stair wound in a spiral and was quite steep. The storm that raged around them grew louder and louder, until they stepped onto a landing and were suddenly right in the middle of it. The wind was so strong it nearly lifted them off their feet. Nerissa let go of the sheet, and took her wand out of her mouth.

"Parasol!" she shouted.

Meri opened the parasol and swung it up over both of them.

Nerissa drew a few runes in the air in front of them, creating a bubble of protection. The sound of the storm's rage receded to a dim roar. The air heated, the wind stopped trying to sweep them over the side of the rail, and it was safe to speak.

"I apologize," she said. "I did not know it was quite this bad up here, or I would have waited."

"I don't mind," said Meri. "I've been in stronger water. I've felt stronger currents."

"I know," said Nerissa. The parasol that still protected them from the rain beating down was small. Meri was pressed all along her body, and their faces were so close Nerissa could feel soft puffs of Meri's breath against her forehead. "Well, this is the lantern room. It is... not much of a room. It is open to the elements."

"But there is a real light here!" Meri said.

"Of course there is," said Nerissa, blinking.

"I didn't think this was an actual... I didn't know this was an actual lighthouse," said Meri.

Nerissa stretched out her arm, pointing in the direction of the sea. "You cannot see it with the storm raging and at night, but this is a perilous section of water for ships. Cliffs jut out. There are unexpected shallows, and if the tide is right – or wrong, as the case may be – there are hundreds of rocks that lurk just under the water, ready to tear apart a hull. This lighthouse was built for a *purpose*. It was here long before I was. No captain could memorize every location of the hidden dangers; the coast here is much too complex for that. This was built to be a guide, just as all lighthouses are."

Meri made a helpless gesture. "I guess I didn't expect you to… tend to the needs of sailors."

Nerissa lifted her hand and stroked her thumb along Meri's jaw. "I do not," she said, with as much gentleness as she possessed. "If at times I light the lantern, it is not because I desire to guide a ship safely along its watery path." The souls of her cormorant servants had to come from *somewhere*. As it happened, luring a ship to a dangerous shore was the easiest way to do it.

"But… ah," said Meri. Though Nerissa watched her closely, she did not seem much disturbed by the idea. The silence that followed was more thoughtful than apprehensive.

And it was Nerissa who broke it. "I made this my home some centuries ago," she said. "I do not allow humans here; I believe they have forgotten there used to be a lighthouse here, for they built another a few miles down the coast. Outside of my demesne."

"Do you like it here?" Meri asked.

It was an unexpected question. Nerissa's gaze flitted away, to watch the lightning arc between clouds, and then flitted back. "It is a place to be, and it is a place to exist." There were other reasons why she stayed here. Nerissa did not believe she could stay away from the cove below. It would always draw her back, no matter how far she roamed. These things, and the reason why, she did not want to tell Meri.

Goosebumps that had nothing to do with the cold erupted on Nerissa's arm as Meri's touch swept up it. Nerissa swallowed and looked at her.

"You sound as lonely as I am," said the mermaid.

And Nerissa cupped the back of her head, shoved lingering thoughts of Dianora away, and stretched upward to meet Meri's lips with her own. The mermaid stiffened for a heartbeat, and then flung herself at Nerissa with an enthusiasm that made Nerissa's head spin. Her tongue was in Meri's mouth – no, *Meri's* tongue was in *her* mouth – and it was a burning sort of pleasure. Desire arced through her body as they kissed. Frantic, she pulled Meri's blanket down, and kneaded her breasts in her hands. Had she noticed how perfectly-sized they were?

For a brief moment, they pulled apart.

"You were right," said Meri, gasping for air.

"I was right?" Nerissa asked.

"They're sensitive, so sensitive," said Meri. She moaned when Nerissa rubbed her nipples with her thumb.

"They are," said Nerissa.

"The serving girl… she was touching them. When the other one was kissing her."

Their eyes met and tangled together. Nerissa knew what she was going to ask a moment before she asked it.

"Will you… my lady, will you… kiss me?" Meri asked. Her head fell back. "Ah, lords of the deep, I can feel it when you kiss me. When you touch me."

"Here?" asked Nerissa. She ran her hand up Meri's thigh and under her blanket. Meri's center was hot and wet. "You can feel it here? Or you want me to kiss you here?"

"Yes," said Meri.

"I will kiss you everywhere," said Nerissa, solemn. Then she bent her head and took a nipple into her mouth.

The parasol clattered to the floor. Nerissa froze, lips still surrounding Meri's sweet-tasting nipple, as an icy water soaked her. The cold penetrated the heat of her thoughts, and she realized she had her fingers between Meri's thighs and her mouth on her breast outside in the midst of a storm. She pulled away, now drenched.

"No—what?"

"Downstairs," said Nerissa. "We will continue downstairs. Where it is warm. Safe."

The trip back down the stairs was a blur. Her arms ached from the tension of wanting to have Meri back in her arms and it was all she could do not to push the mermaid up against the wall. It was a relief when they were once more in the warmth of Nerissa's bedroom. She tugged the blanket Meri wore all the way off, and dropped her own sheet.

"You are certain?" Nerissa asked.

Meri gazed at her. "Oh, yes. I am certain, my lady."

Nerissa slid down Meri's body. Her resolution not to think of Dianora held: it was Meri she thought of as she parted Meri's wet folds, and placed the instrument against tender flesh. It was Meri's scent — light and spicy — that lingered around her. Unable to help herself, she pressed a kiss to the crease of her thigh. When she licked it, Meri's taste was tart on her tongue.

"Hmmm," she murmured, when she finally returned to her task. Meri's center was flushed and pink. The silvery glow emanating from the sigil was stronger and it pulsated lightly. Beneath it, was the tender swell of Meri's pearl. "It has nearly been coaxed out," Nerissa said. "This happened so much quicker than I expected!"

"I could feel it, I think," said Meri, breathless. "I think I could feel it when you kissed me."

In reply, Nerissa kissed her again, this time on her mound. Through the soft skin, she felt the pulse of the instrument at work. This time, she did not bother to keep distant. Her fingers worked inside Meri, pumping along with the suction. Nerissa found a spot that made Meri cry out; she lingered there until the mermaid was writhing under her touch.

"Oh, sea stars, my lady," she said. "That is no passing pleasure." Her thighs quivered under Nerissa as her instincts caught her up. "Oh, my *lady*."

"Just there?" Nerissa asked.

Meri cried out an answer, but it was at that moment the instrument fell away. Nerissa looked up at her, past the white belly and breasts and into her eyes. They burned into her, a silent plea. Nerissa smiled, tossed the instrument aside, and pressed her lips against Meri's center.

A great shuddering cry erupted from the mermaid, and continued as Nerissa suckled on the newly revealed pearl. Her tongue flicked against it, and all of Nerissa's senses were focused on this one point, this one task she had.

Hands gripped her head, pulling her closer. Nerissa obeyed the silent command, lapping at her, showing her exactly what she had been missing all this time.

"Oh, my lady, oh, my lady," Meri chanted.

Nerissa had to pin her hips to the bed.

Meri's passion caught her up in it. Strong thighs clamped down around Nerissa's head, but she kept at it, kept suckling on that pearl, flicking it with her tongue, guided by Meri's rising cries. Fingers twisted in her hair, pulling upward, and keeping Nerissa tight against Meri's center. Then she felt it – Meri's pearl gave a great jerk under her tongue, a scream echoed in her ears, and a new taste flooded on her tongue: honey and Meri and desire. Mindless now with her own need, Nerissa took it all in: she licked, she suckled, she had Meri's taste and scent all over her, but she wanted more…

"My lady," said Meri. Her voice was hoarse. It hardly penetrated the haze of desire around Nerissa at all. "My lady. *Nerissa.*"

At that, Nerissa pulled back and looked up at her. Pale blond hair was a tangled halo around her lovely face. Her bottom lip was glossy and red, as though she'd been biting it, and her eyes… those impossibly wide, impossibly blue eyes were *radiating* an emotion Nerissa could not immediately name.

After that, it was a haze. Meri expressed some sort of foolish worry that she'd somehow offended Nerissa somehow, as though it had not been the most erotic and gratifying experience Nerissa had had in the last century. In order to soothe her, Nerissa had kissed her. Kissed her the way she had on the topmost deck. Meri was just as eager, just as sweet as she had been then.

And still, Nerissa was surprised when the mermaid toppled her onto her back and proceeded to kiss her way down Nerissa's own body. It was on the tip of her tongue to tell her to stop, tell her she did not need to do this… but instead she was spreading her own legs and canting her hips upward, so eager to feel Meri's lips and tongue at her center she could not think in straight lines. Everything spiraled downward, to the sensation of Meri breathing against her core, nuzzling her pearl… nothing else mattered.

Later, much later, after Nerissa had examined Meri's pearl several more times, and each time taught the mermaid more about the pleasures of her new body, and the sky was lightening in the east, a thought prodded her. Nerissa sighed.

"What is it?" Meri asked.

Their bodies were curved together. The sheets and blankets were entirely off the bed; they were tangled together in a sweaty mess on the floor. Nerissa closed her eyes; the wish that she were mortal swelled up inside her. Meri would forget about their love-making. Nerissa would never be able to.

Everything has a price.

"Thoughts intrude, as they do," Nerissa said finally.

Meri's fingers brushed over her nipple, which tightened in response. The mermaid was a swift learner.

"What thoughts?" said Meri.

Nerissa took in a deep breath and blew it out. "The price," she said. "Your pearl is no longer hidden. I have fulfilled my end of our bargain." This was a small lie. Nerissa had promised her help, and she'd said it thrice. There had not been limits placed on that. "As much as I wish it were otherwise, I must now... perhaps not this precise moment, but it approaches as swift as the sunrise... I must now turn my thoughts to the debt between us, and the price you will pay."

CHAPTER FIVE

The change was instantaneous.

The words left Nerissa's mouth and Meri sat up. "The price?" she said.

"Indeed," said Nerissa. "I cannot work a magic for free. You knew this."

"I... you are right," said Meri. "Forgive me." Her throat worked and her gaze flitted away from Nerissa and to the window. "I forgot. I forgot that I – I was in bed with you for... I am *silly* but I forgot we—"

"You are not silly," said Nerissa. She caught Meri's gaze and cupped her chin in her hands. "I wish there had been naught but pleasure between us. But I am a *witch*, Meri. I must never forget that. To do so... it would *harm* you if I allowed you to walk free from here. There would be a debt between us; it is a bond."

"I would not mind so much the bond between us," said Meri, who seemed determined to be stubborn. "It is far and away a better bond between than that between the *prince* and I."

Moonlight turned her skin luminescent. Nerissa was transfixed by it, even as the words slashed through her. Near choking on foreboding, Nerissa said: "You must not say that." She scrambled off the bed as though singed. "You must not *say* that, Meri."

"Why?" Meri challenged, scrambling after her.

Damn that book. The savage thought struck her, and Nerissa wished she had never created such a thing. In its pages, Meri had read the words that could bring about her doom. She knew of the bond between herself and the prince. She already wished it away. How long before she sought to make a bargain with another witch? Cold ripples shuddered over the skin of her back.

Afraid, now, she gathered up a quilt from the chest at the foot of her bed and tossed it at Meri, then led her down. Down the stairs that led to the quiet, dark kitchen. And then down even further into the catacomb of caverns Nerissa had carved into the cliffs surrounding her lighthouse. The air was cool around Nerissa's naked flesh, but she ignored this. Instead, visions of Meri flung themselves at her one by one.

Meri, in the middle of carnage, weeping.

Meri, on her back, bleeding out through the strange sigil carved upon her chest and belly.

Meri, eyes flat and black, blood on her teeth. They were serrated and terrifying... she was the worst of them, the worst kind of witch, the kind that made the debt paid for magic as cruel as could be.

The visions chased her all the way down to her workroom, nipping at her ankles, and harrying her. So sharp in her mind were they, that when she saw the conch shell sitting on the shelf, she let out a small moan of relief.

"What is it?" Meri demanded. "What has *happened?*"

Nerissa turned to her, now clutching the shell so tightly the spines and ridges dug into her palm. "We are supposed to offer you a choice," she said, very swiftly. "It is the rules. It is an old, old law. But Meri – I know what price you should pay."

"A choice?" said Meri. There was a sharp edge on her voice that reminded Nerissa what was buried in the wall behind her.

"Yes," said Nerissa. "I know you know this, I know you know far more about witches than these – these humans around us." She held up the shell. "That story you read in the book... it is true, as I think you know. It is a deep truth that when transformations like this occur, the magic of it needs to be anchored to another soul. It is a bond – a deep, deep bond."

"Like the story," said Meri. "I suspected it was true. It was the first time you didn't look so composed, it was... I had thought you lovely, but that crack... it made you even more beautiful." Her pale, slim brow winged upward at the corner. "You are afraid I won't wish to break it? I swear, I—"

"*No,*" said Nerissa. "*No,* do not swear to me what I think you are about to." She swallowed. "I would *never* allow you to break the bond—"

"—*allow* me?"

"—I would *never* allow you to experience that," said Nerissa. Thought Meri stood whole and hale in front of her, in her mind's eye, Nerissa could see the imprint of the sigil over the quilt. So immersed in her own private nightmare was she that she missed the warning signs of the brewing storm.

"You would make my choice for me?"

The fury in Meri's voice lashed out.

Nerissa stumbled backward an inch at the force of it. "I would not have you be forced to—"

"You would make my choice for me," said Meri. Flames bloomed in her cheeks and lightning crashed in her eyes. "You would take away what little choice I have in *my own life. You* would do this to me?" Hurt and rage mingled together it; the combination stunned Nerissa and made it impossible to speak. "*You?* My lady, you would act as the others? You would play the part of the old king, the prince, and my own father?"

"No, just your memories," said Nerissa. "It is so dangerous for you to remember me; it is especially dangerous for you to remember that story. You have no idea. You never have to." Imploring, now, she gestured toward Meri with the shell. "You are whole now, Meri. You may learn to desire your husband—"

"I never want to find myself in the prince's bed again," Meri said. "After what we shared? And you are going to take that from me as the sea witch stole memories of my sister?"

"It is for your protection," said Nerissa. Her lips were numb.

"From *you?*" Meri cried out. "From *this?* From wanting to make my own choices, for not wanting to be bound to the prince – the prince who is the puppet of the old king, that old man who *bought* me as a slave to his family?" The air around her seemed to sizzle. "You want me to forget that I ever dreamed of something better. You're *just like them?*"

These last words snapped Nerissa out of the near trance she had been in as Meri's wrath broke over her as a tidal wave.

"Apologize!" Nerissa snapped. The shelves of her workroom shook and thunder rolled through the room. "Do *not* mistake me for the old king or one of his. You know I am a witch. You knew you were incurring a debt. You *know* that I have to collect it."

And witches are the debt collectors. There was a sharp pain in her breast. Her breath grew labored.

Meri remained stubborn. Her body seemed even more delicate, swallowed as it was by the quilt she'd drawn around her. A storm rolled in her eyes. "Everything I have ever heard about witches is that they will offer a choice as to how one pays one's debt. You haven't offered me a *choice.*" Fire flickered at the backs of her eyes. "Instead, you *tell* me what price I am to pay. And I'll tell you – I may have forgotten my sister. There is a person whose existence has been wiped from my memory. But I *dream* about her. I know I do. When I wake, there are tears on my pillow and I *ache.*"

"Losing the memory of me and what has happened out here on this peninsula is the kindest price I can offer you," Nerissa said. A jar behind her shattered and lightning arced across the ceiling. This, she ignored.

"And I just told you it isn't kind at all," Meri said. Her retort cracked out like a whip. "And I will *not* apologize. Perhaps it is only sea witches who offer a choice. Perhaps *land* witches are the same as the old king. Only a select few are offered a choice and the rest of us have to suffer." Angry color bloomed in her cheeks. "You are going to steal the best memories of my life."

Best memories of my life.

The words barely penetrated the haze of anger that surrounded Nerissa. "I am not a land witch—"

"Well, you certainly aren't a sea witch—"

"I am neither," Nerissa said in a cold voice.

"But I—"

"I am a witch of the margins," said Nerissa. "I am *the* witch of the margins, as I have never met another."

"Witch of the – of the margins or witch of the land, you are still not offering me a *choice*," said Meri.

"I am trying to protect you," Nerissa said.

"*Protect* me?" Meri said.

It was the disbelief and the rising lack of faith in Meri's tone that did it. The storm raged around and through Nerissa. Meri well and truly believed that Nerissa was like them… that she was trying to exert control over Meri's life the way the old king had. A burning smell filled her nostrils. The wind was at her back, and the sea swelled at her feet. Her power swelled in her. It was the power of the places in the margins: the places that were not quite one thing or the other, the places where boundaries blurred, and where things could be two different things at once. It was where sand met sea and where both met sky… where dreams met memories… where life met death.

It was the place where a witch could be both former human… and former mermaid.

Nerissa's place in the world had been hard won.

"Let me show you what I am protecting you from," Nerissa said, as something inside her breast twanged and snapped. "Let me show you what happens when mermaids make all the wrong decisions."

"I hardly think I—"

"Not you," said Nerissa. Her whole existence narrowed to where she stood, poised between gentleness and cruelty. "Me." It took quick work with her knife to slice her skin. Blood welled and ran down. Wordless, she offered it to Meri.

Her eyes were wide with shock.

"Come look at my memories," Nerissa offered. "Experience them."

Her face tightened, and she drew a ragged breath. Up until Meri's lips clamped over her cut, Nerissa was certain the mermaid would refuse. And what would she do then? If she erased Meri's memories of this peninsula, of what they had shared in the private sanctuary of Nerissa's bedroom, it would also erase this fight. Meri would not know that she had accused Nerissa of negating her choices. She would not know that Nerissa had done exactly that.

But Nerissa would know.

She would see the conch on her shelf whenever she came to her workroom. She would hear these accusations if she held the shell up to her ear. Instead of the ocean, she would hear Meri's voice, sharp and accusing. Worse, would be upstairs, where Meri's scent would linger. She would fall asleep with the aroma around her, and the knowledge that it would eventually fade. Even with enchantments, eventually it would dissipate.

All this flashed through her mind, and then Meri's tongue lapped at her blood.

Fearless Meri.

The mermaid lifted her head. The coppery scent of blood filled the air between them. It smeared on her lips, giving her beauty and grace a savagery that weakened Nerissa's knees. When she reached out and stroked her thumb across Meri's brow, her hand trembled. When she spoke the enchantment that would show Meri the memory, her voice was strong.

They were both so young.

The small, red-haired girl laughed and splashed in a safe tide pool. Another girl, this one with a fin instead of legs, watched her. After a while, the sun came out, and this girl too began to laugh. It was the first meeting between girl and mermaid. But it wasn't the last. Begun with fear, it ended with the first buds of friendship.

Her head broke the surface of the water, following that taste. But what could it be? It was not anything from the sea, Nerissa knew. She was nearly to shore, having to bob around the rocks. It was instinctive for her, and something her mother had taught her to do since she was tiny.

The taste was growing stronger, though, and Nerissa was so distracted that she did not flit out of the way of a heavy block of wood. It slammed into her belly and kept pushing at her until something sharp bit into the tender flesh of her back. Without conscious thought, the pain in her back spreading over her and blanking her mind, she gave three great strokes of her fin, and forced her way against rock, wood, and wave to the surface. Fingers bit into unforgiving stone, her head crested the surface, and she pulled herself out of the water.

Her heart pounded in time with the waves and her whole body trembled. Her body had been pinned against a rock — that was how folk died! All because of that sweet taste on the water. Shivering, she hunched in on herself. The wood could have held her next to the rocks. The waves would have kept coming, driving her into the rocks again and again and again. Her body would have broken apart... what would her sisters have said?

It took some time before she calmed. A swift wind blew her hair around, keeping her eyes veiled in darkness, and it wasn't until long minutes had passed before she dragged it away from her face and peered around her.

Nerissa was at the shore.

Not just at where the waves broke, but she was close enough to the shore to see the wavelets running up to the sand, the cormorants diving for quicksilver fish, and what had to be the flotsam of a shipwreck. A mast with heavy sails buffeted up against the sand in a chaotic rhythm. Great chunks of wood floated everywhere near here. And Nerissa herself shared a rock with a cask that leaked amber liquid into the sea.

Her nose twitched. Whatever that amber liquid was, it was what had made the current taste so sweet! She caught a bit of it on her fingers and sucked them into her mouth. Flavor burst on her tongue: hot and sweet, it lingered in her mouth.

She had never tasted anything like it.

What is this?

"I believe it is mead," said a small, piping voice. "And you are a mermaid."

Panic seized Nerissa. The rock dug into her palms, slicing it, and it was all she could do not to push herself off and dive into the churning sea, where the wreckage would smash her against the rocks. The instinct was strong, even though death was a near certainty. But this was a land creature. This was a human. This was a—

—small creature with bright red hair.

Astonished, Nerissa could only stare.

Her whole body was covered in white cloth and her hair was like blood against it.

"I will not hurt you," said the girl. "My name is Dianora. I would never hurt you." Then she made her way to the rocks where Nerissa was. "It is the wood in the water, is it not? It hurt you, and that is why you came out of the water."

"Yes," said Nerissa. Her voice was very small. "I have heard you—"

With a cry of effort, Nerissa pulled back from the memory. Her whole body was shaking. Meri's presence *did* something. It was no mere memory. She felt as though she were *reliving* that first meeting. Frantic, needing to show Meri, but needing a boundary between life and memory, Nerissa scooped up seawater in her cupped hands and splashed herself and Meri with it.

"We do not need the memory so strong," Nerissa said through clenched teeth. "The seawater will give us some distance." *I hope.* She drew a sigil in the air with her driftwood wand and bit her lip.

This time, when she drew Meri into her memories, it was hazy and dreamlike. They stood at the shore of the forbidden cove. Their feet were in the water, but they did not feel wet. Their hair was unstirred by the wind. And they no longer saw through the eyes of a foolish young mermaid, but looked upon her without *being* her.

Time flickered by in the memory like sunlight rippling over the water.

"Betimes I think you are not real," said the red-haired girl. She was old enough her body was blossoming. It fascinated the mermaid, who never took her eyes off her.

"I am just as real as you, Dianora," said the mermaid.

"I know," she said. "I know you are real, Nerissa, but none of my brothers would ever believe me!" The brief moment of reflection disappeared, and her face flickered with laughter once more. "You are my secret. My secret friend."

A pale hand crept out of the water. The mermaid and the human girl clasped hands.

Some time later, the secret cove became a sanctuary for more than a secret friendship.

Memories whirled. That afternoon was but the first of many during which the mermaid gave Dianora pleasure. Seasons passed.

Then, one day, when the wind blew in cold off the sea, the mermaid sat waiting for Dianora. The sun was sunk low in the sky by the time a small figure approached the secret cove. The only thing recognizable was the bright red of her hair. Her gown was long and heavy with sand and was ornate with decoration.

"Dianora?" said the mermaid.

"It is me, Nerissa," said Dianora. Her face was very pale.

"I have missed you," said Nerissa. "It was spring since you were here last. It is winter now."

A smile flickered on Dianora's face. It disappeared just as quickly. "I... my life has changed." Tears welled in her eyes and spilled over, but when Nerissa reached for her, she stepped back further on the sand where the mermaid could not go. "I never told you, but... my grandfather's brother was king here. He has died in an earthquake, and his sons with him. My father is now king..."

Nerissa stared at her, uncomprehending.

"I am a princess now, and... my life has changed," said Dianora. Tears slipped down her cheeks. "I can no longer come here and be with you. This place on the margins, this place where we can be together... I can no longer come here. It is too much of a danger. I have guards, now, and if they see you... your life would be at risk."

"My life is at risk? Why?"

Dianora knelt on the sand. Wavelets rushed up to greet her and wet her beautiful gown. "I have been selfish these years... you are wondrous, Nerissa. Men would kill to have you. Remember that day we met so long ago? Two lonely little girls? I ought to have told you to swim out to see... never come to the shore again. But I could not. And now I live in terror, for what if someone has followed me even now?" Fingers sunk into her red hair and pulled. "I realize now I could be the cause of your death..."

"I do not understand," said Nerissa. It hurt her palms to flatten them on the sand and press forward, to try to reach Dianora. Tiny rocks dug into her fin, scraping away her scales. "Dianora, you could never hurt me."

"Not with my own hand," said Dianora. "Never with my own hand."

"So you will not be able to come very often?" Nerissa asked. "You will have to come only when your guards are busy elsewhere?"

Dianora looked at her. "Oh, Nerissa. I cannot risk ever coming again."

"Never again?" Puzzlement knit her brow together. "But how will I see you?"

Dianora put her hands over her face and sobbed. Her cries echoed off the cliffs and the birds began to call down to her. It took long, long moments, but darkness fell over Nerissa's face the moment she understood what Dianora was saying as though a candle had been suddenly, inexplicably blown out. Grief poured out of Dianora and she crawled forward close enough to the water she could press kisses against Nerissa's mouth.

"I love you," she said, twining her hands in Nerissa's wet hair. "I love you. I wish I did not have to leave you... Oh, Nerissa. You have made my life a joy, my secret friend. My – my lover. If you were human, I..."

With a wrench and a wordless cry, Nerissa pulled out of the memory, dragging Meri along with her in her wake. The loss of Dianora, the memories of the two of them as children, as adolescents, as much lovers as they could be despite their differences... it welled up in Nerissa. It was an old wound, this. Centuries old, and it still hurt. Nerissa gasped from the pain of it, pressing her hand against her chest, nearly unable to breathe.

"You did it for love."

All Nerissa could do was nod.

"She bade you become human," said Meri.

"She – she did not," said Nerissa. The pain was at its highest tide. "It was not commonly known that someone had made the transition from mermaid to human. It was something we spoke about under the waves – it was a cautionary tale against rousing the sea witches to wrath. Look what had been done! The pain of the transformation... it was a nightmare told in the sea, but it did not touch the humans. They were none the wiser that a mermaid had fallen in love with a prince, and was cursed because of it. How could they know?"

"They know now," said Meri.

"Because of me," said Nerissa. "My transformation was not so quiet as the first."

"It was your story," said Meri. "Your enchanted book. It told me *your* story."

"Indeed," said Nerissa. "Everyone assumed it was the prince I loved. That day on the beach... Dianora had just been engaged to him. He was a distant cousin of hers, if I remember correctly. There was unrest in the kingdom when the former king and all his heirs died in the earthquake. It was whispered that it was the doing of witches – the whispers accused Dianora's father of being in league with them. I never found out the truth of the rumors. It did not matter to me, other than that Dianora was forced to marry a man from a noble house loyal to the old line."

"Humans," Meri said with a great deal of disgust.

"I came to shore the week before her wedding," said Nerissa.

"My lady. Nerissa."

It was the first time Meri spoke her name.

Nerissa just looked at her.

"Show me," said Meri. "Take us back into your memories. I – I need to understand. *Please* don't tell me it doesn't matter. It *does* matter. I need to understand what happened. I need to understand what you're trying to protect me from."

She pulled a deep breath into her lungs. The cold spot at her back reminded her of the obsidian knife. Memories of the pleasure and intimacy that she and Dianora had shared had pulled them back into living Nerissa's memories, despite her cautions. The jagged, destructive edges of the knife would pull them back in.

> "I see a mermaid besieged with regrets."
> The sea witch bobbed on the waves.
> "I did not call you," Nerissa said to her. "I do not need you here."
> "You would become foam upon the waves and the breeze over the oar?"
> "I know what the price for returning would be, and I refuse to pay it," said Nerissa. "Keep your knife of obsidian. I will not strike my love down. She – she did not want this." There was so much of this human world that did not make sense to Nerissa. The sounds, the sights... everything was foreign. But she knew Dianora. She knew her heart. She had known it since they were both children. "I have been told the love between us is forbidden..."
> "Such a willing sacrifice," said the sea witch. Her cruelty sunk into Nerissa's skin.
> Water splashed against the deck of the ship. When the wave receded, the knife of obsidian lay at Nerissa's feet.
> "In case you change your mind," said the sea witch.
> "I will not," Nerissa said calmly.
> Something ugly glittered in the witch's eyes. Clouds blotted out the moon. "Careful, mermaid," she said. "You thought your transformation painful to become a mere human? There are other, crueler transitions. You will not like the path you are walking."
> "I will not hurt her," said Nerissa.
> "You will not have to," said the sea witch. A terrible smile bloomed, revealing a mouth full of serrated teeth. "Someone else is doing that for you."
> There was time for a breath before a scream ripped apart the night.
> "NO!" The word flung out of her. That was Dianora's voice. It was her scream of pain – of terror – that fractured her. With a fluid gesture, Nerissa reached down and grasped the stone hilt of the knife.

While her mind was numb and uncomprehending, her body knew what it was doing as she moved at speed away from the prow, through a knot of sailors, and down the hatch that led to—

Red surged at the corners of the memory.

The stateroom door opened and what greeted Nerissa nearly brought her to her knees.

Strange symbols marked the walls – they were painted in blood and dripped down the walls. On the bed was—

"No," Dianora moaned.

"No!" Nerissa screamed. It was Dianora – beautiful Dianora, and she was... the flesh of her chest gaped open. Blood gushed out of her, pooling on the white quilt.

"How dare you enter here?"

It was the prince. He was naked and covered in the same symbols that were on the walls. They seemed like living things, crawling over him like worms. He did this. The thought rang through Nerissa like a bell. The rage was a small transformation in itself. It rushed through her body, wreaking destruction, melding with the love she had for Dianora until it somehow became one single emotion.

The next moment, Nerissa flung herself at the prince. The obsidian knife was raised and it arced toward his chest. Kill. Kill. Kill. In her madness, it was the only thought she had... seeing this prince's blood fountaining from his body was the only purpose Nerissa now had... her path forward was clear: kill the prince. And try to follow Dianora down her own path.

Except when the knife finally came down, it did not slice into the prince's flesh.

There was a moment of utter incomprehension. It was Dianora –

Horror suffused her limbs and she ripped the obsidian knife out of Dianora. Someone was jeering. Someone was laughing, and it was the prince. All Nerissa could do was stare into those eyes. The brightness dimmed. There was blood on Dianora's lips. She mouthed something to Nerissa and then—

Thunder clapped and lightning struck.

Red erupted. Screams once more rent the night.

Lightning struck Nerissa again and again. It bolted through her, racing through her veins, burning everything inside it. The laughter from the prince had been cut off as surely as the screams of dying sailors, but it still echoed through her. It sounded the way the lightning felt. There was nothing so painful as that lightning. Nothing so painful as that laughter.

The world disappeared, fading to black, as the ship around Nerissa exploded.

And her transformation began as fingers of lightning came down to strike every part of her body. Pain stitched her back together and her mortal body was hollowed out and filled with the mandate of the gods. Sigils burned in front of her closed eyes and her mind flew into pieces—

Just as a powerful voice began to speak, Nerissa and Meri were thrown out of the memory. Shuddering with remembered pain – the transformation was like dying a thousand times but never being allowed a rest – Nerissa fell heavily against the wall.

It was near unbelievable to Nerissa that the workroom around her was unchanged. The memory had been so powerful that she expected to see destruction around her. Instead, the shelves sat sturdy on the walls, supporting Nerissa's belongings, just as they had always done. The wispy cloud that hung over the table was precisely the same shape. The tide continued to move in its basin. Nerissa's entire core had been shaken. A part of her still clung to the wreckage of the ship, stunned and bleeding from wounds that did not come from her body.

The sound of muffled sobs brought her all the way back to her present body.

Meri knelt on the floor, weeping into her hands. Her pale hair hung forward and covered her like a shroud.

It was this that restored Nerissa to clarity. It took more than a minute to lift the enchantments that hid the obsidian knife within the walls of her workroom. It was the first thing she'd placed here, this weapon, the one that had destroyed Dianora. However unknowing Nerissa had been, however much she could not have guessed that a bridegroom would use his bride's body as a shield, a certain awareness pulsed through her.

The *knife* had known. It had always known.

"I never found out why," Nerissa whispered, half to herself. "I never found out what the sigils meant. I do know that the prince had married Dianora in order to perform some sort of ritual. My first century as a witch was spent trying to discover exactly what that was… and who had taught him blood magic like that. He was no witch, Meri… I looked and I looked for answers. Everyone on that ship died that night. You know, you felt it. You saw it. Even *I* died. Imagine my surprise when I opened my eyes some time later to find myself floating on a wooden plank."

"I don't understand…" said Meri.

"It is a mystery," said Nerissa. "Witches are immortal creatures, as you know. But every witch I have spoken to has experienced a death like mine." It was becoming slightly easier to breathe. Nerissa braced herself against the wall, just at where it pulsed with cold, and kept her head down. "No matter how many cities I searched, monasteries I raided, people I killed… the answer never came to me." Her voice shuddered. "I came to this place. And I hid the knife here. The knife that killed Dianora. The knife that broke the bond between us."

Nerissa murmured a word and drew a sigil in the wall with her fingernail.

A hole in the wall appeared. Inside it was a roughly made box – Nerissa had fashioned it out of the plank of wood that had brought her to shore after the ship had been destroyed. The knife itself was wrapped in seaweed. It decayed in her hands leaving only the stone hilt and the sharp black blade. It emanated cold.

"I have learned a little what this kind of knife means," Nerissa said, breaking the silence. "All I knew when I was so young and foolish was that it was a black knife. I did not know of the properties the blade has."

Meri gave no sign of hearing her.

"Obsidian is… as wide and vast as the sea is, its depth does not go on forever," said Nerissa. Her tone took on that of a teacher and only shook a little. Below it, there is more earth and stone. And below that… there is another sea."

Meri's head lifted. "Another *sea*?" she asked.

"Not of water and salt," said Nerissa. "It is a sea of fire – a fire so hot it moves like water. It is made of melted stone. At times, it finds a crack in the earth and it begins to push upward. There is no greater destructive force than that. Tempest. Avalanche. Earthquake. None of these compare to the volcano. And yet, when the belowsea – the one made of rock and fire – comes out, it doesn't burn forever. It cools eventually – and when it cools, it turns to rock. Imagine an entire forest or an entire city covered in stone. Utterly destroyed and encased in stone."

Meri's face was transfixed in a look of horror.

"Obsidian comes from that stone," said Nerissa. "It is not all obsidian – where the fire was the hottest, this is what becomes black as deepest night."

"But it's so cold," Meri said. "I can feel its cold from here."

"It has to be cold," said Nerissa. "Otherwise the heat would burn the world." She knelt and let the mermaid see the knife up close. The bite of chill in the air increased. "As I said, there is nothing that is more destructive. What witch decided to create a weapon from it... I would like to have a few sharp words with that witch. Obsidian retains the quality of the lava – the molten stone. It destroys everything in its path. It breaks every bond – including that between human and mermaid."

Slim, pale fingers reached out.

A flicker of red erupted in the depths of the glossy black.

Meri drew back, a sharp, graceless gesture. The tips of her fingers turned a bright red and she sucked them into her mouth. "That was – that was *hot*."

"It remembers when it once was molten," said Nerissa. She shut the lid of the box with a snap and replaced it in the wall. She did not bother replacing the enchantments. Her energy left her in a rush and there was nothing more she wanted than to get back into bed. "One thing that must be remembered of the molten stone – it is so hot that once you have seen it, it is already nearly too late."

Meri nodded, but Nerissa knew she did not comprehend.

"There is nothing I can do now to take this choice away from you," said Nerissa. "Even if I took your memories, you would still be drawn here. Even if I left this place and took the knife with me... I think you would find some way to follow. You have seen the memory of molten stone in the obsidian knife... you are already in danger."

Blue eyes widened. In them, Nerissa thought she saw a flicker of red.

"My choice," said Meri. "My choice is to lose my memories of you. Or break the bond between myself and the prince." She swallowed and her eyes fluttered closed. When she opened them, they were her own blue and grey again. "I never *wanted* to be bound to the prince. After being here... I can't abide the idea of going back into his bed. I can't *abide* it." The blue shattered and broke. "I didn't *want* him. I didn't love him the way you love Dianora. I don't. And I never will."

"It is no small thing to take a man's life," said Nerissa.

Meri ignored this. "I think... I think I could love you like that. I think I already do."

Blood roared in Nerissa's ears.

"But I know you love Dianora," said Meri. "I know I'm just… someone who asked you for help. And you've been so kind… so gentle. And you love Dianora—"

"I did love Dianora," Nerissa said. "A part of me always will. A part of me will always be stuck in those last moments with her. But I have lived a very long time, Meri—"

"And I know I must be too – too silly, too young," said Meri. Small, nervous fingers worried at the blanket still wrapped around her. "And my hair is not nearly as interesting, I've never seen such a color, you know, except maybe in sunsets."

"Dianora did have lovely hair," Nerissa conceded. "But—"

"And you were just *helping* me, I realize," interrupted Meri. Her head tilted back, and her body curved into the shape of a supplicant, kneeling on the floor, begging.

Nerissa took her hands and raised her to her feet. The blanket, no longer anchored to her body, drifted to the floor. Chaotic color flushed Meri's cheeks and she was beautiful. "You took my breath away the first moment I saw you," said Nerissa. She cupped Meri's chin. Unable to resist, she pressed a quick kiss on her lips. She tasted herself on them. "You took my breath away. I did love Dianora, Meri. But that was life-times ago. I do believe it has been time enough to love again."

Meri melted into her and Nerissa wrapped her arms around her. The cold emanating from the knife at her back receded in her aware-ness. For long, quiet moments, she held the mermaid. It felt like the first time, and she let her hands roam over her silky, smooth back. Meri's head tucked into the curve of Nerissa's neck, and her breath was warm and damp against the naked skin. For long minutes, it was all she allowed herself to feel: Meri in her arms.

Finally, she disentangled herself, enough to lead Meri from the workroom and back to her bed.

Later, when it was night, and both of them were spent of their pas-sion, Nerissa stroked Meri's pale hair, sifting it through her fingers and playing with it. Licking her lips, she could taste Meri's passion on them. Her body remembered the feel of Meri's fingernails digging into her flesh; the lingering echoes of her cries reverberated in her bones. And yet… her mind had once more returned to the obsidian knife, and the choice Meri now had to make.

Nerissa cleared the rust from her throat. "I can give you a year and a day," she said finally.

"Pardon?" Meri turned her head and blinked sleepy eyes at her. "A year and a day?" Then, as though struck, she sat upright. "I can only be with you a year and a day? Just a year and a day?" A thread of hurt wound through her tone. "That's all? Then—"

Nerissa laid a finger over the mermaid's lips. "No. I can give you a year and a day to make your choice," she said. "You do not have to choose tonight. You do not have to choose tomorrow. You will not have to take up the obsidian knife – if that is what you choose – until a year from tomorrow."

Her brow creased with indignation. "I already made my choice!" she said, indignant. "I will not have my memories of you taken away."

"Meri," said Nerissa. "This... it is for my benefit, not yours. I will need to know that you do this of your own will. I need to know that you do it with full knowledge of what becoming a witch means."

"So I'm to toddle back to the city and wait a year and a day to be with you again?" Meri demanded. "Are you hoping time will do the choosing for you, and I'll forget about you? I will tell you this moment that is impossible—"

"Hush," said Nerissa. "I am going with you."

Meri's mouth dropped open. "You're coming *with* me? To the *city*?"

Nerissa nodded. There was no path she could see branching forward that did not include keeping Meri in her life as long as possible. The plan sprang into her mind, fully formed. "You will return by yourself. But I will follow you. I will become your maidservant – there I will stay, at your side, until a year from tomorrow."

"But... no one will know you are a witch?" Meri asked.

"No," said Nerissa. "Have trust in me. The people of the city... the people of your husband's castle... they do not need to know I am about. It will be safer for everyone."

Meri snuggled back into her arms. "My own secret witch," she murmured.

"For a year and a day, that is what I will be," said Nerissa. Her hand found Meri's hair again. In the quiet darkness, she painted a picture for Meri as to what that would be like. It did not take long before the mermaid's breathing evened out and deepened. It was Nerissa who remained awake, trying to pierce the veils of the future to see where their path would lead them. With Meri as a witch?

The questions still plagued her when, three days later – two days after she had said goodbye to Meri – she stood at the bottom of the path that led to her lighthouse. Her cormorants flew around her; the sun flickered off them, filling them with a light that was nearly painful to Nerissa's eyes.

"I will be gone from this place for nearly a year," she told them. They shone like jewels and were entirely too bright for such a somber occasion. Only the first, flecked with ebony, was appropriately garbed. It was partly why she was taking him with her. "You are to guard this place from intruders. Do not allow humans here. Harry them away from our nest."

The ruby cormorant screeched at her.

"Unless it is Meri," Nerissa allowed. "I do not expect her to come here. But if she does need sanctuary for any reason, you will allow her to find it here." She flicked her fingers at them. "Go on, then. Resume your posts. I have left you before, you will be fine."

As one, the flock of stone cormorants flew away – except for her first.

Instead, he perched on the statue and cocked his head at her. The single garnet eye winked at her.

"You are right to assume you are coming with me," said Nerissa. With a smooth, practiced gesture, she hoisted her small bag over her shoulder.

There were two items of particular importance in Nerissa's bag: an empty conch shell and the obsidian knife. Both were painful in their own ways. *Neither will be relevant for nearly a year,* she told herself. Putting both objects out of her mind – for now – she took a deep breath and crossed the boundary between her demesne and the human world.

The hairs on her arms and the back of her neck lifted. The power of crossing margin hummed through her, lifting her spirits, and setting a smile on her face. Still, she allowed herself one last look of her home. The lighthouse stood white and lovely against the sharp blue of sky and sea. Grass rippled with the wind. Her cormorants were bright splashes of color. There was a pang inside her, knowing she would be gone so long from this peaceful place. Her heart skipped a beat and she sighed, shook her head, and whispered the enchantments that would hide this place from prying eyes.

The promontory, the lighthouse, the cormorants... everything dropped out of view, leaving behind a curiously blank hill.

And then Nerissa turned on her heel and started down the overgrown path to the city.

To Meri.

Authors

K.D. West is a teacher, an editor, and the author of *By the Numbers, Wild West,* and *The Visitor Comes for Good,* as well as other fantastical and steamy stories at **StillpointEros.com/kdwest.** You can find West's fanfiction under the pen name Antosha on Archive of Our Own, Phoenix Song, and many other archives.

Shannon Meyers considers herself entirely too awkward to try to explain herself to potential readers. At any given moment, she'd rather be hiding in a corner with a good book, living in a world that doesn't demand her to make eye-contact or try to remember appropriate small-talk topics. She hopes that her story can offer someone the brief, but magical break that she so often seeks herself.

TheWordsinMyHead is a relatively new writer, still exploring all the worlds she wants to create and looking for new ways to get them out onto the page. When she isn't writing, she enjoys baking and generally being happier than her dark and depressing story suggests. She's done talking about herself now, but hopes you'll enjoy the story.

LegendDairy is a born and raised Canadian creative writer who finds long, ocean-side walks on the beach generally too windy and dirty to be enjoyable. Bored with her choice of employment she turned to the Potterverse to keep her brain from turning to mush. This anthology was a lovely opportunity to try out an original piece.

Arden Wiles is an aspiring writer and is studying to become a physician. Her other interests include her literary podcast, her scientific research, cooking, and baking. In her free time, she likes to spend time with her child, long-term partner, and their corgi and cat. She cannot live without her family, friends, or coffee.

Deadwoodpecker is working on a companion piece to *The Witch of the Margins,* in which two more young victims of the old king, who was so cruel to Meri, are featured. She has a cat.

Keep an eye out for

Into the Mystic 2

Coming Autumn, 2020!

more magic

more romance

more wonderful new authors

stillpointdigital.com/aphrodite

CPSIA information can be obtained
at www.ICGtesting.com
Printed in the USA
BVHW031500290620
582558BV00001B/154